Vampires: First Blood

Volume I

The Vampire Lords

Edited by James Grant Goldin

A Basilisk Book

WITH THANKS TO THE WORKS OF

William K. Everson
Denis Gifford
Peter Haining
Raymond T. McNally
Radu Florescu

To Mr. Lugosi and Mr. Frid

NOTES ON THE TEXTS:

Since the stories and poems in this anthology were first published, there have been some changes in the conventions of punctuation and spelling. This edition makes a few—but only a few—concessions to 21st century tastes.

Nineteenth-century versions of words like "some one," "every one," "to-day," "to-morrow," etc., have been mostly modernized to "someone," "everyone," "today," "tomorrow," and so forth.

The original British spellings of words like "ardour," "glamour," etc. have usually been kept, but less familiar British versions have been Americanized; so "shew" is "show," "surprize" is "surprise," etc. The use of long dashes to conceal profanity, a date or a name ("D—", "the year 17—", "the little village of C——") has been happily retained.

A glossary is provided at the end of each story or poem to explain various now-obscure terms.

INTRODUCTION:
FIRST BLOOD

Something connects all vampires—at least all the star vampires, the leading men of the undead, whether on page, stage, or screens of any size—and this "something" isn't blood-lust or superhuman strength or even sexiness.

It's class.

I don't mean just "style," or "manners," although of course leading man vampires have that, too. While werewolves never dress for dinner and zombies generally can't carry on a conversation, a vampire knows which wine to order—even if he never drinks it. A vampire will open a door for a lady—although he may then lock it behind her.

Because, above everything else, a vampire is an aristocrat.

Dracula is *Count* Dracula, and other movie vampires have included Count Mora, Count Karnstein, Count Von Krolock, Count Yorga, and Baron Meinster, as well as Blacula, who was originally an African prince. Anne Rice's Lestat was the Marquis di Lioncourt; Deborah Harkness's Matthew Clairmont has a French lineage going back over 1500 years; Joss Whedon's Angel was an Irish aristocrat. (Spike was a poet—a natural aristocrat—vampirized by an actual aristocrat.) Nick Knight, modern vampire detective, was a noble in medieval Europe.

Female vampires have been equally well-born: two of the best known are Sheridan Le Fanu's Carmilla, a countess; and Anne Rice's Akasha, an ancient queen.

The United States has no titles of nobility, but American vampires tend to come from old, rich, powerful families, often in parts of the U.S. once ruled by landed gentry. Barnabas Collins of *Dark Shadows* is of old New England stock, Bill Compton of *True Blood* and Stefan and Damon Salvatore of *The Vampire Diaries* are linked to old

Southern families; Edward Cullen of *Twilight* is certainly upper middle class, and has spent decades at some of the best schools in the country.

Yes, there are exceptions; vampire fiction has featured bloodsuckers from every social class and line of work. The broad fact remains that vampiric leading men either have an attitude of aristocratic superiority, or are actual noblemen. Star vampires may thirst for red blood; but their own blood is blue.

To some extent, this is the result of the influence of Count Dracula. But the noble *nosferatu* predates Bram Stoker's Transylvanian. In Stoker's early drafts, he was going to call his protagonist Count Wampyr; then he learned of Vlad the Impaler, the 15th century Wallachian ruler who was famous for his cruel punishments (although Vlad was never accused of vampirism). Vlad's father was known as Vlad Dracul—"Dracul" meaning both "dragon" and "devil"—and so the Impaler was called "son of Dracul" or Dracula. Obviously, "Dracula" is a much better name than "Wampyr." But Stoker's vampire's *title* was there from the beginning. He was *always* going to be *Count* Something.

That was because, in 1897, it was *expected* that a vampire would be an aristocrat.

But it wasn't always so.

Surprisingly, the vampire we recognize today—aristocratic, elegant, pale, and so forth—is a fairly recent development.

The earliest vampires not only weren't aristocrats; they were never human. They were winged demons who haunted the ancient Near Eastern nights, killing babies or draining vitality (not necessarily blood) from sleeping men. With the exception of Lilith (who is dealt with in Volume II of this anthology), these proto-vampires—including the later Roman *lamiae*—had no more individuality than a pack of wolves or a flock of bats.

In the early Middle Ages, we sometimes read of corpses coming out of their graves and walking around, spreading illness or calling people to join them in death. Some of these walking corpses show up in the Viking Sagas; in the early 1190's, the English chronicler William of

Newburgh, in *De Nugis Curialium ("Courtiers' Trifles")*, related how the knight Sir William Laudun cut off the head of a Welsh revenant who was terrorizing the village of Hereford and spreading pestilence. There were other reports in 1196 of walking corpses. These revenants were human, but not high-born, and perhaps closer to zombies than vampires; none of them drank blood, but they were disposed of in ways that would later be used against vampires, like impalement and decapitation.

For some reason, though, the idea of the walking corpse faded in England and Northern and Western Europe in the late Middle Ages; and the belief in human vampires—walking corpses out for blood—gained strength in Eastern and Central Europe. But while tales were told around cooking-fires, there were no written stories of vampires. Just four hundred years ago, nobody in Western Europe had even heard of vampires. Poets and playwrights were familiar with witches, wizards, devils, demons, spectres, succubi, incubi, mermaids, goblins, fairies, reanimated corpses, and even lycanthropes; certainly, after Chapman's translation of Homer's *Odyssey* (1614-1616), they knew about ghosts drinking blood—but the word "vampire" would have meant nothing to Marlowe, Spenser, Shakespeare, Jonson, Webster, Donne, Milton, Dryden, or Daniel Defoe.

It was only in the last years of the 17th century that rumors of human vampires began spreading west. Then, in the first three decades of the 18th century, alleged outbreaks of vampirism in parts of the Habsburg Empire were seriously investigated by local authorities, just as middle class people in Western Europe were making newspapers and magazines part of their intellectual lives. In 1732 vampires suddenly became part of the mainstream news in Germany, France, and England. Ironically, it was in these three countries—where the superstition had never existed—that writers would turn the vampire into a mass-marketed literary figure.

The fictional vampire is, therefore, an example of cultural appropriation; although appropriation might be "appropriate" for a being that survives on the life force of others. Looked at another way, the vampire is a form of cultural conquest from the East: an idea that, like a vampire's bite, infected the minds of one writer after another, creating a new genre in a new environment.

The key to the success of the vampire as a literary figure would be an overall upgrade in status. The "real" vampires of the early 1700's were peasants, like the men and women who believed in them; and might as easily attack a cow or a goat as bite a neck. So—how did writers turn the vampire into an aristocrat—and why? The answer lies in the vampires you'll find in these pages—the literary bloodsuckers of the 18th and 19th centuries, who, despite being almost been lost in the huge shadow cast by Dracula's cape, set the stage for Bram Stoker's creation.

This volume focuses on the male vampire; Volume II covers the evolution of the female vampire; but both the vampire lords and the vampire ladies underwent a similar transformation from peasants to patricians. That upgrade in status was the key to the vampire's continuing popularity, as will be discussed in more detail later. First, a few more words about the gradual evolution of the literary vampire.

As one vampire sires another, so one literary effort can inspire the next. If you look at the pre-Dracula vampires in this anthology, you'll see the seeds of almost everything in modern vampire fiction. There's the gender-fluid sexuality of the vampire; the pain of addiction; the problems of immortality; the opposition to established Christianity; and more. And, while vampires had not yet been transformed from monsters into ideal boyfriends, we see the first glimmerings of that notion, too.

On a more practical level, we'll see how different writers deal with the question of how a vampire gets in and out of his resting-place; with the physicality of a vampire; with different powers and weaknesses; and we'll meet the first vampire with fangs.

You won't find some now-familiar tropes: sunlight is not fatal to these early vampires, and there is no mention of garlic. No one in these pages turns into a bat. There are crosses, but the symbol is not yet the universal go-to defense; there are a fair number of stakes, but they aren't all made of wood.

And with regards to what else *isn't* in this book:

While the vampire's multi-media career covered poetry and prose, plays and operas, and while some notable 19th century stage productions are discussed in the introductions and afterwords, the scripts are not reproduced here, primarily for reasons of length.

There is also not a single word from what *might* be the very first vampire novel—Ignaz Ferdinand Arnold's *Der Vampir (The Vampire)*, published in German in 1801—because there seem to be no surviving copies of the book. Historians don't even know for sure if the book really deals with the undead, or if the title is a metaphor, like Marie Nizet's 1879 French novel *Le Capitaine Vampire*. The title character, a Russian officer, is nicknamed "Captain Vampire" because of his fearsome qualities, but you won't find him in these pages.

Several Russian and French stories that are sometimes classified as "vampiric" (such as *Viy* by Nikolai Gogol, or the French vampire novels of Paul Féval) have been left out, either because no public domain translation is available, or because their "vampires" blur the line between witches, warlocks, and the undead. That last consideration applies to Edgar Allan Poe's *Morella* and *Ligeia,* featuring characters who may not be quite dead but who do not drain the blood of the living. Rising from the grave and even making people ill is not enough for admission into these pages. There must be blood.

And now, let's go back to the early part of the 18th century—when there were strange reports of mysterious happenings in Central Europe…before vampires were creatures of fiction…

When they were *news*…

ARNOLD PAUL

…upon digging up his corpse forty days after his burial, he was found to have all the marks of an arch-vampire.

*A*mold Paul is in some ways the most unusual vampire in this collection—because he's real. At least, his story was presented as a documented case of vampirism that occurred in what is now Serbia in 1725 or 1726.

He was a "Heyduke," a kind of freelance militiaman who took up arms, sometimes as part of a guerrilla band, against the Turks of the Ottoman Empire. ("Heyduke" is sometimes translated as "bandit.") According to the report, Paul claimed to have been infected by a Turkish vampire while he was away from his native village, and, against his will, brought the contagion home.

Exactly how Paul became vampirized is somewhat obscure, but the details of his destruction are elaborately, if not lovingly, laid out, and would be repeated again and again, with only slight variations, in later tales of vampires. You'll find echoes of Arnold Paul throughout these volumes.

Paul (possibly originally Paole or Pavle) was not the only reported vampire during this period, but his story became the most detailed and best-known account.

The first selection is from an English newspaper, The London Journal, *published on March 11, 1732. (Although the report itself is dated two months earlier.) The story was copied or reprinted in other periodicals and for the first time presented vampires as a topic of conversation in Western Europe. (The early 1700's spelling and some of the punctuation have been modernized.)*

The second excerpt, which covers the same events, is a slightly edited version of a 1759 English translation of a 1746 French text. The author was a Benedictine monk named Dom Augustin Calmet, who, in his wildly popular Dissertations on the Revenants and Vampires of Hungary, Bohemia, Moravia and Silesia, *used the same official sources as the English newspaper. Calmet's book was by no means the first book on "real" vampires, but it became the most popular, and was the major source of information on vampires for many writers. Calmet provides more details than the earlier English report; he gives a greater sense of vampirism as a contagion—and also suggests, to the careful reader, that there's a strong sexual element to it.*

ARNOLD PAUL

From The London Journal, March 11, 1732

Extract of a Private Letter from Vienna:

Medreyga in Hungary, Jan. 7, 1732. Upon a current report, that in the Village of Medreyga certain dead bodies (called here *Vampyres*) had killed several persons by sucking out all their blood, the present enquiry was made by the Honourable Commander in Chief; and Capt. Gorschutz of the Company of Stallater, the *Hadnagi* Bariacrar, and the Senior Heyduke of the village, were severally examined: Who unanimously declared, that about five years ago a certain Heyduke named Arnold Paul was killed by the overturning of a cartload of hay, who in his life-time was often heard to say that he had been tormented near Caschaw, and upon the borders of Turkish Servia, by a *Vampyre*; and that to extricate himself, he had eaten some of the earth of the *Vampyres'* graves, and rubbed himself with their blood.

That twenty or thirty days after the decease of the said Arnold Paul, several persons complained that they were tormented; and that, in short, he had taken away the lives of four persons. In order, therefore, to put a stop to such a calamity, the inhabitants of the place, having consulted their *Hadnagi*, caused the body of the said Arnold Paul to be taken up, forty days after he had been dead; and found the same to be fresh and free of all manner of corruption; that he bled at the nose, mouth, ears, as pure and florid blood as ever was seen; and that his shroud and winding sheet were all over bloody; and, lastly, his finger and toe nails were fallen off, and new ones grown in their room.

As they observed from all these circumstances that he was a *Vampyre*, they according to custom drove a stake through his heart, at which he gave a horrid groan, and lost a great deal of blood. Afterwards they burnt his body to ashes the same day, and threw them into his grave.

These good men say farther, that all such as have been tormented or killed by the *Vampyres* become *Vampyres* when they are dead; and therefore they served several other dead bodies as they had Arnold Paul's, for tormenting the living.

Signed,

Battauer, First Lieutenant of the Regiment of Alexander

Flickhenger, surgeon-major to the Regiment of Frustemburch,

________ three other surgeons,

Guoichitz, captain at Stallach

Excerpt from "Dissertations on the Revenants and Vampires of Hungary, Bohemia, Moravia and Silesia"

Dom Augustin Calmet

In the part of Hungary known in Latin by the name of *Oppida Heidonum*, on the other side of the Tibiscus, vulgarly called the Teyss; that is, between that part of this river which waters the happy country of Tockay, and the frontiers of Transylvania, the people named Heydukes have a notion that there are dead persons, called by them vampires, which suck the blood of the living, so as to make them fall away visibly to skin and bones, while the carcasses themselves, like leeches, are filled with blood to such a degree that it comes out all the apertures of their body.

This notion has lately been confirmed by several facts, which I think we cannot doubt the truth of, considering the witnesses who attest them. Some of the most considerable of these facts I shall now relate.

A Heyduke named Arnold Paul, an inhabitant of Medreiga, was killed by a cart full of hay that fell upon him. About thirty days after his death, four persons died suddenly, with all the symptoms usually attending those who are killed by vampires.

It was then remembered that this Arnold Paul had frequently told a story of his having been tormented by a Turkish vampire, in the neighbourhood of Cassova, upon the borders of Turkish Servia (for the notion is that those who have been passive vampires in their life-time become active ones after death; or, in other words, that those who have had their blood sucked become suckers in their turn) but that he had been cured by eating some of the earth upon the vampire's grave, and by rubbing himself with his blood.

This precaution, however, did not hinder him from being guilty himself after his death; for, upon digging up his corpse forty days after his burial, he was found to have all the marks of an arch-vampire. His body was fresh and ruddy, his hair, beard, and nails were grown, and his veins were full of fluid blood, which ran from all parts of his body upon the shroud that he was buried in.

The *hadnagy*, or bailiff of the village, who was present at the digging up of the corpse, and was very expert in the whole business of vampirism, ordered a sharp stake to be drove quite through the body of the deceased, and to let it pass through his heart, which was attended with a hideous cry from the carcass, as if it had been alive.

This ceremony being performed, they cut off the head, and burnt the body to ashes.

After this, they proceeded in the same manner with the four other persons that died of vampirism, lest they also should be troublesome.

But all these executions could not hinder this dreadful prodigy from appearing again five years from its first breaking out.

In the space of three months, seventeen persons of different ages and sexes died of vampirism, some without any previous illness, and others after languishing two or three days.

Among others, it was said, that a girl named Stanoska, daughter of the Heyduke Jotuitzo, went to bed in perfect health, but awoke in the middle of the night, trembling, and crying out that the son of the Heyduke Millo, who died about nine weeks before, had almost strangled her while she was asleep. From that time she fell into a languishing state, and died at three days' end. Her evidence against Millo's son was looked upon as a proof of his being a vampire, and, upon digging up his body, he was found to be such.

At a consultation of the principal inhabitants of the place, attended by physicians and surgeons, it was considered how it was possible that the plague of vampirism should break out afresh, after the precautions that had been taken some years before: and, at last, it was found out that the original offender, Arnold Paul, had not only destroyed the four persons mentioned above, but had killed several beasts, which the late vampires, and particularly the son of Millo, had fed upon.

Upon this foundation a resolution was taken to dig up all the persons that had died within a certain time.

Out of forty were found seventeen, with all the evident tokens of vampirism; and they all had stakes driven through their hearts, their heads cut off, their bodies burnt, and their ashes thrown into the river. All these several enquiries and executions were carried on with all the forms of law, and attested by several officers who were in garrison in that country, by the surgeon-majors of the regiments, and by the principal inhabitants of the place. The original papers were all sent to the Imperial council of war at Vienna, which had issued out a commission to several officers to enquire into the truth of the fact.

GLOSSARY

Cashcaw and *Cassova*: Kosovo.

Hadnagy: Or Hadnagi; a town official or magistrate.

Medreiga, Medreyga: Currently Medveda, in Trstenik, Serbia.

Oppida Heidonum: The towns of Heydon.

Servia: Serbia, under the rule of the Ottoman Turks from 1496 to 1817.

Teyss: A river flowing through Romania and Serbia, called Tibiscus by the Romans and Timis or Temesch today.

AFTERWORD

Some researchers theorize that the "vampires" of Medreyga were actually victims of a rabies epidemic. Possibly. Others suggest diseases like pellagra (a skin condition sometimes associated with dementia) or porphyria (which can cause the gums to recede, making teeth look unnaturally long) were responsible for the physical characteristics exhibited by the unearthed corpses. Again—possibly.

Dom Calmet himself wasn't quite sure whether or not vampires were real. One thing that puzzled him was how a corpse could get in and out of its grave without disturbing the earth around it. Some supernatural theorists suggested that vampires could become immaterial, but Church teaching denied the possibility of physical beings changing their forms.

As noted earlier, the staking and destruction of Arnold Paul were repeated, with some variations, in vampire deaths for the next two centuries and more. Other aspects of his story, like the dangers of eating vampire-infected livestock, never really caught on among writers. Paul himself was apparently a man in a great deal of psychological anguish; but his character didn't become the basis for the modern vampire in fiction. After all. he was a peasant, killed by an overturned hay wagon; not a good template for a brooding anti-hero.

There had been a previous report from Kisiljevo, another Serbian village, more than 180 miles from where Paul lived. In 1725, about the same time as the Paul case, nine people in Kisiljevo were said to have died over the space of eight days, each after an illness lasting 24 hours. They all said that a peasant named Petar Blagojevic (sometimes Westernized as Peter Plogojowitz), who had died a few days earlier, had come back from the dead to suffocate them. (He also asked his widow to give him back his shoes.) The villagers, claiming that something similar had happened a few years earlier, demanded that a government official named Frombald allow them to dig up Blagojevic's body and destroy it. Frombald was reluctant and urged them to wait until he presented the case to his superiors; but the villagers insisted there was no time to lose. The vampire had to be destroyed right away—or everyone would desert Kisiljevo and move somewhere else.

Frombald reluctantly agreed. In his official account, printed in the Viennese newspaper Wienerisches Diarium, *(still published today as* Die Wiener Zeitung), *Frombald wrote:*

> *And since with such beings (which they call vampires) various symptoms are to be seen, such as: the body undecomposed, the skin, hair, beard, and nails growing; the villagers resolved, unanimously, to open the grave of Peter Plogojowitz, and to see if such above-mentioned signs were truly to be found on him....*

> *I did not detect the slightest odor that is otherwise characteristic of the dead; and the body (except for the nose, which was fallen away a little) was completely fresh, even the hair and beard. The nails, of which the old ones had fallen away, were grown on*

him. The old skin, which was somewhat white, had peeled away, and a new one had grown under it. The face, hands, feet, and the whole body were so constituted that they could not have been more perfect in his lifetime. In his mouth I saw, not without astonishment, some fresh blood, which, according to the general testimony, had been sucked from the people he had killed.

In short, all the indications were present as such spirits (as mentioned above) are supposed to have. After both the priest and I had seen this spectacle, the people grew more outraged than distressed; all the subjects hurriedly sharpened a stake to pierce the corpse to the heart.

Whereupon, as he was pierced, not only did blood, completely fresh, flow from his ears and mouth, but still other wild signs (which I pass over out of high respect). These things happened. Finally...they burned the above-mentioned body, in hoc casu [in this case] *to ashes; of which I informed the most laudable Administration; at the same time, I would like to request, obediently and humbly, that if a mistake was made in this matter, it should be attributed, not to me, but to the rabble, who were beside themselves with fear.*

In 2018, Kisiljevo started promoting the story to boost tourism.

For Western Europeans. vampires were examples of a previously unknown creature of fable and fancy. The vampire was more physical than the ghost and more complicated than the werewolf. At first, the most fascinating aspect seemed to be the unearthing of the lifelike corpse and the second killing of a dead man...

...but there was more to the vampire than that. In Germany, one young

poet read the reports of vampires sneaking into bedrooms and thought, "That sounds interesting..."

OSSENFELDER'S VAMPIRE

For thus shall I be kissing
And death's threshold thou'lt be crossing...

he 18th century was a time when "ghost stories" began to become popular entertainment in Western Europe, as actual belief in the supernatural began to fade. (Voltaire, who knew Calmet personally, mocked the belief in vampires in his Philosophical Dictionary *in 1764. That was the same year Horace Walpole started the genre of the Gothic novel with his supernatural-themed* The Castle of Otranto.) *None of the writers who took up the vampire theme in poetry or prose actually believed in such creatures—but they were intrigued by what the vampire could represent, in terms of life, death…and sex.*

Der Vampir (The Vampire) *was written in 1748, by the young German poet Heinrich August Ossenfelder. It's the first poem about a vampire—well, almost. The first-person narrator isn't an actual vampire; instead, impatient that a young woman named Christine refuses to sleep with him, he imagines getting drunk and raping her with the power and invulnerability of a vampire.*

While the poem was clearly influenced by the Arnold Paul account (note the reference to a "Heyduck," or Heyduke), Ossenfelder's vampire is presented, not as a blood-mad peasant clawing his way out of the filthy earth, but—for the first time ever—as a drunken rapist…or, as the poem would have it, as a sexy seducer…

THE VAMPIRE

Heinrich August Ossenfelder

My dear young maiden clingeth
Unbending fast and firm
To all the long-held teaching
Of a mother ever true;
As in vampires unmortal
Folk on Theyse's portal
Heyduck-like do believe.
But my Christine thou dost dally,
And wilt my loving parry
Till I myself avenging
To a vampire's health a-drinking
Him toast in pale tockay.
And as softly thou art sleeping
To thee shall I come creeping
And thy life's blood drain away.
And so shalt thou be trembling
For thus shall I be kissing
And death's threshold thou'lt be crossing
With fear, in my cold arms.
And last shall I thee question
Compared to such instruction
What are a mother's charms?

GLOSSARY

Heyduck: Or Heyduk, Heyduke, Haiduk; an irregular soldier in Hungary.

Theyse: Or Tisza; a large river in Hungary.

Tockay: Or Tokay; a sweet Hungarian wine from Tokaj.

AFTERWORD

Vampirism and sex had been linked before, most notably in the demons of the Near East who exhausted sleeping men in the night. And there were clearly sexual aspects to 18th century vampires, such as when "Stanoska, daughter of the Heyduke Jotuitzo," claimed that "the son of the Heyduke Millo, who died about nine weeks before, had almost strangled her while she was asleep." But Ossenfelder was the first writer to deliberately combine sex and bloodsucking vampirism, even in a metaphorical way. Christine will bleed from the loss of her virginity—but she'll enjoy it, because "dying" is an old poetic metaphor for orgasm. Ossenfelder's narrator, as the vampire, represents a liberating sexuality opposed to a suffocating Christianity that stifles feelings and natural urges. It's rape as liberation. Or, liberation as rape.

Before the 1960's, the sexual aspect of the vampire was rarely discussed openly (although it's very strongly indicated in. for example, Orson Welles's 1938 radio adaptation of Dracula*). The vampire often hypnotized his lovely female victim before biting her; part of the horror was the loss of free will, something very much on people's minds, especially in the 1930's and 1940's, when several highly influential vampire movies came out, most featuring Dracula. The vampire, often presented as a foreign aristocrat, symbolized the old, undemocratic order that modern Britons and Americans, who prized individualism and free will above all else, had to fight against. But it wasn't as simple as that. While the battle against vampires from the Depression through the Cold War might be a struggle for individuality, the battle was* fought with crosses, holy water, and communion wafers—tools of a faith that had almost been set aside by a secular Protestant society. The vampire was a kind of anti-Christ who rose from the dead and promised eternal life in exchange for blood and obedience; but if an anti-Christ was real, then Christ had to be real, as well. The vampire was both a threat to modern secular society and an implied criticism of it.

In the 1960's and 1970's, society was more secular than ever; people were turning against old notions of religion and sexual restraint; in the new vampire tales, women might willingly offer their necks to their undead lovers or masters without being hypnotized, and the use of Catholic paraphernalia began to wane. Once again, Christianity was seen as hypocritical and suffocating. Once again, vampires were exemplars of individualism and a free and open sexuality. In fact, maybe vampires were real and Christianity was the superstition. All of that is prefigured in Ossenfelder's poem from 1748.

But Ossenfelder's poem is more than a challenge to social conformity. It is, fundamentally, a heterosexual rape fantasy. The "vampire" becomes Christine's master, introducing her into a new life of mental and physical service to an eternal patriarchy. She might enjoy it because it's "for her own good," but her wishes are, really, entirely beside the point.

Because the vampire is after blood, the gender of the victim is immaterial. Arnold Paul, after all, was "tormented" by the mysterious male Turkish vampire. The idea that vampires had a taste for their own kind forms the basis of the next poem, which is probably the first piece of vampire fiction with an obvious gay subtext...

SIGISMUND

"From the drear mansion of the tomb,
From the low regions of the dead,
The ghost of Sigismund doth roam,
And dreadful haunts me in my bed…"

When the reports of Arnold Paul and the vampire plague reached England in 1732, the response wasn't horror—but amusement. After all, the last witch in Britain had been burned way, way back in 1727, so six or seven years later, it was easy to mock the credulous bumpkins from those strange-sounding countries. (It should be said, though, the laughter was louder in the city; in rural England, suicides were still forbidden burial in consecrated ground, and might be buried at a crossroads with a stake through their bodies. England's last crossroads staking took place in 1823, after which the practice was made illegal.)

But the English language is always on the lookout for new words, and "vampire" quickly became a satiric political metaphor. Businesses that took money from people and gave little or nothing in return were vampires; excessive taxes were vampiric, writers were vampirized by publishers who didn't pay royalties on time, and so forth.

In 1765, the composer William Hayes presented a little ditty called The Thirsty Vampires, a comic song about drinking. In his introduction, Hayes explained that the song "alludes to a Notion receiv'd in Poland & other Countries, that some Persons, after they are dead & buried, have a Power of sucking the Blood of others till they die; a consumptive Person is therefore said to be sucked by some Vampire: for so they call those who are supposed to have this Faculty."

> The thirsty Vampires, some believe,
> Their Graves can pierce and Coffins leave,
> To suck poor Mortals dry.
>
> If I've the Luck to drink when dead,
> My Liquor shan't be Blood tho' red.
>
> The Juice of Grapes best suits to me,
> To some huge Cask of Wine I'll be,
> I'll be a Vampire when I die.

The English kept laughing through most of the 1700's. But by the beginning of the 19th century, two literary movements began altering attitudes about the supernatural.

As though opposing the rationalism of the Enlightenment and the growing power of the Industrial Revolution, literature became fascinated with feelings. "Gothic" novels found chills and thrills in ancient castles and moonlit graveyards; two or three decades later, the Romantic movement celebrated feelings of every kind—including feelings of horror and terror. So, some poets thought, maybe living corpses who drank blood were scary, after all...

Robert Southey's poetic epic Thalaba the Destroyer (1801) featured a terrifying female vampire (see Volume II; The Vampire Ladies); and in 1812, a minor poet named John Stagg wrote the first stand-alone poem in English about a vampire. Stagg, who lived in Manchester most of his life with his wife and seven children, was known as "The Blind Bard," having lost his sight through an injury as a boy. "The Vampyre" is the poem for which he's chiefly remembered—an eerie anecdote clearly inspired by Arnold Paul. Judging by the names of the characters (Herman, Gertrude, Sigismund), the events take place in a German-speaking part of Europe.

Out of the grave, Sigismund the vampire (or "vampyre," the spelling that for some reason became popular in England for the first half of the 19th century) is both a solid figure and a phantom. He's draining Herman every night; but Herman's wife Gertrude, in the same bed, is unaware of what's happening...

THE VAMPYRE

John Stagg

"Why looks my lord so deadly pale?
Why fades the crimson from his cheek?
What can my dearest husband ail?
Thy heartfelt cares, O Herman, speak!

"Why, at the silent hour of rest,
Dost thou in sleep so sadly mourn?
As tho' with heaviest grief oppress'd,
Griefs too distressful to be borne.

"Why heaves thy breast? — why throbs thy heart?
O speak! and if there be relief
Thy Gertrude solace shall impart,
If not, at least shall share thy grief.

"Wan is that cheek, which once the bloom
Of manly beauty sparkling show'd;
Dim are those eyes, in pensive gloom,
That late with keenest lustre glow'd.

"Say why, too, at the midnight hour,
You sadly pant and tug for breath,
As if some supernat'ral pow'r
Were pulling you away to death?
"Restless, tho' sleeping, still you groan,
And with convulsive horror start;
O Herman! to thy wife make known
That grief which preys upon thy heart."

"O Gertrude! how shall I relate
Th' uncommon anguish that I feel;
Strange as severe is this my fate, —
A fate I cannot long conceal.

"In spite of all my wonted strength,
Stern destiny has seal'd my doom;
The dreadful malady at length
Will drag me to the silent tomb!"

"But say, my Herman, what's the cause
Of this distress, and all thy care.
That, vulture-like, thy vitals gnaws,
And galls thy bosom with despair?

"Sure this can be no common grief,
Sure this can be no common pain?
Speak, if this world contain relief,
That soon thy Gertrude shall obtain."

"O Gertrude, 'tis a horrid cause,
O Gertrude, 'tis unusual care,
That, vulture-like, my vitals gnaws,
And galls my bosom with despair.

"Young Sigismund, my once dear friend,
But lately he resign'd his breath;
With others I did him attend
Unto the silent house of death.

"For him I wept, for him I mourn'd,
Paid all to friendship that was due;
But sadly friendship is return'd,
Thy Herman he must follow too!

"Must follow to the gloomy grave,
In spite of human art or skill;
No pow'r on earth my life can save,
'Tis fate's unalterable will!

"Young Sigismund, my once dear friend,
But now my persecutor foul,
Doth his malevolence extend
E'en to the torture of my soul.

"By night, when, wrapt in soundest sleep,
All mortals share a soft repose,
My soul doth dreadful vigils keep,
More keen than which hell scarcely knows.

"From the drear mansion of the tomb,
From the low regions of the dead,
The ghost of Sigismund doth roam,
And dreadful haunts me in my bed!

"There, vested in infernal guise,
(By means to me not understood,)
Close to my side the goblin lies,
And drinks away my vital blood!
"Sucks from my veins the streaming life,
And drains the fountain of my heart!
O Gertrude, Gertrude! dearest wife!
Unutterable is my smart.

"When surfeited, the goblin dire,
With banqueting by suckled gore,
Will to his sepulchre retire,
Till night invites him forth once more.

"Then will he dreadfully return,
And from my veins life's juices drain;
Whilst, slumb'ring, I with anguish mourn,
And toss with agonizing pain!

"Already I'm exhausted, spent;
His carnival is nearly o'er,
My soul with agony is rent,
To-morrow I shall be no more!

"But, O my Gertrude! dearest wife!
The keenest pangs hath last remain'd—
When dead, I too shall seek thy life,
Thy blood by Herman shall be drain'd!

"But to avoid this horrid fate,
Soon as I'm dead and laid in earth,
Drive thro' my corpse a jav'lin straight; —
This shall prevent my coming forth.

"O watch with me, this last sad night,
Watch in your chamber here alone,
But carefully conceal the light
Until you hear my parting groan.

"Then at what time the vesper-bell
Of yonder convent shall be toll'd,
That peal shall ring my passing knell,
And Herman's body shall be cold!

"Then, and just then, thy lamp make bare,
The starting ray, the bursting light,
Shall from my side the goblin scare,

And show him visible to sight!"

The live-long night poor Gertrude sate,
Watch'd by her sleeping, dying lord;
The live-long night she mourn'd his fate,
The object whom her soul ador'd.

Then at what time the vesper-bell
Of yonder convent sadly toll'd,
Then, then was peal'd his passing knell,
The hapless Herman he was cold!

Just at that moment Gertrude drew
From 'neath her cloak the hidden light;
When, dreadful! she beheld in view
The shade of Sigismund! — sad sight!

Indignant roll'd his ireful eyes,
That gleam'd with wild horrific stare;
And fix'd a moment with surprise,
Beheld aghast th' enlight'ning glare.
His jaws cadaverous were besmear'd
With clott'd carnage o'er and o'er,
And all his horrid whole appear'd
Distent, and fill'd with human gore!

With hideous scowl the spectre fled;
She shriek'd aloud; — then swoon'd away!
The hapless Herman in his bed,
All pale, a lifeless body lay!

Next day in council 'twas decreed,
(Urg'd at the instance of the state,)
That shudd'ring nature should be freed

From pests like these ere 'twas too late.

The choir then burst the fun'ral dome
Where Sigismund was lately laid,
And found him, tho' within the tomb,
Still warm as life, and undecay'd.

With blood his visage was distain'd,
Ensanguin'd were his frightful eyes,
Each sign of former life remain'd,
Save that all motionless he lies.

The corpse of Herman they contrive
To the same sepulchre to take,
And thro' both carcasses they drive,
Deep in the earth, a sharpen'd stake!

By this was finish'd their career,
Thro' this no longer they can roam;
From them their friends have nought to fear,
Both quiet keep the slumb'ring tomb.

GLOSSARY

Vesper: Evening prayer.
Wonted: Usual, regular.

AFTERWORD

So, Herman and Sigismund are going to spend eternity one on top of the other, with no indication that their souls have been released to eternal rest, or that Herman will ever be reunited with Gertrude in the grave, let alone the afterlife.

Is the image supposed to be shameful? Has an infectious disease been stopped in a rather extreme way? Or are the poem's two real lovers united until the end of time?

In most of the "real" cases of infectious walking corpses or vampires, it can seem that gender is no more important than the question of whether a male or female wolf is attacking you. But there does seem to be something more going on here, even if it's unconscious.

While later vampire tales would echo Stagg's homoeroticism, either celebrating it or using it as another element of horror, his idea of a human community justly and wisely uniting against a vampire—doubtless taken from the stories Calmet collected—all but disappears from the genre. By the mid-19th century, if an outraged community does gather together to do away with a vampire, they do so as a lynch mob without any sort of official approval. Even in stories where the hero assembles a small group of like-minded men to righteously seek out and kill the vampire (as in Dracula), they act in secret, as vigilantes outside the law.

The main reason not to involve the authorities is that, by the second half of the 19th century, it was taken for granted that nobody believed in such things, and that complaining of vampires to the local policeman or town council would be useless.

This change is implicit in the following stories, when the modern literary vampire really comes into recognizable form for the first time. We're no longer in Central Europe, but central London—in a hard, glittering, cynical society, where the vampire's existence is something no rational person would ever suspect...

DARVELL

*Where there is mystery, it is generally supposed
there must be evil...*

"*It is my destiny to ruin all I come near.*" Not exactly something a wife wants to hear from her husband. But that was what England's most notorious poet, George Gordon, Lord Byron (1788-1824) wrote to Lady Byron, as one reason why their marriage wouldn't work out. That sentiment would also become attached to the classic image of the male vampire—an image which owes a very great deal to the man one ex-lover, Lady Caroline Lamb, called "mad, bad, and dangerous to know."

Byron was a genius, tall, dark, handsome, and far busier sexually, with both women and men, than was safe for him. Pursued by scandals political and sexual (including rumors of incest with his half-sister), he left England for the Continent. In the public eye—and sometimes, perhaps, in his own mind—his life merged with the heroes of his poems Childe Harold's Pilgrimage and Manfred: driven, doomed, brooding men. The Byronic Hero became an archetype, reflected in endless stories, novels, movies and TV shows. (The screenwriter William Goldman has summarized the Byronic Hero as "a tall, dark man with a past.")

The Byronic Hero would also become the foundation of every modern vampire. This is how it happened:

Lord Byron knew about vampires. In 1813, he wrote a long poem set in the Middle East called The Giaour (a Turkish word for "infidel") that included these lines—as one of the characters calls down a curse upon the hero:

> But first, on earth as vampire sent,
> Thy corse shall from its tomb be rent:
> Then ghastly haunt thy native place,
> And suck the blood of all thy race;
> . . . . Yet loathe the banquet which perforce
> Must feed thy livid living corse:
> Thy victims ere they yet expire
> Shall know the demon for their sire,
>
> As cursing thee, thou cursing them,

Thy flowers are withered on the stem.
. . . Then stalking to thy sullen grave,
Go - and with Ghouls and Affits rave;
Till these in horror shrink away
From spectre more accursed than they!

This is the first time that such self-loathing was attached to a vampire;
a far cry from Ossenfelder's confident seducer.

Although English people had first heard of vampires more than eighty
years earlier, undead bloodsuckers were still new enough for Byron to
include a few ethnographic comments on the subject in the notes to his
poem:

> *"The Vampire superstition is still general in the*
> *Levant....I recollect a whole family being terrified by*
> *the scream of a child, which they imagined must*
> *proceed from such a visitation...The stories told in*
> *Hungary and Greece of these foul feeders are*
> *singular, and some of them most incredibly attested."*

(The Greek vampire, by the way, is the vrykolakas, sometimes spelled
vorvolakas, vourdoulakas or even broukolakas.)

In 1816, three years after writing The Giaour, *Byron was staying at the*
Villa Diodati, a rented mansion on the shores of Switzerland's Lake
Geneva, with some friends, including the poet Percy Shelley; his soon-
to-be-wife, Mary Godwin (later Mary Shelley); Mary's stepsister Claire
Clairmont (who was carrying Byron's child), and Dr. John William
Polidori, Lord Byron's young physician.

The year before, the Indonesian volcano Mt. Tambora had erupted in
an explosion so gigantic that it affected the world's weather. 1816 was
known as "the year without a summer," and Byron and company spent
a lot of time indoors during the rainy days and nights. They read
horror stories and poems (including Coleridge's Christabel, *featuring a*
seductive female demon with some vampire-ish qualities, although she
doesn't drink blood), and, as Mary Shelley later remembered:

" 'We will each write a ghost story,' said Lord Byron,
and his proposition was acceded to."

Mary, all of 18 years old, ended up writing Frankenstein. Clair wrote nothing; Polidori started a "terrible idea about a skull-headed lady" (to quote Mary) that may never have been finished. As for Lord Byron and Percy Shelley, again quoting Mary Shelley:

"The illustrious poets also, annoyed by the platitudes
of prose, speedily relinquished their uncongenial
task."

Byron wrote fewer than 2,000 words before giving up. The unfinished and untitled effort has been published as either A Fragment or The Burial. If Byron had completed it, it might have been the first prose vampire story. (Although, to be fair, there are some reservations on this point, to be discussed in the Afterword.)

Byron's main character is presented through the prism of Byron's own person and personality. (Which is only to be expected.) Augustus Darvell is nothing like Arnold Paul or his contemporaries. He's not from the Middle East or Central Europe; but, as his name indicates, from old Anglo-Norman stock.

More importantly, Darvell is no peasant like Arnold Paul or Petar Blagojevic. Augustus Darvell would never get close enough to a hay wagon to risk being killed by one, and he wouldn't return from the dead to ask his wife for his old shoes; he'd order a new pair from his London bootmaker.

Darvell is not in any obvious way a "foul feeder," but rather "a being of no common order." He and the unnamed narrator live in the hot-house world of England's upper classes, where the strongest relationships are between men, and male bonding includes not asking personal questions...even if, perhaps, one really should.

The incomplete tale only hints at what might have been, and it breaks off before Byron even gets to the actual vampire part! Nevertheless, the "fragment" of narrative sets the stage for the next two centuries and *beyond of vampire tales. The blood of Byron courses through the veins of Dracula, Barnabas, Lestat, Edward and others.*

THE BURIAL:

A FRAGMENT

George Gordon, Lord Byron

In the year 17__ , having for some time determined on a journey through countries not hitherto much frequented by travelers, I set out, accompanied by a friend, whom I shall designate by the name of Augustus Darvell. He was a few years my elder, and a man of considerable fortune and ancient family, advantages which an extensive capacity prevented him alike from undervaluing and overrating. Some peculiar circumstances in his private history had rendered him to me an object of attention, of interest, and even of regard, which neither the reserve of his manners, not occasional indication of an inquietude at times approaching to alienation of mind, could extinguish.

I was yet young in life, which I had begun early; but my intimacy with him was of a recent date: we had been educated at the same schools and university; but his progress through these had preceded mine, and he had been deeply initiated into what is called the world, while I was yet in my noviciate. While thus engaged, I had heard much both of his past and present life; and although in these accounts there were many and irreconcilable contradictions, I could still gather from the whole that he was a being of no common order, and one who, whatever pains he might take to avoid remark, would still be remarkable. I had cultivated his acquaintance subsequently, and endeavoured to obtain his friendship, but this last appeared to be unattainable; whatever affections he might have possessed seemed now, some to have been extinguished, and others to be concentred: that his feelings were acute, I had sufficient opportunities of observing; for, although he could control, he could not altogether disguise them: still he had a power of giving to one passion the appearance of another in such a manner that it was difficult to define the nature of what was working within him; and the expressions of his features would vary so rapidly, though slightly, that it was useless to trace them to their sources. It was evident that he was a prey to some cureless disquiet; but whether it arose from ambition, love, remorse, grief, from one or all of these, or merely from a morbid temperament akin to disease, I could not discover: there were circumstances alleged, which might have justified the application to each of these causes; but, as I have before said, these were so contradictory and contradicted, that none could be fixed upon with accuracy. Where there is mystery, it is generally supposed that there must also be evil: I know not how this may be, but in him there certainly was the one, though I could not ascertain the extent of the other—and felt loth, as far as regarded himself, to believe in its existence. My advances were received with sufficient coldness; but I was young, and not easily discouraged, and at length succeeded in obtaining, to a certain degree, that common-place intercourse and moderate confidence of common and every day concerns, created and cemented by similarity of pursuit and frequency of meeting, which is called intimacy, or friendship, according to the ideas of him who uses those words to express them.

Darvell had already travelled extensively; and to him I had applied for information with regard to the conduct of my intended journey. It was my secret wish that he might be prevailed on to accompany me: it was also a probable hope, founded upon the shadowy restlessness which I had observed in him, and to which the animation which he appeared to feel on such subjects, and his apparent indifference to all by which he was more immediately surrounded, gave fresh strength. This wish I first hinted, and then expressed: his answer, though I had partly expected it, gave me all the pleasure of surprise—he consented; and, after the requisite arrangements, we commenced our voyages. After journeying through various countries of the south of Europe, our attention was turned towards the East, according to our original destination; and it was in my progress through those regions that the incident occurred upon which will turn what I may have to relate.

The constitution of Darvell, which must from his appearance have been in early life more than usually robust, had been for some time gradually giving way, without the intervention of any apparent disease: he had neither cough nor hectic, yet he became daily more enfeebled: his habits were temperate, and he neither declined nor complained of fatigue, yet he was evidently wasting away: he became more and more silent and sleepless, and at length so seriously altered, that my alarm grew proportionate to what I conceived to be his danger.

We had determined, on our arrival at Smyrna, on an excursion to the ruins of Ephesus and Sardis, from which I endeavoured to dissuade him in his present state of indisposition -- but in vain: there appeared to be an oppression on his mind, and a solemnity in his manner, which ill corresponded with his eagerness to proceed on what I regarded as a mere party of pleasure, little suited to a valetudinarian; but I opposed him no longer—and in a few days we set off together, accompanied only by a serrugee and a single janizary.

We had passed halfway towards the remains of Ephesus, leaving behind us the more fertile environs of Smyrna, and were entering upon that wild and tenantless track through the marshes and defiles which lead to the few huts yet lingering over the broken columns of Diana— the roofless walls of expelled Christianity, and the still more recent but complete desolation of abandoned mosques—when the sudden and rapid illness of my companion obliged us to halt at a Turkish cemetery, the turbaned tombstones of which were the sole indication that human life had ever been a sojourner in this wilderness. The only caravansera we had seen was left some hours behind us, not a vestige of a town or even cottage was within sight or hope, and this "city of the dead" appeared to be the sole refuge for my unfortunate friend, who seemed on the verge of becoming the last of its inhabitants.

In this situation, I looked round for a place where he might most conveniently repose:—contrary to the usual aspect of Mahometan burial-grounds, the cypresses were in this few in number, and these thinly scattered over its extent: the tombstones were mostly fallen, and worn with age:—upon one of the most considerable of these, and beneath one of the most spreading trees, Darvell supported himself, in a half-reclining posture, with great difficulty. He asked for water. I had some doubts of our being able to find any, and prepared to go in search of it with hesitating despondency—but he desired me to remain; and turning to Suleiman, our janizary, who stood by us smoking with great tranquility, he said, "*Suleiman, verbana su,*" (i.e. bring some water,) and went on describing the spot where it was to be found with great minuteness, at a small well for camels, a few hundred yards to the right: the janizary obeyed. I said to Darvell, "How did you know this?"—He replied, "From our situation; you must perceive that this place was once inhabited, and could not have been so without springs: I have also been here before."

"You have been here before!—How came you never to mention this to me? and what could you be doing in a place where no one would remain a moment longer than they could help it?"

To this question I received no answer. In the meantime Suleiman returned with the water, leaving the serrugee and the horses at the fountain. The quenching of his thirst had the appearance of reviving him for a moment; and I conceived hopes of his being able to proceed, or at least to return, and I urged the attempt. He was silent—and appeared to be collecting his spirits for an effort to speak. He began.

"This is the end of my journey, and of my life—I came here to die: but I have a request to make, a command—for such my last words must be—You will observe it?"

"Most certainly; but have better hopes."

"I have no hopes, nor wishes, but this—conceal my death from every human being."

"I hope there will be no occasion; that you will recover, and—"

"Peace!—it must be so: promise this."

"I do."

"Swear it, by all that"—He here dictated an oath of great solemnity.

"There is no occasion for this—I will observe your request; and to doubt me is—"

"It cannot be helped, —you must swear."

I took the oath: it appeared to relieve him. He removed a seal ring from his finger, on which were some Arabic characters, and presented it to me. He proceeded—

"On the ninth day of the month, at noon precisely (what month you please, but this must be the day), you must fling this ring into the salt springs which run into the Bay of Eleusis: the day after, at the same hour, you must repair to the ruins of the temple of Ceres, and wait one hour."

"Why?"

"You will see."

"The ninth day of the month, you say?"

"The ninth."

As I observed that the present was the ninth day of the month, his countenance changed, and he paused. As he sat, evidently becoming more feeble, a stork, with a snake in her beak, perched upon a tombstone near us; and, without devouring her prey, appeared to be steadfastly regarding us. I know not what impelled me to drive it away, but the attempt was useless; she made a few circles in the air, and returned exactly to the same spot. Darvell pointed to it, and smiled: he spoke—I know not whether to himself or to me—but the words were only, "'Tis well!"

"What is well? what do you mean?"

"No matter: you must bury me here this evening, and exactly where that bird is now perched. You know the rest of my injunctions."

He then proceeded to give me several directions as to the manner in which his death might be best concealed. After these were finished, he exclaimed, "You perceive that bird?"

"Certainly."

"And the serpent writhing in her beak?"

"Doubtless: there is nothing uncommon in it; it is her natural prey. But it is odd that she does not devour it."

He smiled in a ghastly manner, and said, faintly, "It is not yet time!" As he spoke, the stork flew away. My eyes followed it for a moment, it could hardly be longer than ten might be counted. I felt Darvell's weight, as it were, increase upon my shoulder, and, turning to look upon his face, perceived that he was dead!

I was shocked with the sudden certainty which could not be mistaken—his countenance in a few minutes became nearly black. I should have attributed so rapid a change to poison, had I not been aware that he had no opportunity of receiving it unperceived. The day was declining, the body was rapidly altering, and nothing remained but to fulfil his request. With the aid of Suleiman's ataghan and my own sabre, we scooped a shallow grave upon the spot which Darvell had indicated: the earth easily gave way, having already received some Mahometan tenant. We dug as deeply as the time permitted us, and throwing the dry earth upon all that remained of the singular being so lately departed, we cut a few sods of greener turf from the less withered soil around us, and laid them upon his sepulchre.

Between astonishment and grief, I was tearless.

GLOSSARY

Afrit: In Arabic legend, a kind of evil genie (djinn).

Ataghan: Or yataghan; a curved, single-bladed Turkish sword.

Bay of Eleusis: Eleusis itself was the site of an ancient temple in Greece dedicated to Demeter (Ceres) where the highly secret "Eleusinian Mysteries" were performed. Demeter was the goddess of agriculture and the harvest, and was connected with Classical ideas of rebirth or resurrection. (It's also the name of the Russian schooner that brings Count Dracula to England in Stoker's novel.)

Caravansera: Caravan.

Corse: Corpse.

Ephesus: In Izmir Province, Turkey. Ancient Ionian Greek city, once the site of the Temple of Artemis (Roman Diana), one of the Seven Wonders of the Ancient World.

Janizary: Also "janissary," a member of the Sultan's guard in Turkey from the 14th-19th centuries.

Mahometan: Muslim.

Ninth Day of the Month: In ancient Roman calendars, the 9th day of a month was the "nones," originally a day dedicated to the half moon.

Sardis: Ancient city, now part of Turkey; one of the Seven Churches of Asia in the Biblical *Book of Revelation.*

Serrugee: The driver of the horses.

Smyrna: An ancient harbor city in Eastern Turkey (Izmir Province), originally settled circa 6500 BC. At the time of the story, the center of a large Greek community.

Stork, with a snake in her beak: With the story unfinished, the meaning of this is ultimately unclear; but the stork was associated with rebirth—and so is the snake, because it sheds its skin. However, a stork eating a snake was sometimes seen as symbolizing the defeat of the Devil.

Valetudinarian: Someone overly-concerned about their health, but not quite a hypochondriac.

AFTERWORD

If Byron had written his fragmentary account of Augustus Darvell in private, without discussing it with any friends or hangers-on who would remember it later, then we would have no idea what the story was really about.

Thanks to Dr. Polidori, we know, at least in general, where Byron would have taken the tale:

"...his Lordship had said that it was his intention of writing a ghost story, depending for interest upon the circumstances of two friends leaving England, and one dying in Greece, the other finding him alive, upon his return, and making love to his sister."

So Polidori wrote in 1819. But notice that the word "vampire" is missing from that synopsis. Did Byron intend to make Darvell a vampire, or only some other kind of revenant—the type that doesn't drink blood? (Another mystery: What, if anything, was the secret of the ring with the "Arabic characters"?)

We'll never know for sure; but, as noted above, Byron certainly knew about vampires, and had written of them tangentially in The Giaour; *and Darvell's sudden deterioration when he "dies" may be the first example of the "rapid decay" vampire trope. There are also hints that Darvell is connected with ancient pre-Christian rites—something that Anne Rice would make much of with her vampires.*

But all this is supposition. Fundamentally, the unfinished tale of Augustus Darvell is included as a vampire story in this collection because Polidori used Byron's fragment, rather closely in some respects, as the basis for his own story, boldly titled The Vampyre, *which would inspire the world of fantastic fiction for the next quarter of a century...*

LORD RUTHVEN

...that mystery, which to his exalted imagination began to assume the appearance of something supernatural.

In the summer of 1816, Dr. Polidori's attempts at writing a ghost story earned him nothing but ridicule at the Villa Diodati. He desperately wanted Lord Byron's approval, to compete in his circle—and he never got it. Byron would call him "Polly-dolly" and mock everything from his literary pretensions to his love-life. Sometimes Polidori took it, other times he called Byron a "cold-hearted monster." Eventually, Polidori got his revenge and a chance at fame— or so he thought.

He took the outline of Byron's fragment—the aristocratic vampire who travels to Greece with a younger man, seems to die, makes the young man swear not to reveal the death for a time, and then returns from the grave to pursue the man's sister—and added elements of Byron himself to the vampire—or "vampyre."

Polidori called his vampyre Lord Ruthven. Many people pronounce this "Ruth-ven," either with a long "u" like "truth" or a short "u" like "stuff." But Ruthven is an actual title of Scottish nobility, and the Scottish pronunciation is apparently "Riven" or "Ruh-ven." One pronunciation brings up the association of something ruthless; the other, of a torn and riven soul.

By using the Lord Ruthven name, Polidori was making the true identity of the vampyre even clearer. In 1816, Byron's jilted mistress, Lady Caroline Lamb, had written a roman-a-clef about the affair called Glenarvon; *she gave her heartless Byron stand-in the title of Lord Ruthven.*

Polidori claimed that he more or less dashed off the actual story "in two idle mornings" with "a lady" by his side. In another account, he claims it took three mornings. The "lady" may have been the Countess of Breuss, a Russian living near the Villa Diodati. Exactly what happened then is a little murky. Polidori may have given the story to the Countess, who had it passed on to Henry Colburn, the London publisher of The New Monthly Magazine. The Vampyre: A Tale *was first published in the April 1819 issue of that magazine, and the literary world had its first true vampire craze...*

THE VAMPYRE;
A TALE.

John William Polidori

It happened that in the midst of the dissipations attendant upon a London winter, there appeared at the various parties of the leaders of the town a nobleman more remarkable for his singularities than his rank. He gazed upon the mirth around him as if he could not participate therein. Apparently, the light laughter of the fair only attracted his attention that he might by a look quell it, and throw fear into those breasts where thoughtlessness reigned. Those who felt this sensation of awe, could not explain whence it arose: some attributed it to the dead grey eye, which, fixing upon the object's face, did not seem to penetrate, and at one glance to pierce through to the inward workings of the heart; but fell upon the cheek with a leaden ray that weighed upon the skin it could not pass. His peculiarities caused him to be invited to every house; all wished to see him, and those who had been accustomed to violent excitement, and now felt the weight of ennui, were pleased at having something in their presence capable of engaging their attention. In spite of the deadly hue of his face, which never gained a warmer tint, either from the blush of modesty, or from the strong emotion of passion, though its form and outline were beautiful, many of the female hunters after notoriety attempted to win his attentions, and gain, at least, some marks of what they might term affection: Lady Mercer, who had been the mockery of every monster shown in drawing-rooms since her marriage, threw herself in his way, and did all but put on the dress of a mountebank, to attract his notice:—though in vain:—when she stood before him, though his eyes were apparently fixed upon hers, still it seemed as if they were unperceived;—even her unappalled impudence was baffled, and she left the field. But though the common adulteress could not influence even the guidance of his eyes, it was not that the female sex was indifferent to him: yet such was the apparent caution with which he spoke to the virtuous wife and innocent daughter, that few knew he ever addressed himself to females. He had, however, the reputation of a winning tongue; and whether it was that it even overcame the dread of his singular character, or that they were moved by his apparent hatred of vice, he was as often among those females who form the boast of their sex from their domestic virtues, as among those who sully it by their vices.

About the same time, there came to London a young gentleman of the name of Aubrey: he was an orphan left with an only sister in the possession of great wealth, by parents who died while he was yet in childhood. Left also to himself by guardians, who thought it their duty merely to take care of his fortune, while they relinquished the more important charge of his mind to the care of mercenary subalterns, he cultivated more his imagination than his judgment. He had, hence, that high romantic feeling of honour and candour which daily ruins so many milliners' apprentices. He believed all to sympathise with virtue, and thought that vice was thrown in by Providence merely for the picturesque effect of the scene, as we see in romances: he thought that the misery of a cottage merely consisted in the vesting of clothes, which were as warm, but which were better adapted to the painter's eye by their irregular folds and various coloured patches. He thought, in fine, that the dreams of poets were the realities of life. He was handsome, frank, and rich: for these reasons, upon his entering into the gay circles, many mothers surrounded him, striving which should describe with least truth their languishing or romping favourites: the daughters at the same time, by their brightening countenances when he approached, and by their sparkling eyes, when he opened his lips, soon led him into false notions of his talents and his merit. Attached as he was to the romance of his solitary hours, he was startled at finding, that, except in the tallow and wax candles that flickered, not from the presence of a ghost, but from want of snuffing, there was no foundation in real life for any of that congeries of pleasing pictures and descriptions contained in those volumes, from which he had formed his study. Finding, however, some compensation in his gratified vanity, he was about to relinquish his dreams, when the extraordinary being we have above described, crossed him in his career.

He watched him; and the very impossibility of forming an idea of the character of a man entirely absorbed in himself, who gave few other signs of his observation of external objects, than the tacit assent to their existence, implied by the avoidance of their contact: allowing his imagination to picture everything that flattered its propensity to extravagant ideas, he soon formed this object into the hero of a romance, and determined to observe the offspring of his fancy, rather than the person before him. He became acquainted with him, paid him attentions, and so far advanced upon his notice, that his presence was always recognised. He gradually learnt that Lord Ruthven's affairs were embarrassed, and soon found, from the notes of preparation in ——— Street, that he was about to travel. Desirous of gaining some information respecting this singular character, who, till now, had only whetted his curiosity, he hinted to his guardians, that it was time for him to perform the tour, which for many generations has been thought necessary to enable the young to take some rapid steps in the career of vice towards putting themselves upon an equality with the aged, and not allowing them to appear as if fallen from the skies, whenever scandalous intrigues are mentioned as the subjects of pleasantry or of praise, according to the degree of skill shewn in carrying them on. They consented: and Aubrey immediately mentioning his intentions to Lord Ruthven, was surprised to receive from him a proposal to join him. Flattered by such a mark of esteem from him, who, apparently, had nothing in common with other men, he gladly accepted it, and in a few days they had passed the circling waters.

Hitherto, Aubrey had had no opportunity of studying Lord Ruthven's character, and now he found that, though many more of his actions were exposed to his view, the results offered different conclusions from the apparent motives to his conduct. His companion was profuse in his liberality;—the idle, the vagabond, and the beggar, received from his hand more than enough to relieve their immediate wants. But Aubrey could not avoid remarking that it was not upon the virtuous, reduced to indigence by the misfortunes attendant even upon virtue, that he bestowed his alms;—these were sent from the door with hardly suppressed sneers; but when the profligate came to ask something, not to relieve his wants, but to allow him to wallow in his lust, or to sink him still deeper in his iniquity, he was sent away with rich charity. This was, however, attributed by him to the greater importunity of the vicious, which generally prevails over the retiring bashfulness of the virtuous indigent. There was one circumstance about the charity of his Lordship, which was still more impressed upon his mind: all those upon whom it was bestowed, inevitably found that there was a curse upon it, for they were all either led to the scaffold, or sunk to the lowest and the most abject misery. At Brussels and other towns through which they passed, Aubrey was surprised at the apparent eagerness with which his companion sought for the centers of all fashionable vice; there he entered into all the spirit of the faro table: he betted, and always gambled with success, except where the known sharper was his antagonist, and then he lost even more than he gained; but it was always with the same unchanging face, with which he generally watched the society around: it was not, however, so when he encountered the rash youthful novice, or the luckless father of a numerous family; then his very wish seemed fortune's law—this apparent abstractedness of mind was laid aside, and his eyes sparkled with more fire than that of the cat whilst dallying with the half-dead mouse. In every town, he left the formerly affluent youth, torn from the circle he adorned, cursing, in the solitude of a dungeon, the fate that had drawn him within the reach of this fiend; whilst many a father sat frantic, amidst the speaking looks of mute hungry children, without a single farthing of his late immense wealth, wherewith to buy even sufficient to satisfy their present craving. Yet he took no money from the gambling table; but immediately lost, to the ruiner of many, the last gilder he had just snatched from the convulsive grasp of the innocent:

this might but be the result of a certain degree of knowledge, which was not, however, capable of combating the cunning of the more experienced. Aubrey often wished to represent this to his friend, and beg him to resign that charity and pleasure which proved the ruin of all, and did not tend to his own profit;—but he delayed it—for each day he hoped his friend would give him some opportunity of speaking frankly and openly to him; however, this never occurred. Lord Ruthven in his carriage, and amidst the various wild and rich scenes of nature, was always the same: his eye spoke less than his lip; and though Aubrey was near the object of his curiosity, he obtained no greater gratification from it than the constant excitement of vainly wishing to break that mystery, which to his exalted imagination began to assume the appearance of something supernatural.

They soon arrived at Rome, and Aubrey for a time lost sight of his companion; he left him in daily attendance upon the morning circle of an Italian countess, whilst he went in search of the memorials of another almost deserted city. Whilst he was thus engaged, letters arrived from England, which he opened with eager impatience; the first was from his sister, breathing nothing but affection; the others were from his guardians, the latter astonished him; if it had before entered into his imagination that there was an evil power resident in his companion, these seemed to give him sufficient reason for the belief. His guardians insisted upon his immediately leaving his friend, and urged, that his character was dreadfully vicious, for that the possession of irresistible powers of seduction, rendered his licentious habits more dangerous to society. It had been discovered, that his contempt for the adulteress had not originated in hatred of her character; but that he had required, to enhance his gratification, that his victim, the partner of his guilt, should be hurled from the pinnacle of unsullied virtue, down to the lowest abyss of infamy and degradation: in fine, that all those females whom he had sought, apparently on account of their virtue, had, since his departure, thrown even the mask aside, and had not scrupled to expose the whole deformity of their vices to the public gaze.

Aubrey determined upon leaving one, whose character had not yet shown a single bright point on which to rest the eye. He resolved to invent some plausible pretext for abandoning him altogether, purposing, in the meanwhile, to watch him more closely, and to let no slight circumstances pass by unnoticed. He entered into the same circle, and soon perceived, that his Lordship was endeavouring to work upon the inexperience of the daughter of the lady whose house he chiefly frequented. In Italy, it is seldom that an unmarried female is met with in society; he was therefore obliged to carry on his plans in secret; but Aubrey's eye followed him in all his windings, and soon discovered that an assignation had been appointed, which would most likely end in the ruin of an innocent though thoughtless girl. Losing no time, he entered the apartment of Lord Ruthven, and abruptly asked him his intentions with respect to the lady, informing him at the same time that he was aware of his being about to meet her that very night. Lord Ruthven answered, that his intentions were such as he supposed all would have upon such an occasion; and upon being pressed whether he intended to marry her, merely laughed. Aubrey retired; and, immediately writing a note, to say, that from that moment he must decline accompanying his Lordship in the remainder of their proposed tour, he ordered his servant to seek other apartments, and calling upon the mother of the lady, informed her of all he knew, not only with regard to her daughter, but also concerning the character of his Lordship. The assignation was prevented. Lord Ruthven next day merely sent his servant to notify his complete assent to a separation; but did not hint any suspicion of his plans having been foiled by Aubrey's interposition.

Having left Rome, Aubrey directed his steps towards Greece, and crossing the Peninsula, soon found himself at Athens. He then fixed his residence in the house of a Greek; and soon occupied himself in tracing the faded records of ancient glory upon monuments that apparently, ashamed of chronicling the deeds of freemen only before slaves, had hidden themselves beneath the sheltering soil or many coloured lichen. Under the same roof as himself, existed a being, so beautiful and delicate, that she might have formed the model for a painter wishing to portray on canvas the promised hope of the faithful in Mahomet's paradise, save that her eyes spoke too much mind for anyone to think she could belong to those who had no souls. As she danced upon the plain, or tripped along the mountain's side, one would have thought the gazelle a poor type of her beauties; for who would have exchanged her eye, apparently the eye of animated nature, for that sleepy luxurious look of the animal suited but to the taste of an epicure. The light step of Ianthe often accompanied Aubrey in his search after antiquities, and often would the unconscious girl, engaged in the pursuit of a Kashmere butterfly, show the whole beauty of her form, floating as it were upon the wind, to the eager gaze of him, who forgot the letters he had just decyphered upon an almost effaced tablet, in the contemplation of her sylph-like figure. Often would her tresses falling, as she flitted around, exhibit in the sun's ray such delicately brilliant and swiftly fading hues, it might well excuse the forgetfulness of the antiquary, who let escape from his mind the very object he had before thought of vital importance to the proper interpretation of a passage in Pausanias. But why attempt to describe charms which all feel, but none can appreciate?—It was innocence, youth, and beauty, unaffected by crowded drawing-rooms and stifling balls. Whilst he drew those remains of which he wished to preserve a memorial for his future hours, she would stand by, and watch the magic effects of his pencil, in tracing the scenes of her native place; she would then describe to him the circling dance upon the open plain, would paint, to him in all the glowing colours of youthful memory, the marriage pomp she remembered viewing in her infancy; and then, turning to subjects that had evidently made a greater impression upon her mind, would tell him all the supernatural tales of her nurse. Her earnestness and apparent belief of what she narrated, excited the interest even of Aubrey; and often as she told him the tale of the living vampyre, who had passed years amidst his friends, and dearest ties, forced every year, by feeding upon the life of a lovely female to prolong his existence for the ensuing months, his blood would run cold, whilst he attempted to laugh her out of such idle and horrible fantasies; but Ianthe cited to him the names of old men, who had at last detected one living among themselves, after several of their near relatives and children had been found marked with the stamp of the fiend's appetite; and when she found him so incredulous, she begged of him to believe her, for it had been, remarked, that those who had dared to question their existence, always had some proof given, which obliged them, with grief and heartbreaking, to confess it was true. She detailed to him the traditional appearance of these monsters, and his horror was increased, by hearing a pretty accurate description of Lord Ruthven; he, however, still persisted in persuading her, that there could be no truth in her fears, though at the same time he wondered at the many coincidences which had all tended to excite a belief in the supernatural power of Lord Ruthven.

Aubrey began to attach himself more and more to Ianthe; her innocence, so contrasted with all the affected virtues of the women among whom he had sought for his vision of romance, won his heart; and while he ridiculed the idea of a young man of English habits, marrying an uneducated Greek girl, still he found himself more and more attached to the almost fairy form before him. He would tear himself at times from her, and, forming a plan for some antiquarian research, he would depart, determined not to return until his object was attained; but he always found it impossible to fix his attention upon the ruins around him, whilst in his mind he retained an image that seemed alone the rightful possessor of his thoughts. Ianthe was unconscious of his love, and was ever the same frank infantile being he had first known. She always seemed to part from him with reluctance; but it was because she had no longer any one with whom she could visit her favourite haunts, whilst her guardian was occupied in sketching or uncovering some fragment which had yet escaped the destructive hand of time. She had appealed to her parents on the subject of Vampyres, and they both, with several present, affirmed their existence, pale with horror at the very name. Soon after, Aubrey determined to proceed upon one of his excursions, which was to detain him for a few hours; when they heard the name of the place, they all at once begged of him not to return at night, as he must necessarily pass through a wood, where no Greek would ever remain, after the day had closed, upon any consideration. They described it as the resort of the vampyres in their nocturnal orgies, and denounced the most heavy evils as impending upon him who dared to cross their path. Aubrey made light of their representations, and tried to laugh them out of the idea; but when he saw them shudder at his daring thus to mock a superior, infernal power, the very name of which apparently made their blood freeze, he was silent.

Next morning Aubrey set off upon his excursion unattended; he was surprised to observe the melancholy face of his host, and was concerned to find that his words, mocking the belief of those horrible fiends, had inspired them with such terror. When he was about to depart, Ianthe came to the side of his horse, and earnestly begged of him to return, ere night allowed the power of these beings to be put in action;—he promised. He was, however, so occupied in his research, that he did not perceive that day-light would soon end, and that in the horizon there was one of those specks which, in the warmer climates, so rapidly gather into a tremendous mass, and pour all their rage upon the devoted country.—He at last, however, mounted his horse, determined to make up by speed for his delay: but it was too late. Twilight, in these southern climates, is almost unknown; immediately the sun sets, night begins: and ere he had advanced far, the power of the storm was above—its echoing thunders had scarcely an interval of rest—its thick heavy rain forced its way through the canopying foliage, whilst the blue forked lightning seemed to fall and radiate at his very feet. Suddenly his horse took fright, and he was carried with dreadful rapidity through the entangled forest. The animal at last, through fatigue, stopped, and he found, by the glare of lightning, that he was in the neighbourhood of a hovel that hardly lifted itself up from the masses of dead leaves and brushwood which surrounded it. Dismounting, he approached, hoping to find someone to guide him to the town, or at least trusting to obtain shelter from the pelting of the storm. As he approached, the thunders, for a moment silent, allowed him to hear the dreadful shrieks of a woman mingling with the stifled, exultant mockery of a laugh, continued in one almost unbroken sound;—he was startled: but, roused by the thunder which again rolled over his head, he, with a sudden effort, forced open the door of the hut. He found himself in utter darkness: the sound, however, guided him. He was apparently unperceived; for, though he called, still the sounds continued, and no notice was taken of him. He found himself in contact with someone, whom he immediately seized; when a voice cried, "Again baffled!" to which a loud laugh succeeded; and he felt himself grappled by one whose strength seemed superhuman: determined to sell his life as dearly as he could, he struggled; but it was in vain: he was lifted from his feet and hurled with enormous force against the ground:—his enemy threw himself upon him, and kneeling upon his breast, had placed his hands upon his throat—when the glare of many torches penetrating through the hole that gave light in the day, disturbed him;—he instantly rose, and, leaving his prey, rushed through the door, and in a moment the crashing of the branches, as he broke through the wood, was no longer heard. The storm was now still; and Aubrey, incapable of moving, was soon heard by those without. They entered; the light of their torches fell upon the mud walls, and the thatch loaded on every individual straw with heavy flakes of soot. At the desire of Aubrey they searched for her who had attracted him by her cries; he was again left in darkness; but what was his horror, when the light of the torches once more burst upon him, to perceive the airy form of his fair conductress brought in a lifeless corse. He shut his eyes, hoping that it was but a vision arising from his disturbed imagination; but he again saw the same form, when he unclosed them, stretched by his side. There was no colour upon her cheek, not even upon her lip; yet there was a stillness about her face that seemed almost as attaching as the life that once dwelt there:—upon her neck and breast was blood, and upon her throat were the marks of teeth having opened the vein:—to this the men pointed, crying, simultaneously struck with horror, "A Vampyre! a Vampyre!" A litter was quickly formed, and Aubrey was laid by the side of her who had lately been to him the object of so many bright and fairy visions, now fallen with the flower of life that had died within her. He knew not what his thoughts were—his mind was benumbed and seemed to shun reflection, and take refuge in vacancy—he held almost unconsciously in his hand a naked dagger of a particular construction, which had been found in the hut. They were soon met by different parties who had been engaged in the search of her whom a mother had missed. Their lamentable cries, as they approached the city, forewarned the parents of some dreadful catastrophe. —To describe their grief would be impossible; but when they ascertained the cause of their child's death, they looked at Aubrey, and pointed to the corse. They were inconsolable; both died broken-hearted.

Aubrey being put to bed was seized with a most violent fever, and was often delirious; in these intervals he would call upon Lord Ruthven and upon Ianthe—by some unaccountable combination he seemed to beg of his former companion to spare the being he loved. At other times he would imprecate maledictions upon his head, and curse him as her destroyer. Lord Ruthven, chanced at this time to arrive at Athens, and, from whatever motive, upon hearing of the state of Aubrey, immediately placed himself in the same house, and became his constant attendant. When the latter recovered from his delirium, he was horrified and startled at the sight of him whose image he had now combined with that of a Vampyre; but Lord Ruthven, by his kind words, implying almost repentance for the fault that had caused their separation, and still more by the attention, anxiety, and care which he showed, soon reconciled him to his presence. His lordship seemed quite changed; he no longer appeared that apathetic being who had so astonished Aubrey; but as soon as his convalescence began to be rapid, he again gradually retired into the same state of mind, and Aubrey perceived no difference from the former man, except that at times he was surprised to meet his gaze fixed intently upon him, with a smile of malicious exultation playing upon his lips: he knew not why, but this smile haunted him. During the last stage of the invalid's recovery, Lord Ruthven was apparently engaged in watching the tideless waves raised by the cooling breeze, or in marking the progress of those orbs, circling, like our world, the moveless sun;—indeed, he appeared to wish to avoid the eyes of all.

Aubrey's mind, by this shock, was much weakened, and that elasticity of spirit which had once so distinguished him now seemed to have fled forever. He was now as much a lover of solitude and silence as Lord Ruthven; but much as he wished for solitude, his mind could not find it in the neighbourhood of Athens; if he sought it amidst the ruins he had formerly frequented, Ianthe's form stood by his side—if he sought it in the woods, her light step would appear wandering amidst the underwood, in quest of the modest violet; then suddenly turning round, would show, to his wild imagination, her pale face and wounded throat, with a meek smile upon her lips. He determined to fly the scenes, every feature of which created such bitter associations in his mind. He proposed to Lord Ruthven, to whom he held himself bound by the tender care he had taken of him during his illness, that they should visit those parts of Greece neither had yet seen. They travelled in every direction, and sought every spot to which a recollection could be attached: but though they thus hastened from place to place, yet they seemed not to heed what they gazed upon. They heard much of robbers, but they gradually began to slight these reports, which they imagined were only the invention of individuals, whose interest it was to excite the generosity of those whom they defended from pretended dangers. In consequence of thus neglecting the advice of the inhabitants, on one occasion they travelled with only a few guards, more to serve as guides than as a defense. Upon entering, however, a narrow defile, at the bottom of which was the bed of a torrent, with large masses of rock brought down from the neighboring precipices, they had reason to repent their negligence; for scarcely were the whole of the party engaged in the narrow pass, when they were startled by the whistling of bullets close to their heads, and by the echoed report of several guns. In an instant their guards had left them, and, placing themselves behind rocks, had begun to fire in the direction whence the report came. Lord Ruthven and Aubrey, imitating their example, retired for a moment behind the sheltering turn of the defile: but ashamed of being thus detained by a foe, who with insulting shouts bade them advance, and being exposed to unresisting slaughter, if any of the robbers should climb above and take them in the rear, they determined at once to rush forward in search of the enemy. Hardly had they lost the shelter of the rock, when Lord Ruthven received a shot in the shoulder, which brought him to the ground. Aubrey hastened to his assistance; and, no longer heeding the contest or his own peril, was soon surprised by seeing the robbers' faces around him—his guards having, upon Lord Ruthven's being wounded, immediately thrown up their arms and surrendered.

By promises of great reward, Aubrey soon induced them to convey his wounded friend to a neighbouring cabin; and having agreed upon a ransom, he was no more disturbed by their presence—they being content merely to guard the entrance till their comrade should return with the promised sum, for which he had an order. Lord Ruthven's strength rapidly decreased; in two days mortification ensued, and death seemed advancing with hasty steps. His conduct and appearance had not changed; he seemed as unconscious of pain as he had been of the objects about him: but towards the close of the last evening, his mind became apparently uneasy, and his eye often fixed upon Aubrey, who was induced to offer his assistance with more than usual earnestness— "Assist me! you may save me—you may do more than that—I mean not my life, I heed the death of my existence as little as that of the passing day; but you may save my honour, your friend's honour."

"How? tell me how? I would do anything," replied Aubrey.

"I need but little—my life ebbs apace—I cannot explain the whole— but if you would conceal all you know of me, my honour were free from stain in the world's mouth—and if my death were unknown for some time in England—I—I—but life."

"It shall not be known."

"Swear!" cried the dying man, raising himself with exultant violence, "Swear by all your soul reveres, by all your nature fears, swear that, for a year and a day you will not impart your knowledge of my crimes or death to any living being in any way, whatever may happen, or whatever you may see." His eyes seemed bursting from their sockets.

"I swear!" said Aubrey; he sunk laughing upon his pillow, and breathed no more.

Aubrey retired to rest, but did not sleep; the many circumstances attending his acquaintance with this man rose upon his mind, and he knew not why; when he remembered his oath a cold shivering came over him, as if from the presentiment of something horrible awaiting him. Rising early in the morning, he was about to enter the hovel in which he had left the corpse, when a robber met him, and informed him that it was no longer there, having been conveyed by himself and comrades, upon his retiring, to the pinnacle of a neighbouring mount, according to a promise they had given his lordship, that it should be exposed to the first cold ray of the moon that rose after his death. Aubrey astonished, and taking several of the men, determined to go and bury it upon the spot where it lay. But, when he had mounted to the summit he found no trace of either the corpse or the clothes, though the robbers swore they pointed out the identical rock on which they had laid the body. For a time his mind was bewildered in conjectures, but he at last returned, convinced that they had buried the corpse for the sake of the clothes.

Weary of a country in which he had met with such terrible misfortunes, and in which all apparently conspired to heighten that superstitious melancholy that had seized upon his mind, he resolved to leave it, and soon arrived at Smyrna. While waiting for a vessel to convey him to Otranto, or to Naples, he occupied himself in arranging those effects he had with him belonging to Lord Ruthven. Amongst other things there was a case containing several weapons of offence, more or less adapted to ensure the death of the victim. There were several daggers and ataghans. Whilst turning them over, and examining their curious forms, what was his surprise at finding a sheath apparently ornamented in the same style as the dagger discovered in the fatal hut—he shuddered—hastening to gain further proof, he found the weapon, and his horror may be imagined when he discovered that it fitted, though peculiarly shaped, the sheath he held in his hand. His eyes seemed to need no further certainty—they seemed gazing to be bound to the dagger; yet still he wished to disbelieve; but the particular form, the same varying tints upon the haft and sheath were alike in splendour on both, and left no room for doubt; there were also drops of blood on each.

He left Smyrna, and on his way home, at Rome, his first inquiries were concerning the lady he had attempted to snatch from Lord Ruthven's seductive arts. Her parents were in distress, their fortune ruined, and she had not been heard of since the departure of his lordship. Aubrey's mind became almost broken under so many repeated horrors; he was afraid that this lady had fallen a victim to the destroyer of Ianthe. He became morose and silent; and his only occupation consisted in urging the speed of the postilions, as if he were going to save the life of someone he held dear. He arrived at Calais; a breeze, which seemed obedient to his will, soon wafted him to the English shores; and he hastened to the mansion of his fathers, and there, for a moment, appeared to lose, in the embraces and caresses of his sister, all memory of the past. If she before, by her infantine caresses, had gained his affection, now that the woman began to appear, she was still more attaching as a companion.

Miss Aubrey had not that winning grace which gains the gaze and applause of the drawing-room assemblies. There was none of that light brilliancy which only exists in the heated atmosphere of a crowded apartment. Her blue eye was never lit up by the levity of the mind beneath. There was a melancholy charm about it which did not seem to arise from misfortune, but from some feeling within, that appeared to indicate a soul conscious of a brighter realm. Her step was not that light footing, which strays where'er a butterfly or a colour may attract—it was sedate and pensive. When alone, her face was never brightened by the smile of joy; but when her brother breathed to her his affection, and would in her presence forget those griefs she knew destroyed his rest, who would have exchanged her smile for that of the voluptuary? It seemed as if those eyes,—that face were then playing in the light of their own native sphere. She was yet only eighteen, and had not been presented to the world, it having been thought by her guardians more fit that her presentation should be delayed until her brother's return from the continent, when he might be her protector. It was now, therefore, resolved that the next drawing-room, which was fast approaching, should be the epoch of her entry into the "busy scene." Aubrey would rather have remained in the mansion of his fathers, and fed upon the melancholy which overpowered him. He could not feel interest about the frivolities of fashionable strangers, when his mind had been so torn by the events he had witnessed; but he determined to sacrifice his own comfort to the protection of his sister. They soon arrived in town, and prepared for the next day, which had been announced as a drawing-room.

The crowd was excessive—a drawing-room had not been held for a long time, and all who were anxious to bask in the smile of royalty, hastened thither. Aubrey was there with his sister. While he was standing in a corner by himself, heedless of all around him, engaged in the remembrance that the first time he had seen Lord Ruthven was in that very place—he felt himself suddenly seized by the arm, and a voice he recognized too well, sounded in his ear—"Remember your oath." He had hardly courage to turn, fearful of seeing a spectre that would blast him, when he perceived, at a little distance, the same figure which had attracted his notice on this spot upon his first entry into society. He gazed till his limbs almost refusing to bear their weight, he was obliged to take the arm of a friend, and forcing a passage through the crowd, he threw himself into his carriage, and was driven home. He paced the room with hurried steps, and fixed his hands upon his head, as if he were afraid his thoughts were bursting from his brain. Lord Ruthven again before him—circumstances started up in dreadful array—the dagger—his oath.—He roused himself, he could not believe it possible—the dead rise again!—He thought his imagination had conjured up the image his mind was resting upon. It was impossible that it could be real—he determined, therefore, to go again into society; for though he attempted to ask concerning Lord Ruthven, the name hung upon his lips, and he could not succeed in gaining information. He went a few nights after with his sister to the assembly of a near relation. Leaving her under the protection of a matron, he retired into a recess, and there gave himself up to his own devouring thoughts. Perceiving, at last, that many were leaving, he roused himself, and entering another room, found his sister surrounded by several, apparently in earnest conversation; he attempted to pass and get near her, when one, whom he requested to move, turned round, and revealed to him those features he most abhorred. He sprang forward, seized his sister's arm, and, with hurried step, forced her towards the street: at the door he found himself impeded by the crowd of servants who were waiting for their lords; and while he was engaged in passing them, he again heard that voice whisper close to him—"Remember your oath!"—He did not dare to turn, but, hurrying his sister, soon reached home.

Aubrey became almost distracted. If before his mind had been absorbed by one subject, how much more completely was it engrossed, now that the certainty of the monster's living again pressed upon his thoughts. His sister's attentions were now unheeded, and it was in vain that she intreated him to explain to her what had caused his abrupt conduct. He only uttered a few words, and those terrified her. The more he thought, the more he was bewildered. His oath startled him;— was he then to allow this monster to roam, bearing ruin upon his breath, amidst all he held dear, and not avert its progress? His very sister might have been touched by him. But even if he were to break his oath, and disclose his suspicions, who would believe him? He thought of employing his own hand to free the world from such a wretch; but death, he remembered, had been already mocked. For days he remained in this state; shut up in his room, he saw no one, and ate only when his sister came, who, with eyes streaming with tears, besought him, for her sake, to support nature. At last, no longer capable of bearing stillness and solitude, he left his house, roamed from street to street, anxious to fly that image which haunted him. His dress became neglected, and he wandered, as often exposed to the noon-day sun as to the midnight damps. He was no longer to be recognized; at first he returned with the evening to the house; but at last he laid him down to rest wherever fatigue overtook him. His sister, anxious for his safety, employed people to follow him; but they were soon distanced by him who fled from a pursuer swifter than any—from thought. His conduct, however, suddenly changed. Struck with the idea that he left by his absence the whole of his friends, with a fiend amongst them, of whose presence they were unconscious, he determined to enter again into society, and watch him closely, anxious to forewarn, in spite of his oath, all whom Lord Ruthven approached with intimacy. But when he entered into a room, his haggard and suspicious looks were so striking, his inward shudderings so visible, that his sister was at last obliged to beg of him to abstain from seeking, for her sake, a society which affected him so strongly. When, however, remonstrance proved unavailing, the guardians thought proper to interpose, and, fearing that his mind was becoming alienated, they thought it high time to resume again that trust which had been before imposed upon them by Aubrey's parents.

Desirous of saving him from the injuries and sufferings he had daily encountered in his wanderings, and of preventing him from exposing to the general eye those marks of what they considered folly, they engaged a physician to reside in the house, and take constant care of him. He hardly appeared to notice it, so completely was his mind absorbed by one terrible subject. His incoherence became at last so great, that he was confined to his chamber. There he would often lie for days, incapable of being roused. He had become emaciated, his eyes had attained a glassy lustre;—the only sign of affection and recollection remaining displayed itself upon the entry of his sister; then he would sometimes start, and, seizing her hands, with looks that severely afflicted her, he would desire her not to touch him. "Oh, do not touch him—if your love for me is aught, do not go near him!" When, however, she inquired to whom he referred, his only answer was, "True! True!" and again he sank into a state, whence not even she could rouse him. This lasted many months: gradually, however, as the year was passing, his incoherences became less frequent, and his mind threw off a portion of its gloom, whilst his guardians observed, that several times in the day he would count upon his fingers a definite number, and then smile.

The time had nearly elapsed, when, upon the last day of the year, one of his guardians entering his room, began to converse with his physician upon the melancholy circumstance of Aubrey's being in so awful a situation, when his sister was going next day to be married. Instantly Aubrey's attention was attracted; he asked anxiously to whom. Glad of this mark of returning intellect, of which they feared he had been deprived, they mentioned the name of the Earl of Marsden. Thinking this was a young Earl whom he had met with in society, Aubrey seemed pleased, and astonished them still more by his expressing his intention to be present at the nuptials, and desiring to see his sister. They answered not, but in a few minutes his sister was with him. He was apparently again capable of being affected by the influence of her lovely smile; for he pressed her to his breast, and kissed her cheek, wet with tears, flowing at the thought of her brother's being once more alive to the feelings of affection. He began to speak with all his wonted warmth, and to congratulate her upon her marriage with a person so distinguished for rank and every accomplishment; when he suddenly perceived a locket upon her breast; opening it, what was his surprise at beholding the features of the monster who had so long influenced his life. He seized the portrait in a paroxysm of rage, and trampled it under foot. Upon her asking him why he thus destroyed the resemblance of her future husband, he looked as if he did not understand her—then seizing her hands, and gazing on her with a frantic expression of countenance, he bade her swear that she would never wed this monster, for he—— But he could not advance— it seemed as if that voice again bade him remember his oath—he turned suddenly round, thinking Lord Ruthven was near him but saw no one. In the meantime the guardians and physician, who had heard the whole, and thought this was but a return of his disorder, entered, and forcing him from Miss Aubrey, desired her to leave him. He fell upon his knees to them, he implored, he begged of them to delay but for one day. They, attributing this to the insanity they imagined had taken possession of his mind, endeavoured to pacify him, and retired.

Lord Ruthven had called the morning after the drawing-room, and had been refused with everyone else. When he heard of Aubrey's ill health, he readily understood himself to be the cause of it; but when he learned that he was deemed insane, his exultation and pleasure could hardly be concealed from those among whom he had gained this information. He hastened to the house of his former companion, and, by constant attendance, and the presence of great affection for the brother and interest in his fate, he gradually won the ear of Miss Aubrey. Who could resist his power? His tongue had dangers and toils to recount—could speak of himself as of an individual having no sympathy with any being on the crowded earth, save with her to whom he addressed himself;—could tell how, since he knew her, his existence, had begun to seem worthy of preservation, if it were merely that he might listen to her soothing accents;—in fine, he knew so well how to use the serpent's art, or such was the will of fate, that he gained her affections. The title of the elder branch falling at length to him, he obtained an important embassy, which served as an excuse for hastening the marriage, (in spite of her brother's deranged state,) which was to take place the very day before his departure for the continent.

Aubrey, when he was left by the physician and his guardians, attempted to bribe the servants, but in vain. He asked for pen and paper; it was given him; he wrote a letter to his sister, conjuring her, as she valued her own happiness, her own honour, and the honour of those now in the grave, who once held her in their arms as their hope and the hope of their house, to delay but for a few hours that marriage, on which he denounced the most heavy curses. The servants promised they would deliver it; but giving it to the physician, he thought it better not to harass any more the mind of Miss Aubrey by, what he considered, the ravings of a maniac. Night passed on without rest to the busy inmates of the house; and Aubrey heard, with a horror that may more easily be conceived than described, the notes of busy preparation. Morning came, and the sound of carriages broke upon his ear. Aubrey grew almost frantic. The curiosity of the servants at last overcame their vigilance, they gradually stole away, leaving him in the custody of an helpless old woman. He seized the opportunity, with one bound was out of the room, and in a moment found himself in the apartment where all were nearly assembled. Lord Ruthven was the first to perceive him: he immediately approached, and, taking his arm by force, hurried him from the room, speechless with rage. When on the staircase, Lord Ruthven whispered in his ear—"Remember your oath, and know, if not my bride today, your sister is dishonoured. Women are frail!" So saying, he pushed him towards his attendants, who, roused by the old woman, had come in search of him. Aubrey could no longer support himself; his rage not finding vent, had broken a blood-vessel, and he was conveyed to bed. This was not mentioned to his sister, who was not present when he entered, as the physician was afraid of agitating her. The marriage was solemnized, and the bride and bridegroom left London.

Aubrey's weakness increased; the effusion of blood produced symptoms of the near approach of death. He desired his sister's guardians might be called, and when the midnight hour had struck, he related composedly what the reader has perused—he died immediately after.

The guardians hastened to protect Miss Aubrey; but when they arrived, it was too late. Lord Ruthven had disappeared, and Aubrey's sister had glutted the thirst of a VAMPYRE!

GLOSSARY

Affairs were embarrassed: Lord Ruthven apparently had some financial debts, and it was a good idea for him to get out of town for awhile to escape his creditors.

Ataghan: Or "yataghan," a curved, single-bladed Turkish sword.

Corse: Corpse.

Dress of a mountebank: A flamboyant outfit.

Ianthe: Several women in Greek mythology were named Ianthe; one was a sea nymph; another was a beautiful girl from Crete who married Iphis, a woman pretending to be a man who, at their wedding, was transformed by the Egyptian goddess Isis into a real man. Ianthe was also Byron's nickname for Charlotte Harley, the 11-year-old daughter of his mistress Lady Oxford. Byron met Charlotte in 1812 and dedicated the 7th printing of *Childe Harold's Pilgrimage* to her as "Ianthe," who was *"fair in form...pure of heart..."* In 1813, Byron wrote to another mistress, Lady Melbourne, "I could love [Charlotte] forever if she could always be only 11 years old, and whom I shall probably marry when she is old enough, and bad enough to be made into a modern wife." Byron, however, never saw Charlotte again. In 1816, Byron's estranged wife Annabella claimed Byron had once admitted to her that Lady Oxford surprised him while he was forcing himself on the 11-year-old. Historians have debated whether or not Byron raped the girl; but it would be an amazing coincidence if name— and the allegation—did not lie behind Polidori's portrayal of the seduction and murder of the young Greek woman by Lord Ruthven. Charlotte Harley herself seems to have kept several mementoes from Byron throughout an eventful life. She married a hero of the Napoleonic Wars, Anthony Bacon, and shared many adventures with him. She spent some of her later years in Australia, and part of the Finke River in the Northern Territory was named Charlotte Waters after her. Charlotte died in 1880; the *Times* of London remembered her as Byron's "Ianthe."

Kashmere: Kashmir, in what is now Pakistan. The Kashmir butterfly has wings of white and black or dark brown.

Mahomet: Muhammad the Prophet.

Otranto: A seaside town in Italy. Possibly a reference to Horace Walpole's pioneering Gothic novel, *The Castle of Otranto,* or to Byron's poetic drama *Manfred*; the titular Byronic hero rules Otranto.

Pausanias: A 2nd Century Greek historian and geographer.

Smyrna: An ancient harbor city in Eastern Turkey; since 1930, the Turkish city of Izmir. At the time of the story, Smyrna was the center of a large Greek community.

The tour: At around the age of 21, the wealthy children of the British upper classes went on a "Grand Tour" of Europe, with stops at sites of Classical significance. The practice was common from the 1660's to the 1840's. Also, of course, an element in Byron's "fragment."

"…your sister is dishonoured. Women are frail!": Ruthven has already had sex with Aubrey's sister and this will presumably be revealed if the wedding is put off. By the rules of society, marriage is the only way to make an "honest woman" of the young lady. As we learn in the final line, however, she is killed on her wedding night. (It's unclear why Lord Ruthven would want to go through a wedding ceremony to be joined in holy matrimony with a woman he intends to kill a few hours later; possibly it's just a vampiric joke, or a demonstration of how outside of and above the Byronic vampire is to the conventions of society.)

AFTERWORD

Polidori introduced several key elements that would become standard in vampire fiction:

- *Ruthven is always pale (although he doesn't fear the sun).*
- *Ruthven's strength is superhuman.*
- *Ruthven leaves bite marks on the throat (although Ruthven is not specifically said to have fangs).*

- *Ruthven feeds specifically to sustain his life for a few more months—and therefore can presumably reach an advanced age (although we don't know how long Lord Ruthven has been a vampire).*

The literary vampire, however, is still a work in progress: Ruthven is vulnerable to ordinary weapons. And—in an invention of Polidori's—he needs moonlight to return from the dead. This would become less important to literary vampires—as the moon was claimed more exclusively by literary werewolves, and as vampires became harder to kill.

But Polidori's key contribution was to match the predatory nature of a vampire with Byron's aristocratic temperament, along with, crucially, Byron's aristocratic title.

Aristocrats once had a real place in European society. They owned the land and provided warriors for the king. But, by the early 19th century, with the first Industrial Revolution accompanied by the spread of democracy, capitalism and permanent armies, lords and ladies were becoming things of the past. And yet, they never completely disappeared. In spite of real social changes, lords and ladies continued to wield power and live well—while millions struggled. They enjoyed half-hidden yet glittering lives, feeding off the work of others.

So of course *aristocrats were vampires.*

But aristocrats were also envied and respected by the rising middle classes. A lord, vampire or not, was deferred to, invited into a middle-class home, maybe introduced to the eldest daughter...

Even without their former political clout, aristocrats still exercised social dominance; they embodied unseen power—which was something Romantics loved: the personal authority that bent others to a superior will. (No wonder that, when hypnotism was developed in the mid-19th century, it was added to the vampire's abilities, turning a masterful personality into an actual supernatural power.)

Aristocracy also takes care of the problem that Dom Calmet fretted over: how, exactly, a vampire gets in and out of his grave. Aristocrats have no need to dematerialize through four tons of earth (although, much later, Dracula will be able to assume the form of mist). An aristocratic vampire would naturally be laid to rest in an expensive above-ground family vault or mausoleum. Then it's just a matter of lifting the coffin lid. Not much more difficult than opening a door. (That said, Lord Ruthven doesn't seem to worry about going to and from a grave, and seems able to sleep anywhere; but an early aristocratic vampire burial occurs in the 1833 poem The Vampire Bride, *featured in* Volume II: The Vampire Ladies.*)*

An aristocrat also has money with which to travel and buy things, and this helps writers move the story along. Lord Ruthven can take off for Greece at a moment's notice; Dracula *begins with the Count negotiating an expensive real estate deal.*

Aristocratic wealth also means a vampire has free time to brood over the dark destiny that has sealed them off from the rest of humanity. When an aristocrat moodily broods over his fate, it's romantic— perhaps the black-clad Prince Hamlet set the mood for that. People who clean restrooms and make cold calls from "boiler room" phone centers also brood when they have a spare moment, but audiences don't seem to find that very romantic. This says something rather unpleasant about the ongoing snobbery of modern society…

…but, then, so do vampires. Because, in vampire literature, and Gothic and romantic fiction in general, the veneer of "class" has been used, consciously or unconsciously, to soften the edges of the rape fantasy central to the male vampire storyline. Rape is a crime; but an aristocratic rape, with flowing cloaks and nightgowns, rich velvet and fine lace, and the submission to an overpowering will rather than crude brute force or a sedative…Well, rapists and writers can try to pass that off as seduction, which implies at a least a last-minute consent on the part of the woman. Readers will often forgive and even relish violence and crime if it's presented with style. Nobody in the 18th or 19th century applauded the petty thieves who skulked in alleys, bashing people on

the head and robbing them; but highwaymen, with their horses and masks and cloaks and pistol butts a-twinkle, became celebrities.

This attitude helped make the dashing Lord Ruthven an immediate sensation—although Polidori's sudden, shocking ending, with evil utterly triumphant, clearly frustrated some readers—and writers. (At least highwaymen ended up on the gallows.) A year after its publication, an unauthorized French sequel (Lord Ruthwen, ou les Vampires—note the different spelling) had Aubrey surviving his burst blood-vessel and pursuing the vampiric lord through Venice and the Middle East. The same year saw separate French and English plays loosely adapting The Vampyre as The Vampire. The setting was changed to Scotland, with a plaid-clad Lord Ruthven. Why? Apparently, either Scottish plays were popular at the time, or the theatre had a lot of unused Scottish costumes lying around.

The plot of The Vampire, or The Bride of the Isles has almost nothing to do with the Polidori story, other than the name of the vampire and the oath before dying. Lord Ruthven, wounded by a pistol, is dying at the end of the first act; but before he expires, he enacts an oath of secrecy from his friend Lord Ronald—the father of the young woman Ruthven is pursuing. Ronald swears the oath Aubrey takes in the novella, and Ruthven dies in the light of a stage moon. He reappears in Act Two, and whispers "Your oath!" to a horrified and mystified Lord Ronald. At the end, the wicked Lord Ruthven is carried away to Hell—making an instantaneous disappearance thanks to a new kind of trap door, that would be known thereafter as a "vampire."

The next year, 1821, saw a German stage version, and in 1828 there were two separate German operas based on The Vampyre (with the setting changed from Scotland to Hungary). In his 1845 novel, The Count of Monte Cristo, Alexandre Dumas had a character compare the brooding, mysterious Count with Lord Ruthven. In 1851, Dumas and his collaborator August Macquet added to Ruthven's multimedia success with a new play (Le Vampire) that teamed Ruthven with a female ghoul.

In 1852, the Anglo-Irish actor-manager Dion Boucicault adapted the story again, as the play The Vampire, in which the Lord Ruthven figure became Sir Alan Raby. Raby didn't drink blood, but, like Darvell and Ruthven, as he seems to die, he imposes an oath of secrecy on one of the other characters. Just before the Act One curtain, moonlight bathes the corpse, and Sir Alan rises from the dead to hail the lunar power:

> "Fountain of my life! Once more thy rays restore me!
> Death—! I defy thee!"

So, for more than thirty years, Lord Ruthven was a multi-media success. Polidori might have become rich and renowned…if he had been universally acclaimed as the actual author, which he wasn't, and if copyright laws had really been in force, which they weren't.

One of the problems was that The New Monthly Magazine listed the author as Lord Byron himself!

Whether this was a mistake or a deliberate lie by the publisher, the idea that Byron had written a vampire story captured the imagination of Europe. Goethe thought it was Byron's best work! When Polidori tried to come forth as the author, he was actually accused of plagiarism. He did receive proper credit when The Vampyre was reprinted later in 1819, but the damage was done. Some sources would continue to list Byron as the author well into the 20th century.

Byron himself had no interest in being associated with Ruthven. On the 27th of April, 1819—twenty-six days after Polidori's story appeared—he wrote a letter of complaint to a publisher in Paris (note how Byron spells "vampire" as opposed to the way Polidori does):

> Sir—In various numbers of your journal I have seen a
> work entitled "The Vampire," with the addition of my
> name as that of the author. I am not the author, and
> never heard of the work in question until now. In a
> more recent paper I perceive a formal annunciation of
> "The Vampire," with the addition of my "residence in

*the island of Mitylene," an island which I have
occasionally sailed by in the course of travelling some
years ago in the Levant, and where I should have no
objection to reside—but where I have never yet
resided. Neither of these performances are mine; and
I presume it is neither unjust nor ungracious that you
will favour me by contradicting the advertisement to
which I allude. If the book is clever, it would be base
to deprive the real writer, whoever he may be, of his
honours; and if stupid, I desire the responsibility of
nobody's dullness but my own.*

*You will forgive the trouble I give you: the imputation
is of no great importance, and as long as it was
confined to surmises and reports I should have
received it as I have received many others—in silence;
but the formality of a public advertisement of a book I
never wrote , and a residence where I never resided, is
a little too much, particularly as I have no notion of
the contents of the one nor the incidents of the other.
I have besides a personal dislike to "Vampires," and
the little acquaintance I have with them would by no
means induce me to divulge their secrets...*

*This statement, of course, only adds to the mystery of whether
Augustus Darvell was going to be an actual vampire.*

Interestingly, Byron published his A Fragment *as an appendage to his
poem* Mazeppa *in July, 1819, just three months after Polidori's* The
Vampyre. *But that might have compounded the authorship error in the
public's mind, since the story of Augustus Darvell was clearly similar to
the story of Lord Ruthven...and Ruthven was undoubtedly Lord Byron,
regardless of who the author might be.*

After The Vampyre *failed to bring Polidori the success he craved, the
young physician was so upset he tried to escape into a monastery...but
the abbot, who* did *know that Polidori wrote* The Vampyre, *refused to*

admit the author of such a scandalous work. Polidori tried different careers: first the law, then gambling. He failed at both. Beset by gambling debts and other burdens, Polidori died in August 1821 at the age of 25. The coroner was persuaded to ascribe his demise to "natural causes," but there was strong reason to suspect that Polidori killed himself by swallowing cyanide.

Byron's reaction was like a vampire recalling a long-ago victim:

> "Poor Polidori. It seems that disappointment was the cause of this rash act. He had entertained too sanguine hopes of literary fame."

Lord Ruthven is barely remembered today, and, if he is, it's as a footnote to Dracula. In 1945, science fiction writer Leigh Brackett loosely adapted Polidori's novel—with a version of the deathbed vow and the revival by moonlight—as a B-picture titled The Vampire's Ghost, set in then-contemporary colonial Africa; it incorporated tropes that were, by then, standard in vampire stories: the lack of reflection in mirrors, hypnotic abilities, vulnerability to silver, etc.

In 1973, The Vampyre was partially adapted into comic book form by writer Roy Thomas and artist Win Mortimer in the first issue of Marvel Comics' Vampire Tales. On the cover, Lord Ruthven is heralded as "The first, most fearsome VAMPYRE of all!" As in the novel, Ruthven is temporarily killed with a knife—but the adaptation makes it a silver knife; by then, every reader knew that no ordinary weapon could harm a vampire.

Since then, Ruthven has popped up as a side character in other comics, as well as novels and games, but it's unlikely that the original Byronic vampire will ever emerge from the shadow of Count Dracula and step again into the limelight he once enjoyed.

GORCHA

" 'Corpse!' George shouted at the old man.
'What did you do with my eldest son?' "

*L*ord Ruthven's influence in the early 1800's extended into Russia; where writers could look to Slavic folklore and find further inspiration for their vampire stories.

The Family of the Vourdalak *was written by Count Alexei Tolstoy, a second cousin of Count Leo Tolstoy, author of* Anna Karenina *and* War and Peace. *Count Alexei was one of the most important playwrights and poets of Tsarist Russia. Tolstoy wrote the story in French, which all Russians of his class read and spoke fluently. But the story was never published during his lifetime. In 1884, nine years after Tolstoy's death (and thirteen years before* Dracula*), it was translated into Russian—but still remained unpublished. In 1906 (nine years after* Dracula*), a shortened version (also in Russian) finally appeared in print in 1906. It made almost no literary impact.*

In 1950, Tolstoy's original version was finally published in the French journal Revue des études slaves (The Review of Slavic Studies). *It was subsequently translated into other languages and, in 1963, was filmed in Italy as part of Mario Bava's* Three Faces of Fear *(retitled* Black Sabbath *in England and America, and, yes, that's where Ozzy Osbourne got the name for his band). In the Bava film, Gorcha was played by Boris Karloff—his only appearance as a vampire. The adaptation revived interest in the original. Like a true vampire, Tolstoy's* Vourdalak *lay buried for more than a century before taking its place in the literature of terror.*

Tolstoy probably got the word "vourdalak" from an article by his fellow author Alexander Pushkin; there is some controversy as to whether the vourdalak (or vurdulak) is a genuine Slavic superstition with Indo-European roots, or if Pushkin just mixed together legends about vampires and werewolves. The setting is deep in Serbia, in the heart of Central Europe, and clearly draws on aspects of the Arnold Paul case. The vampire, here, is not *an aristocrat—although he is the patriarch of his family. The name Gorcha, by the way, should be pronounced "Gorka," and the lovely Sdenka would be "Zdenya." Also, the wooden stake that plays a crucial role in the story shouldn't be pictured as a simple hand-held implement, but something the length of a fencepost.*

THE FAMILY OF THE VOURDALAK

Count Alexei Konstantinovich Tolstoy

The year 1815 brought together in Vienna all the best minds in Europe, the most distinguished scholars and the most skillful diplomats. At the conclusion of the Congress, the royalist emigrants prepared to return to their native castles, the Russian warriors to see their abandoned homes, and some unhappy Poles to take to Krakow their love of liberty, to shelter it under the doubtful independence which the Prince of Metternich, the Prince of Hardenberg, and the Count of Nesselrode had assured them.

Like the end of a lively ball, the meeting, once so noisy, had been reduced to a small number of pleasure-seekers, who, fascinated by the charms of the Austrian ladies, were slow to pack their bags and go their separate ways.

This merry society, of which I was a part, met twice a week in the castle of Madame the Dowager Princess of Schwarzenberg, a few miles from the town, beyond a small village named Hitzing. The great manners of the mistress of the place, relieved by her gracious amiability and the delicacy of her wit, made staying at her residence extremely pleasant.

Our mornings were devoted to walks; we dined together, either in the chateau or in the neighborhood, and in the evening, seated near a hearty fireplace, we amused ourselves by chatting and telling stories. It was strictly forbidden to talk politics. Everyone had had enough of that, and our stories were borrowed either from the legends of our respective countries, or from our own memories.

One evening, when everyone had already told some stories, and our minds were in that state of tension that usually increases darkness and silence, the Marquis d'Urfe, an old émigré whom we all loved because of his youthful cheerfulness and the piquant manner in which he spoke of his old good fortune, took advantage of a moment of silence and spoke:

"Your stories, gentlemen," he said, "are probably amazing, but it is my opinion that they lack an essential point, I mean that of authenticity, because I do not know that any of you have seen with your own eyes the marvelous things which you have just narrated, nor that you can affirm the truth of you word as a gentleman."

We were obliged to agree, and the old man continued, adjusting his cravat:

"As for me, gentlemen, I know only one adventure of this kind, but it is at once so strange, so horrible, and so true, that it alone would suffice to strike the imagination of the most incredulous. I have unfortunately been a witness and an actor at the same time, and although, ordinarily, I do not like to remember it, I shall willingly make the effort this time, if of course the ladies will permit it."

The assent was unanimous. True, a few fearful glances turned to the luminous squares on the floor which the moonlight began to shine on, but soon our little circle gathered silently around the marquis to listen to his story. M. d'Urfe took a pinch of snuff, slowly inhaled it, and began as follows:

"Above all, ladies, I beg your pardon if, in the course of my narration, I sometimes speak of my affairs of the heart more often than it would suit a man of my age. But I will have to mention it for the intelligence of my story. Moreover, it is forgivable for old age to have moments of forgetfulness, and it will be your fault, ladies, if, seeing you so beautiful in front of me, I am still tempted to believe me a young man. I will tell you, without further preamble, that in the year 1759 I was madly in love with the pretty Duchesse de Gramont. This passion, which I then believed to be profound and lasting, gave me neither day nor night repose, and the duchess, as the pretty women often do, was pleased by her coquetry to add to my torment. So that, in a moment of spite, I came to solicit and obtain a diplomatic mission to the

Gospodar, that is, the Lord, of Moldavia, then in talks with the cabinet of Versailles for cases of which it would be as boring as useless to tell you. The day before I left, I went to see the Duchess. She received me with a less mocking air than usual and said to me in a voice which had a certain emotion in it:

" 'D'Urfe, you are doing a great madness here. But I know you and I know you will never go back on a resolution made. Thus, I ask you only one thing: accept this little cross as a pledge of my friendship and carry it on you until your return. It is a family relic to which we attach a great price.'

"With a gallantry perhaps displaced at such a moment, I kissed not the relic, but the charming hand that presented it to me, and I put on my neck the cross which has never left it since.

"I will not tire you ladies with the details of my journey, nor of the observations which I made on the Hungarians and the Serbs, those poor and ignorant people—but brave and honest, and who, enslaved as they were by the Turks had forgotten neither their dignity nor their former independence. It will be enough for me to say that, having learned a little Polish during a stay I had made in Warsaw, I soon became acquainted with Serbian, for these two idioms, as well as Russian and Bohemian, are, as you probably know, branches of the Slavonic language.

"Now, I knew enough to make myself understood, when one day I arrived in a village whose name would hardly interest you. I found the inhabitants of the house where I went down in a consternation that seemed all the more strange to me as it was a Sunday, a day when the Serbian people used to indulge in different pleasures, such as dancing, target practice, wrestling, etc. I attributed the attitude of my guests to some newly arrived misfortune, and I was about to retire when a man of about thirty, of tall stature and imposing figure, approached me and took me by the hand.

"Come in, come in, stranger," said he, "do not be put off by our sadness; you will understand it when you know the cause."

He told me then that his old father, whose name was Gorcha, a man of a restless and uncomfortable character, had risen one day from his bed and had taken from the wall his long Turkish musket.

" 'Children,' he had said to his two sons, George and Peter, 'I am going away from the mountains to join the brave men who hunt this dog Alibek.' That was the name of a Turkish brigand who for some time had devastated the country. 'Wait for me for ten days, and if I do not return the tenth, say a death mass, because then I will be killed. But,' added old Gorcha, taking his most serious look, 'if, God keep you, I came back after the ten days, for your salvation do not let me enter. I order you in this case to forget that I was your father and to pierce me with an aspen stake, whatever I may say or do, because then I would be a cursed vourdalak who would suck your blood!'

"I should tell you, ladies, that the vourdalaks, or vampires of the Slav peoples, are, in the opinion of the country, nothing other than dead bodies risen from their graves to suck the blood of the living. Until then their habits are those of all vampires, but they have another one that only makes them more formidable. The vourdalaks, ladies, prefer to suck the blood of their closest relatives and their most intimate friends who, once dead, become vampires in turn. So it is claimed that whole villages in Bosnia and Hungary have been transformed into vourdalaks. Father Augustin Calmet, in his curious work on apparitions, quotes frightening examples. The emperors of Germany several times appointed commissions to investigate cases of vampirism. Minutes were drawn up, corpses were exhumed to be found gorged with blood, and burned in the public squares after having pierced their hearts. Magistrates who witnessed these executions say that they heard the corpses scream as the executioner pushed a stake into their chest. They made the formal statement and corroborated it with their oath and signature.

"According to this information, it will be easy for you to understand, ladies, the effect produced by the words of old Gorcha on his sons. The two of them had thrown themselves at his feet and begged him to let them go in his place, but, for all answer, he had turned his back on them and had gone away singing the chorus of an old ballad. The day I arrived in the village was exactly the one where Gorcha's term was to expire, and I had no difficulty in explaining to myself the anxiety of his children.

"It was a good and honest family. George, the eldest of the two sons, seemed a serious and resolute man, with well-marked masculine features. He was married with two children. His brother Peter, a handsome young man of eighteen, betrayed in his countenance more gentleness than boldness, and appeared the favorite of a younger sister, called Sdenka, who might well have passed for the very picture of Slav beauty. Besides this incontestable loveliness in all respects, a distant resemblance to the Duchesse de Gramont struck me at first sight. Above all, there was a delicate line on both their brows; in all my life, I only found it in these two people. This trait might not please at first glance, but I was irresistibly attached to it as soon as I had been seen it a few times.

"Whether I was very young then, or that this resemblance, joined to an original and naive spirit, created a really irresistible effect, I had not been with Sdenka for two minutes when I felt for her a sympathy so bright that it would threaten to change into a more tender feeling if I prolonged my stay in this village.

"We were all gathered in front of the house around a table topped with cheese and slices of milk. Sdenka was spinning; her sister-in-law was preparing supper for the children, who were playing in the sand; Peter, with an affected carelessness, hissed while cleaning a yataghan, or long Turkish knife. George, leaning on the table, his head in his hands, was anxiously devouring the high road with his eyes—and saying nothing.

"As for me, overcome by the general sorrow, I looked sadly at the evening clouds framing the golden background of the sky and the silhouette of a monastery that a black pine forest half masked.

"This convent, I learned later, had once enjoyed great celebrity because of a miraculous image of the Virgin, which, according to legend, had been brought by angels and appeared on an oak tree. But in the beginning of the last century, the Turks had made an invasion in the country; they had slaughtered the monks and ransacked the monastery. All that remained were the walls and a chapel served by a kind of hermit. The latter gave the curious tours of the ruins and gave hospitality to the pilgrims who, on their way from one place of worship to another, loved to stop at the monastery of the Virgin of the Oak. As I said, I only learned about it later, because that night I had something else in mind besides the archaeology of Serbia. As often happens when one lets go of one's imagination, I thought of the time spent, the beautiful days of my childhood, of my beautiful France, which I had left for a distant and savage country.

"I thought of the Duchesse de Gramont and—why not admit it—I also thought of some other contemporaries of your grandmothers, whose pictures, without my knowledge, had crept into my heart as a result of that of the charming duchess.

"Soon I had forgotten my hosts and their worry. Suddenly, George broke the silence.

" 'Woman,' he said, 'what time did the old man leave?'

" 'At eight o'clock,' replied the woman. 'I heard the bell of the monastery ring well.'

" 'Well, that's fine,' said George, 'it can't be more than seven-thirty.' And he was silent, fixing his eyes again on the great road that was lost in the forest.

"I forgot to tell you, ladies, that when the Serbs suspect someone of vampirism, they avoid naming him by his name or designating him in a direct way, because they think it would raise him from the tomb. So, for some time now, George, in speaking of his father, called him only 'the old man.'

"There was a moment of silence. Suddenly one of the children said—

" 'Aunt, when will Grandpa come home?'

"A blow from George was the answer to this untimely question.

"The child began to cry, but his little brother said with a look at once astonished and fearful:

" 'Why, father, do you forbid us to talk about Grandpa?'

"Another blow closed his mouth. The two children screamed and all the adults crossed themselves.

"We were there when I heard the monastery clock slowly ring eight. As soon as the first blow had sounded in our ears, we saw a human form coming off the wood and advancing towards us.

" 'It's him! God be praised!' exclaimed Sdenka, Peter, and his sister-in-law.

" 'God has us in His holy guard!' said George solemnly. 'How can we know if the ten days have or have not passed?'

"Everyone looked at him with horror. However, the human form was still advancing. He was a tall old man with a silver mustache, a pale, severe face, and dragging himself with difficulty with a stick. As he advanced, George became darker. When the newcomer was near us, he stopped and looked at his family who did not move or speak.

" 'Well,' he said in a hollow voice, 'no one gets up to receive me? What does this silence mean? Do not you see that I am hurt?'

"I saw then that the left side of the old man was bloody.

" 'Help your father, then,' I said to George, 'and you, Sdenka, you ought to give him some spirts, he's ready to collapse!'

" 'My father,' said George, approaching Gorcha, 'show me your wound, and I will dress it.'

"He tried to open the coat, but the old man pushed him back roughly and covered his side with both hands.

" 'Go, clumsy one!' he said. 'You hurt me!'

" 'But you've been wounded near the heart!' cried George, all pale; 'Come, come, take off your coat, you must, you must, I tell you!'

"The old man got up straight and stiff. 'Take care of yourself,' he said in a low voice. 'If you touch me, I curse you!'

"Peter stood between George and his father. 'Leave him,' he told his brother, 'you see that he is suffering!'

" 'Do not displease him,' added his wife, 'you know he never tolerated it!'

"At that moment we saw a flock coming back from the pasture and walking towards the house in a cloud of dust. Either the dog that accompanied them had not recognized his old master, or he was driven by another motive, for as he got near to Gorcha, he stopped, his hair bristling, and began to howl as if he saw something supernatural.

" 'What's wrong with this dog?' said the old man, with an air more and more dissatisfied, 'What does all this mean? Am I a stranger in my own home? Have ten days spent in the mountains changed me to the point that my dogs themselves do not recognize me?'

" 'Do you hear it?' said George to his wife.

" 'What ?'

" 'He confesses that the ten days have passed!'

" 'But no, since he has returned in time!'

" 'Never mind, never mind, I know what to do.'

"As the dog continued to howl, 'I want him killed!' exclaimed Gorcha. 'Well, do you hear me?'

"George did not move; but Peter rose, with tears in his eyes, and, seizing his father's musket, he shot the dog, who rolled in the dust. 'He was my favorite dog,' he said in a low voice. 'I do not know why father wanted him killed…'

" 'Because that's what he deserved!' said Gorcha. 'Now it's cold out here! Let's get inside!'

"Sdenka had prepared a tea made of boiled spirits with pears, honey and raisins, but her father pushed it away in disgust. He showed the same aversion to the dish of mutton and rice George presented to him, and went to sit at the corner of the hearth, murmuring unintelligible words between his teeth.

"A fire of pines sparkled in the hearth, and animated with its trembling light the face of the old man, so pale and so defeated that, without this light, it might have been mistaken for that of a dead man.

"Sdenka came to sit beside him. 'My father,' said she, 'you will not eat or drink or rest; will you tell us about your adventures in the mountains?'

"In saying this, the girl knew that she was touching a chord, for the old man liked to talk about wars and fights. So, a kind of smile appeared on his discolored lips, without his eyes taking part, and he answered by passing his hand on his beautiful white hair: 'Yes, my daughter, yes, Sdenka, I want to tell you what happened to me in the mountains, but it will be another time, because I am tired today. I will tell you, however, that Alibek is no more and that it is from my hand that he perished. If anyone doubts it,' continued the old man, looking at his family, 'here is the proof!' He undid a satchel which hung behind his back, and drew a livid and bloody head which was not yet pallid! We turned away with horror, but Gorcha, giving it to Peter, said, 'Here, nail it up above the door outside, so that all the passers-by will learn that Alibek is killed, and that the roads are purged of robbers, if I except the janissaries of the Sultan!'

"Peter obeyed with disgust. 'I understand everything now,' said he, 'that poor dog that I killed was only screaming because it smelled the dead flesh!'

" 'Yes, he could smell the dead flesh,' replied George, with a gloomy air. He had left without anyone being aware of it, and now returned holding an object in his hand and placing it in a corner. I thought it was a stake.

" 'George,' said his wife, in a low voice, 'you do not want to do this, I hope…'

" 'My brother,' added his sister, 'what do you want to do? But no, no, you will not do anything, will you?'

" 'Leave me,' George said. 'I know what I have to do, and I will do nothing that is not necessary.'

"The night having come, the family went to bed in a part of the house which was separated from my room only by a very thin partition. I admit that what I saw in the evening impressed my imagination. My light was out, the moon was right in a small low window, close to my bed, and threw on the floor and the walls gloomy lights, much like she does now, ladies, in the living room where we are. I wanted to sleep and could not. I attributed my insomnia to the light of the moon; I looked for something that could serve as a curtain, but I found nothing. Then, hearing confused voices behind the partition, I began to listen.

" 'Lie down, woman,' said George, 'and you, Peter, and you, Sdenka.

Do not worry about anything, I'll watch for you.'

" 'But, George,' said his wife, 'I should watch. You worked last night, you must be tired. Besides, I must watch our eldest. You know he's not doing well since yesterday!'

" 'Be calm and lie down,' said George, 'I will watch for both of us!'

" 'But, my brother,' said Sdenka, in her sweetest voice, 'it seems to me that it would be useless to watch. Our father is already asleep, and see how calm and peaceful he looks.'

" 'You do not understand either,' said George in a tone that did not admit of a reply. 'I tell you to go to bed and let me watch!'

"Then there was a deep silence. Soon I felt my eyelids grow heavy and sleep seized my senses. I thought I saw my door open slowly and old Gorcha appear on the doorstep. But I suspected his form rather than seeing it, because it was very dark in the room from which he came. It seemed to me that his dim eyes sought to guess my thoughts and followed the movement of my breathing. Then he put one foot forward, then the other. Then, with extreme caution, he began to step towards me. Then he rose up beside my bed. I felt inexpressible anxieties, yet an invisible force kept me motionless. The old man leaned over me and put his livid face so close to mine that I thought I felt his cadaverous breath. So I made a superhuman effort and woke up, bathed in sweat.

"There was no one in my room. But, glancing at the window, I clearly saw old Gorcha, who had pressed his face against the glass and stared at me with frightening eyes.

"I had the strength not to scream and the presence of mind to remain in bed, as if I had not seen anything. However, the old man seemed to have come only to make sure that I was asleep, for he made no attempt to enter, but, after having examined me well, he walked away from the window and I heard him walking in the next room. George had fallen asleep and he was snoring to shake the walls. The child coughed in that moment and I could hear Gorcha's voice.

" 'You're not sleeping, little one?'

" 'No, Grandpa,' replied the child, 'and I would like to talk to you!'

" 'Ah, you want to talk to me, and what are we talking about?'

" 'I would like you to tell me how you fought with the Turks, for I, too, would fight with the Turks!'

" 'I thought about it, child, and I brought you a little yataghan that I will give you tomorrow.'

" 'Ah, Grandpa, give it to me right now, since you're not sleeping.'

" 'But why, little one, did you not speak to me while it was daylight?'

" 'Because papa forbade me!'

" 'He's careful, your papa. So, would you like to have your little yataghan?'

" 'Oh yes, I would, but not here, because papa could wake up!'

" 'But where then?'

" 'If we go out, I promise you to be very good and not to make any noise!'

"I thought I heard a low laugh from Gorcha, and I heard the child get up. I did not believe in vampires, but the nightmare that I had just had acted on my nerves and, rather than reproach myself later, I got up and slammed my hand against the wall. It would have been enough to wake the Seven Sleepers, but the family didn't seem to hear it. I threw myself toward the door, determined to save the child, but found it locked from the outside, and it did not give way to my efforts. While I was trying to push it open, I saw the old man passing in front of my window with the child in his arms.

" 'Get up, get up!' I shouted with all my strength, and I shook the wall with my blows. Only then did George wake up.

" 'Where is the old man?' he said.

" 'Come out quickly,' I cried, 'he has just carried away your child!'

" 'With a kick George knocked open his door, which, like mine, had been locked from the outside, and he began to run in the direction of the wood.

"I finally managed to wake Peter, his sister-in-law and Sdenka. We gathered in front of the house and, after a few minutes of waiting, we saw George come back with his son. He had found him unconscious on the main road, but soon he recovered his senses and did not look any the worse. In response to all our questions, he said that his grandfather had done him no harm, that they had gone out together to talk better at their ease, but that once outside he had lost consciousness, without remembering how. As for Gorcha, he was gone.

"After that, it was a sleepless night, as one can imagine. The next day I learned that the Danube, which cut the main road a quarter of a league from the village, had begun to freeze over, which always happens in these countries in the late autumn and early spring. The river was cut off for a few days, so I could not think of leaving. Besides, even if I could have done so, curiosity would have kept me there—combined with a more powerful attraction.

"The more I saw Sdenka, the more I felt inclined to love her. I am not one of those, ladies, who believe in the sudden and irresistible passions of which novels give us examples; but I think there are cases where love develops faster than usual. Sdenka's beauty, her singular resemblance to the Duchesse de Gramont, whom I had fled Paris to escape, and whom I found here, in a picturesque costume, speaking a foreign and harmonious language, that delicate line on her brow which, in France, made me want to kill myself twenty times—all this, together with the singularity of my situation and the mysteries surrounding me, contributed to a feeling growing in me which, in other circumstances, would never have happened; or only in a vague and fleeting way.

"In the course of the day I heard Sdenka conversing with her younger brother.

" 'What do you think of all this?' she said, 'Do you also suspect our father?'

" 'I do not dare to suspect him,' replied Peter, 'especially since the child says that he has not hurt him. And as for his disappearance, you know that he's never told us about where he goes.'

" 'I know,' said Sdenka, 'but then you have to save it, because you know George—'

" 'Yes, yes, I know him. Talking to him would be useless, but we'll hide the stake, and he won't look for another one, for on this side of the mountains there is not a single trembling aspen leaf!'

" 'Yes, hide the stake, but don't tell the children, because they could talk to George!'

" 'It'll be all right,' Peter said. And they parted.

"The night came without us having learned anything about old Gorcha. I was again lying on my bed and the moon was right in my room. When sleep began to cloud my ideas, I felt, as if by instinct, the approach of the old man. I opened my eyes and saw his livid face pressed against my window.

"This time I wanted to get up, but that was impossible. It seemed to me that all my limbs were paralyzed. After looking at me well, the old man went away. I heard him go around the house and knock softly at the window of the room where George and his wife were sleeping. The child turned in his bed and moaned in a dream. A few minutes of silence passed, then I heard another knock at the window. Then the child moaned again and awoke.

" 'Is that you, Grandpa?' he said.

" 'It's me,' replied a dull voice, 'and I bring you your little yataghan.'

" 'But I dare not go out, Daddy told me not to!'

" 'You don't need to go out, just open the window and come and kiss me!'

"The child stood up and I heard him open the window. With every ounce of strength I had, I jumped off my bed and ran to bang on the wall.

"In a minute George was up. I heard him swear, his wife uttered a loud cry, and soon the whole house was gathered around the motionless child. Gorcha had disappeared as the day before. By dint of care we managed to get the child to regain consciousness, but he was very weak and breathed with difficulty. The poor little one did not know the cause of his fainting. His mother and Sdenka attributed it to the fright of being surprised talking with his grandfather. I did not say anything. However, the child calmed down , and everyone except George went back to bed.

"Towards daybreak I heard him waking his wife. They whispered to each other. Sdenka joined them and I heard her sobbing, as did her sister-in-law.

"The child was dead.

"I shall not describe the family's agony. No one, however, attributed the cause to old Gorcha. At least, we did not talk about it openly.

"George was silent, but his still dark expression was now something terrible. For two days the old man did not reappear. In the night after the third (the day the burial took place) I thought I heard footsteps around the house and an old man's voice calling the little brother of the deceased. It seemed to me also for a moment that I saw the figure of Gorcha glued to my window, but I could not tell if it was real or the effect of my imagination, because that night the moon was veiled. I thought, however, of my duty to speak to George about it. He questioned the child, and the boy replied that he had indeed heard his grandfather call him and saw him looking through the window. George urged his son to wake him up if the old man appeared again.

"All these circumstances did not prevent my affection for Sdenka from developing ever more. I could not talk to her without witnesses that day. When night came, the thought of my upcoming departure was heartbreaking. Sdenka's room was separated from mine only by a sort of corridor overlooking the street on one side and the courtyard on the other. The rest of the family were in bed, when it occurred to me to take a walk in the country to distract me. Entering the corridor, I saw that the door of Sdenka was ajar.

"I stopped involuntarily. A well-known dress rustle made my heart beat. Then I heard Sdenka singing in a low voice. It was the farewell that a Serbian king, going to war, addressed to his beloved. The old king says—

" 'Oh, my young poplar,
I'm going to war and you'll forget me!
The trees growing at the foot of the mountain
are slender and flexible,
but you are lovelier than they!
The fruits of the mountain ash

that the wind swings
are red but your lips are redder than the fruits of the mountain ash!
And I am like an old oak tree stripped of leaves,
and my beard is whiter than the foam of the Danube!
And you will forget me, O my soul,
and I will die of sorrow,
for the enemy will not dare to kill the old king!'

"And the beloved replies—

" *'I swear to remain faithful to you*
and not to forget you.
If I fail in my oath, may you, after your death,
come and suck all the blood of my heart!'

"And the old king said, '*So be it!*' And he went to war. And soon his beloved forgot him!

"Here Sdenka stopped, as if she were afraid of finishing the ballad. I restrained myself no longer. That voice, so sweet, so expressive, was the voice of the Duchesse de Gramont. Without thinking of anything, I pushed open the door and entered. Sdenka had just removed a kind of jacket worn by the women of his country. Her shirt, embroidered with gold and red silk, bound tight around her waist by a simple plaid skirt, made up all her costume. Her beautiful blond tresses were untied and her neglected hair only enhanced her attractions. She was not irritated by my sudden entrance, but she seemed confused and blushed slightly.

" 'Oh,' she said to me, 'why are you here? What would you think of me if someone came in?'

" 'Sdenka, my soul,' I said to her, 'be quiet, everything is sleeping around us, there is only the cricket in the grass and the beetle in the air that can hear what I have to say to you.'

" 'Oh, my friend, run away, run away! If my brother surprises us, I'm lost!'

" 'Sdenka, I will not go until you promise to love me always, as the beloved promised to the king of the ballad. I'm leaving soon, Sdenka, who knows when we'll see each other again? Sdenka, I love you more than my soul, more than my salvation ...'

" 'Many things can happen in an hour,' said Sdenka thoughtfully; but she left her hand in mine. 'You do not know my brother,' she continued, shuddering; 'I have a presentiment that he will come.'

" 'Calm down, my Sdenka,' I said to her, 'your brother is exhausted from his watches, he has been lulled to sleep by the wind playing in the trees; how heavy is his sleep, long is the night, and I only ask you an hour! And then, goodbye...maybe forever!'

" 'Oh, no, no, not forever!' said Sdenka quickly; then she recoiled as frightened of her own voice.

" 'Oh! Sdenka,' I cried, 'I see only you, I only hear you, I am no longer master of myself, I obey a superior force, forgive me, Sdenka!' And like a madman I hugged her against my heart.

" 'Oh, you are not my friend!' she said, pulling away from my arms. She went to take refuge in the back of the room. I do not know what I told her, for I myself was confused by my daring—not that on such occasions it did not sometimes succeed—but because, despite my passion, I had a sincere respect for Sdenka's innocence. I did, it is true, start using some of those phrases of gallantry that did not displease the beautiful of our time, but soon I was ashamed, and I gave up, seeing that the simplicity of the young girl prevented her from understanding me—though I see by your smiles that you, ladies, guess what I meant.

"I was there in front of her, not knowing what to say to her, when suddenly I saw her flinch and stare at the window with a look of terror. I followed the direction of her eyes and I distinctly saw the motionless figure of Gorcha watching us from outside.

"At the same moment, I felt a heavy hand resting on my shoulder. I turned around. It was George.

" 'What are you doing here?' he asked me.

Disconcerted, I showed him his father, who was looking out of the window and who disappeared as soon as George saw him. 'I heard the old man and I came to tell your sister,' I said.

"George looked at me as if trying to read my soul. Then he took me by the arm, led me to my room, and went away without uttering a word.

"The next day, the family was gathered in the front of the house around a table laden with milk and cheese.

" 'Where is the child?' said George.

" 'He is in the yard,' replied his mother, 'he's playing his favorite game: fighting the Turks.'

"No sooner had she uttered these words than to our utter amazement we saw, coming from out of the woods, the tall figure of Gorcha, who walked slowly to our group and sat at the table as he had done the day of my arrival.

" 'My father, welcome,' murmured his daughter-in-law in a voice scarcely intelligible.

" 'Welcome, my father,' said Sdenka and Peter in low voices.

" 'My father,' said George, in a firm voice, although his face had lost its color, 'we are waiting for you to say grace!'

"The old man turned away, frowning.

" 'Say grace, right now!' repeated George, and make the sign of the cross. 'Or by St. George...'

"Sdenka and her sister-in-law leaned over the old man and begged him to say the prayer.

" 'No, no, no,' said the old man, 'he has no right to command me, and if he insists, I curse him!'

George got up and ran into the house. Soon he came back, fury in his eyes.

" 'Where is the stake?' he exclaimed. 'Where did you hide the stake?'

Sdenka and Peter exchanged a look.

" 'Corpse!' George shouted at the old man. 'What did you do with my eldest son? Why did you kill my child? Give me back my son, corpse!'

"And speaking thus, he grew more and more pale, and his eyes became more animated.

"The old man looked at him with a bad look and did not move.

" 'Oh! the stake, the stake!' exclaimed George. 'May he who hid it answer for the misfortunes that await us!'

"At that moment we heard the joyous bursts of laughter of the youngest child, and we saw him riding on a great stake, which he dragged on, prancing on it, and uttering with his little voice the war cry of the Serbs when they attacked the enemy.

"At this sight George's eyes lit up. He snatched the stake from the child and rushed to his father. Gorcha screamed and ran in the direction of the woods with a speed so little in keeping with his age that it seemed supernatural.

"George pursued him across the fields, and soon we lost sight of them.

"The sun had gone down when George came home, pale as death and with bristling hair. He sat by the fire and I thought I heard his teeth chatter. Nobody dared to question him. About the time when the family was about to part, he seemed to recover all his energy and, taking me aside, he told me in the most natural way,—

" 'My dear guest, I have just seen the river. There is no more ice, the way is free, nothing prevents your departure. It is not necessary,' he added, glancing at Sdenka, 'to take leave of my family. She wishes you all the happiness you can desire here, and I hope you too will have a good memory. Tomorrow, at break of day, you will find your saddled horse and your guide ready to follow you. Farewell, remember sometimes your host and forgive him if your stay here was not as free of tribulations as he would have liked.'

"George's rough features were at this moment almost cordial. He took me to my room and shook my hand one last time. Then he flinched and his teeth chattered as if shivering with cold.

"Alone, I did not think of going to bed as you think. Other ideas worried me. I had loved several times in my life. I had had fits of tenderness, spite and jealousy, but never, not even when I left the Duchesse de Gramont, had I felt a sadness like that which was tearing my heart at that moment. Before the sun had appeared, I put on my traveling clothes and wanted to try a last interview with Sdenka. But George was waiting for me in the vestibule. There was no possibility of seeing her alone again.

"I jumped on my horse and kicked its sides. I promised myself, on my return from Jassy, to come back to this village, and this hope, however remote it was, gradually drove away my worries. I was already thinking about my return, and my imagination recounted in advance all the details, when a sudden movement of the horse nearly made me lose hold of the pommel. The animal stopped short, stiffened on its front hooves, and whinnied in alarm. I looked carefully and saw, a hundred steps in front of me, a wolf digging the ground. Hearing me, he fled. I plunged my spurs into the flanks of my mount and urged him forward. I then saw that the wolf had been digging into what looked like a fresh grave. It also seemed that I could see the end of a wooden stake protruding a few inches from the earth which the wolf had just stirred. However, I could not confirm it, for I passed very quickly by this place."

Here the marquis was silent, and took a pinch of snuff.

"Is this all?" asked the ladies.

"Alas no!" replied M. d'Urfe. "What I have to tell you now is for me a much more painful memory, and I would give much to be delivered from it.

"The business that brought me to Jassy kept me there longer than I expected. I did not finish until six months later. What will I say to you? It is a sad truth to confess, but it is nonetheless a truth that there are few lasting feelings here below. The success of my negotiations, the encouragement I received from the cabinet of Versailles, the policy in a word, this ugly policy, which has so much bothered us lately, soon weakened the memory of Sdenka in my mind. Then, the wife of the Gospodar, who was very beautiful and spoke French perfectly, had given, on my arrival, the honour of distinguishing me among some other young foreigners who were staying at Jassy. Raised, as I have been, in the principles of French gallantry, my Gallic blood would have revolted at the idea of paying ingratitude for the benevolence of beauty. So I courteously responded to the advances made to me, and to put myself in a position to assert the interests and rights of France, I began by identifying myself with all those of the Gospodar.

"Called back to my country, I took the road that had brought me to

Jassy.

"I no longer thought of Sdenka or her family, when one evening, crossing the country, I heard a bell ringing eight o'clock. This sound did not seem unfamiliar to me, and my guide told me that it came from a monastery not far away. I asked him for the name, and I learned that it was that of the Virgin of the Oak. I pressed the pace of my horse and soon we knocked on the door of the monastery. The hermit came to open us and led us to the foreigners' apartment. I found it so full of pilgrims that I lost the urge to spend the night, and asked if I could find a lodging in the village.

" 'You will find more than one,' replied the hermit, with a deep sigh; thanks to the disbeliever Gorcha, there are no empty houses!'

" 'What do you say?' I asked. 'Is old Gorcha still alive?'

" 'Oh, no, that one is properly buried with a stake in his heart! But he had sucked the blood of George's son. The child came back one night, crying at the door, saying he was cold and wanted to go home. His foolish mother, though she had buried him herself, did not have the courage to send him back to the cemetery and opened the door for him. Then he threw himself on her and sucked her to death. Buried in her turn, she returned to suck the blood of her second son, and then that of her husband, and then that of her brother-in-law. All have passed.'

" 'And Sdenka?' I said.

" 'Oh, that one went mad with pain; poor child, do not talk to me about it!'

"The hermit's response was so forceful, I did not have the courage to repeat my question.

" 'Vampirism is contagious,' continued the hermit, crossing himself; 'Many families in the village are affected, many families have died to their last member, and if you want to believe me, you will stay the night here at the monastery, because in the village, even if you are not devoured by the vourdalaks, the constant fear of them will be enough to whiten your hair before I have finished ringing matins. I am only a poor monk,' he went on, 'but the generosity of the travelers has enabled me to provide for them. I have exquisite cheeses, raisins that will make your mouth water just to see them, and a few bottles of Tokay wine that does not bow to anything that is served to His Holiness the Patriarch!'

"It seemed to me at this moment that the hermit had become an innkeeper! I thought that he had purposely told me a ghost story to give me the opportunity to make myself agreeable to heaven by imitating the generosity of the travelers who had placed the holy man in a position to provide for their needs.

"Also, the word fear has always had on me the effect of the bugle on a warhorse. I would have been ashamed of myself if I had not left immediately.

"My guide, trembling, begged to stay behind, and I gladly agreed.

"It took me about half an hour to get to the village. I found it deserted. No light shone on the windows, no song was heard. I passed in silence in front of all these houses, most of which were known to me, and I finally arrived at George's. Either because of sentimental memory or a young man's temerity, I decided to spend the night there.

"I dismounted and knocked at the gate. Nobody answered. I pushed the door. It opened, groaning on its hinges, and I entered the courtyard.

"I tied my saddled horse under a shed, where I found a sufficient supply of oats for one night, and advanced resolutely towards the house.

"No door was closed, yet all the rooms seemed uninhabited. That of Sdenka seemed to have been abandoned only the day before. Some clothes were still lying on the bed. Some jewels which I had given her, among which I recognized a small enameled cross which I had bought while passing by Pesth, shone on a table by the light of the moon. I could not help but hold my heart, though my love was gone. However, I wrapped myself in my cloak and lay down on the bed. Soon sleep won over me. I do not remember the details of my dream, but I know that I saw Sdenka again, beautiful, naive and loving as in the past. I reproached myself, on seeing her, for my selfishness and inconstancy.

How could I, I wondered, abandon this poor child who loved me, how could I forget her? Then her face became confused with that of the Duchesse de Gramont, and I saw in these two images only one and the same person. I threw myself at Sdenka's feet and implored her forgiveness. All my being, all my soul was confused in an ineffable feeling of melancholy and happiness.

"I was still dreaming, when I was half awakened by a harmonious sound, like the rustle of a field of wheat stirred by the light breeze. It seemed to me that the ears of wheat clanged melodiously and the song of the birds mingled with the rolling of a waterfall and the whispering of the trees. Then, it seemed to me that all these confused sounds were only the rustle of a woman's dress, and I stopped at this idea.

"I opened my eyes and saw Sdenka beside my bed.

"The moon shone so vividly that I could see in every detail the adorable features that had once been so dear to me, that I had prized even more in my dream. I found Sdenka more beautiful and more captivating than ever. She had the same simple costume as the last time I saw her alone: a simple shirt embroidered with gold and silk, and then a tight-fitting skirt over the hips.

" 'Sdenka!' I said, rising to my feet, 'Is it really you, Sdenka?'

" 'Yes, it's me,' she answered in a soft, sad voice, 'it's your Sdenka, whom you've forgotten. Ah, why did not you come back sooner? All is finished now, you must go; one more moment and you are lost! Farewell, my friend, goodbye forever!'

" 'Sdenka,' said I, 'you have had many misfortunes, I am told! Come, we will talk together and that will relieve you!'

" 'Oh, my friend,' said she, 'we must not believe everything we say about ourselves; but leave, leave as quickly as possible, for if you stay here, your doom is certain.'

" 'But, Sdenka, what is this danger that threatens me? Cannot you give me an hour, just an hour to talk with you?'

"Sdenka flinched, and a strange revolution took place in her whole person.

" 'Yes,' said she, '*an hour, an hour*, is it not, as when I was singing
the old king's ballad and you entered my room? That's what you mean? Tell, either way, I give you an hour! But no, no,' she said, recovering, 'go, go! Leave soon, I tell you, run away! As far as you can!'

"A savage energy animated her features. I did not understand what made her speak like that, but she was so beautiful that I resolved to stay in spite of herself. Finally yielding to my entreaties, she sat down beside me, spoke to me of past times, and confessed to me, blushing, that she had loved me from the day of my arrival. However, little by little, I noticed a change in Sdenka. Her former reserve had given way to a strange indifference. Her gaze, once so timid, had something bold in it. Finally, I saw with surprise that she had lost the modesty that had once distinguished her.

" 'Is it possible,' I asked myself, 'that Sdenka was not the pure and innocent girl she seemed to be? Would she have only pretended to be, for fear of her brother? Would I have been so grossly duped by her false virtue? But why demand that I leave? Is it perhaps some new refinement of coquetry? And I thought I knew her! But no matter! If Sdenka is not a Diana, as I thought, I can compare her to another deity, no less lovable—and, praise God, I prefer the role of Adonis to that of Actaeon!'

" 'If this classic phrase that I addressed to myself seems out of season, ladies, please think that what I have the honor to tell you happened in the year of grace 1759. Mythology then was the order of the day, and I did not desire to go faster than my century. Things have changed since then, and it was not long ago that the Revolution, by reversing the memories of paganism, along with the Christian religion, had put the goddess Reason in their place. This goddess, ladies, was never my mistress when I found myself in your presence; and at the time of which I speak, I was less disposed than ever to offer her sacrifices. I surrendered unreservedly to the inclination that led me to Sdenka, and I went happily to meet her advances.

"After some time, I amused myself by dressing Sdenka with all her jewels. As part of this, I wanted to put the small enamel cross I had found on the table around her neck.

"Sdenka shrank back.

" 'Enough childishness, my friend,' she said to me, 'leave these trinkets and talk about you and your projects!' Sdenka's unease made me think. Examining it carefully, I noticed that she no longer carried around her neck, as in the past, a host of small images, reliquaries and sachets filled with incense that the Serbs have the habit of wearing from their childhood and that they leave only at their death.

" 'Sdenka,' said I, 'where are the icons you had around your neck?'

" 'I lost them,' she replied impatiently, and she immediately changed her conversation.

"I do not know what vague presentiment, which I did not realize, seized me. I wanted to leave, but Sdenka held me back. 'What?' she said. 'You asked me for an hour, and now you're leaving after a few minutes!'

" 'Sdenka,' I said, 'you were right to ask me to leave; I think I hear some noise and I'm afraid we will be found out!'

" 'Be quiet, my friend, everything is sleeping around us, there is only the cricket in the grass and the beetle in the air that can hear what I have to say to you!'

" 'No, no, Sdenka, I must leave!'

" 'Stop, stop,' said Sdenka, 'I love you more than my soul, more than my salvation, you told me that your life and your blood were mine!'

" 'But your brother, your brother, Sdenka, I have a feeling that he will come!'

" 'Calm down, my soul, my brother was put to sleep by the wind playing in the trees; how heavy is his sleep, how long is the night, and I only ask you for an hour!'

"Sdenka said that; and she was so beautiful that the vague terror that agitated me began to yield to the desire to stay with her. A mixture of fear and voluptuousness impossible to describe filled my whole being. As I weakened, Sdenka became more tender, so I decided to give in while promising to keep myself on my guard. However, as I said earlier, I have never been half wise, and when Sdenka, noting my reserve, proposed to put off the cold of the night with a few glasses of a wine that a generous hermit had given her, I accepted her proposal with an eagerness that made her smile.

"The wine produced its effect. From the second glass the bad impression made on me by the circumstance of the cross and the images completely faded away; Sdenka, in the disorder of her dress, with her beautiful half-braided hair, with her jewels illuminated by the moon, seemed to me irresistible. I no longer held back, and pressed her in my arms.

"Then, ladies, took place one of those mysterious revelations which I can never explain, but which experience has compelled me to believe, although until then I had been little inclined to admit such things.

"The strength with which I clasped my arms around Sdenka brought into my breast one of the points of the cross which you have just seen, and which the Duchesse de Gramont had given me upon my departure. The acute pain I felt was like a ray of light that went right through me. I looked at Sdenka and saw that her features, although still beautiful, were contracted as if by death. Her eyes were blank, and her smile was a convulsion, printed by agony on the figure of a corpse. At the same time, I felt in the room that nauseating odor which is usually spread by ill-closed vaults. The frightful truth stood before me in all its ugliness, and I remembered too late the hermit's warnings.

"I realized how precarious my position was and I felt that everything depended on my courage and my coolness. I turned away from Sdenka to hide the horror that my features had to express. My eyes, then, fell on the window and I saw the infamous Gorcha, leaning on a bleeding stake and staring at me with hyena eyes. The other window was occupied by the pale figure of George, who at that moment had a terrifying likeness with his father. Both seemed to be watching my movements, and I did not doubt that they would leap upon me at the slightest attempt at flight. I pretended not to see them, but, making a violent effort, I continued, yes, ladies, I continued to lavish on Sdenka the same caresses that I wished to do before my terrible discovery!

"Meanwhile, I thought with anxiety of escaping. I noticed that Gorcha and George were signaling to Sdenka and that they were becoming impatient. I heard a woman's voice and the cries of children outside, but so awful that they could have been mistaken them for the cries of wildcats.

" 'It is time to get out of here,' I said to myself, 'and the sooner the better!'

"Addressing myself then to Sdenka, I told her, loudly enough for her hideous family to hear:

" 'I am very tired, my child, I would like to go to bed and sleep a few hours, but first I must go and see if my horse has eaten his food. Please do not go away and wait for my return.'

"I then pressed my lips to her cold, discolored lips and went out.

"I found my horse covered with foam and struggling under the shed. He had not touched the oats, but the neighing he uttered when he saw me coming gave me goosebumps, for I feared he would betray my intentions. However, the vampires, who had probably heard my conversation with Sdenka, did not raise any alarm. I made sure that the door was open, and, throwing myself into the saddle, I plunged my spurs into the sides of my horse.

"I had time to perceive, on leaving the door, that the troop assembled near the house, most of whose faces were glued to the windows, was very numerous. I think that my abrupt departure surprised them at first, because for a time I could not hear, in the silence of the night, anything but the uniform gallop of my horse. I already thought I could congratulate myself on my cunning, when all of a sudden I heard a noise like a hurricane in the mountains behind me. A thousand confused voices screamed, screamed, and seemed to argue with each other. Then all were silent, as if by mutual agreement, and I heard a hurried tramp as if a troop of infantry approached at a running pace.

"I pressed my horse enough to tear his sides. An ardent fever made my heart pound, and, while I was exhausting myself in unheard-of efforts to preserve my presence of mind, I heard behind me a voice that cried out to me:

" 'Stop, stop, my friend! I love you more than my soul, I love you more than my salvation! stop, stop, your blood is mine!'

"At the same time, a cold breath touched my ear and I felt Sdenka jump on my back.

" 'My heart, my soul!' she said to me, 'I see only you, I feel only you, I am not mistress of myself, I am slave to a superior force, forgive me, my friend, forgive me!'

"And, embracing me in her arms, she tried to pull me back and bite me by the throat. A terrible struggle broke out between us.

"For a long time I defended myself with difficulty, but at last I managed to seize Sdenka with one hand by her waist and with the other by her braids, and, standing on my stirrups, I threw her to the ground!

"Immediately my strength abandoned me and the delirium took hold of me. A thousand mad and terrible grimacing forms pursued me. First George and his brother Peter were walking along the road and trying to cut me off. They could not do it, and I was just about to rejoice when, turning around, I saw old Gorcha, who was using his stake to leap like the Tyrolean mountaineers when they cross the abysses. But I also left Gorcha behind. Then his daughter-in-law, who was dragging her children after her, threw one to him, which he received at the end of his stake. Using it as a catapult, he threw the child after me with all his strength. I avoided the blow, but with a fanatical instinct, the little toad clung to my horse's neck, and I had difficulty in tearing it away. The other child was sent to me in the same way, but he fell beyond the horse and was crushed.

"I do not know how it is that I am still living, but when I came back to me it was a great day and I found myself lying on the road next to my exhaling horse.

"Thus ends, ladies, a love that should have healed me forever from the desire to seek new ones. Some contemporaries of your grandmothers could tell you if I was wiser in the future.

"Be that as it may, I still shudder at the thought that if I had succumbed to my enemies, I would have become a vampire myself; but heaven did not allow things to come to this point, and far from thirsting for your blood, ladies, I ask nothing better, old as I am, than to pour mine for your service!"

GLOSSARY

Actaeon: In Greek and Roman mythology, a hunter who stumbled on the goddess Artemis (Diana) while she was bathing. The goddess turned him into a stag and his hunting dogs tore Actaeon apart.

Adonis: In Greek and Roman mythology, the handsomest young man in the world, who was pursued by the lusty goddess Aphrodite (Venus)—and then killed by a boar. By comparing himself to Actaeon and Adonis, D'Urfe is saying that, if he has to die, he'd rather have sex first with a willing beauty.

Aspen: The stake in the story is made of aspen—because according to one legend, Christ's cross was made of aspen. Aspen leaves tremble in the lightest breeze—or, according to legend, because the tree is still nervous about participating in the Crucifixion.

Congress of Vienna: The Conference in 1815 that restructured Europe after the defeat of Napoleon at Waterloo.

Janissaries: Elite Turkish infantry before 1826.

Jassy: Capital of Moldavia, 1564-1859.

Pesth: Pest, the eastern part of the Budapest, Hungary. The two sections are separated by the Danube river.

Reason: Opposition to the Catholic Church was one of the driving forces of some radical elements of the French Revolution, and from 1792-1794 some revolutionaries tried to replace Christianity with a Cult of Reason. Many churches—including Notre Dame—were rededicated as "Temples of Reason." At these "Temples," Festivals of Reason were celebrated, and women dressed up in togas to personify the goddess. (This avoided the use of statues to Reason, which would have encouraged idolatry.) The Revolutionary leader Robespierre dismantled the Cult of Reason and set up his own Cult of the Supreme Being, before being guillotined. Napoleon outlawed the Cults and Catholicism returned to France.

Seven Sleepers: In Islamic myth, seven young men who, to escape religious persecution circa 250 AD, hide—and sleep, in a kind of suspended animation—in a cave outside the Greek city of Ephesus, and wake up three centuries later.

Yataghan: A curved, single-bladed Turkish sword.

AFTERWORD

Tolstoy is unclear on exactly how Gorcha becomes a vourdalak, although it's likely that Alibek, the Turkish bandit, was a vourdalak and bit Gorcha before getting beheaded.

Note the use of Christian iconography in the story; in this case, though, the cross doesn't hurt the vampire, but prods d'Urfe into seeing what Sdenka has become.

TELYAEV

"Notice the way, when they meet each other, they click their tongues."

In 1841, two years after The Family of the Vourdalak, *Tolstoy returned to the subject of vampires, this time with a short novel. Unlike his earlier attempt, this was written in Russian and actually published, although under a pseudonym.*

Critical reception was mixed. Unlike the dreadful old Gorcha, Telyaev and his vampiric brethren are not to be taken entirely seriously; they're intended to be more absurd than genuinely frightening.

While Tolstoy's earlier story was set in a peasant village in deepest Serbia, his new vampire story picked up the theme of aristocracy established by Lord Ruthven—and expanded on it.

Instead of a single vampire lord secretly stalking high society, Tolstoy presents us with an entire society of aristocratic vampires, almost out in the open in the heart of Moscow. And yet, they are unsuspected by ordinary people. At first, only one stranger, as mysterious as the vampires themselves, is aware of the truth.

The secret vampire society is a theme that would be picked up by later writers, especially by Anne Rice and those who followed in her wake.

The title of the novella is Upyr, *which is a little confusing. An upyr is a creature in Russian folklore that is very similar to the vampire, although "ghoul" is probably a better translation. However, the undead in Tolstoy's story are clearly vampires; and the novella has been translated as both* Ghoul *and* The Vampire. *The story starts off with a tongue-in-cheek discussion of what the proper (and properly Russian) word should be used for these bloodsuckers. Again, there's a note of absurdity rather than horror.*

Currently, Ghoul/The Vampire *is hard to find, and there is no full English translation in the public domain. Only the opening sequence, newly translated by the editor, is presented here, to give readers a taste of the piece.*

It's a short but fascinating scene in terms of the literary development of the vampire. Here is the first "vampire ball," and it confirms the fact that, in Russia as in England, vampires had apparently secured their places in high society in the first half of the 19th century.

GHOUL

(OR, THE VAMPIRE)

Count Alexei Konstantinovich Tolstoy

The ball was very crowded. After a rather noisy waltz, Runevsky escorted his latest dancing partner back to her place and began to walk around the rooms, looking at the various groups of guests.

His eye fell upon a man, apparently still young, but pale and almost completely white-haired. The man stood leaning against the fireplace, all his attention trained on the opposite side of the hall—so much so that he did not notice that the hem of his tail coat had gotten too close to the fire and had begun to smoke.

Runevsky, fascinated by the strange behavior, took the opportunity to have a conversation with the man.

"While you're looking for somebody," he said, "your clothes are about to burn."

The stranger looked around, stepped away from the fireplace and looked intently at Runevsky.

"No, I'm not looking for anyone; I'm just surprised at how many ghouls there are at the ball!"

"Ghouls?" Runevsky repeated. "You mean—ghouls?"

"Ghouls," replied the stranger very cold-bloodedly. "You, God knows why, call them vampires. They are real—and *upyr*, 'ghoul,' is their real name, their Russian name, since they are of purely Slavic origin; although they are found throughout Europe and even in Asia, it is unjustified to use the name, warped by Hungarian monks who thought to turn everything into Latin and made a *vampire* out of an *upyr*. A vampire, a vampire!" he repeated with contempt. "It is as though in Russian we didn't say *prizrak*, 'ghost', but spoke of a 'phantom' or 'revenant!' "

"Yes, well," said Runevsky, "but, whatever you call them, how do you know that there are vampires or ghouls here?"

Instead of answering, the stranger held out his hand and pointed to an elderly lady, who was talking in friendly tones to another lady and a young girl sitting next to her. The conversation, obviously, concerned the girl because she smiled from time to time and blushed slightly.

"Do you know this old woman?" the stranger asked Runevsky.

"That's Madame Suglobina, widow of the brigadier general Suglobin," he said. "I don't know her personally, but I was told that she is very rich and that she has a lovely cottage not far from Moscow—not at all decorated in the style you'd expect a Brigadier to approve of."

"Yes, she was definitely Suglobina a few years ago, but now she's nothing more or less than the most heinous ghoul, whose only desire is to satiate herself with human blood. Look at the way she looks at that poor girl. Her own granddaughter! Listen to what the old woman says: she sings her praises and persuades her to come for two weeks to her cottage, the very cottage you spoke of; but I assure you that it will not be three days before the poor thing dies. Doctors will say it's fever or an inflammation in the lungs; but don't you believe them!"

Runevsky listened and could not believe his ears.

"Do you doubt it?" continued the stranger. "No one, however, knows better than I can that Suglobina is a ghoul, for I was at her funeral. If I had been able to do what I wanted then, she would have been impaled with an aspen stake between her shoulders to keep her in her grave!"

At that moment a man in a frock-coat approached the old woman. He wore a wig, with a large Vladimir cross on his neck and a decoration representing forty-five years of blameless service. He held a golden snuff-box with both hands and as Runevsky watched from across the room, he opened it for the general's widow.

"And he is also a vampire?" asked Runevsky.

"Without a doubt," answered the stranger. "This is the state councilor Telyaev; he was a great friend of Suglobina and died two weeks before her."

Telyaev smiled and shifted his bearing from foot to foot. The old woman smiled and dropped her fingers into the snuffbox.

"With clover, my dear sir?" she asked.

"With clover, madam," Telyaev answered in a sweet voice.

"Do you hear?" said the stranger to Runevsky. "It's word for word a conversation they had when they were still alive. Every time Telyaev met with Suglobina, he brought her a snuffbox, from which she took a pinch, asking in advance, if the tobacco was made with clover? Then Telyaev answered that it was, and sat next to her."

"Tell me," asked Runevsky, "how can you tell who's a vampire and who isn't?"

"That's easy. As for these two, I can't be mistaken, because I knew them before their deaths. Many who knew them are surprised to see them, and I have to admit, this takes some remarkable audacity on their part—But you ask how to recognize ghouls? Notice the way, when they meet each other, they click their tongues. It's not really clicking, it's a sound similar to the one produced by the lips when one sucks an orange. It's their password, their secret greeting, so they can recognize each other...."

GLOSSARY

Vladimir cross: An award established by Catherine the Great in 1782, consisting of a red cross with black and gold edges. It should be noted that this is not a religious cross like the worn by d'Urfe in *The Family of the Vourdalak.*

AFTERWORD

While the idea of a secret underground society of vampires would become very popular later on, in the 1840's, the solitary Byronic vampire—or "vampyre"—would once more be set loose in polite society...in a pulp epic that introduced vampire tropes that are still familiar today...

VARNEY

"Is he a vampyre?" he asked himself. "Are there vampyres, and is this man of fashion—this courtly, talented, educated gentleman one?" It was a perfectly hideous question.

*V*arney, the Vampyre; or the Feast of Blood *was published in England in a series of "penny dreadful" magazines. The weekly installments ran between 1845 and 1847, adding up to an epic of approximately 667,000 words...eighty-three times the length of Polidori's tale and longer than all four* Twilight *books put together. What follows is only about 10% of the whole—the first twenty chapters, followed by the thirty-fourth chapter.*

Most of Chapter XIX has been edited out, as it primarily consists of the heroine, Flora, reading a totally unrelated horror story. This was originally to pad out the chapter until the next installment. (The excisions are indicated with four asterisks.)

Varney is more properly Sir Francis Varney, as aristocratic as Darvell or Ruthven, and Varney the Vampyre *continues the evolution of the aristocratic, Byronic vampire. But, as the story develops, there is a new factor that will become key to vampire stories from the late 20ᵗʰ century onward: the experience of immortality.*

We don't know how old Darvell or Lord Ruthven are, although it's probable that they've "died" before. The key element in The Vampyre *is the return from death, not endless survival. But what if a vampire did live for centuries? How would that affect his character?*

Part of the appeal of the Gothic literature of the 18ᵗʰ and 19ᵗʰ centuries, of which the vampire was a part, was on an awareness of the past as a truly different time. In Europe, while ancient Greece and Rome were naturally "the past," it wasn't until the late 1700's—when a new sensibility found beauty in ruined castles and churches—that the more recent centuries were seen as a narrative of progress, development, and change. What, then, would it be like to be an immortal who remembered when the ruins were new? In 1820—one year after The Vampyre—*the Gothic novel* Melmoth the Wanderer, *by Charles Maturin, featured a 17ᵗʰ century man who makes a pact with Satan to live for an extra 150 years, interacting with various significant historical people and events. The idea was clearly applicable to a vampire, and Rymer makes some use of this with Sir Francis Varney.*

The timeline of Varney the Vampyre *is unclear; parts of the story seem to take place in the early 1700's, while others must be almost contemporaneous with the publication; at various points, Varney himself says he became a vampire either in the 17th century or sometime around 1400! As often happens with storylines that just keep going and going, week after week, month after month, writers have to keep generating new ideas, and if they forget or ignore continuity, they have to hope their audience will, too. Characters and motivations change—sometimes for reasons that seem psychologically consistent, sometimes because the writer or writers just have different ideas. Whatever the details, though, Varney's essentially immortal life is part and parcel of his character, and became a major trope in vampire fiction.*

Despite Sir Francis Varney's pedigree, his bloodsucking, at least in the early sections, doesn't have any hint of elegant seduction about it; the heroine, Flora, is in no sense a willing victim; she isn't caught up in an irresistible sexual attraction. Vampirism in Varney *is very much an allegory of rape...At least, it starts out that way. Rymer's ideas changed over the course of writing the weekly installments, and Varney's aims change from bloodlust to a desire to take over his ancestral home. He becomes less of a monster and more of a Byronic anti-hero. You can see the beginning of that change of character, or change of direction, in the 63,000 words that follow...*

Excerpts from

VARNEY, THE VAMPYRE;
OR
THE FEAST OF BLOOD
A ROMANCE

James Malcolm Rymer

CHAPTER I.

> ———*"How graves give up their dead.*
> *And how the night air hideous grows*
> *With shrieks!"*

MIDNIGHT.—THE HAIL-STORM.—THE DREADFUL VISITOR.—THE VAMPYRE.

The solemn tones of an old cathedral clock have announced midnight—the air is thick and heavy—a strange, death like stillness pervades all nature. Like the ominous calm which precedes some more than usually terrific outbreak of the elements, they seem to have paused even in their ordinary fluctuations, to gather a terrific strength for the great effort. A faint peal of thunder now comes from far off. Like a signal gun for the battle of the winds to begin, it appeared to awaken them from their lethargy, and one awful, warring hurricane swept over a whole city, producing more devastation in the four or five minutes it lasted, than would a half century of ordinary phenomena.

It was as if some giant had blown upon some toy town, and scattered many of the buildings before the hot blast of his terrific breath; for as suddenly as that blast of wind had come did it cease, and all was as still and calm as before.

Sleepers awakened, and thought that what they had heard must be the confused chimera of a dream. They trembled and turned to sleep again.

All is still—still as the very grave. Not a sound breaks the magic of repose. What is that—a strange, pattering noise, as of a million of fairy feet? It is hail—yes, a hail-storm has burst over the city. Leaves are dashed from the trees, mingled with small boughs; windows that lie most opposed to the direct fury of the pelting particles of ice are broken, and the rapt repose that before was so remarkable in its intensity, is exchanged for a noise which, in its accumulation, drowns every cry of surprise or consternation which here and there arose from persons who found their houses invaded by the storm.

Now and then, too, there would come a sudden gust of wind that in its strength, as it blew laterally, would, for a moment, hold millions of the hailstones suspended in mid air, but it was only to dash them with redoubled force in some new direction, where more mischief was to be done.

Oh, how the storm raged! Hail—rain—wind. It was, in very truth, an awful night.

There is an antique chamber in an ancient house. Curious and quaint carvings adorn the walls, and the large chimney-piece is a curiosity of itself. The ceiling is low, and a large bay window, from roof to floor, looks to the west. The window is latticed, and filled with curiously painted glass and rich stained pieces, which send in a strange, yet beautiful light, when sun or moon shines into the apartment. There is but one portrait in that room, although the walls seem panelled for the express purpose of containing a series of pictures. That portrait is of a young man, with a pale face, a stately brow, and a strange expression about the eyes, which no one cared to look on twice.

There is a stately bed in that chamber, of carved walnut-wood is it made, rich in design and elaborate in execution; one of those works of art which owe their existence to the Elizabethan era. It is hung with heavy silken and damask furnishing; nodding feathers are at its corners—covered with dust are they, and they lend a funereal aspect to the room. The floor is of polished oak.

God! how the hail dashes on the old bay window! Like an occasional discharge of mimic musketry, it comes clashing, beating, and cracking upon the small panes; but they resist it—their small size saves them; the wind, the hail, the rain, expend their fury in vain.

The bed in that old chamber is occupied. A creature formed in all fashions of loveliness lies in a half sleep upon that ancient couch—a girl young and beautiful as a spring morning. Her long hair has escaped from its confinement and streams over the blackened coverings of the bedstead; she has been restless in her sleep, for the clothing of the bed is in much confusion. One arm is over her head, the other hangs nearly off the side of the bed near to which she lies. A neck and bosom that would have formed a study for the rarest sculptor that ever Providence gave genius to, were half disclosed. She moaned slightly in her sleep, and once or twice the lips moved as if in prayer—at least one might judge so, for the name of Him who suffered for all came once faintly from them.

She has endured much fatigue, and the storm does not awaken her; but it can disturb the slumbers it does not possess the power to destroy entirely. The turmoil of the elements wakes the senses, although it cannot entirely break the repose they have lapsed into.

Oh, what a world of witchery was in that mouth, slightly parted, and exhibiting within the pearly teeth that glistened even in the faint light that came from that bay window. How sweetly the long silken eyelashes lay upon the cheek. Now she moves, and one shoulder is entirely visible—whiter, fairer than the spotless clothing of the bed on which she lies, is the smooth skin of that fair creature, just budding into womanhood, and in that transition state which presents to us all the charms of the girl—almost of the child, with the more matured beauty and gentleness of advancing years.

Was that lightning? Yes—an awful, vivid, terrifying flash—then a roaring peal of thunder, as if a thousand mountains were rolling one over the other in the blue vault of Heaven! Who sleeps now in that ancient city? Not one living soul. The dread trumpet of eternity could not more effectually have awakened anyone.

The hail continues. The wind continues. The uproar of the elements seems at its height. Now she awakens—that beautiful girl on the antique bed; she opens those eyes of celestial blue, and a faint cry of alarm bursts from her lips. At least it is a cry which, amid the noise and turmoil without, sounds but faint and weak. She sits upon the bed and presses her hands upon her eyes. Heavens! what a wild torrent of wind, and rain, and hail! The thunder likewise seems intent upon awakening sufficient echoes to last until the next flash of forked lightning should again produce the wild concussion of the air. She murmurs a prayer—a prayer for those she loves best; the names of those dear to her gentle heart come from her lips; she weeps and prays; she thinks then of what devastation the storm must surely produce, and to the great God of Heaven she prays for all living things. Another flash—a wild, blue, bewildering flash of lightning streams across that bay window, for an instant bringing out every colour in it with terrible distinctness. A shriek bursts from the lips of the young girl, and then, with eyes fixed upon that window, which, in another moment, is all darkness, and with such an expression of terror upon her face as it had never before known, she trembled, and the perspiration of intense fear stood upon her brow.

"What—what was it?" she gasped; "real, or a delusion? Oh, God, what was it? A figure tall and gaunt, endeavouring from the outside to unclasp the window. I saw it. That flash of lightning revealed it to me.

It stood the whole length of the window."

There was a lull of the wind. The hail was not falling so thickly—moreover, it now fell, what there was of it, straight, and yet a strange clattering sound came upon the glass of that long window. It could not be a delusion—she is awake, and she hears it. What can produce it? Another flash of lightning—another shriek—there could be now no delusion.

A tall figure is standing on the ledge immediately outside the long window. It is its finger-nails upon the glass that produces the sound so like the hail, now that the hail has ceased. Intense fear paralysed the limbs of that beautiful girl. That one shriek is all she can utter—with hands clasped, a face of marble, a heart beating so wildly in her bosom, that each moment it seems as if it would break its confines, eyes distended and fixed upon the window, she waits, froze with horror. The pattering and clattering of the nails continue. No word is spoken, and now she fancies she can trace the darker form of that figure against the window, and she can see the long arms moving to and fro, feeling for some mode of entrance. What strange light is that which now gradually creeps up into the air? red and terrible—brighter and brighter it grows. The lightning has set fire to a mill, and the reflection of the rapidly consuming building falls upon that long window. There can be no mistake. The figure is there, still feeling for an entrance, and clattering against the glass with its long nails, that appear as if the growth of many years had been untouched. She tries to scream again but a choking sensation comes over her, and she cannot. It is too dreadful—she tries to move—each limb seems weighed down by tons of lead—she can but in a hoarse faint whisper cry,—

"Help—help—help—help!"

And that one word she repeats like a person in a dream. The red glare of the fire continues. It throws up the tall gaunt figure in hideous relief against the long window. It shows, too, upon the one portrait that is in the chamber, and that portrait appears to fix its eyes upon the attempting intruder, while the flickering light from the fire makes it look fearfully lifelike. A small pane of glass is broken, and the form from without introduces a long gaunt hand, which seems utterly destitute of flesh. The fastening is removed, and one-half of the window, which opens like folding doors, is swung wide open upon its hinges.

And yet now she could not scream—she could not move. "Help!—help!—help!" was all she could say. But, oh, that look of terror that sat upon her face, it was dreadful—a look to haunt the memory for a lifetime—a look to obtrude itself upon the happiest moments, and turn them to bitterness.

The figure turns half round, and the light falls upon the face. It is perfectly white—perfectly bloodless. The eyes look like polished tin; the lips are drawn back, and the principal feature next to those dreadful eyes is the teeth—the fearful looking teeth—projecting like those of some wild animal, hideously, glaringly white, and fang-like. It approaches the bed with a strange, gliding movement. It clashes together the long nails that literally appear to hang from the finger ends. No sound comes from its lips. Is she going mad—that young and beautiful girl exposed to so much terror? She has drawn up all her limbs; she cannot even now say help. The power of articulation is gone, but the power of movement has returned to her; she can draw herself slowly along to the other side of the bed from that towards which the hideous appearance is coming.

But her eyes are fascinated. The glance of a serpent could not have produced a greater effect upon her than did the fixed gaze of those awful, metallic-looking eyes that were bent on her face. Crouching down so that the gigantic height was lost, and the horrible, protruding, white face was the most prominent object, came on the figure. What was it?—what did it want there?—what made it look so hideous—so unlike an inhabitant of the earth, and yet to be on it?

Now she has got to the verge of the bed, and the figure pauses. It seemed as if when it paused she lost the power to proceed. The clothing of the bed was now clutched in her hands with unconscious power. She drew her breath short and thick. Her bosom heaves, and her limbs tremble, yet she cannot withdraw her eyes from that marble-looking face. He holds her with his glittering eye.

The storm has ceased—all is still. The winds are hushed; the church clock proclaims the hour of one: a hissing sound comes from the throat of the hideous being, and he raises his long, gaunt arms—the lips move. He advances. The girl places one small foot from the bed on to the floor. She is unconsciously dragging the clothing with her. The door of the room is in that direction—can she reach it? Has she power to walk?—can she withdraw her eyes from the face of the intruder, and so break the hideous charm? God of Heaven! is it real, or some dream so like reality as to nearly overturn the judgment forever?

The figure has paused again, and half on the bed and half out of it that young girl lies trembling. Her long hair streams across the entire width of the bed. As she has slowly moved along she has left it streaming across the pillows. The pause lasted about a minute—oh, what an age of agony. That minute was, indeed, enough for madness to do its full work in.

With a sudden rush that could not be foreseen—with a strange howling cry that was enough to awaken terror in every breast, the figure seized the long tresses of her hair, and twining them round his bony hands he held her to the bed. Then she screamed—Heaven granted her then power to scream. Shriek followed shriek in rapid succession. The bed-clothes fell in a heap by the side of the bed—she was dragged by her long silken hair completely on to it again. Her beautifully rounded limbs quivered with the agony of her soul. The glassy, horrible eyes of the figure ran over that angelic form with a hideous satisfaction—horrible profanation. He drags her head to the bed's edge. He forces it back by the long hair still entwined in his grasp. With a plunge he seizes her neck in his fang-like teeth—a gush of blood, and a hideous sucking noise follows. *The girl has swooned, and the vampyre is at his hideous repast!*

CHAPTER II.

THE ALARM. —THE PISTOL SHOT. —THE PURSUIT AND ITS CONSEQUENCES.

Lights flashed about the building, and various room doors opened; voices called one to the other. There was an universal stir and commotion among the inhabitants.

"Did you hear a scream, Harry?" asked a young man, half-dressed, as he walked into the chamber of another about his own age.

"I did—where was it?"

"God knows. I dressed myself directly."

"All is still now."

"Yes; but unless I was dreaming there was a scream."

"We could not both dream there was. Where did you think it came from?"

"It burst so suddenly upon my ears that I cannot say."

There was a tap now at the door of the room where these young men were, and a female voice said,—

"For God's sake, get up!"

"We are up," said both the young men, appearing.

"Did you hear anything?"

"Yes, a scream."

"Oh, search the house—search the house; where did it come from— can you tell?"

"Indeed we cannot, mother."

Another person now joined the party. He was a man of middle age, and, as he came up to them, he said,

"Good God! what is the matter?"

Scarcely had the words passed his lips, than such a rapid succession of shrieks came upon their ears, that they felt absolutely stunned by them. The elderly lady, whom one of the young men had called mother, fainted, and would have fallen to the floor of the corridor in which they all stood, had she not been promptly supported by the last comer, who himself staggered, as those piercing cries came upon the night air. He, however, was the first to recover, for the young men seemed paralysed.

"Henry," he cried, "for God's sake support your mother. Can you doubt that these cries come from Flora's room?"

The young man mechanically supported his mother, and then the man who had just spoken darted back to his own bed-room, from whence he returned in a moment with a pair of pistols, and shouting,—

"Follow me, who can!" he bounded across the corridor in the direction of the antique apartment, from whence the cries proceeded, but which were now hushed.

That house was built for strength, and the doors were all of oak, and of considerable thickness.

Unhappily, they had fastenings within, so that when the man reached the chamber of her who so much required help, he was helpless, for the door was fast.

"Flora! Flora!" he cried; "Flora, speak!"

All was still.

"Good God!" he added; "we must force the door."

"I hear a strange noise within," said the young man, who trembled violently.

"And so do I. What does it sound like?"

"I scarcely know; but it nearest resembles some animal eating, or sucking some liquid."

"What on earth can it be? Have you no weapon that will force the door? I shall go mad if I am kept here."

"I have," said the young man. "Wait here a moment."

He ran down the staircase, and presently returned with a small, but powerful, iron crow-bar. "This will do," he said.

"It will, it will.—Give it to me."

"Has she not spoken?"

"Not a word. My mind misgives me that something very dreadful must have happened to her."

"And that odd noise!"

"Still goes on. Somehow, it curdles the very blood in my veins to hear it."

The man took the crow-bar, and with some difficulty succeeded in introducing it between the door and the side of the wall—still it required great strength to move it, but it did move, with a harsh, crackling sound.

"Push it!" cried he who was using the bar, "push the door at the same time."

The younger man did so. For a few moments the massive door resisted. Then, suddenly, something gave way with a loud snap—it was a part of the lock,—and the door at once swung wide open.

How true it is that we measure time by the events which happen within a given space of it, rather than by its actual duration.

To those who were engaged in forcing open the door of the antique chamber, where slept the young girl whom they named Flora, each moment was swelled into an hour of agony; but, in reality, from the first moment of the alarm to that when the loud cracking noise heralded the destruction of the fastenings of the door, there had elapsed but very few minutes indeed.

"It opens—it opens," cried the young man.

"Another moment," said the stranger, as he still plied the crowbar— "another moment, and we shall have free ingress to the chamber. Be patient."

This stranger's name was Marchdale; and even as he spoke, he succeeded in throwing the massive door wide open, and clearing the passage to the chamber.

To rush in with a light in his hand was the work of a moment to the young man named Henry; but the very rapid progress he made into the apartment prevented him from observing accurately what it contained, for the wind that came in from the open window caught the flame of the candle, and although it did not actually extinguish it, it blew it so much on one side, that it was comparatively useless as a light.

"Flora—Flora!" he cried.

Then with a sudden bound something dashed from off the bed. The concussion against him was so sudden and so utterly unexpected, as well as so tremendously violent, that he was thrown down, and, in his fall, the light was fairly extinguished.

All was darkness, save a dull, reddish kind of light that now and then, from the nearly consumed mill in the immediate vicinity, came into the room. But by that light, dim, uncertain, and flickering as it was, someone was seen to make for the window.

Henry, although nearly stunned by his fall, saw a figure, gigantic in height, which nearly reached from the floor to the ceiling. The other young man, George, saw it, and Mr. Marchdale likewise saw it, as did the lady who had spoken to the two young men in the corridor when first the screams of the young girl awakened alarm in the breasts of all the inhabitants of that house.

The figure was about to pass out at the window which led to a kind of balcony, from whence there was an easy descent to a garden.

Before it passed out they each and all caught a glance of the side-face, and they saw that the lower part of it and the lips were dabbled in blood. They saw, too, one of those fearful-looking, shining, metallic eyes which presented so terrible an appearance of unearthly ferocity.

No wonder that for a moment a panic seized them all, which paralysed any exertions they might otherwise have made to detain that hideous form.

But Mr. Marchdale was a man of mature years; he had seen much of life, both in this and in foreign lands; and he, although astonished to the extent of being frightened, was much more likely to recover sooner than his younger companions, which, indeed, he did, and acted promptly enough.

"Don't rise, Henry," he cried. "Lie still."

Almost at the moment he uttered these words, he fired at the figure, which then occupied the window, as if it were a gigantic figure set in a frame.

The report was tremendous in that chamber, for the pistol was no toy weapon, but one made for actual service, and of sufficient length And bore of barrel to carry destruction along with the bullets that came from it.

"If that has missed its aim," said Mr. Marchdale, "I'll never pull a trigger again."

As he spoke he dashed forward, and made a clutch at the figure he felt convinced he had shot.

The tall form turned upon him, and when he got a full view of the face, which he did at that moment, from the opportune circumstance of the lady returning at the instant with a light she had been to her own chamber to procure, even he, Marchdale, with all his courage, and that was great, and all his nervous energy, recoiled a step or two, and uttered the exclamation of, "Great God!"

That face was one never to be forgotten. It was hideously flushed with colour—the colour of fresh blood; the eyes had a savage and remarkable lustre; whereas, before, they had looked like polished tin— they now wore a ten times brighter aspect, and flashes of light seemed to dart from them. The mouth was open, as if, from the natural formation of the countenance, the lips receded much from the large canine-looking teeth.

A strange howling noise came from the throat of this monstrous figure, and it seemed upon the point of rushing upon Mr. Marchdale. Suddenly, then, as if some impulse had seized upon it, it uttered a wild and terrible shrieking kind of laugh; and then turning, dashed through the window, and in one instant disappeared from before the eyes of those who felt nearly annihilated by its fearful presence.

"God help us!" ejaculated Henry.

Mr. Marchdale drew a long breath, and then, giving a stamp on the floor, as if to recover himself from the state of agitation into which even he was thrown, he cried,—

"Be it what or who it may, I'll follow it."

"No—no—do not," cried the lady.

"I must, I will. Let who will come with me—I follow that dreadful form."

As he spoke, he took the road it took, and dashed through the window into the balcony.

"And we, too, George," exclaimed Henry; "we will follow Mr. Marchdale. This dreadful affair concerns us more nearly than it does him."

The lady who was the mother of these young men, and of the beautiful girl who had been so awfully visited, screamed aloud, and implored of them to stay. But the voice of Mr. Marchdale was heard exclaiming aloud,—

"I see it—I see it; it makes for the wall."

They hesitated no longer, but at once rushed into the balcony, and from thence dropped into the garden.

The mother approached the bed-side of the insensible, perhaps the murdered girl; she saw her, to all appearance, weltering in blood, and, overcome by her emotions, she fainted on the floor of the room.

When the two young men reached the garden, they found it much lighter than might have been fairly expected; for not only was the morning rapidly approaching, but the mill was still burning, and those mingled lights made almost every object plainly visible, except when deep shadows were thrown from some gigantic trees that had stood for centuries in that sweetly wooded spot. They heard the voice of Mr. Marchdale, as he cried,—

"There—there—towards the wall. There—there—God! how it bounds along."

The young men hastily dashed through a thicket in the direction from whence his voice sounded, and then they found him looking wild and terrified, and with something in his hand which looked like a portion of clothing.

"Which way, which way?" they both cried in a breath.

He leant heavily on the arm of George, as he pointed along a vista of trees, and said in a low voice,—

"God help us all. It is not human. Look there—look there—do you not see it?"

They looked in the direction he indicated. At the end of this vista was the wall of the garden. At that point it was full twelve feet in height, and as they looked, they saw the hideous, monstrous form they had traced from the chamber of their sister, making frantic efforts to clear the obstacle. Then they saw it bound from the ground to the top of the wall, which it very nearly reached, and then each time it fell back again into the garden with such a dull, heavy sound, that the earth seemed to shake again with the concussion. They trembled—well indeed they might, and for some minutes they watched the figure making its fruitless efforts to leave the place.

"What—what is it?" whispered Henry, in hoarse accents. "God, what can it possibly be?"

"I know not," replied Mr. Marchdale. "I did seize it. It was cold and clammy like a corpse. It cannot be human."

"Not human?"

"Look at it now. It will surely escape now."

"No, no—we will not be terrified thus—there is Heaven above us. Come on, and, for dear Flora's sake, let us make an effort yet to seize this bold intruder."

"Take this pistol," said Marchdale. "It is the fellow of the one I fired. Try its efficacy."

"He will be gone," exclaimed Henry, as at this moment, after many repeated attempts and fearful falls, the figure reached the top of the wall, and then hung by its long arms a moment or two, previous to dragging itself completely up.

The idea of the appearance, be it what it might, entirely escaping, seemed to nerve again Mr. Marchdale, and he, as well as the two young men, ran forward towards the wall. They got so close to the figure before it sprang down on the outer side of the wall, that to miss killing it with the bullet from the pistol was a matter of utter impossibility, unless willfully.

Henry had the weapon, and he pointed it full at the tall form with a steady aim. He pulled the trigger—the explosion followed, and that the bullet did its office there could be no manner of doubt, for the figure gave a howling shriek, and fell headlong from the wall on the outside.

"I have shot him," cried Henry, "I have shot him."

CHAPTER III.

THE DISAPPEARANCE OF THE BODY.—FLORA'S RECOVERY AND MADNESS.—THE OFFER OF ASSISTANCE FROM SIR FRANCIS VARNEY.

"He is human!" cried Henry; "I have surely killed him."

"It would seem so," said Mr. Marchdale. "Let us now hurry round to the outside of the wall, and see where he lies."

This was at once agreed to, and the whole three of them made what expedition they could towards a gate which led into a paddock, across which they hurried, and soon found themselves clear of the garden wall, so that they could make way towards where they fully expected to find the body of him who had worn so unearthly an aspect, but who it would be an excessive relief to find was human.

So hurried was the progress they made, that it was scarcely possible to exchange many words as they went; a kind of breathless anxiety was upon them, and in the speed they disregarded every obstacle, which would, at any other time, have probably prevented them from taking the direct road they sought.

It was difficult on the outside of the wall to say exactly which was the precise spot which it might be supposed the body had fallen on; but, by following the wall in its entire length, surely they would come upon it.

They did so; but, to their surprise, they got from its commencement to its further extremity without finding any dead body, or even any symptoms of one having lain there.

At some parts close to the wall there grew a kind of heath, and, consequently, the traces of blood would be lost among it, if it so happened that at the precise spot at which the strange being had seemed to topple over, such vegetation had existed. This was to be ascertained; but now, after traversing the whole length of the wall twice, they came to a halt, and looked wonderingly in each other's faces.

"There is nothing here," said Harry.

"Nothing," added his brother.

"It could not have been a delusion," at length said Mr. Marchdale, with a shudder.

"A delusion?" exclaimed the brother! "That is not possible; we all saw it."

"Then what terrible explanation can we give?"

"By heavens! I know not," exclaimed Henry. "This adventure surpasses all belief, and but for the great interest we have in it, I should regard it with a world of curiosity."

"It is too dreadful," said George; "for God's sake, Henry, let us return to ascertain if poor Flora is killed."

"My senses," said Henry, "were all so much absorbed in gazing at that horrible form, that I never once looked towards her further than to see that she was, to appearance, dead. God help her! poor—poor, beautiful Flora. This is, indeed, a sad, sad fate for you to come to. Flora—Flora—"

"Do not weep, Henry," said George. "Rather let us now hasten home, where we may find that tears are premature. She may yet be living and restored to us."

"And," said Mr. Marchdale, "she may be able to give us some account of this dreadful visitation."

"True—true," exclaimed Henry; "we will hasten home."

They now turned their steps homeward, and as they went they much blamed themselves for all leaving home together, and with terror pictured what might occur in their absence to those who were now totally unprotected.

"It was a rash impulse of us all to come in pursuit of this dreadful figure," remarked Mr. Marchdale; "but do not torment yourself, Henry. There may be no reason for your fears."

At the pace they went, they very soon reached the ancient house, and when they came in sight of it, they saw lights flashing from the windows, and the shadows of faces moving to and fro, indicating that the whole household was up, and in a state of alarm.

Henry, after some trouble, got the hall door opened by a terrified servant, who was trembling so much that she could scarcely hold the light she had with her.

"Speak at once, Martha," said Henry. "Is Flora living?"

"Yes; but—"

"Enough—enough! Thank God she lives; where is she now?"

"In her own room, Master Henry. Oh, dear—oh, dear, what will become of us all?"

Henry rushed up the staircase, followed by George and Mr. Marchdale, nor paused he once until he reached the room of his sister.

"Mother," he said, before he crossed the threshold, "are you here?"

"I am, my dear—I am. Come in, pray come in, and speak to poor Flora."

"Come in, Mr. Marchdale," said Henry—"come in; we make no stranger of you."

They all then entered the room.

Several lights had been now brought into that antique chamber, and, in addition to the mother of the beautiful girl who had been so fearfully visited, there were two female domestics, who appeared to be in the greatest possible fright, for they could render no assistance whatever to anybody.

The tears were streaming down the mother's face, and the moment she saw Mr. Marchdale, she clung to his arm, evidently unconscious of what she was about, and exclaimed,—

"Oh, what is this that has happened—what is this? Tell me, Marchdale! Robert Marchdale, you whom I have known even from my childhood, you will not deceive me. Tell me the meaning of all this?"

"I cannot," he said, in a tone of much emotion. "As God is my judge, I am as much puzzled and amazed at the scene that has taken place here to-night as you can be."

The mother wrung her hands and wept.

"It was the storm that first awakened me," added Marchdale; "and then I heard a scream."

The brothers tremblingly approached the bed. Flora was placed in a sitting, half-reclining posture, propped up by pillows. She was quite insensible, and her face was fearfully pale; while that she breathed at all could be but very faintly seen. On some of her clothing, about the neck, were spots of blood, and she looked more like one who had suffered some long and grievous illness, than a young girl in the prime of life and in the most robust health, as she had been on the day previous to the strange scene we have recorded.

"Does she sleep?" said Henry, as a tear fell from his eyes upon her pallid cheek.

"No," replied Mr. Marchdale. "This is a swoon, from which we must recover her."

Active measures were now adopted to restore the languid circulation, and, after persevering in them for some time, they had the satisfaction of seeing her open her eyes.

Her first act upon consciousness returning, however, was to utter a loud shriek, and it was not until Henry implored her to look around her, and see that she was surrounded by none but friendly faces, that she would venture again to open her eyes, and look timidly from one to the other. Then she shuddered, and burst into tears as she said,—

"Oh, Heaven, have mercy upon me—Heaven, have mercy upon me, and save me from that dreadful form."

"There is no one here, Flora," said Mr. Marchdale, "but those who love you , and who, in defense of you, if needs were would lay down their lives."

"Oh, God! Oh, God!"

"You have been terrified. But tell us distinctly what has happened? You are quite safe now."

She trembled so violently that Mr. Marchdale recommended that some stimulant should be given to her, and she was persuaded, although not without considerable difficulty, to swallow a small portion of some wine from a cup. There could be no doubt but that the stimulating effect of the wine was beneficial, for a slight accession of colour visited her cheeks, and she spoke in a firmer tone as she said,—

"Do not leave me. Oh, do not leave me, any of you. I shall die if left alone now. Oh, save me—save me. That horrible form! That fearful face!"

"Tell us how it happened, dear Flora?" said Henry.

"Or would you rather endeavour to get some sleep first?" suggested Mr. Marchdale.

"No—no—no," she said, "I do not think I shall ever sleep again."

"Say not so; you will be more composed in a few hours, and then you can tell us what has occurred."

"I will tell you now. I will tell you now." She placed her hands over her face for a moment, as if to collect her scattered thoughts, and then she added,—

"I was awakened by the storm, and I saw that terrible apparition at the window. I think I screamed, but I could not fly. Oh, God! I could not fly. It came—it seized me by the hair. I know no more. I know no more."

She passed her hand across her neck several times, and Mr. Marchdale said, in an anxious voice,

"You seem, Flora, to have hurt your neck—there is a wound."

"A wound!" said the mother, and she brought a light close to the bed, where all saw on the side of Flora's neck a small punctured wound; or, rather two, for there was one a little distance from the other. It was from these wounds the blood had come which was observable upon her night clothing.

"How came these wounds?" said Henry.

"I do not know," she replied. "I feel very faint and weak, as if I had almost bled to death."

"You cannot have done so, dear Flora, for there are not above half-a-dozen spots of blood to be seen at all."

Mr. Marchdale leaned against the carved head of the bed for support, and he uttered a deep groan. All eyes were turned upon him, and Henry said, in a voice of the most anxious inquiry,—

"You have something to say, Mr. Marchdale, which will throw some light upon this affair."

"No, no, no, nothing!" cried Mr. Marchdale, rousing himself at once from the appearance of depression that had come over him. "I have nothing to say, but that I think Flora had better get some sleep if she can."

"No sleep—no sleep for me," again screamed Flora. "Dare I be alone to sleep?"

"But you shall not be alone, dear Flora," said Henry. "I will sit by your bedside and watch you."

She took his hand in both hers, and while the tears chased each other down her cheeks, she said,—

"Promise me, Henry, by all your hopes of Heaven, you will not leave me."

"I promise!"

She gently laid herself down, with a deep sigh, and closed her eyes.

"She is weak, and will sleep long," said Mr. Marchdale.

"You sigh," said Henry. "Some fearful thoughts, I feel certain, oppress your heart."

"Hush-hush!" said Mr. Marchdale, as he pointed to Flora. "Hush! not here—not here."

"I understand," said Henry. "Let her sleep."

There was a silence of some few minutes duration. Flora had dropped into a deep slumber. That silence was first broken by George, who said,—

"Mr. Marchdale, look at that portrait." He pointed to the portrait in the frame to which we have alluded, and the moment Marchdale looked at it he sunk into a chair as he exclaimed,—

"Gracious Heaven, how like!"

"It is—it is," said Henry. "Those eyes—"

"And see the contour of the countenance, and the strange shape of the mouth."

"Exact—exact."

"That picture shall be moved from here. The sight of it is at once sufficient to awaken all her former terrors in poor Flora's brain if she should chance to awaken and cast her eyes suddenly upon it."

"And is it so like him who came here?" said the mother.

"It is the very man himself," said Mr. Marchdale. "I have not been in this house long enough to ask any of you whose portrait that may be?"

"It is," said Henry, "the portrait of Sir Runnagate Bannerworth, an ancestor of ours, who first, by his vices, gave the great blow to the family prosperity."

"Indeed. How long ago?"

"About ninety years."

"Ninety years. 'Tis a long while—ninety years."

"You muse upon it."

"No, no. I do wish, and yet I dread—"

"What?"

"To say something to you all. But not here—not here. We will hold a consultation on this matter tomorrow. Not now—not now."

"The daylight is coming quickly on," said Henry; "I shall keep my sacred promise of not moving from this room until Flora awakens; but there can be no occasion for the detention of any of you. One is sufficient here. Go all of you, and endeavour to procure what rest you can."

"I will fetch you my powder-flask and bullets," said Mr. Marchdale; "and you can, if you please, reload the pistols. In about two hours more it will be broad daylight."

This arrangement was adopted. Henry did reload the pistols, and placed them on a table by the side of the bed, ready for immediate action, and then, as Flora was sleeping soundly, all left the room but himself.

Mrs. Bannerworth was the last to do so. She would have remained, but for the earnest solicitation of Henry, that she would endeavour to get some sleep to make up for her broken night's repose, and she was indeed so broken down by her alarm on Flora's account, that she had not power to resist, but with tears flowing from her eyes, she sought her own chamber.

And now the calmness of the night resumed its sway in that evil-fated mansion; and although no one really slept but Flora, all were still.

Busy thought kept everyone else wakeful. It was a mockery to lie down at all, and Henry, full of strange and painful feelings as he was, preferred his present position to the anxiety and apprehension on Flora's account which he knew he should feel if she were not within the sphere of his own observation, and she slept as soundly as some gentle infant tired of its playmates and its sports.

CHAPTER IV.

THE MORNING. —THE CONSULTATION. —THE FEARFUL SUGGESTION.

What wonderfully different impressions and feelings, with regard to the same circumstances, come across the mind in the broad, clear, and beautiful light of day to what haunt the imagination, and often render the judgment almost incapable of action, when the heavy shadow of night is upon all things.

There must be a downright physical reason for this effect—it is so remarkable and so universal. It seems that the sun's rays so completely alter and modify the constitution of the atmosphere, that it produces, as we inhale it, a wonderfully different effect upon the nerves of the human subject.

We can account for this phenomenon in no other way. Perhaps never in his life had he, Henry Bannerworth, felt so strongly this transition of feeling as he now felt it, when the beautiful daylight gradually dawned upon him, as he kept his lonely watch by the bedside of his slumbering sister.

That watch had been a perfectly undisturbed one. Not the least sight or sound of any intrusion had reached his senses. All had been as still as the very grave.

And yet while the night lasted, and he was more indebted to the rays of the candle, which he had placed upon a shelf, for the power to distinguish objects than to the light of the morning, a thousand uneasy and strange sensations had found a home in his agitated bosom.

He looked so many times at the portrait which was in the panel that at length he felt an undefined sensation of terror creep over him whenever he took his eyes off it.

He tried to keep himself from looking at it, but he found it vain, so he adopted what, perhaps, was certainly the wisest, best plan, namely, to look at it continually.

He shifted his chair so that he could gaze upon it without any effort, and he placed the candle so that a faint light was thrown upon it, and there he sat, a prey to many conflicting and uncomfortable feelings, until the daylight began to make the candle flame look dull and sickly.

Solution for the events of the night he could find none. He racked his imagination in vain to find some means, however vague, of endeavouring to account for what occurred, and still he was at fault.

All was to him wrapped in the gloom of the most profound mystery.

And how strangely, too, the eyes of that portrait appeared to look upon him—as if instinct with life, and as if the head to which they belonged was busy in endeavouring to find out the secret communings of his soul. It was wonderfully well executed that portrait; so life-like, that the very features seemed to move as you gazed upon them.

"It shall be removed," said Henry. "I would remove it now, but that it seems absolutely painted on the panel, and I should awake Flora in any attempt to do so."

He arose and ascertained that such was the case, and that it would require a workman, with proper tools adapted to the job, to remove the portrait.

"True," he said, "I might now destroy it, but it is a pity to obscure a work of such rare art as this is; I should blame myself if I were. It shall be removed to some other room of the house, however."

Then, all of a sudden, it struck Henry how foolish it would be to remove the portrait from the wall of a room which, in all likelihood, after that night, would be uninhabited; for it was not probable that Flora would choose again to inhabit a chamber in which she had gone through so much terror.

"It can be left where it is," he said, "and we can fasten up, if we lease, even the very door of this room, so that no one need trouble themselves any further about it."

The morning was now coming fast, and just as Henry thought he would partially draw a blind across the window, in order to shield from the direct rays of the sun the eyes of Flora, she awoke.

"Help—help!" she cried, and Henry was by her side in a moment.

"You are safe, Flora—you are safe," he said.

"Where is it now?" she said.

"What—what, dear Flora?"

"The dreadful apparition. Oh, what have I done to be made thus perpetually miserable?"

"Think no more of it, Flora."

"I must think. My brain is on fire! A million of strange eyes seem gazing on me."

"Great Heaven! She raves," said Henry.

"Hark—hark—hark! He comes on the wings of the storm. Oh, it is most horrible—horrible!"

Henry rang the bell, but not sufficiently loudly to create any alarm. The sound reached the waking ear of the mother, who in a few moments was in the room.

"She has awakened," said Henry, "and has spoken, but she seems to me to wander in her discourse. For God's sake, soothe her, and try to bring her mind round to its usual state."

"I will, Henry—I will."

"And I think, mother, if you were to get her out of this room, and into some other chamber as far removed from this one as possible, it would tend to withdraw her mind from what has occurred."

"Yes; it shall be done. Oh, Henry, what was it—what do you think it was?"

"I am lost in a sea of wild conjecture. I can form no conclusion; where is Mr. Marchdale?"

"I believe in his chamber."

"Then I will go and consult with him."

Henry proceeded at once to the chamber, which was, as he knew, occupied by Mr. Marchdale; and as he crossed the corridor, he could not but pause a moment to glance from a window at the face of nature. As is often the case, the terrific storm of the preceding evening had cleared the air, and rendered it deliciously invigorating and lifelike. The weather had been dull, and there had been for some days a certain heaviness in the atmosphere, which was now entirely removed.

The morning sun was shining with uncommon brilliancy, birds were singing in every tree and on every bush; so pleasant, so spirit-stirring, health-giving a morning, seldom had he seen. And the effect upon his spirits was great, although not altogether what it might have been, had all gone on as it usually was in the habit of doing at that house. The ordinary little casualties of evil fortune had certainly from time to time, in the shape of illness, and one thing or another, attacked the family of the Bannerworths in common with every other family, but here suddenly had arisen a something at once terrible and inexplicable.

He found Mr. Marchdale up and dressed, and apparently in deep and anxious thought. The moment he saw Henry, he said,—

"Flora is awake, I presume."

"Yes, but her mind appears to be much disturbed."

"From bodily weakness, I dare say."

"But why should she be bodily weak? she was strong and well, aye, as well as she could ever be in all her life. The glow of youth and health was on her cheeks. Is it possible that, in the course of one night, she should become bodily weak to such an extent?"

"Henry," said Mr. Marchdale, sadly, "Sit down. I am not, as you know, a superstitious man."

"You certainly are not."

"And yet, I never in all my life was so absolutely staggered as I have been by the occurrences of to-night."

"Say on."

"There is a frightful, a hideous solution of them; one which every consideration will tend to add strength to, one which I tremble to name now, although, yesterday, at this hour, I should have laughed it to scorn."

"Indeed!"

"Yes, it is so. Tell no one that which I am about to say to you. Let the dreadful suggestion remain with ourselves alone, Henry Bannerworth."

"I—I am lost in wonder."

"You promise me?"

"What—what?"

"That you will not repeat my opinion to anyone."

"I do."

"On your honour."

"On my honour, I promise."

Mr. Marchdale rose, and proceeding to the door, he looked out to see that there were no listeners near. Having ascertained then that they were quite alone, he returned, and drawing a chair close to that on which Henry sat, he said,—

"Henry, have you never heard of a strange and dreadful superstition which, in some countries, is extremely rife, by which it is supposed that there are beings who never die."

"Never die!"

"Never. In a word, Henry, have you never heard of—of—I dread to pronounce the word."

"Speak it. God of Heaven! let me hear it."

"A *vampyre!*"

Henry sprung to his feet. His whole frame quivered with emotion; the drops of perspiration stood upon his brow, as, in, a strange, hoarse voice, he repeated the words,—

"A vampyre!"

"Even so; one who has to renew a dreadful existence by human blood—one who lives on forever, and must keep up such a fearful existence upon human gore—one who eats not and drinks not as other men—a vampyre."

Henry dropped into his seat, and uttered a deep groan of the most exquisite anguish.

"I could echo that groan," said Marchdale , "but that I am so thoroughly bewildered I know not what to think."

"Good God—good God!"

"Do not too readily yield belief in so dreadful a supposition, I pray you."

"Yield belief!" exclaimed Henry, as he rose, and lifted up one of his hands above his head. "No; by Heaven, and the great God of all, who there rules, I will not easily believe aught so awful and so monstrous."

"I applaud your sentiment, Henry; not willingly would I deliver up myself to so frightful a belief—it is too horrible. I merely have told you of that which you saw was on my mind. You have surely before heard of such things."

"I have—I have."

"I much marvel, then, that the supposition did not occur to you, Henry."

"It did not—it did not, Marchdale. It—it was too dreadful, I suppose, to find a home in my heart. Oh! Flora, Flora, if this horrible idea should once occur to you, reason cannot, I am quite sure, uphold you against it."

"Let no one presume to insinuate it to her, Henry. I would not have it mentioned to her for worlds."

"Nor I—nor I. Good God! I shudder at the very thought—the mere possibility; but there is no possibility, there can be none. I will not believe it."

"Nor I."

"No; by Heaven's justice, goodness, grace, and mercy, I will not believe it."

"'Tis well sworn, Henry; and now, discarding the supposition that Flora has been visited by a vampyre, let us seriously set about endeavouring, if we can, to account for what has happened in this house."

"I—I cannot now."

"Nay, let us examine the matter; if we can find any natural explanation, let us cling to it, Henry, as the sheet-anchor of our very souls."

"Do as you think. You are fertile in expedients. Do as you think, Marchdale; and, for Heaven's sake, and for the sake of our own peace, find out some other way of accounting for what has happened, than the hideous one you have suggested."

"And yet my pistol bullets hurt him not; he has left the tokens of his presence on the neck of Flora."

"Peace, oh! peace. Do not, I pray you, accumulate reasons why I should receive such a dismal, awful superstition. Oh, do not, Marchdale, as you love me!"

"You know that my attachment to you," said Marchdale, "is sincere; and yet, Heaven help us!" His voice was broken by grief as he spoke, and he turned aside his head to hide the bursting tears that would, despite all his efforts, show themselves in his eyes.

"Marchdale," added Henry, after a pause of some moments' duration, "I will sit up to-night with my sister."

"Do—do!"

"Think you there is a chance it may come again?"

"I cannot—I dare not speculate upon the coming of so dreadful a visitor, Henry; but I will hold watch with you most willingly."

"You will, Marchdale?"

"My hand upon it. Come what dangers may, I will share them with you, Henry."

"A thousand thanks. Say nothing, then, to George of what we have been talking about. He is of a highly susceptible nature, and the very idea of such a thing would kill him."

"I will; be mute. Remove your sister to some other chamber, let me beg of you, Henry; the one she now inhabits will always be suggestive of horrible thoughts."

"I will; and that dreadful-looking portrait, with its perfect likeness to him who came last night."

"Perfect indeed. Do you intend to remove it?"

"I do not. I thought of doing so; but it is actually on the panel in the wall, and I would not willingly destroy it, and it may as well remain where it is in that chamber, which I can readily now believe will become henceforward a deserted one in this house."

"It may well become such."

"Who comes here? I hear a step."

There was a tip at the door at this moment, and George made his appearance in answer to the summons to come in. He looked pale and ill; his face betrayed how much he had mentally suffered during that night, and almost directly he got into the bed-chamber he said,—

"I shall, I am sure, be censured by you both for what I am going to say; but I cannot help saying it, nevertheless, for to keep it to myself would destroy me."

"Good God, George! what is it?" said Mr. Marchdale.

"Speak it out!" said Henry.

"I have been thinking of what has occurred here, and the result of that thought has been one of the wildest suppositions that ever I thought I should have to entertain. Have you never heard of a vampyre?"

Henry sighed deeply, and Marchdale was silent.

"I say a vampyre," added George, with much excitement in his manner. "It is a fearful, a horrible supposition; but our poor, dear Flora has been visited by a vampyre, and I shall go completely mad!"

He sat down, and covering his face with his hands, he wept bitterly and abundantly.

"George," said Henry, when he saw that the frantic grief had in some measure abated—"be calm, George, and endeavour to listen to me."

"I hear, Henry."

"Well, then, do not suppose that you are the only one in this house to whom so dreadful a superstition has occurred."

"Not the only one?"

"No; it has occurred to Mr. Marchdale also."

"Gracious Heaven!"

"He mentioned it to me; but we have both agreed to repudiate it with horror."

"To—repudiate—it?"

"Yes, George."

"And yet—and yet—"

"Hush, hush! I know what you would say. You would tell us that our repudiation of it cannot affect the fact. Of that we are aware; but yet will we disbelieve that which a belief in would be enough to drive us mad."

"What do you intend to do?"

"To keep this supposition to ourselves, in the first place; to guard it most zealously from the ears of Flora."

"Do you think she has ever heard of vampyres?"

"I never heard her mention that in all her reading she had gathered even a hint of such a fearful superstition. If she has, we must be guided by circumstances, and do the best we can."

"Pray Heaven she may not!"

"Amen to that prayer, George," said Henry. "Mr. Marchdale and I intend to keep watch over Flora to-night."

"May not I join you?"

"Your health, dear George, will not permit you to engage in such matters. Do you seek your natural repose, and leave it to us to do the best we can in this most fearful and terrible emergency."

"As you please, brother, and as you please, Mr. Marchdale. I know I am a frail reed, and my belief is that this affair will kill me quite. The truth is, I am horrified—utterly and frightfully horrified. Like my poor, dear sister, I do not believe I shall ever sleep again."

"Do not fancy that, George," said Marchdale. "You very much add to the uneasiness which must be your poor mother's portion, by allowing this circumstance to so much affect you. You well know her affection for you all, and let me therefore, as a very old friend of hers, entreat you to wear as cheerful an aspect as you can in her presence."

"For once in my life," said George, sadly, "I will; to my dear mother, endeavour to play the hypocrite."

"Do so," said Henry. "The motive will sanction any such deceit as that, George, be assured."

The day wore on, and Poor Flora remained in a very precarious situation. It was not until mid-day that Henry made up his mind he would call in a medical gentleman to her, and then he rode to the neighbouring market-town, where he knew an extremely intelligent practitioner resided. This gentleman Henry resolved upon, under a promise of secrecy, makings confidant of; but, long before he reached him, he found he might well dispense with the promise of secrecy.

He had never thought, so engaged had he been with other matters, that the servants were cognizant of the whole affair, and that from them he had no expectation of being able to keep the whole story in all its details. Of course such an opportunity for tale-bearing and gossiping was not likely to be lost; and while Henry was thinking over how he had better act in the matter, the news that Flora Bannerworth had been visited in the night by a vampyre—for the servants named the visitation such at once—was spreading all over the county.

As he rode along, Henry met a gentleman on horseback who belonged to the county, and who, reining in his steed, said to him, "Good morning, Mr. Bannerworth."

"Good morning," responded Henry, and he would have ridden on, but the gentleman added,—

"Excuse me for interrupting you, sir; but what is the strange story that is in everybody's mouth about a vampyre?"

Henry nearly fell off his horse, he was so much astonished, and, wheeling the animal around, he said,—

"In everybody's mouth!"

"Yes; I have heard it from at least a dozen persons."

"You surprise me."

"It is untrue? Of course I am not so absurd as really to believe about the vampyre; but is there no foundation at all for it? We generally find that at the bottom of these common reports there is a something around which, as a nucleus, the whole has formed."

"My sister is unwell."

"Ah, and that's all. It really is too bad, now."

"We had a visitor last night."

"A thief, I suppose?"

"Yes, yes—I believe a thief. I do believe it was a thief, and she was terrified."

"Of course, and upon such a thing is grafted a story of a vampyre, and the marks of his teeth being in her neck, and all the circumstantial particulars."

"Yes, yes."

"Good morning, Mr. Bannerworth."

Henry bade the gentleman good morning, and much vexed at the publicity which the affair had already obtained, he set spurs to his horse, determined that he would speak to no one else upon so uncomfortable a theme. Several attempts were made to stop him, but he only waved his hand and trotted on, nor did he pause in his speed till he reached the door of Mr. Chillingworth, the medical man whom he intended to consult.

Henry knew that at such a time he would be at home, which was the case, and he was soon closeted with the man of drugs. Henry begged his patient hearing, which being accorded, he related to him at full length what had happened, not omitting, to the best of his remembrance, any one particular. When he had concluded his narration, the doctor shifted his position several times, and then said,—

"That's all?"

"Yes—and enough too."

"More than enough, I should say, my young friend. You astonish me."

"Can you form any supposition, sir, on the subject?"

"Not just now. What is your own idea?"

"I cannot be said to have one about it. It is too absurd to tell you that my brother George is impressed with a belief a vampyre has visited the house."

"I never in all my life heard a more circumstantial narrative in favour of so hideous a superstition."

"Well, but you cannot believe—"

"Believe what?"

"That the dead can come to life again, and by such a process keep up vitality."

"Do you take me for a fool?"

"Certainly not."

"Then why do you ask me such questions?"

"But the glaring facts of the case."

"I don't care if they were ten times more glaring, I won't believe it. I would rather believe you were all mad, the whole family of you—that at the full of the moon you all were a little cracked."

"And so would I."

"You go home now, and I will call and see your sister in the course of two hours. Something may turn up yet, to throw some new light upon this strange subject."

With this understanding Henry went home, and he took care to ride as fast as before, in order to avoid questions, so that he got back to his old ancestral home without going through the disagreeable ordeal of having to explain to anyone what had disturbed the peace of it.

When Henry reached his home, he found that the evening was rapidly coming on, and before he could permit himself to think upon any other subject, he inquired how his terrified sister had passed the hours during his absence.

He found that but little improvement had taken place in her, and that she had occasionally slept, but to awaken and speak incoherently, as if the shock she had received had had some serious affect upon her nerves. He repaired at once to her room, and, finding that she was awake, he leaned over her, and spoke tenderly to her.

"Flora," he said, "dear Flora, you are better now?"

"Harry, is that you?"

"Yes, dear."

"Oh, tell me what has happened?"

"Have you not a recollection, Flora?"

"Yes, yes, Henry; but what was it? They none of them will tell me what it was, Henry."

"Be calm, dear. No doubt some attempt to rob the house."

"Think you so?"

"Yes; the bay window was peculiarly adapted for such a purpose; but now that you are removed here to this room, you will be able to rest in peace."

"I shall die of terror, Henry. Even now those eyes are glaring on me so hideously. Oh, it is fearful—it is very fearful, Henry. Do you not pity me, and no one will promise to remain with me at night."

"Indeed, Flora, you are mistaken, for I intend to sit by your bedside armed, and so preserve you from all harm."

She clutched his hand eagerly, as she said,—

"You will, Henry. You will, and not think it too much trouble, dear Henry."

"It can be no trouble, Flora."

"Then I shall rest in peace, for I know that the dreadful vampyre cannot come to me when you are by—"

"The what, Flora!"

"The vampyre, Henry. It was a vampyre."

"Good God, who told you so?"

"No one. I have read of them in the book of *Travels in Norway*, which Mr. Marchdale lent us all."

"Alas, alas!" groaned Henry. "Discard, I pray you, such a thought from your mind."

"Can we discard thoughts. What power have we but from that mind, which is ourselves?"

"True, true."

"Hark, what noise is that? I thought I heard a noise. Henry, when you go, ring for someone first. Was there not a noise?"

"The accidental shutting of some door, dear."

"Was it that?"

"It was."

"Then I am relieved. Henry, I sometimes fancy I am in the tomb, and that someone is feasting on my flesh. They do say, too, that those who in life have been bled by a vampyre, become themselves vampyres, and have the same horrible taste for blood as those before them. Is it not horrible?”

“You only vex yourself by such thoughts, Flora. Mr. Chillingworth is coming to see you.”

“Can he minister to a mind diseased?”

“But yours is not, Flora. Your mind is healthful, and so, although his power extends not so far, we will thank Heaven, dear Flora, that you need it not.”

She sighed deeply, as she said,—

“Heaven help me! I know not, Henry. The dreadful being held on by my hair. I must have it all taken off. I tried to get away, but it dragged me back—a brutal thing it was. Oh, then at that moment, Henry, I felt as if something strange took place in my brain, and that I was going mad! I saw those glazed eyes close to, mine—I felt a hot, pestiferous breath upon my face—help—help!”

“Hush! my Flora, hush! Look at me.”

“I am calm again. It fixed its teeth in my throat. Did I faint away?”

“You did, dear; but let me pray you to refer all this to imagination; or at least the greater part of it.”

“But you saw it.”

“Yes—”

“All saw it.”

“We all saw some man—a housebreaker—It must have been some housebreaker. What more easy, you know, dear Flora, than to assume some such disguise?”

“Was anything stolen?”

“Not that I know of; but there was an alarm, you know.”

Flora shook her head, as she said, in a low voice,—

“That which came here was more than mortal. Oh, Henry, if it had but killed me, now I had been happy; but I cannot live—I hear it breathing now.”

“Talk of something else, dear Flora,” said the much distressed Henry; “you will make yourself much worse, if you indulge yourself in these strange fancies.”

"Oh, that they were but fancies!"

"They are, believe me."

"There is a strange confusion in my brain, and sleep comes over me suddenly, when I least expect it. Henry, Henry, what I was, I shall never, never be again."

"Say not so. All this will pass away like a dream, and leave so faint a trace upon your memory, that the time will come when you will wonder it ever made so deep an impression on your mind."

"You utter these words, Henry," she said, "but they do not come from your heart. Ah, no, no, no! Who comes?"

The door was opened by Mrs. Bannerworth, who said,—

"It is only me, my dear. Henry, here is Dr. Chillingworth in the dining-room."

Henry turned to Flora, saying,—

"You will see him, dear Flora? You know Mr. Chillingworth well."

"Yes, Henry, yes, I will see him, or whoever you please."

"Show Mr. Chillingworth up," said Henry to the servant.

In a few moments the medical man was in the room, and he at once approached the bedside to speak to Flora, upon whose pale countenance he looked with evident interest, while at the same time it seemed mingled with a painful feeling—at least so his own face indicated.

"Well, Miss Bannerworth," he said, "what is all this I hear about an ugly dream you have had?"

"A dream?" said Flora, as she fixed her beautiful eyes on his face.

"Yes, as I understand."

She shuddered, and was silent.

"Was it not a dream, then?" added Mr. Chillingworth.

She wrung her hands, and in a voice of extreme anguish and pathos, said,—

"Would it were a dream—would it were a dream! Oh, if anyone could but convince me it was a dream!"

"Well, will you tell me what it was?"

"Yes, sir, it was a vampyre."

Mr. Chillingworth glanced at Henry, as he said, in reply to Flora's words,—

"I suppose that is, after all, another name, Flora, for the nightmare?"

"No—no—no!"

"Do you really, then, persist in believing anything so absurd, Miss Bannerworth?"

"What can I say to the evidence of my own senses?" she replied. "I saw it, Henry saw it, George saw, Mr. Marchdale, my mother—all saw it. We could not all be at the same time the victims of the same delusion."

"How faintly you speak."

"I am very faint and ill."

"Indeed. What wound is that on your neck?"

A wild expression came over the face of Flora; a spasmodic action of the muscles, accompanied with a shuddering, as if a sudden chill had come over the whole mass of blood took place, and she said,—

"It is the mark left by the teeth of the vampyre."

The smile was a forced one upon the face of Mr. Chillingworth.

"Draw up the blind of the window, Mr. Henry," he said, "and let me examine this puncture to which your sister attaches so extraordinary a meaning."

The blind was drawn up, and a strong light was thrown into the room. For full two minutes Mr. Chillingworth attentively examined the two small wounds in the neck of Flora. He took a powerful magnifying glass from his pocket, and looked at them through it, and after his examination was concluded, he said,—

"They are very trifling wounds, indeed."

"But how inflicted?" said Henry.

"By some insect, I should say, which probably—it being the season for many insects—has flown in at the window."

"I know the motive," said Flora. "which prompts all these suggestions it is a kind one, and I ought to be the last to quarrel with it; but what I have seen, nothing can make me believe I saw not, unless I am, as once or twice I have thought myself, really mad."

"How do you now feel in general health?"

"Far from well; and a strange drowsiness at times creeps over me. Even now I feel it." She sunk back on the pillows as she spoke and closed her eyes with a deep sigh.

Mr. Chillingworth beckoned Henry to come with him from the room, but the latter had promised that he would remain with Flora; and as Mrs. Bannerworth had left the chamber because she was unable to control her feelings, he rang the bell, and requested that his mother would come.

She did so, and then Henry went downstairs along with the medical man, whose opinion he was certainly eager to be now made acquainted with.

As soon as they were alone in an old-fashioned room which was called the oak closet, Henry turned to Mr. Chillingworth, and said,—

"What, now, is your candid opinion, sir? You have seen my sister, and those strange indubitable evidences of something wrong."

"I have; and to tell you candidly the truth, Mr. Henry, I am sorely perplexed."

"I thought you would be."

"It is not often that a medical man likes to say so much, nor is it, indeed, often prudent that he should do so, but in this case I own I am much puzzled. It is contrary to all my notions upon all such subjects."

"Those wounds, what do you think of them?"

"I know not what to think. I am completely puzzled as regards them."

"But, but do they not really bear the appearance of being bites?"

"They really do."

"And so far, then, they are actually in favour of the dreadful supposition which poor Flora entertains."

"So far they certainly are. I have no doubt in the world of their being bites; but we not must jump to a conclusion that the teeth which inflicted them were human. It is a strange case, and one which I feel assured must give you all much uneasiness, as, indeed, it gave me; but, as I said before, I will not let my judgment give in to the fearful and degrading superstition which all the circumstances connected with this strange story would seem to justify."

"It is a degrading superstition."

"To my mind your sister seems to be labouring under the effect of some narcotic."

"Indeed!"

"Yes; unless she really has lost a quantity of blood, which loss has decreased the heart's action sufficiently to produce the languor under which she now evidently labours."

"Oh, that I could believe the former supposition, but I am confident she has taken no narcotic; she could not even do so by mistake, for there is no drug of the sort in the house. Besides, she is not heedless by any means. I am quite convinced she has not done so."

"Then I am fairly puzzled, my young friend, and I can only say that I would freely have given half of what I am worth to see that figure you saw last night."

"What would you have done?"

"I would not have lost sight of it for the world's wealth."

"You would have felt your blood freeze with horror. The face was terrible."

"And yet let it lead me where it liked I would have followed it."

"I wish you had been here."

"I wish to Heaven I had. If I thought there was the least chance of another visit I would come and wait with patience every night for a month."

"I cannot say," replied Henry. "I am going to sit up to-night with my sister, and I believe, our friend Mr. Marchdale will share my watch with me."

Mr. Chillingworth appeared to be for a few moments lost in thought, and then suddenly rousing himself, as if he found it either impossible to come to any rational conclusion upon the subject, or had arrived at one which he chose to keep to himself, he said,—

"Well, well, we must leave the matter at present as it stands. Time may accomplish something towards its development, but at present so palpable a mystery I never came across, or a matter in which human calculation was so completely foiled."

"Nor I—nor I."

"I will send you some medicines, such as I think will be of service to Flora, and depend upon seeing me by ten o'clock to-morrow morning."

"You have, of course, heard something," said Henry to the doctor, as he was pulling on his gloves, "about vampyres."

"I certainly have, and I understand that in some countries, particularly Norway and Sweden, the superstition is a very common one."

"And in the Levant."

"Yes. The ghouls of the Mahometans are of the same description of beings. All that I have heard of the European vampyre has made it a being which can be killed, but is restored to life again by the rays of a full moon falling on the body."

"Yes, yes, I have heard as much."

"And that the hideous repast of blood has to be taken very frequently, and that if the vampyre gets it not he wastes away, presenting the appearance of one in the last stage of a consumption, and visibly, so to speak, dying."

"That is what I have understood."

"Tonight, do you know, Mr. Bannerworth, is the full of the moon."

Henry started.

"If now you had succeeded in killing—. Pshaw, what am I saying. I believe I am getting foolish, and that the horrible superstition is beginning to fasten itself upon me as well as upon all of you. How strangely the fancy will wage war with the judgment in such a way as this."

"The full of the moon," repeated Henry, as he glanced towards the window, "and the night is near at hand."

"Banish these thoughts from your mind," said the doctor, "or else, my young friend, you will make yourself decidedly ill. Good evening to you, for it is evening. I shall see you to-morrow morning."

Mr. Chillingworth appeared now to be anxious to go, and Henry no longer opposed his departure; but when he was gone a sense of great loneliness came over him.

"Tonight," he repeated, "is the full of the moon. How strange that this dreadful adventure should have taken place just the night before. 'Tis very strange. Let me see—let me see."

He took from the shelves of a bookcase the work which Flora had mentioned, entitled *Travels in Norway*, in which work he found some account of the popular belief in vampyres.

He opened the work at random, and then some of the leaves turned over of themselves to a particular place, as the leaves of a book will frequently do when it has been kept open a length of time at that part, and the binding stretched there more than anywhere else. There was a note at the bottom of one of the pages at this part of the book, and Henry read as follows:—

> *"With regard to these vampyres, it is believed by those who are inclined to give credence to so dreadful a superstition, that they always endeavour to make their feast of blood, for the revival of their bodily powers, on some evening immediately preceding a full moon, because if any accident befall them, such as being shot, or otherwise killed or wounded, they can recover by lying down somewhere where the full moon's rays will fall upon them."*

Henry let the book drop from his hands with a groan and a shudder.

CHAPTER V.

THE NIGHT WATCH. —THE PROPOSAL. —THE MOONLIGHT. —THE FEARFUL ADVENTURE.

A kind of stupefaction came over Henry Bannerworth, and he sat for about a quarter of an hour scarcely conscious of where he was, and almost incapable of anything in the shape of rational thought. It was his brother, George, who roused him by saying, as he laid his hand upon his shoulder,—

"Henry, are you asleep?"

Henry had not been aware of his presence, and he started up as if he had been shot.

"Oh, George, is it you?" he said.

"Yes, Henry, are you unwell?"

"No, no; I was in a deep reverie."

"Alas! I need not ask upon what subject," said George, sadly. "I sought you to bring you this letter."

"A letter to me?"

"Yes, you see it is addressed to you, and the seal looks as if it came from someone of consequence."

"Indeed!"

"Yes, Henry. Read it, and see from whence it comes."

There was just sufficient light by going to the window to enable Henry to read the letter, which he did aloud. It ran thus:—

> *"Sir Francis Varney presents his compliments to Mr. Beaumont, and is much concerned to hear that some domestic affliction has fallen upon him. Sir Francis hopes that the genuine and loving sympathy of a neighbour will not be regarded as an intrusion, and begs to proffer any assistance or counsel that may be within the compass of his means.*
> *Ratford Abbey."*

"Sir Francis Varney!" said Henry, "Who is he?"

"Do you not remember, Henry," said George, "we were told a few days ago, that a gentleman of that name had become the purchaser of the estate of Ratford Abbey."

"Oh, yes, yes. Have you seen him?"

"I have not."

"I do not wish to make any new acquaintance, George. We are very poor—much poorer indeed than the general appearance of this place, which, I fear, we shall soon have to part with, would warrant anyone believing. I must, of course, return a civil answer to this gentleman, but it must be such as one as shall repress familiarity."

"That will be difficult to do while we remain here, when we come to consider the very close proximity of the two properties, Henry."

"Oh, no, not at all. He will easily perceive that we do not want to make acquaintance with him, and then, as a gentleman, which doubtless he is, he will give up the attempt."

"Let it be so, Henry. Heaven knows I have no desire to form any new acquaintance with anyone, and more particularly under our present circumstances of depression. And now, Henry, you must permit me, as I have had some repose, to share with you your night watch in Flora's room."

"I would advise you not, George; your health, you know, is very far from good."

"Nay, allow me. If not, then the anxiety I shall suffer will do me more harm than the watchfulness I shall keep up in her chamber."

This was an argument which Henry felt himself the force of too strongly not to admit it in the case of George, and he therefore made no further opposition to his wish to make one in the night watch.

"There will be an advantage, " said George, "you see, in three of us being engaged in this matter, because, should anything occur, two can act together, and yet Flora may not be left alone."

"True, true, that is a great advantage."

Now a soft gentle silvery light began to spread itself over the heavens. The moon was rising, and as the beneficial effects of the storm of the preceding evening were still felt in the clearness of the air, the rays appeared to be more lustrous and full of beauty than they commonly were.

Each moment the night grew lighter, and by the time the brothers were ready to take their places in the chamber of Flora, the moon had risen considerably.

Although neither Henry nor George had any objection to the company of Mr. Marchdale, yet they gave him the option, and rather in fact urged him not to destroy his night's repose by sitting up with them; but he said,—

"Allow me to do so; I am older, and have calmer judgment than you can have. Should anything again appear, I am quite resolved that it shall not escape me."

"What would you do?"

"With the name of God upon my lips," said Mr. Marchdale, solemnly, "I would grapple with it."

"You laid hands upon it last night."

"I did, and have forgotten to show you what I tore from it. Look here,—what should you say this was?"

He produced a piece of cloth, on which was an old-fashioned piece of lace, and two buttons. Upon a close inspection, this appeared to be a portion of the lapel of a coat of ancient times, and suddenly, Henry, with a look of intense anxiety, said,—

"This reminds me of the fashion of garments very many years ago, Mr. Marchdale."

"It came away in my grasp as if rotten and incapable of standing any rough usage."

"What a strange unearthly smell it has!"

"Now you mention it yourself," added Mr. Marchdale, "I must confess it smells to me as if it had really come from the very grave."

"It does—it does. Say nothing of this relic of last night's work to anyone."

"Be assured I shall not. I am far from wishing to keep up in anyone's mind proofs of that which I would fain, very fain refute."

Mr. Marchdale replaced the portion of the coat which the figure had worn in his pocket, and then the whole three proceeded to the chamber of Flora.

It was within a very few minutes of midnight, the moon had climbed high in the heavens, and a night of such brightness and beauty had seldom shown itself for a long period of time.

Flora slept, and in her chamber sat the two brothers and Mr. Marchdale, silently, for she had shown symptoms of restlessness, and they much feared to break the light slumber into which she had fallen.

Occasionally they had conversed in whispers, which could not have the effect of rousing her, for the room, although smaller than the one she had before occupied, was still sufficiently spacious to enable them to get some distance from the bed.

Until the hour of midnight now actually struck, they were silent, and when the last echo of the sounds had died away, a feeling of uneasiness came over them, which prompted some conversation to get rid of it.

"How bright the moon is now," said Henry, in a low tone.

"I never saw it brighter," replied Marchdale. "I feel as if I were assured that we shall not to-night be interrupted."

"It was later than this," said Henry.

"It was—it was."

"Do not then yet congratulate us upon no visit."

"How still the house is!" remarked George; "it seems to me as if I had never found it so intensely quiet before."

"It is very still."

"Hush! she moves."

Flora moaned in her sleep, and made a slight movement. The curtains were all drawn closely round the bed to shield her eyes from the bright moonlight which streamed into the room so brilliantly. They might have closed the shutters of the window, but this they did not like to do, as it would render their watch there of no avail at all, inasmuch as they would not be able to see if any attempt was made by anyone to obtain admittance.

A quarter of an hour longer might have thus passed when Mr. Marchdale said in a whisper,—

"A thought has just struck me that the piece of coat I have, which I dragged from the figure last night, wonderfully resembles in colour and appearance the style of dress of the portrait in the room which Flora lately slept in.”

“I thought of that,” said Henry, “when first I saw it; but, to tell the honest truth, I dreaded to suggest any new proof connected with last night’s visitation.”

“Then I ought not to have drawn your attention to it,” said Mr. Marchdale, “and regret I have done so.”

“Nay, do not blame yourself on such an account,” said Henry. “You are quite right, and it is I who am too foolishly sensitive. Now, however, since you have mentioned it, I must own I have a great desire to test the accuracy of the observation by a comparison with the portrait.”

“That may easily be done.”

“I will remain here,” said George, “in case Flora awakens, while you two go if you like. It is but across the corridor.”

Henry immediately rose, saying—

“Come, Mr. Marchdale, come. Let us satisfy ourselves at all events upon this point at once. As George says it is only across the corridor, and we can return directly.”

“I am willing,” said Mr. Marchdale, with a tone of sadness.

There was no light needed, for the moon stood suspended in a cloudless sky, so that from the house being a detached one, and containing numerous windows, it was as light as day.

Although the distance from one chamber to the other was only across the corridor, it was a greater space than these words might occupy, for the corridor was wide, neither was it directly across, but considerably slanting. However, it was certainly sufficiently close at hand for any sound of alarm from one chamber to reach another without any difficulty.

A few moments sufficed to place Henry and Mr. Marchdale in that antique room, where, from the effect of the moonlight which was streaming over it, the portrait on the panel looked exceedingly life like.

And this effect was probably the greater because the rest of the room was not illuminated by the moon’s rays, which came through a window in the corridor, and then at the open door of that chamber upon the portrait.

Mr. Marchdale held the piece of cloth he had close to the dress of the portrait, and one glance was sufficient to show the wonderful likeness between the two.

"Good God!" said Henry, "It is the same."

Mr. Marchdale dropped the piece of cloth and trembled.

"This fact shakes even your skepticism," said Henry.

"I know not what to make of it."

"I can tell you something which bears upon it. I do not know if you are sufficiently aware of my family history to know that this one of my ancestors, I wish I could say worthy ancestors, committed suicide, and was buried in his clothes."

"You—you are sure of that?"

"Quite sure."

"I am more and more bewildered as each moment some strange corroborative fact of that dreadful supposition we so much shrink from seems to come to light and to force itself upon our attention."

There was a silence of a few moments' duration, and Henry had turned towards Mr. Marchdale to say something, when the cautious tread of a footstep was heard in the garden, immediately beneath that balcony.

A sickening sensation came over Henry, and he was compelled to lean against the wall for support, as in scarcely articulate accents he said—

"The vampyre—the vampyre! God of heaven, it has come once again!"

"Now, Heaven inspire us with more than mortal courage," cried Mr. Marchdale, and he dashed open the window at once, and sprang into the balcony. Henry in a moment recovered himself sufficiently to follow him, and when he reached his side in the balcony, Marchdale said, as he pointed below,—

"There is someone concealed there."

"Where—where?"

"Among the laurels. I will fire a random shot, and we may do some execution."

"Hold!" said a voice from below; "don't do any such thing, I beg of you."

"Why, that is Mr. Chillingworth's voice," cried Henry.

"Yes, and it's Mr. Chillingworth's person, too," said the doctor, as he emerged from among some laurel bushes.

"How is this?" said Marchdale.

"Simply that I made up my mind to keep watch and ward tonight outside here, in the hope of catching the vampyre. I got into here by climbing the gate."

"But why did you not let me know?" said Henry.

"Because I did not know myself, my young friend, till an hour and a half ago."

"Have you seen anything?"

"Nothing. But I fancied I heard something in the park outside the wall."

"Indeed!"

"What say you, Henry," said Mr. Marchdale, "to descending and taking a hasty examination of the garden and grounds?"

"I am willing; but first allow me to speak to George, who otherwise might be surprised at our long absence."

Henry walked rapidly to the bed chamber of Flora, and he said to George,—

"Have you any objection to being left alone here for about half an hour, George, while we make an examination of the garden?"

"Let me have some weapon and I care not. Remain here while I fetch a sword from my own room."

Henry did so, and when George returned with a sword, which he always kept in his bed-room, he said,—

"Now go, Henry. I prefer a weapon of this description to pistols much. Do not be longer gone than necessary."

"I will not, George, be assured."

George was then left alone, and Henry returned to the balcony, where Mr. Marchdale was waiting for him. It was a quicker mode of descending to the garden to do so by clambering over the balcony than any other, and the height was not considerable enough to make it very objectionable, so Henry and Mr. Marchdale chose that way of joining Mr. Chillingworth.

"You are, no doubt, much surprised at finding me here," said the doctor; "but the fact is, I half made up my mind to come while I was here; but I had not thoroughly done so, therefore I said nothing to you about it."

"We are much indebted to you," said Henry, "for making the attempt."

"I am prompted to it by a feeling of the strongest curiosity."

"Are you armed, sir?" said Marchdale.

"In this stick," said the doctor, "is a sword, the exquisite temper of which I know I can depend upon, and I fully intended to run through any one whom I saw that looked in the least of the vampyre order."

"You would have done quite right," replied Mr. Marchdale. "I have a brace of pistols here, loaded with ball; will you take one, Henry, if you please, and then we shall be all armed."

Thus, then, prepared for any exigency, they made the whole round of the house; but found all the fastenings secure, and everything as quiet as possible.

"Suppose, now, we take a survey of the park outside the garden wall," said Mr. Marchdale.

This was agreed to; but before they had proceeded far, Mr. Marchdale said,—

"There is a ladder lying on the wall; would it not be a good plan to place it against the very spot the supposed vampyre jumped over last night, and so, from a more elevated position, take a view of the open meadows. We could easily drop down on the outer side, if we saw anything suspicious."

"Not a bad plan," said the doctor. "Shall we do it?"

"Certainly," said Henry; and they accordingly carried the ladder, which had been used for pruning the trees, towards the spot at the end of the long walk, at which the vampyre had made good, after so many fruitless efforts, his escape from the premises.

They made haste down the long vista of trees until they reached the exact spot, and then they placed the ladder as near as possible, exactly where Henry, in his bewilderment on the evening before, had seen the apparition from the grave spring to.

"We can ascend singly," said Marchdale; "but there is ample space for us all there to sit on the top of the wall and make our observations."

This was seen to be the case, and in about a couple of minutes they had taken up their positions on the wall, and, although the height was but trifling, they found that they had a much more extensive view than they could have obtained by any other means.

"To contemplate the beauty of such a night as this," said Mr. Chillingworth, "is amply sufficient compensation for coming the distance I have."

"And who knows," remarked Marchdale, "we may yet see something which may throw a light upon our present perplexities. God knows that I would give all I can call mine in the world to relieve you and your sister, Henry Bannerworth, from the fearful effect which last night's proceedings cannot fail to have upon you."

"Of that I am well assured, Mr. Marchdale," said Henry. "If the happiness of myself and family depended upon you, we should be happy indeed."

"You are silent, Mr. Chillingworth," remarked Marchdale, after a slight pause.

"Hush!" said Mr. Chillingworth—"hush—hush!"

"Good God, what do you hear?" cried Henry.

The doctor laid his hand upon Henry's arm as he said,—

"There is a young lime tree yonder to the right."

"Yes—yes."

"Carry your eye from it in a horizontal line, as near as you can, towards the wood."

Henry did so, and then he uttered a sudden exclamation of surprise, and pointed to a rising spot of ground, which was yet, in consequence of the number of tall trees in its vicinity, partially enveloped in shadow.

"What is that?" he said.

"I see something," said Marchdale. "By Heaven! It is a human form lying stretched there."

"It is—as if in death."

"What can it be?" said Chillingworth.

"I dread to say," replied Marchdale; "but to my eyes, even at this distance, it seems like the form of him we chased last night."

"The vampyre?"

"Yes—yes. Look, the moonbeams touch him. Now the shadows of the trees gradually recede. God of Heaven! the figure moves."

Henry's eyes were riveted to that fearful object, and now a scene presented itself which filled them all with wonder and astonishment, mingled with sensations of the greatest awe and alarm.

As the moonbeams, in consequence of the luminary rising higher and higher in the heavens, came to touch this figure that lay extended on the rising ground, a perceptible movement took place in it. The limbs appeared to tremble, and although it did not rise up, the whole body gave signs of vitality.

"The vampyre—the vampyre!" said Mr. Marchdale. "I cannot doubt it now. We must have hit him last night with the pistol bullets, and the moonbeams are now restoring him to a new life."

Henry shuddered, and even Mr. Chillingworth turned pale. But he was the first to recover himself sufficiently to propose some course of action, and he said—

"Let us descend and go up to this figure. It is a duty we owe to ourselves as much as to society."

"Hold a moment," said Mr. Marchdale, as he produced a pistol. "I am an unerring shot, as you well know, Henry. Before we move from this position we now occupy, allow me to try what virtue may be in a bullet to lay that figure low again.”

“He is rising!” exclaimed Henry.

Mr. Marchdale levelled the pistol—he took a sure and deliberate aim, and then, just as the figure seemed to be struggling to its feet, he fired, and, with a sudden bound, it fell again.

“You have hit it,” said Henry.

“You have indeed,” exclaimed the doctor. “I think we can go now.”

“Hush!" said Marchdale—“Hush! Does it not seem to you that, hit it as often as you will, the moonbeams will recover it?”

“Yes—yes,” said Henry, “they will—they will.”

“I can endure this no longer,” said Mr. Chillingworth, as he sprung from the wall. “Follow me or not, as you please, I will seek the spot where this being lies.”

“Oh, be not rash.” cried Marchdale. “See, it rises again, and its form looks gigantic.”

“I trust in Heaven and a righteous cause,” said the doctor, as he drew the sword he had spoken of from the stick, and threw away the scabbard. “Come with me if you like, or I go alone.”

Henry at once jumped down from the wall, and then Marchdale followed him, saying,—

“Come on; I will not shrink.”

They ran towards the piece of rising ground; but before they got to it, the form rose and made rapidly towards a little wood which was in the immediate neighbourhood of the hillock.

“It is conscious of being pursued,” cried the doctor. “See how it glances back, and then increases its speed.”

“Fire upon it, Henry,” said Marchdale.

He did so; but either his shot did not take effect, or it was quite unheeded if it did, by the vampyre, which gained the wood before they could have a hope of getting sufficiently near it to effect, or endeavour to effect, a capture.

"I cannot follow it there," said Marchdale. "In open country I would have pursued it closely; but I cannot follow it into the intricacies of a wood."

"Pursuit is useless there," said Henry. "It is enveloped in the deepest gloom."

"I am not so unreasonable," remarked Mr. Chillingworth, "as to wish you to follow into such a place as that. I am confounded utterly by this affair."

"And I," said Marchdale. "What on earth is to be done?"

"Nothing—nothing!" exclaimed Henry, vehemently; "and yet I have, beneath the canopy of Heaven, declared that I will, so help me God! spare neither time nor trouble in the unravelling of this most fearful piece of business. Did either of you remark the clothing which this spectral appearance wore?"

"They were antique clothes," said Mr. Chillingworth, "such as might have been fashionable a hundred years ago, but not now."

"Such was my impression," added Marchdale.

"And such my own," said Henry, excitedly. "Is it at all within the compass of the wildest belief that what we have seen is a vampyre, and no other than my ancestor who, a hundred years ago, committed suicide?"

There was so much intense excitement, and evidence of mental suffering, that Mr. Chillingworth took him by the arm, saying,—

"Come home—come home; no more of this at present; you will but make yourself seriously unwell."

"No—no—no."

"Come home now, I pray you; you are by far too much excited about this matter to pursue it with the calmness which should be brought to bear upon it."

"Take advice, Henry," said Marchdale, "take advice, and come home at once."

"I will yield to you; I feel that I cannot control my own feelings—I will yield to you, who, as you say, are cooler on this subject than I can be. Oh, Flora, Flora, I have no comfort to bring to you now."

Poor Henry Bannerworth appeared to be in a complete state of mental prostration, on account of the distressing circumstances that had occurred so rapidly and so suddenly in his family, which had had quite enough to contend with without having superadded to every other evil the horror of believing that some preternatural agency was at work to destroy every hope of future happiness in this world, under any circumstances.

He suffered himself to be led home by Mr. Chillingworth and Marchdale; he no longer attempted to dispute the dreadful fact concerning the supposed vampyre; he could not contend now against all the corroborating circumstances that seemed to collect together for the purpose of proving that which, even when proved, was contrary to all his notions of Heaven, and at variance with all that was recorded and established is part and parcel of the system of nature.

"I cannot deny," he said, when they had reached home, "that such things are possible; but the probability will not bear a moment's investigation."

"There are more things," said Marchdale, solemnly, "in Heaven, and on earth, than are dreamed of in our philosophy."

"There are indeed, it appears," said Mr. Chillingworth.

"And are you a convert?" said Henry, turning to him.

"A convert to what?"

"To a belief in—in—these vampyres?"

"I? No, indeed; if you were to shut me up in a room full of vampyres, I would tell them all to their teeth that I defied them."

"But after what we have seen to-night?"

"What have we seen?"

"You are yourself a witness."

"True; I saw a man lying down, and then I saw a man get up; he seemed then to be shot, but whether he was or not he only knows; and then I saw him walk off in a desperate hurry. Beyond that, I saw nothing."

"Yes; but, taking such circumstances into combination with others, have you not a terrible fear of the truth of the dreadful appearance?"

"No—no; on my soul, no. I will die in my disbelief of such an outrage upon Heaven as one of these creatures would most assuredly be."

"Oh! that I could think like you; but the circumstance strikes too nearly to my heart."

"Be of better cheer, Henry—be of better cheer," said Marchdale; "there is one circumstance which we ought to consider, it is that, from all we have seen, there seems to be some things which would favour an opinion, Henry, that your ancestor, whose portrait hangs in the chamber which was occupied by Flora, is the vampyre."

"The dress was the same," said Henry.

"I noted it was."

"And I."

"Do you not, then, think it possible that something might be done to set that part of the question at rest?"

"What—what?"

"Where is your ancestor buried?"

"Ah! I understand you now."

"And I," said Mr. Chillingworth; "you would propose a visit to his mansion?"

"I would," added Marchdale; "anything that may in any way tend to assist in making this affair clearer, and divesting it of its mysterious circumstances, will be most desirable."

Henry appeared to rouse for some moments and then he said,—

"He, in common with many other members of the family, no doubt occupies place in the vault under the old church in the village."

"Would it be possible," asked Marchdale, "to get into that vault without exciting general attention?"

"It would," said Henry; "the entrance to the vault is in the flooring of the pew which belongs to the family in the old church."

"Then it could be done?" asked Mr. Chillingworth.

"Most undoubtedly."

"Will you undertake such an adventure?" said Mr. Chillingworth. "It may ease your mind."

"He was buried in the vault, and in his clothes," said Henry, musingly; "I will think of it. About such a proposition I would not decide hastily. Give me leave to think of it until to-morrow."

"Most certainly."

They now made their way to the chamber of Flora, and they heard from George that nothing of an alarming character had occurred to disturb him on his lonely watch. The morning was now again dawning, and Henry earnestly entreated Mr. Marchdale to go to bed, which he did, leaving the two brothers to continue as sentinels by Flora's bed side, until the morning light should banish all uneasy thoughts.

Henry related to George what had taken place outside the house, and the two brothers held a long and interesting conversation for some hours upon that subject, as well as upon others of great importance to their welfare. It was not until the sun's early rays came glaring in at the casement that they both rose, and thought of awakening Flora, who had now slept soundly for so many hours.

CHAPTER VI.

A GLANCE AT THE BANNERWORTH FAMILY. —THE PROBABLE CONSEQUENCES OF THE MYSTERIOUS APPARITION'S APPEARANCE.

Having thus far, we hope, interested our readers in the fortunes of a family which had become subject to so dreadful a visitation, we trust that a few words concerning them, and the peculiar circumstances in which they are now placed, will not prove altogether out of place, or unacceptable. The Bannerworth family then were well known in the part of the country where they resided. Perhaps, if we were to say they were better known by name than they were liked, on account of that name, we should be near the truth, for it had unfortunately happened that for a very considerable time past the head of the family had been the very worst specimen of it that could be procured. While the junior branches were frequently amiable and most intelligent, and such in mind and manner as were calculated to inspire goodwill in all who knew them, he who held the family property, and who resided in the house now occupied by Flora and her brothers, was a very so-so sort of character.

This state of things, by some strange fatality, had gone on for nearly a hundred years, and the consequence was what might have been fairly expected, namely—that, what with their vices and what with their extravagances, the successive heads of the Bannerworth family had succeeded in so far diminishing the family property that, when it came into the hands of Henry Bannerworth, it was of little value, on account of the numerous encumbrances with which it was saddled.

The father of Henry had not been a very brilliant exception to the general rule, as regarded the head of the family. If he were not quite so bad as many of his ancestors, that gratifying circumstance was to be accounted for by the supposition that he was not quite so bold, and that the change in habits, manners, and laws, which had taken place in a hundred years, made it not so easy for even a landed proprietor to play the petty tyrant.

He had, to get rid of those animal spirits which had prompted many of his predecessors to downright crimes, had recourse to the gaming-table, and, after raising whatever sums he could upon the property which remained, he naturally, and as might have been fully expected, lost them all.

He was found lying dead in the garden of the house one day, and by his side was his pocket-book, on one leaf of which, it was the impression of the family, he had endeavoured to write something previous to his decease, for he held a pencil firmly in his grasp.

The probability was that he had felt himself getting ill, and, being desirous of making some communication to his family which pressed heavily upon his mind, he had attempted to do so, but was stopped by the too rapid approach of the hand of death.

For some days previous to his decease, his conduct had been extremely mysterious. He had announced an intention of leaving

England for ever—of selling the house and grounds for whatever they would fetch over and above the sums for which they were mortgaged, and so clearing himself of all encumbrances.

He had, but a few hours before he was found lying dead, made the following singular speech to Henry,—

"Do not regret, Henry, that the old house which has been in our family so long is about to be parted with. Be assured that, if it is but for the first time in my life, I have good and substantial reasons now for what I am about to do. We shall be able to go some other country, and there live like princes of the land."

Where the means were to come from to live like a prince, unless Mr. Bannerworth had some of the German princes in his eye, no one knew but himself, and his sudden death buried with him that most important secret.

There were some words written on the leaf of his pocket-book, but they were of by far too indistinct and ambiguous a nature to lead to anything. They were these:—

The money is ——————

And then there was a long scrawl of the pencil, which seemed to have been occasioned by his sudden decease.

Of course nothing could be made of these words, except in the way of a contradiction as the family lawyer said, rather more facetiously than a man of law usually speaks, for if he had written *"The money is not,"* he would have been somewhere remarkably near the truth. However, with all his vices he was regretted by his children, who chose rather to remember him in his best aspect than to dwell upon his faults.

For the first time then, within the memory of man, the head of the family of the Bannerworths was a gentleman, in every sense of the word. Brave, generous, highly educated, and full of many excellent and noble qualities—for such was Henry, whom we have introduced to our readers under such distressing circumstances.

And now, people said, that the family property having been all dissipated and lost, there would take place a change, and that the Bannerworths would have to take to some course of honourable industry for a livelihood, and that then they would be as much respected as they had before been detested and disliked.

Indeed, the position which Henry held was now a most precarious one—for one of the amazingly clever acts of his father had been to encumber the property with overwhelming claims, so that when Henry administered to the estate, it was doubted almost by his attorney if it were at all desirable to do so.

An attachment, however, to the old house of his family, had induced the young man to hold possession of it as long as he could, despite any adverse circumstance which might eventually be connected with it.

Some weeks, however, only after the decease of his father, and when he fairly held possession, a sudden and a most unexpected offer came to him from a solicitor in London, of whom he knew nothing, to purchase the house and grounds, for a client of his, who had instructed him so to do, but whom he did not mention.

The offer made was a liberal one, and beyond the value of the place. The lawyer who had conducted Henry's affairs for him since his father's decease, advised him by all means to take it; but after a consultation with his mother and sister, and George, they all resolved to hold by their own house as long as they could, and, consequently, he refused the offer.

He was then asked to let the place, and to name his own price for the occupation of it; but that he would not do: so the negotiation went off altogether, leaving only, in the minds of the family, much surprise at the exceeding eagerness of someone, whom they knew not, to get possession of the place on any terms.

There was another circumstance perhaps which materially aided in producing a strong feeling on the minds of the Bannerworths, with regard to remaining where they were.

That circumstance occurred thus: a relation of the family, who was now dead, and with whom had died all his means, had been in the habit, for the last half dozen years of his life, of sending a hundred pounds to Henry, for the express purpose of enabling him and his brother George and his sifter Flora to take a little continental or home tour, in the autumn of the year.

A more acceptable present, or for a more delightful purpose, to young people, could not be found; and, with the quiet, prudent habits of all three of them, they contrived to go far and to see much for the sum which was thus handsomely placed at their disposal.

In one of those excursions, when among the mountains of Italy, an adventure occurred which placed the life of Flora in imminent hazard.

They were riding along a narrow mountain path, and, her horse slipping, she fell over the ledge of a precipice.

In an instant, a young man, a stranger to the whole party, who was travelling in the vicinity, rushed to the spot, and by his knowledge and exertions, they felt convinced her preservation was effected.

He told her to lie quiet; he encouraged her to hope for immediate succour; and then, with much personal exertion, and at immense risk to himself, he reached the ledge of rock on which she lay, and then he supported her until the brothers had gone to a neighbouring house, which, bye-the-bye, was two good English miles off, and got assistance.

There came on, while they were gone, a terrific storm, and Flora felt that but for him who was with her she must have been hurled from the rock, and perished in an abyss below, which was almost too deep for observation.

Suffice it to say that she was rescued; and he who had, by his intrepidity, done so much towards saving her, was loaded with the most sincere and heartfelt acknowledgments by the brothers as well as by herself.

He frankly told them that his name was Holland; that he was travelling for amusement and instruction, and was by profession an artist.

He travelled with them for some time; and it was not at all to be wondered at, under the circumstances, that an attachment of the tenderest nature should spring up between him and the beautiful girl, who felt that she owed to him her life.

Mutual glances of affection were exchanged between them, and it was arranged that when he returned to England, he should come at once as an honoured guest to the house of the family of the Bannerworths.

All this was settled satisfactorily with the full knowledge and acquiescence of the two brothers, who had taken a strange attachment to the young Charles Holland, who was indeed in every way likely to propitiate the good opinion of all who knew him.

Henry explained to him exactly how they were situated, and told him that when he came he would find a welcome from all, except possibly his father, whose wayward temper he could not answer for.

Young Holland stated that he was compelled to be away for a term of two years, from certain family arrangements he had entered into, and that then he would return and hope to meet Flora unchanged as he should be.

It happened that this was the last of the continental excursions of the Bannerworths, for, before another year rolled round, the generous relative who had supplied them with the means of making such delightful trips was no more; and, likewise, the death of the father had occurred in the manner we have related, so that there was no chance as had been anticipated and hoped for by Flora, of meeting Charles Holland on the continent again, before his two years of absence from England should be expired.

Such, however, being the state of things, Flora felt reluctant to give up the house, where he would be sure to come to look for her, and her happiness was too dear to Henry to induce him to make any sacrifice of it to expediency.

Therefore was it that Bannerworth Hall, as it was sometimes called, was retained, and fully intended to be retained at all events until after Charles Holland had made his appearance, and his advice (for he was, by the young people, considered as one of the family) taken, with regard to what was advisable to be done.

With one exception this was the state of affairs at the hall, and that exception relates to Mr. Marchdale.

He was a distant relation of Mrs. Bannerworth, and, in early life, had been sincerely and tenderly attached to her. She, however, with the want of steady reflection of a young girl, as she then was, had, as is generally the case among several admirers, chosen the very worst: that is, the man who treated her with the most indifference, and who paid her the least attention, was of course, thought the most of, and she gave her hand to him.

That man was Mr. Bannerworth. But future experience had made her thoroughly awake to her former error; and, but for the love she bore her children, who were certainly all that a mother's heart could wish, she would often have deeply regretted the infatuation which had induced her to bestow her hand in the quarter she had done so.

About a month after the decease of Mr. Bannerworth, there came one to the hall, who desired to see the widow. That one was Mr. Marchdale.

It might have been some slight tenderness towards him which had never left her, or it might be the pleasure merely of seeing one whom she had known intimately in early life, but, be that as it may, she certainly gave him a kindly welcome; and he, after consenting to remain for some time as a visitor at the hall, won the esteem of the whole family by his frank demeanour and cultivated intellect.

He had travelled much and seen much, and he had turned to good account all he had seen, so that not only was Mr. Marchdale a man of sterling sound sense, but he was a most entertaining companion.

His intimate knowledge of many things concerning which they knew little or nothing; his accurate modes of thought, and a quiet, gentlemanly demeanour, such as is rarely to be met with, combined to make him esteemed by the Bannerworths. He had a small independence of his own, and being completely alone in the world, for he had neither wife nor child, Marchdale owned that he felt a pleasure in residing with the Bannerworths.

Of course he could not, in decent terms, so far offend them as to offer to pay for his subsistence, but he took good care that they should really be no losers by having him as an inmate, a matter which he could easily arrange by little presents of one kind and another, all of which he managed should be such as were not only ornamental, but actually spared his kind entertainers some positive expense which otherwise they must have gone to.

Whether or not this amiable piece of maneuvering was seen through by the Bannerworths it is not our purpose to inquire. If it was seen through, it could not lower him in their esteem, for it was probably just what they themselves would have felt a pleasure in doing under similar circumstances, and if they did not observe it, Mr. Marchdale would, probably, be all the better pleased.

Such then may be considered by our readers as a brief outline of the state of affairs among the Bannerworths—a state which was pregnant with changes, and which changes were now likely to be rapid and conclusive.

How far the feelings of the family towards the ancient house of their race would be altered by the appearance at it of so fearful a visitor as a vampyre, we will not stop to inquire, inasmuch as such feelings will develop themselves as we proceed.

That the visitation had produced a serious effect upon all the household was sufficiently evident, as well among the educated as among the ignorant. On the second morning, Henry received notice to quit his service from the three servants he with difficulty had contrived to keep at the hall. The reason why he received such notice he knew well enough, and therefore he did not trouble himself to argue about a superstition to which he felt now himself almost, compelled to give way; for how could he say there was no such thing as a vampyre, when he had, with his own eyes, had the most abundant evidence of the terrible fact?

He calmly paid the servants, and allowed them to leave him at once without at all entering into the matter, and, for the time being, some men were procured, who, however, came evidently with fear and trembling, and probably only took the place, on account of not being able, to procure any other. The comfort of the household was likely to be completely put an end to, and reasons now for leaving the hall appeared to be most rapidly accumulating.

CHAPTER VII.
THE VISIT TO THE VAULT OF THE BANNERWORTHS, AND ITS UNPLEASANT RESULT. —THE MYSTERY.

Henry and his brother roused Flora, and after agreeing together that it would be highly imprudent to say anything to her of the proceedings of the night, they commenced a conversation with her in encouraging and kindly accents.

"Well, Flora," said Henry, "you see you have been quite undisturbed to-night."

"I have slept long, dear Henry."

"You have, and pleasantly too, I hope."

"I have not had any dreams, and I feel much refreshed, now, and quite well again."

"Thank Heaven!" said George.

"If you will tell dear mother that I am awake, I will get up with her assistance."

The brothers left the room, and they spoke to each other of it as a favourable sign, that Flora did not object to being left alone now, as she had done on the preceding morning.

"She is fast recovering, now, George," said Henry. "If we could now but persuade ourselves that all this alarm would pass away, and that we should hear no more of it, we might return to our old and comparatively happy condition."

"Let us believe, Henry, that we shall."

"And yet, George, I shall not be satisfied in my mind, until I have paid a visit."

"A visit? Where?"

"To the family vault."

"Indeed, Henry! I thought you had abandoned that idea."

"I had. I have several times abandoned it; but it comes across my mind again and again."

"I much regret it."

"Look you, George; as yet, everything that has happened has tended to confirm a belief in this most horrible of all superstitions concerning vampyres."

"It has."

"Now, my great object, George, is to endeavour to disturb such a state of things, by getting something, however slight, or of a negative character, for the mind to rest upon on the other side of the question."

"I comprehend you, Henry."

"You know that at present we are not only led to believe, almost irresistibly that we have been visited here by a vampyre but that that vampyre is our ancestor, whose portrait is on the panel of the wall of the chamber into which he contrived to make his way."

"True, most true."

"Then let us, by an examination of the family vault, George, put an end to one of the evidences. If we find, as most surely we shall, the coffin of the ancestor of ours, who seems, in dress and appearance, so horribly mixed up in this affair, we shall be at rest on that head."

"But consider how many years have elapsed."

"Yes, a great number."

"What then, do you suppose, could remain of any corpse placed in a vault so long ago?"

"Decomposition must of course have done its work, but still there must be a something to show that a corpse has so undergone the process common to all nature. Double the lapse of time surely could not obliterate all traces of that which had been."

"There is reason in that, Henry."

"Besides, the coffins are all of lead, and some of stone, so that they cannot have all gone."

"True, most true."

"If in the one which, from the inscription and the date, we discover to be that of our ancestor whom we seek, we find the evident remains of a corpse, we shall be satisfied that he has rested in his tomb in peace."

"Brother, you seem bent on this adventure," said George; "if you go, I will accompany you."

"I will not engage rashly in it, George. Before I finally decide, I will again consult with Mr. Marchdale. His opinion will weigh much with me."

"And in good time, here he comes across the garden," said George, as he looked from the window of the room in which they sat.

It was Mr. Marchdale, and the brothers warmly welcomed him as he entered the apartment.

"You have been early afoot," said Henry.

"I have," he said. "The fact is, that although at your solicitation I went to bed, I could not sleep, and I went out once more to search about the spot where we had seen the—the I don't know what to call it, for I have a great dislike to naming it a vampyre."

"There is not much in a name," said George.

"In this instance there is," said Marchdale. "It is a name suggestive of horror."

"Made you any discovery?" said Henry.

"None whatever."

"You saw no trace of anyone?"

"Not the least."

"Well, Mr. Marchdale, George and I were talking over this projected visit to the family vault."

"Yes."

"And we agreed to suspend our judgments until we saw you, and learned your opinion."

"Which I will tell you frankly," said Mr. Marchdale, "because I know you desire it freely."

"Do so."

"It is, that you make the visit."

"Indeed."

"Yes, and for this reason. You have now, as you cannot help having, a disagreeable feeling, that you may find that one coffin is untenanted. Now, if you do find it so, you scarcely make matters worse, by an additional confirmation of what already amounts to a strong supposition, and one which is likely to grow stronger by time."

"True, most true."

"On the contrary, if you find indubitable proofs that your ancestor has slept soundly in the tomb, and gone the way of all flesh, you will find yourselves much calmer, and that an attack is made upon the train of events which at present all run one way."

"That is precisely the argument I was using to George," said Henry, "a few moments since."

"Then let us go," said George, "by all means."

"It is so decided then," said Henry.

"Let it be done with caution," replied Mr. Marchdale.

"If anyone can manage it, of course we can."

"Why should it not be done secretly and at night? Of course we lose nothing by making a night visit to a vault into which daylight, I presume, cannot penetrate."

"Certainly not."

"Then let it be at night."

"But we shall surely require the concurrence of some of the church authorities."

"Nay, I do not see that," interposed Mr. Marchdale. "It is the vault actually vested in and belonging to yourself you wish to visit, and, therefore, you have right to visit it in any manner or at any time that may be most suitable to yourself."

"But detection in a clandestine visit might produce unpleasant consequences."

"The church is old," said George, "and we could easily find means of getting into it. There is only one objection that I see, just now, and that is, that we leave Flora unprotected."

"We do, indeed," said Henry. "I did not think of that."

"It must be put to herself, as a matter for her own consideration," said Mr. Marchdale, "if she will consider herself sufficiently safe with the company and protection of your mother only."

"It would be a pity were we not all three present at the examination of the coffin," remarked Henry.

"It would, indeed. There is ample evidence," said Mr. Marchdale, "but we must not give Flora a night of sleeplessness and uneasiness on that account, and the more particularly as we cannot well explain to her where we are going, or upon what errand."

"Certainly not."

"Let us talk to her, then, about it," said Henry. "I confess I am much bent upon the plan, and fain would not forego it; neither should I like other than that we three should go together."

"If you determine, then, upon it," said Marchdale, "we will go tonight; and, from your acquaintance with the place, doubtless you will be able to decide what tools are necessary."

"There is a trap-door at the bottom of the pew," said Henry; "it is not only secured down, but it is locked likewise, and I have the key in my possession."

"Indeed!"

"Yes; immediately beneath is a short flight of stone steps, which conduct at once into the vault."

"Is it large?"

"No; about the size of a moderate chamber, and with no intricacies about it."

"There can be no difficulties, then."

"None whatever, unless we meet with actual personal interruption, which I am inclined to think is very far from likely. All we shall require will be a screwdriver, with which to remove the screws, and then something with which to wrench open the coffin."

"Those we can easily provide, along with lights," remarked Mr. Marchdale.

"I hope to Heaven that this visit to the tomb will have the effect of easing your minds, and enabling you to make a successful stand against the streaming torrent of evidence that has poured in upon us regarding this most fearful of apparitions."

"I do, indeed, hope so," added Henry; "and now I will go at once to Flora, and endeavour to convince her she is safe without us to-night."

"By-the-bye, I think," said Marchdale, "that if we can induce Mr. Chillingworth to come with us, it will be a great point gained in the investigation."

"He would," said Henry, "be able to come to an accurate decision with respect to the remains—if any—in the coffin, which we could not."

"Then have him, by all means," said George. "He did not seem averse last night to go on such an adventure."

"I will ask him when he makes his visit this morning upon Flora; and should he not feel disposed to join us, I am quite sure he will keep the secret of our visit."

All this being arranged, Henry proceeded to Flora, and told her that he and George, and Mr. Marchdale wished to go out for about a couple of hours in the evening after dark, if she felt sufficiently well to feel a sense of security without them.

Flora changed colour, and slightly trembled, and then, as if ashamed of her fears, she said,—

"Go, go; I will not detain you. Surely no harm can come to me in the presence of my mother."

"We shall not be gone longer than the time I mention to you," said Henry.

"Oh, I shall be quite content. Besides, am I to be kept thus in fear all my life? Surely, surely not. I ought, too, to learn to defend myself."

Henry caught at the idea, as he said,—

"If fire-arms were left you, do you think you would have courage to use them?"

"I do, Henry."

"Then you shall have them; and let me beg of you to shoot anyone without the least hesitation who shall come into your chamber."

"I will, Henry. If ever human being was justified in the use of deadly weapons, I am now. Heaven protect me from a repetition of the visit to which I have now been once subjected. Rather, oh, much rather would I die a hundred deaths than suffer what I have suffered."

"Do not allow it, dear Flora, to press too heavily upon your mind in dwelling upon it in conversation. I still entertain a sanguine expectation that something may arise to afford a far less dreadful explanation of what has occurred than what you have put upon it. Be of good cheer, Flora, we shall go one hour after sunset, and return in about two hours from the time at which we leave here, you may be assured."

Notwithstanding this ready and courageous acquiescence of Flora in the arrangement, Henry was not without his apprehension that when the night should come again, her fears would return with it; but he spoke to Mr. Chillingworth upon the subject, and got that gentleman's ready consent to accompany them.

He promised to meet them at the church porch exactly at nine o'clock, and matters were all arranged, and Henry waited with much eagerness and anxiety now for the coming night, which he hoped would dissipate one of the fearful deductions which his imagination had drawn from recent circumstances.

He gave to Flora a pair of pistols of his own, upon which he knew he could depend, and he took good care to load them well, so that there could be no likelihood whatever of their missing fire at a critical moment.

"Now, Flora," he said, "I have seen you use fire-arms when you were much younger than you are now, and therefore I need give you no instructions. If any intruder does come, and you do fire, be sure you take a good aim, and shoot low."

"I will, Henry, I will; and you will be back in two hours?"

"Most assuredly I will."

The day wore on, evening came, and then deepened into night. It turned out to be a cloudy night, and therefore the moon's brilliance was nothing near equal to what it had been on the preceding night. Still, however, it had sufficient power over the vapours that frequently covered it for many minutes together, to produce a considerable light effect upon the face of nature, and the night was consequently very far, indeed, from what might be called a dark one.

George, Henry, and Marchdale, met in one of the lower rooms of the house, previous to starting upon their expedition; and after satisfying themselves that they had with them all the tools that were necessary, inclusive of the same small, but well-tempered iron crow-bar with which Marchdale had, on the night of the visit of the vampyre, forced open the door of Flora's chamber, they left the hall, and proceeded at a rapid pace towards the church.

"And Flora does not seem much alarmed," said Marchdale, "at being left alone?"

"No," replied Henry, "she has made up her mind with a strong natural courage which I knew was in her disposition to resist as much as possible the depressing effects of the awful visitation she has endured."

"It would have driven some really mad."

"It would, indeed; and her own reason tottered on its throne, but, thank Heaven, she has recovered."

"And I fervently hope that, through her life," added Marchdale, "she may never have such another trial."

"We will not for a moment believe that such a thing can occur twice."

"She is one among a thousand. Most young girls would never at all have recovered the fearful shock to the nerves."

"Not only has she recovered," said Henry, "but a spirit, which I am rejoiced to see, because it is one which will uphold her, of resistance now possesses her."

"Yes, she actually—I forgot to tell you before—but she actually asked me for arms to resist any second visitation."

"You much surprise me."

"Yes, I was surprised, as well as pleased, myself."

"I would have left her one of my pistols had I been aware of her having made such a request. Do you know if she can use fire-arms?"

"Oh, yes; well."

"What a pity. I have them both with me."

"Oh, she is provided."

"Provided?"

"Yes; I found some pistols which I used to take with me on the continent, and she has them both well loaded, so that if the vampyre makes his appearance, he is likely to meet with rather a warm reception."

"Good God! was it not dangerous?"

"Not at all, I think."

"Well, you know best, certainly, of course. I hope the vampyre may come, and that we may have the pleasure, when we return, of finding him dead. By-the-bye, I—I—. Bless me, I have forgot to get the materials for lights, which I pledged myself to do."

"How unfortunate."

"Walk on slowly, while I run back and get them."

"Oh, we are too far—"

"Hilloa!" cried a man at this moment, some distance in front of them.

"It is Mr. Chillingworth," said Henry.

"Hilloa," cried the worthy doctor again. "Is that you, my friend, Henry Bannerworth?"

"It is," cried Henry.

Mr. Chillingworth now came up to them and said,—

"I was before my time, so rather than wait at the church porch, which would have exposed me to observation perhaps, I thought it better to walk on, and chance meeting with you."

"You guessed we should come this way?"

"Yes, and so it turns out, really. It is unquestionably your most direct route to the church."

"I think I will go back," said Mr. Marchdale.

"Back!" exclaimed the doctor; "what for?"

"I forgot the means of getting lights. We have candles, but no means of lighting them."

"Make yourselves easy on that score," said Mr. Chillingworth. "I am never without some chemical matches of my own manufacture, so that as you have the candles, that can be no bar to our going on a once."

"That is fortunate," said Henry.

"Very," added Marchdale; "for it seems a mile's hard walking me, or at least half a mile from the hall. Let us now push on."

They did push on, all four walking at a brisk pace. The church, although it belonged to the village, was not in it. On the contrary, it was situated at the end of a long lane, which was a mile nearly from the village, in the direction of the hall, therefore, in going to it from the hall, that amount of distance was saved, although it was always called and considered the village church.

It stood alone, with the exception of a glebe house and two cottages, that were occupied by persons who held situations about the sacred edifice, and who were supposed, being on the spot, to keep watch and ward over it.

It was an ancient building of the early English style of architecture, or rather Norman, with one of those antique, square, short towers, built of flint stones firmly embedded in cement, which, from time, had acquired almost the consistency of stone itself. There were numerous arched windows, partaking something of the more florid gothic style, although scarcely ornamental enough to be called such. The edifice stood in the center of a graveyard, which extended over a space of about half an acre, and altogether it was one of the prettiest and most rural old churches within many miles of the spot.

Many a lover of the antique and of the picturesque, for it was both, went out of his way while travelling in the neighbourhood to look at it, and it had an extensive and well-deserved reputation as a fine specimen of its class and style of building.

In Kent, to the present day, are some fine specimens of the old Roman style of church, building; and, although they are as rapidly pulled down as the abuse of modern architects, and the cupidity of speculators, and the vanity of clergymen can possibly encourage, in order to erect flimsy, Italianised structures in their stead, yet sufficient of them remain dotted over England to interest the traveller.

At Walesden there is a church of this description which will well repay a visit. This, then, was the kind of building into which it was the intention of our four friends to penetrate, not on an unholy, or an unjustifiable errand, but on one which, proceeding from good and proper motives, it was highly desirable to conduct in as secret a manner as possible.

The moon was more densely covered by clouds than it had yet been that evening, when they reached the little wicket-gate which led into the churchyard, through which was a regularly used thoroughfare.

"We have a favourable night," remarked Henry, "for we are not so likely to be disturbed."

"And now, the question is, how are we to get in?" said Mr. Chillingworth, as he paused, and glanced up at the ancient building.

"The doors," said George, "would effectually resist us."

"How can it be done, then?"

"The only way I can think of," said Henry, "is to get out one of the small diamond-shaped panes of glass from one of the low windows, and then we can one of us put in our hands, and undo the fastening, which is very simple, when the window opens like a door, and it is but a step into the church."

"A good way," said Marchdale. "We will lose no time."

They walked round the church till they came to a very low window indeed, near to an angle of the wall, where a huge abutment struck far out into the burial-ground.

"Will you do it, Henry?" said George.

"Yes. I have often noticed the fastenings. Just give me a slight hoist up, and all will be right."

George did so, and Henry with his knife easily bent back some of the leadwork which held in one of the panes of glass, and then got it out whole. He handed it down to George, saying,—

"Take this, George. We can easily replace it when we leave, so that there can be no signs left of any one having been here at all."

George took the piece of thick, dim-coloured glass, and in another moment Henry had succeeded in opening the window, and the mode of ingress to the old church was fair and easy before them all, had there been ever so many.

"I wonder," said Marchdale, "that a place so inefficiently protected has never been robbed."

"No wonder at all," remarked Mr. Chillingworth. "There is nothing to take that I am aware of that would repay anybody the trouble of taking."

"Indeed!"

"Not an article. The pulpit, to be sure, is covered with faded velvet; but beyond that, and an old box, in which I believe nothing is left but some books, I think there is no temptation."

"And that, Heaven knows, is little enough, then."

"Come on," said Henry. "Be careful; there is nothing beneath the window, and the depth is about two feet."

Thus guided, they all got fairly into the sacred edifice, and then Henry closed the window, and fastened it on the inside as he said,—

"We have nothing to do now but to set to work opening a way into the vault, and I trust that Heaven will pardon me for thus desecrating the tomb of my ancestors, from a consideration of the object I have in view by so doing."

"It does seem wrong thus to tamper with the secrets of the tomb," remarked Mr. Marchdale.

"The secrets of a fiddlestick!" said the doctor. "What secrets has the tomb, I wonder?"

"Well, but, my dear sir—"

"Nay, my dear sir, it is high time that death, which is, then, the inevitable fate of us all, should be regarded with more philosophic eyes than it is. There are no secrets in the tomb but such as may well be endeavoured to be kept secret."

"What do you mean?"

"There is one which very probably we shall find unpleasantly revealed."

"Which is that?"

"The not-overpleasant odour of decomposed animal remains—beyond that I know of nothing of a secret nature that the tomb can show us."

"Ah, your profession hardens you to such matters."

"And a very good thing that it does, or else, if all men were to look upon a dead body as something almost too dreadful to look upon, and by far too horrible to touch, surgery would lose its value, and crime, in many instances of the most obnoxious character, would go unpunished."

"If we have a light here," said Henry, "we shall run the greatest chance in the world of being seen, for the church has many windows."

"Do not have one, then, by any means," said Mr. Chillingworth. "A match held low down in the pew may enable us to open the vault."

"That will be the only plan."

Henry led them to the pew which belonged to his family, and in the floor of which was the trap door.

"When was it last opened?" inquired Marchdale.

"When my father died," said Henry; "some ten months ago now, I should think."

"The screws, then, have had ample time to fix themselves with fresh rust."

"Here is one of my chemical matches," said Mr. Chillingworth, as he suddenly irradiated the pew with a clear and beautiful flame, that lasted about a minute.

The heads of the screws were easily discernible, and the short time that the light lasted had enabled Henry to turn the key he had brought with him in the lock.

"I think that without a light now," he said, "I can turn the screws well."

"Can you?"

"Yes; there are but four."

"Try it, then."

Henry did so, and from the screws having very large heads, and being made purposely, for the convenience of removal when required, with deep indentations to receive the screwdriver, he found no difficulty in feeling for the proper places, and extracting the screws without any more light than was afforded to him from the general whitish aspect of the heavens.

"Now, Mr. Chillingworth," he said "another of your matches, if you please. I have all the screws so loose that I can pick them up with my fingers."

"Here," said the doctor.

In another moment the pew was as light as day, and Henry succeeded in taking out the few screws, which he placed in his pocket for their greater security, since, of course, the intention was to replace everything exactly as it was found, in order that not the least surmise should arise in the mind of any person that the vault had been opened, and visited for any purpose whatever, secretly or otherwise.

"Let us descend," said Henry. "There is no further obstacle, my friends. Let us descend."

"If anyone," remarked George, in a whisper, as they slowly descended the stairs which conducted into the vault—"if anyone had told me that I should be descending into a vault for the purpose of ascertaining if a dead body, which had been nearly a century there, was removed or not, and had become a vampyre, I should have denounced the idea as one of the most absurd that ever entered the brain of a human being."

"We are the very slaves of circumstances," said Marchdale, "and we never know what we may do, or what we may not. What appears to us so improbable as to border even upon the impossible at one time, is at another the only course of action which appears feasibly open to us to attempt to pursue."

They had now reached the vault, the floor of which was composed of flat red tiles, laid in tolerable order the one beside the other. As Henry had stated, the vault was by no means of large extent. Indeed, several of the apartments for the living, at the hall, were much larger than was that one destined for the dead.

The atmosphere was damp and noisome, but not by any means so bad as might have been expected, considering the number of months which had elapsed since last the vault was opened to receive one of its ghastly and still visitants.

"Now for one of your lights. Mr. Chillingworth. You say you have the candles, I think, Marchdale, although you forgot the matches."

"I have. They are here." Marchdale took from his pocket a parcel which contained several wax candles, and when it was opened, a smaller packet fell to the ground.

"Why, these are instantaneous matches," said Mr. Chillingworth, as he lifted the small packet up.

"They are; and what a fruitless journey I should have had back to the hall," said Mr. Marchdale, "if you had not been so well provided as you are with the means of getting a light. These matches, which I thought I had not with me, have been, in the hurry of departure, enclosed, you see, with the candles. Truly, I should have hunted for them at home in vain."

Mr. Chillingworth lit the wax candle which was now handed to him by Marchdale, and in another moment the vault from one end of it to the other was quite clearly discernible.

CHAPTER VIII.

THE COFFIN. —THE ABSENCE OF THE DEAD. —THE MYSTERIOUS CIRCUMSTANCE, AND THE CONSTERNATION OF GEORGE.

They were all silent for a few moments as they looked around them with natural feelings of curiosity. Two of that party had of course never been in that vault at all, and the brothers, although they had descended into it upon the occasion, nearly a year before, of their father being placed in it, still looked upon it with almost as curious eyes as they who now had their first sight of it.

If a man be at all of a thoughtful or imaginative cast of mind, some curious sensations are sure to come over him, upon standing in such a place, where he knows around him lie, in the calmness of death, those in whose veins have flowed kindred blood to him—who bore the same name, and who preceded him in the brief drama of his existence, influencing his destiny and his position in life probably largely by their actions compounded of their virtues and their vices.

Henry Bannerworth and his brother George were just the kind of persons to feel strongly such sensations. Both were reflective, imaginative, educated young men, and, as the light from the wax candle flashed upon their faces, it was evident how deeply they felt the situation in which they were placed.

Mr. Chillingworth and Marchdale were silent. They both knew what was passing in the minds of the brothers, and they had too much delicacy to interrupt a train of thought which, although from having no affinity with the dead who lay around, they could not share in, yet they respected. Henry at length, with a sudden start, seemed to recover himself from his reverie.

"This is a time for action, George," he said, "and not for romantic thought. Let us proceed."

"Yes, yes," said George, and he advanced a step towards the center of the vault.

"Can you find out among all these coffins, for there seem to be nearly twenty," said Mr. Chillingworth, "which is the one we seek?"

"I think we may," replied Henry. "Some of the earlier coffins of our race, I know, were made of marble, and others of metal, both of which materials, I expect, would withstand the encroaches of time for a hundred years, at least."

"Let us examine," said George.

There were shelves or niches built into the walls all round, on which the coffins were placed, so that there could not be much difficulty in a minute examination of them all, the one after the other.

When, however, they came to look, they found that "decay's offensive fingers" had been more busy than they could have imagined, and that whatever they touched of the earlier coffins crumbled into dust before their very fingers. In some cases the inscriptions were quite illegible, and, in others, the plates that had borne them had fallen on to the floor of the vault, so that it was impossible to say to which coffin they belonged.

Of course, the more recent and fresh-looking coffins they did not examine, because they could not have anything to do with the object of that melancholy visit.

"We shall arrive at no conclusion," said George. "All seems to have rotted away among those coffins where we might expect to find the one belonging to Marmaduke Bannerworth, our ancestor."

"Here is a coffin plate," said Marchdale, taking one from the floor.

He handed it to Mr. Chillingworth, who, upon an inspection of it, close to the light, exclaimed,—

"It must have belonged to the coffin you seek."

"What says it?"

"*Ye mortale remains of Marmaduke Bannerworth, Yeoman. God reste his soule. A.D. 1640.*"

"It is the plate belonging to his coffin," said Henry, "and now our search is fruitless."

"It is so, indeed," exclaimed George, "for how can we tell to which of the coffins that have lost the plates this one really belongs?"

"I should not be so hopeless," said Marchdale. "I have, from time to time, in the pursuit of antiquarian lore, which I was once fond of, entered many vaults, and I have always observed that an inner coffin of metal was sound and good, while the outer one of wood had rotted away, and yielded at once to the touch of the first hand that was laid upon it."

"But, admitting that to be the case," said Henry, "how does that assist us in the identification of a coffin?"

"I have always, in my experience, found the name and rank of the deceased engraved upon the lid of the inner coffin, as well as being set forth in a much more perishable manner on the plate which was secured to the outer one."

"He is right," said Mr. Chillingworth. "I wonder we never thought of that. If your ancestor was buried in a leaden coffin, there will be no difficulty in finding which it is."

Henry seized the light, and proceeding to one of the coffins, which seemed to be a mass of decay, he pulled away some of the rotted wood work, and then suddenly exclaimed,—

"You are quite right. Here is a firm strong leaden coffin within, which, although quite black, does not otherwise appear to have suffered."

"What is the inscription on that?" said George.

With difficulty the name on the lid was deciphered, but it was found not to be the coffin of him whom they sought.

"We can make short work of this," said Marchdale, "by only examining those leaden coffins which have lost the plates from off their outer cases. There do not appear to be many in such a state."

He then, with another light, which he lighted from the one that Henry now carried, commenced actively assisting in the search, which was carried on silently for more than ten minutes.

Suddenly Mr. Marchdale cried, in a tone of excitement,—

"I have found it. It is here."

They all immediately surrounded the spot where he was, and then he pointed to the lid of a coffin, which he had been rubbing with his handkerchief, in order to make the inscription more legible, and said,—

"See. It is here."

By the combined light of the candles they saw the words,—

Marmaduke Bannerworth, Yeoman, 1640.

"Yes, there can be no mistake here," said Henry. "This is the coffin, and it shall be opened."

"I have the iron crowbar here," said Marchdale. "It is an old friend of mine, and I am accustomed to the use of it. Shall I open the coffin?"

"Do so—do so," said Henry.

They stood around in silence, while Mr. Marchdale, with much care, proceeded to open the coffin, which seemed of great thickness, and was of solid lead.

It was probably the partial rotting of the metal, in consequence of the damps of that place, that made it easier to open the coffin than it otherwise would have been, but certain it was that the top came away remarkably easily. Indeed, so easily did it come off, that another supposition might have been hazarded, namely, that it had never at all been effectually fastened.

The few moments that elapsed were ones of very great suspense to everyone there present; and it would, indeed, be quite sure to assert, that all the world was for the time forgotten in the absorbing interest which appertained to the affair which was in progress.

The candles were now both held by Mr. Chillingworth, and they were so held as to cast a full and clear light upon the coffin. Now the lid slid off, and Henry eagerly gazed into the interior.

There lay something certainly there, and an audible "Thank God!" escaped his lips.

"The body is there!" exclaimed George.

"All right," said Marchdale, "here it is. There is something, and what else can it be?"

"Hold the lights," said Mr. Chillingworth; "hold the lights, some of you; let us be quite certain."

George took the lights, and Mr. Chillingworth, without any hesitation, dipped his hands at once into the coffin, and took up some fragments of rags which were there. They were so rotten, that they fell to pieces in his grasp, like so many pieces of tinder.

There was a death-like pause for some few moments, and then Mr. Chillingworth said, in a low voice,—

"There is not the least vestige of a dead body here."

Henry gave a deep groan, as he said,—

"Mr. Chillingworth, can you take upon yourself to say that no corpse has undergone the process of decomposition in this coffin?"

"To answer your question exactly, as probably in your hurry you have worded it," said Mr. Chillingworth, "I cannot take upon myself to say any such thing; but this I can say, namely, that in this coffin there are no animal remains, and that it is quite impossible that any corpse enclosed here could, in any lapse of time, have so utterly and entirely disappeared."

"I am answered," said Henry.

"Good God!" exclaimed George, "and has this but added another damning proof, to those we have already on our minds, of one of the must dreadful superstitions that ever the mind of man conceived?"

"It would seem so," said Marchdale, sadly.

"Oh, that I were dead! This is terrible. God of heaven, why are these things? Oh, if I were but dead, and so spared the torture of supposing such things possible."

"Think again, Mr. Chillingworth; I pray you think again," cried Marchdale.

"If I were to think for the remainder of my existence," he replied, "I could come to no other conclusion. It is not a matter of opinion; it is a matter of fact."

"You are positive, then," said Henry, "that the dead body of Marmaduke Bannerworth is not rested here?"

"I am positive. Look for yourselves. The lead is but slightly discoloured; it looks tolerably clean and fresh; there is not a vestige of putrefaction—no bones, no dust even."

They did all look for themselves, and the most casual glance was sufficient to satisfy the most skeptical.

"All is over," said Henry; "let us now leave this place; and all I can now ask of you, my friends, is to lock this dreadful secret deep in your own hearts."

"It shall never pass my lips," said Marchdale.

"Nor mine, you may depend," said the doctor. "I was much in hopes that this night's work would have had the effect of dissipating, instead of adding to, the gloomy fancies that now possess you."

"Good heavens!" cried George, "can you call them fancies, Mr. Chillingworth?"

"I do, indeed."

"Have you yet a doubt?"

"My young friend, I told you from the first, that I would not believe in your vampyre; and I tell you now, that if one was to come and lay hold of me by the throat, as long as I could at all gasp for breath I would tell him he was a d——d impostor."

"This is carrying incredulity to the verge of obstinacy."

"Far beyond it, if you please."

"You will not be convinced?" said Marchdale.

"I most decidedly, on this point, will not."

"Then you are one who would doubt a miracle, if you saw it with your own eyes."

"I would, because I do not believe in miracles. I should endeavour to find some rational and some scientific means of accounting for the phenomenon, and that's the very reason why we have no miracles nowadays, between you and I, and no prophets and saints, and all that sort of thing."

"I would rather avoid such observations in such a place as this," said Marchdale.

"Nay, do not be the moral coward," cried Mr. Chillingworth, "to make your opinions, or the expression of them, dependent upon any certain locality."

"I know not what to think," said Henry; "I am bewildered quite. Let us now come away."

Mr. Marchdale replaced the lid of the coffin, and then the little party moved towards the staircase.

Henry turned before he ascended, and glanced back into the vault. "Oh," he said, "if I could but think there had been some mistake, some error of judgment, on which the mind could rest for hope."

"I deeply regret," said Marchdale, "that I so strenuously advised this expedition. I did hope that from it would have resulted much good."

"And you had every reason so to hope," said Chillingworth. "I advised it likewise, and I tell you that its result perfectly astonishes me, although I will not allow myself to embrace at once all the conclusions to which it would seem to lead me."

"I am satisfied," said Henry; "I know you both advised me for the best. The curse of Heaven seems now to have fallen upon me and my house."

"Oh, nonsense!" said Chillingworth. "What for?"

"Alas! I know not."

"Then you may depend that Heaven would never act so oddly. In the first place, Heaven doesn't curse anybody; and, in the second , it is too just to inflict pain where pain is not amply deserved."

They ascended the gloomy staircase of the vault. The countenances of both George and Henry were very much saddened, and it was quite evident that their thoughts were by far too busy to enable them to enter into any conversation. They did not, and particularly George, seem to hear all that was said to them. Their intellects seemed almost stunned by the unexpected circumstance of the disappearance of the body of their ancestor.

All along they had, although almost unknown to themselves, felt a sort of conviction that they must find some remains of Marmaduke Bannerworth, which would render the supposition, even in the most superstitious minds, that he was the vampyre, a thing totally and physically impossible.

But now the whole question assumed a far more bewildering shape.

The body was not in its coffin—it had not there quietly slept the long sleep of death common to humanity. Where was it then? What had become of it? Where, how, and under what circumstances had it been removed? Had it itself burst the bands that held it, and hideously stalked forth into the world again to make one of its seeming inhabitants, and kept up for a hundred years a dreadful existence by such adventures as it had consummated at the hall, where, in the course of ordinary human life, it had once lived?

All these were questions which irresistibly pressed themselves upon the consideration of Henry and his brother. They were awful questions.

And yet, take any sober, sane, thinking, educated man, and show him all that they had seen, subject him to all to which they had been subjected, and say if human reason, and all the arguments that the subtlest brain could back it with, would be able to hold out against such a vast accumulation of horrible evidences, and say—"I don't believe it."

Mr. Chillingworth's was the only plan. He would not argue the question. He said at once,—

"I will not believe this thing—upon this point I will yield to no evidence whatever."

That was the only way of disposing of such a question; but there are not many who could so dispose of it, and not one so much interested in it as were the brothers Bannerworth, who could at all hope to get into such a state of mind.

The boards were laid carefully down again, and the screws replaced. Henry found himself unequal to the task, so it was done by Marchdale, who took pains to replace everything in the same state in which they had found it, even to the laying even the matting at the bottom of the pew.

Then they extinguished the light, and, with heavy hearts, they all walked towards the window, to leave the sacred edifice by the same means they had entered it.

"Shall we replace the pane of glass?" said Marchdale.

"Oh, it matters not—it matters not," said Henry, listlessly; "nothing matters now. I care not what becomes of me—I am getting weary of a life which now must be one of misery and dread."

"You must not allow yourself to fall into such a state of mind as this," said the doctor, "or you will become a patient of mine very quickly."

"I cannot help it."

"Well, but be a man. If there are serious evils affecting you, fight out against them the best way you can."

"I cannot."

"Come, now, listen to me. We need not, I think, trouble ourselves about the pane of glass, so come along."

He took the arm of Henry and walked on with him a little in advance of the others.

"Henry," he said, "the best way, you may depend, of meeting evils, be they great or small, is to get up an obstinate feeling of defiance against them. Now, when anything occurs which is uncomfortable to me, I endeavour to convince myself, and I have no great difficulty in doing so, that I am a decidedly injured man."

"Indeed!"

"Yes; I get very angry, and that gets up a kind of obstinacy, which makes me not feel half so much mental misery as would be my portion, if I were to succumb to the evil, and commence whining over it, as many people do, under the presence of being resigned."

"But this family affliction of mine transcends anything that anybody else ever endured."

"I don't know that; but it is a view of the subject which, if I were you, would only make me more obstinate."

"What can I do?"

"In the first place, I would say to myself, 'There may or there may not be supernatural beings, who, from some physical derangement of the ordinary nature of things, make themselves obnoxious to living people; if there are, d—n them! There may be vampyres; and if there are, I defy them. Let the imagination paint its very worst terrors; let fear do what it will and what it can in peopling the mind with horrors. Shrink from nothing, and even then I would defy them all.' "

"Is not that like defying Heaven?"

"Most certainly not; for in all we say and in all we do we act from the impulses of that mind which is given to us by Heaven itself. If Heaven creates an intellect and a mind of a certain order, Heaven will not quarrel that it does the work which it was adapted to do."

"I know these are your opinions. I have heard you mention them before."

"They are the opinions of every rational person, Henry Bannerworth, because they will stand the test of reason; and what I urge upon you is, not to allow yourself to be mentally prostrated, even if a vampyre has paid a visit to your house. Defy him, say I—fight him. Self-preservation is a great law of nature, implanted in all our hearts; do you summon it to your aid."

"I will endeavor to think as you would have me. I thought more than once of summoning religion to my aid."

"Well, that is religion."

"Indeed!"

"I consider so, and the most rational religion of all. All that we read about religion that does not seem expressly to agree with it, you may consider as an allegory."

"But, Mr. Chillingworth, I cannot and will not renounce the sublime truths of Scripture. They may be incomprehensible; they may be inconsistent; and some of them may look ridiculous; but still they are sacred and sublime, and I will not renounce them although my reason may not accord with them, because they are the laws of Heaven."

No wonder this powerful argument silenced Mr. Chillingworth, who was one of those characters in society who hold most dreadful opinions, and who would destroy religious beliefs, and all the different sects in the world, if they could, and endeavor to introduce instead some horrible system of human reason and profound philosophy.

But how soon the religious man silences his opponent; and let it not be supposed that, because his opponent says no more upon the subject, he does so because he is disgusted with the stupidity of the other; no, it is because he is completely beaten, and has nothing more to say.

The distance now between the church and the hall was nearly traversed, and Mr. Chillingworth, who was a very good man, notwithstanding his disbelief in certain things of course paved the way for him to hell, took a kind leave of Mr. Marchdale and the brothers, promising to call on the following morning and see Flora.

Henry and George then, in earnest conversation with Marchdale, proceeded homewards. It was evident that the scene in the vault had made a deep and saddening impression upon them, and one which was not likely easily to be eradicated.

CHAPTER IX.
THE OCCURRENCES OF THE NIGHT AT THE HALL. —THE SECOND APPEARANCE OF THE VAMPYRE, AND THE PISTOL-SHOT.

Despite the full and free consent which Flora had given to her brothers to entrust her solely to the care of her mother and her own courage at the hall, she felt greater fear creep over her after they were gone than she chose to acknowledge.

A sort of presentiment appeared to come over her that some evil was about to occur, and more than once she caught herself almost in the act of saying,—

"I wish they had not gone."

Mrs. Bannerworth, too, could not be supposed to be entirely destitute of uncomfortable feelings, when she came to consider how poor a guard she was over her beautiful child, and how much terror might even deprive of the little power she had, should the dreadful visitor again make his appearance.

"but it is but for two hours," thought flora, "and two hours will soon pass away."

There was, too, another feeling which gave her some degree of confidence, although it arose from a bad source, inasmuch as it was one which showed powerfully how much her mind was dwelling on the particulars of the horrible belief in the class of supernatural beings, one of whom she believed had visited her.

That consideration was this. The two hours of absence from the hall of its male inhabitants, would be from nine o'clock until eleven, and those were not the two hours during which she felt that she would be most timid on account of the vampyre.

"it was after midnight before," she thought, "when it came, and perhaps it may not be able to come earlier. It may not have the power, until that time, to make its hideous visits, and, therefore, I will believe myself safe."

She had made up her mind not to go to bed until the return of her brothers, and she and her mother sat in a small room that was used as a breakfast-room, and which had a latticed window that opened on to the lawn.

This window had in the inside strong oaken shutters, which had been fastened as securely as their construction would admit of some time before the departure of the brothers and Mr. Marchdale on that melancholy expedition, the object of which, if it had been known to her, would have added so much to the terrors of poor Flora.

It was not even guessed at, however remotely, so that she had not the additional affliction of thinking, that while she was sitting there, a prey to all sorts of imaginative terrors, they were perhaps gathering fresh evidence, as, indeed, they were, of the dreadful reality of the appearance which, but for the collateral circumstances attendant upon its coming and its going, she would fain have persuaded herself was but the vision of a dream.

It was before nine that the brothers started, but in her own mind Flora gave them to eleven, and when she heard ten o'clock sound from a clock which stood in the hall, she felt pleased to think that in another hour they would surely be at home.

"My dear," said her mother, "you look more like yourself, now."

"Do, I, mother?"

"Yes, you are well again."

"Ah, if I could forget—"

"Time, my dear Flora, will enable you to do so, and all the fear of what made you so unwell will pass away. You will soon forget it all."

"I will hope to do so."

"Be assured that, some day or another, something will occur, as Henry says, to explain all that has happened, in some way consistent with reason and the ordinary nature of things, my dear Flora."

"Oh, I will cling to such a belief; I will get Henry, upon whose judgment I know I can rely, to tell me so, and each time that I hear such words from his lips, I will contrive to dismiss some portion of the terror which now, I cannot but confess, clings to my heart."

Flora laid her hand upon her mother's arm, and in a low, anxious tone of voice, said,—"Listen, mother."

Mrs. Bannerworth turned pale, as she said,—"Listen to what, dear?"

"Within these last ten minutes," said Flora, "I have thought three or four times that I heard a slight noise without. Nay, mother, do not tremble—it may be only fancy."

Flora herself trembled, and was of a death-like paleness; once or twice she passed her hand across her brow, and altogether she presented a picture of much mental suffering.

They now conversed in anxious whispers, and almost all they said consisted in anxious wishes for the return of the brothers and Mr. Marchdale.

"You will be happier and more assured, my dear, with some company," said Mrs. Bannerworth.

"Shall I ring for the servants, and let them remain in the room with us, until they who are our best safeguards next to Heaven return?"

"Hush—hush—hush, mother!"

"What do you hear?"

"I thought—I heard a faint sound."

"I heard nothing, dear."

"Listen again, mother. Surely I could not be deceived so often. I have now, at least, six times heard a sound as if someone was outside by the windows."

"No, no, my darling, do not think; your imagination is active and in a state of excitement."

"It is, and yet—"

"Believe me, it deceives you."

"I hope to Heaven it does!"

There was a pause of some minutes' duration, and then Mrs. Bannerworth again urged slightly the calling of some of the servants, for she thought that their presence might have the effect of giving a different direction to her child's thoughts; but Flora saw her place her hand upon the bell, and she said,—

"No, mother, no—not yet, not yet. Perhaps I am deceived."

Mrs. Bannerworth upon this sat down, but no sooner had she done so than she heartily regretted she had not rung the bell, for, before, another word could be spoken, there came too perceptibly upon their ears for there to be any mistake at all about it, a strange scratching noise upon the window outside.

A faint cry came from Flora's lips, as she exclaimed, in a voice of great agony,—

"Oh, God!—oh, God! It has come again!"

Mrs. Bannerworth became faint, and unable to move or speak at all; she could only sit like one paralysed, and unable to do more than listen to and see what was going on.

The scratching noise continued for a few seconds, and then altogether ceased. Perhaps, under ordinary circumstances, such a sound outside the window would have scarcely afforded food for comment at all, or, if it had, it would have been attributed to some natural effect, or to the exertions of some bird or animal to obtain admittance to the house.

But there had occurred now enough in that family to make any little of wonderful importance, and these things which before would have passed completely unheeded, at all events without creating much alarm, were now invested with a fearful interest.

When the scratching noise ceased, Flora spoke in a low, anxious whisper, as she said,—

"Mother, you heard it then?"

Mrs. Bannerworth tried to speak, but she could not; and then suddenly, with a loud clash, the bar, which on the inside appeared to fasten the shutters strongly, fell as if by some invisible agency, and the shutters now, but for the intervention of the window, could be easily pushed open from without.

Mrs. Bannerworth covered her face with her hands, and, after rocking to and fro for a moment, she fell off her chair, having fainted with the excess of terror that came over her.

For about the space of time in which a fast speaker could count twelve, Flora thought her reason was leaving her, but it did not. She found herself recovering; and there she sat, with her eyes fixed upon the window, looking more like some exquisitely-chiselled statue of despair than a being of flesh and blood, expecting each moment to have its eyes blasted by some horrible appearance, such as might be supposed to drive her to madness.

And now again came the strange knocking or scratching against the glass of the window.

This continued for some minutes, during which it appeared likewise to Flora that some confusion was going on at another part of the house, for she fancied she heard voices and the banging of doors.

It seemed to her as if she must have sat looking at the shutters of that window a long time before she saw them shake, and then one wide hinged portion of them slowly opened.

Once again horror appeared to be on the point of producing madness in her brain, and then, as before, a feeling of calmness rapidly ensued.

She was able to see plainly that something was by the window, but what it was she could not plainly discern, in consequence of the lights she had in the room. A few moments, however, sufficed to settle that mystery, for the window was opened and a figure stood before her.

One glance, one terrified glance, in which her whole soul was concentrated, sufficed to show her who and what the figure was. There was the tall, gaunt form—there was the faded ancient apparel—the lustrous metallic-looking eyes—its half-opened month, exhibiting the tusk-like teeth! It was—yes, it was—*the vampyre!*

It stood for a moment gazing at her, and then in the hideous way it had attempted before to speak, it apparently endeavoured to utter some words which it could not make articulate to human ears.

The pistols lay before Flora. Mechanically she raised one, and pointed it at the figure. It advanced a step, and then she pulled the trigger.

A stunning report followed. There was a loud cry of pain, and the vampyre fled. The smoke and the confusion that was incidental to the spot prevented her from seeing if the figure walked or ran away. She thought she heard a crashing sound among the plants outside the window, as if it had fallen, but she did not feel quite sure.

It was no effort of any reflection, but a purely mechanical movement, that made her raise the other pistol, and discharge that likewise in the direction the vampyre had taken. Then casting the weapon away, she rose, and made a frantic rush from the room. She opened the door, and was dashing out, when she found herself caught in the circling arms of someone who either had been there waiting, or who had just at that moment got there.

The thought that it was the vampyre, who by some mysterious

means, had got there, and was about to make her his prey, now overcame her completely, and she sunk into a state of utter insensibility on the moment.

CHAPTER X.

THE RETURN FROM THE VAULT. —THE ALARM, AND THE SEARCH AROUND THE HALL.

It so happened that George and Henry Bannerworth, along with Mr. Marchdale, had just reached the gate which conducted into the garden of the mansion when they all were alarmed by the report of a pistol. Amid the stillness of the night, it came upon them with so sudden a shock, that they involuntarily paused, and there came from the lips of each an expression of alarm.

"Good heavens!" cried George, "can that be Flora firing at any intruder?"

"It must be," cried Henry; "she has in her possession the only weapons in the house."

Mr. Marchdale turned very pale, and trembled slightly, but he did not speak.

"On, on," cried Henry; "for God's sake, let us hasten on."

As he spoke, he cleared the gate at a bound, and at a terrific pace he made towards the house, passing over beds, and plantations, and flowers heedlessly, so that he went the most direct way to it.

Before, however, it was possible for any human speed to accomplish even half of the distance, the report of the other shot came upon his ears, and he even fancied he heard the bullet whistle past his head in tolerably close proximity. This supposition gave him a clue to the direction at all events from whence the shots proceeded, otherwise he knew not from which window they were fired, because it had not occurred to him, previous to leaving home, to inquire in which room Flora and his mother were likely to be seated waiting his return.

He was right as regarded the bullet. It was that winged messenger of death which had passed his head in such very dangerous proximity, and consequently he made with tolerable accuracy towards the open window from whence the shots had been fired.

The night was not near so dark as it had been, although even yet it was very far from being a light one, and he was soon enabled to see that there was a room, the window of which was wide open, and lights burning on the table within. He made towards it in a moment, and entered it. To his astonishment, the first objects he beheld were Flora and a stranger, who was now supporting her in his arms. To grapple him by the throat was the work of a moment, but the stranger cried aloud in a voice which sounded familiar to Harry,—

"Good God, are you all mad?"

Henry relaxed his hold, and looked in his face.

"Gracious heavens, it is Mr. Holland!" he said.

"Yes; did you not know me?"

Henry was bewildered. He staggered to a seat, and, in doing so, he saw his mother, stretched apparently lifeless upon the floor. To raise her was the work of a moment, and then Marchdale and George, who had followed him as fast as they could, appeared at the open window. Such a strange scene as that small room now exhibited had never been equalled in Bannerworth Hall. There was young Mr. Holland, of whom mention has already been made, as the affianced lover of Flora, supporting her fainting form. There was Henry doing equal service to his mother; and on the floor lay the two pistols, and one of the candles which had been upset in the confusion; while the terrified attitudes of George and Mr. Marchdale at the window completed the strange-looking picture.

"What is this—oh! what has happened?" cried George.

"I know not—I know not," said Henry. "Someone summon the servants; I am nearly mad."

Mr. Marchdale at once rang the bell, for George looked so faint and ill as to be incapable of doing so; and he rung it so loudly and so effectually, that the two servants who had been employed suddenly upon the others leaving came with much speed to know what was the matter.

"See to your mistress," said Henry. "She is dead, or has fainted. For God's sake, let who can give me some account of what has caused all this confusion here."

"Are you aware, Henry," said Marchdale, "that a stranger is present in the room?"

He pointed to Mr. Holland as he spoke, who, before Henry could reply, said,—

"Sir, I may be a stranger to you, as you are to me, and yet no stranger to those whose home this is."

"No, no," said Henry, "you are no stranger to us, Mr. Holland, but are thrice welcome—none can be more welcome. Mr. Marchdale, this is Mr. Holland, of whom you have heard me speak."

"I am proud to know you, sir," said Marchdale.

"Sir, I thank you," replied Holland, coldly.

It will so happen; but, at first sight, it appeared as if those two persons had some sort of antagonistic feeling towards each other, which threatened to prevent effectually their ever becoming intimate friends.

The appeal of Henry to the servants to know if they could tell him what had occurred was answered in the negative. All they knew was that they had heard two shots fired, and that, since then, they had remained where they were, in a great fright, until the bell was rung violently. This was no news at all and, therefore, the only chance was, to wait patiently for the recovery of the mother, or of Flora, from one or the other of whom surely some information could be at once then procured.

Mrs. Bannerworth was removed to her own room, and so would Flora have been; but Mr. Holland, who was supporting her in his arms, said,—

"I think the air from the open window is recovering her, and it is likely to do so. Oh, do not now take her from me, after so long an absence. Flora, Flora, look up; do you not know me? You have not yet given me one look of acknowledgment. Flora, dear Flora!"

The sound of his voice seemed to act as the most potent of charms in restoring her to consciousness; it broke through the death-like trance in which she lay, and, opening her beautiful eyes, she fixed them upon his face, saying,—

"Yes, yes; it is Charles—it is Charles."

She burst into a hysterical flood of tears, and clung to him like some terrified child to its only friend in the whole wide world.

"Oh, my dear friends," cried Charles Holland, "do not deceive me; has Flora been ill?"

"We have all been ill," said George.

"All ill?"

"Ay, and nearly mad," exclaimed Harry.

Holland looked from one to the other in surprise, as well he might, nor was that surprise at all lessened when Flora made an effort to extricate herself from his embrace, as she exclaimed,—

"You must leave me—you must leave me, Charles, forever! Oh! never, never look upon my face again!"

"I—I am bewildered," said Charles.

"Leave me, now," continued Flora; "think me unworthy; think what you will, Charles, but I cannot, I dare not, now be yours."

"Is this a dream?"

"Oh, would it were. Charles, if we had never met, you would be happier—I could not be more wretched."

"Flora, Flora, do you say these words of so great cruelty to try my love?"

"No, as Heaven is my judge, I do not."

"Gracious Heaven, then, what do they mean?"

Flora shuddered, and Henry, coming up to her, took her hand in his tenderly, as he said,—

"Has it been again?"

"It has."

"You shot it?"

"I fired full upon it, Henry, but it fled."

"It did—fly?"

"It did, Henry, but it will come again—it will be sure to come again."

"You—you hit it with the bullet?" interposed Mr. Marchdale. "Perhaps you killed it?"

"I think I must have hit it, unless I am mad."

Charles Holland looked from one to the other with such a look of intense surprise, that George remarked it, and said at once to him,—

"Mr. Holland, a full explanation is due to you, and you shall have it."

"You seem the only rational person here," said Charles. "Pray what is it that everybody calls '*it*?'"

"Hush—hush!" said Henry; "you shall hear soon, but not at present."

"Hear me, Charles," said Flora. "From this moment mind, I do release you from every vow, from every promise made to me of constancy and love; and if you are wise, Charles, and will be advised, you will now this moment leave this house never to return to it."

"No," said Charles—"no; by Heaven I love you, Flora! I have come to say again all that in another clime I said with joy to you. When I forget you, let what trouble may oppress you, may God forget me, and my own right hand forget to do me honest service."

"Oh! no more—no more!" sobbed Flora.

"Yes, much more, if you will tell me of words which shall be stronger than others in which to paint my love, my faith, and my constancy."

"Be prudent," said Henry. "Say no more."

"Nay, upon such a theme I could speak for ever. You may cast me off, Flora; but until you tell me you love another, I am yours till the death, and then with a sanguine hope at my heart that we shall meet again, never, dearest, to part."

Flora sobbed bitterly. "Oh!" she said, "this is the unkindest blow of all—this is worse than all."

"Unkind!" echoed Holland.

"Heed her not," said Henry; "she means not you."

"Oh, no—no!" she cried. "Farewell, Charles—dear Charles."

"Oh, say that word again!" he exclaimed, with animation. "It is the first time such music has met my ears."

"It must be the last."

"No, no—oh, no."

"For your own sake I shall be able now, Charles, to show you that I really loved you."

"Not by casting me from you?"

"Yes, even so. That will be the way to show you that I love you."

She held up her hands wildly, as she added, in an excited voice,—

"The curse of destiny is upon me! I am singled out as one lost and accursed. Oh, horror—horror! would that I were dead!"

Charles staggered back a pace or two until he came to the table, at which he clutched for support. He turned very pale as he said, in a faint voice,—

"Is—is she mad, or am I?"

"Tell him I am mad, Henry," cried Flora. "Do not, oh, do not make his lonely thoughts terrible with more than that. Tell him I am mad."

"Come with me," whispered Henry to Holland. "I pray you come with me at once, and you shall know all."

"I—will."

"George, stay with Flora for a time. Come, come, Mr. Holland, you ought, and you shall know all; then you can come to a judgment for yourself. This way, sir. You cannot, in the wildest freak of your imagination, guess that which I have now to tell you."

Never was mortal man so utterly bewildered by the events of the last hour of his existence as was now Charles Holland, and truly he might well be so. He had arrived in England, and made what speed he could to the house of a family whom he admired for their intelligence, their high culture, and in one member of which his whole thoughts of domestic happiness in this world were centered, and he found nothing but confusion, incoherence, mystery, and the wildest dismay.

Well might he doubt if he were sleeping or waking—well might he ask if he or they were mad.

And now, as, after a long, lingering look of affection upon the pale, suffering face of Flora, he followed Henry from the room, his thoughts were busy in fancying a thousand vague and wild imaginations with respect to the communication which was promised to be made to him.

But, as Henry had truly said to him, not in the wildest freak of his imagination could he conceive of anything near the terrible strangeness and horror of that which he had to tell him, and consequently he found himself closeted with Henry in a small private room, removed from the domestic part of the hall, to the full in as bewildered a state as he had been from the first.

CHAPTER XI.

THE COMMUNICATIONS TO THE LOVER. —THE HEART'S DESPAIR.

Consternation is sympathetic, and anyone who had looked upon the features of Charles Holland, now that he was seated with Henry Bannerworth, in expectation of a communication which his fears told him was to blast all his dearest and most fondly cherished hopes for ever, would scarce have recognised in him the same young man who, one short hour before, had knocked so loudly, and so full of joyful hope and expectation, at the door of the hall.

But so it was. He knew Henry Bannerworth too well to suppose that any unreal cause could blanch his cheek. He knew Flora too well to imagine for one moment that caprice had dictated the, to him, fearful words of dismissal she had uttered to him.

Happier would it at that time have been for Charles Holland had she acted capriciously towards him, and convinced him that his true heart's devotion had been cast at the feet of one unworthy of so really noble a gift. Pride would then have enabled him, no doubt, successfully to resist the blow. A feeling of honest and proper indignation at having his feelings trifled with, would, no doubt, have sustained him, but, alas! the case seemed widely different.

True, she implored him to think of her no more—no longer to cherish in his breast the fond dream of affection which had been its guest so long; but the manner in which she did so brought along with it an irresistible conviction, that she was making a noble sacrifice of her own feelings for him, from some cause which was involved in the profoundest mystery.

But now he was to hear all. Henry had promised to tell him, and as he looked into his pale, but handsomely intellectual face, he half dreaded the disclosure he yet panted to hear.

"Tell me all, Henry—tell me all," he said. "Upon the words that come from your lips I know I can rely."

"I will have no reservations with you," said Henry, sadly. "You ought to know all, and you shall. Prepare yourself for the strangest revelation you ever heard."

"Indeed!"

"Ay. One which in hearing you may well doubt; and one which, I hope, you will never find an opportunity of verifying."

"You speak in riddles."

"And yet speak truly, Charles. You heard with what a frantic vehemence Flora desired you to think no more of her?"

"I did—I did."

"She was right. She is a noble-hearted girl for uttering those words. A dreadful incident in our family has occurred, which might well induce you to pause before uniting your fate with that of any member of it."

"Impossible. Nothing can possibly subdue the feelings of affection I entertain for Flora. She is worthy of any one, and, as such, amid all changes—all mutations of fortune, she shall be mine."

"Do not suppose that any change of fortune has produced the scene you were witness to."

"Then, what else?"

"I will tell you, Holland. In all your travels, and in all your reading, did you ever come across anything about vampyres?"

"About what?" cried Charles, drawing his chair forward a little. "About what?"

"You may well doubt the evidence of your own ears, Charles Holland, and wish me to repeat what I said. I say, do you know anything about vampyres?"

Charles Holland looked curiously in Henry's face, and the latter immediately added,—

"I can guess what is passing in your mind at present, and I do not wonder at it. You think I must be mad."

"Well, really, Henry, your extraordinary question—"

"I knew it. Were I you, I should hesitate to believe the tale; but the fact is, we have every reason to believe that one member of our own family is one of those horrible preternatural beings called vampyres."

"Good God, Henry, can you allow your judgment for a moment to stoop to such a supposition?"

"That is what I have asked myself a hundred times; but, Charles Holland, the judgment, the feelings, and all the prejudices, natural and acquired, must succumb to actual ocular demonstration. Listen to me, and do not interrupt me. You shall know all, and you shall know it circumstantially."

Henry then related to the astonished Charles Holland all that had occurred, from the first alarm of Flora, up to that period when he, Holland, caught her in his arms as she was about to leave the room.

"And now," he said, in conclusion, "I cannot tell what opinion you may come to as regards these most singular events. You will recollect that here is the unbiased evidence of four or five people to the facts, and, beyond that, the servants, who have seen something of the horrible visitor."

"You bewilder me, utterly," said Charles Holland.

"As we are all bewildered."

"But—but, gracious Heaven! it cannot be."

"It is."

"No—no. There is—there must be yet some dreadful mistake."

"Can you start any supposition by which we can otherwise explain any of the phenomena I have described to you? If you can, for Heaven's sake do so, and you will find no one who will cling to it with more tenacity than I."

"Any other species or kind of supernatural appearance might admit of argument; but this, to my perception, is too wildly improbable—too much at variance with all we see and know of the operations of nature."

"It is so. All that we have told ourselves repeatedly, and yet is all human reason at once struck down by the few brief words of—'We have seen it.' "

"I would doubt my eyesight."

"One might; but many cannot be labouring under the same delusion."

"My friend, I pray you, do not make me shudder at the supposition that such a dreadful thing as this is at all possible."

"*I* am, believe me, Charles, most unwilling to oppress anyone with the knowledge of these evils; but you are so situated with us, that you ought to know, and you will clearly understand that you may, with perfect honour, now consider yourself free from all engagements you have entered into with Flora."

"No, no! By Heaven, no!"

"Yes, Charles. Reflect upon the consequences now of a union with such a family."

"Oh, Henry Bannerworth, can you suppose me so dead to all good feeling, so utterly lost to honourable impulses, as to eject from my heart her who has possession of it entirely, on such a ground as this?"

"You would be justified."

"Coldly justified in prudence I might be. There are a thousand circumstances in which a man may be justified in a particular course of action, and that course yet may be neither honourable nor just. I love Flora; and were she tormented by the whole of the supernatural world, I should still love her. Nay, it becomes, then, a higher and a nobler duty on my part to stand between her and those evils, if possible."

"Charles—Charles," said Henry, "I cannot of course refuse to you my meed of praise and admiration for your generosity of feeling; but, remember, if we are compelled, despite all our feelings and all our predilections to the contrary, to give in to a belief in the existence of vampyres, why may we not at once receive as the truth all that is recorded of them?"

"To what do you allude?"

"To this. That one who has been visited by a vampyre, and whose blood has formed a horrible repast for such a being, becomes, after death, one of the dreadful race, and visits others in the same way."

"Now this must be insanity," cried Charles.

"It bears the aspect of it, indeed," said Henry; "oh, that you could by some means satisfy yourself that I am mad."

"There may be insanity in this family," thought Charles, with such an exquisite pang of misery, that he groaned aloud.

"Already," added Henry, mournfully, "already the blighting influence of the dreadful tale is upon you, Charles. Oh, let me add my advice to Flora's entreaties. She loves you, and we all esteem you; fly, then, from us, and leave us to encounter our miseries alone. Fly from us, Charles Holland, and take with you our best wishes for happiness which you cannot know here."

"Never," cried Charles; "I devote my existence to Flora. I will not play the coward, and fly from one whom I love, on such grounds. I devote my life to her."

Henry could not speak for emotion for several minutes, and when at length, in a faltering voice, he could utter some words, he said,—

"God of heaven, what happiness is marred by these horrible events? What have we all done to be the victims of such a dreadful act of vengeance?"

"Henry, do not talk in that way," cried Charles. "Rather let us bend all our energies to overcoming the evil, than spend any time in useless lamentations. I cannot even yet give in to a belief in the existence of such a being as you say visited Flora."

"But the evidences."

"Look you here, Henry: until I am convinced that some things have happened which it is totally impossible could happen by any human means whatever, I will not ascribe them to supernatural influence."

"But what human means, Charles, could produce what I have now narrated to you?"

"I do not know, just at present, but I will give the subject the most attentive consideration. Will you accommodate me here for a time?"

"You know you are as welcome here as if the house were your own, and all that it contains."

"I believe so, most truly. You have no objection, I presume, to my conversing with Flora upon this strange subject?"

"Certainly not. Of course you will be careful to say nothing which can add to her fears."

"I shall be most guarded, believe me. You say that your brother George, Mr. Chillingworth, yourself, and this Mr. Marchdale, have all been cognisant of the circumstances."

"Yes—yes."

"Then with the whole of them you permit me to hold free communication upon the subject?"

"Most certainly."

"I will do so then. Keep up good heart, Henry, and this affair, which looks so full of terror at first sight, may yet be divested of some of its hideous aspect."

"I am rejoiced, if anything can rejoice me now," said Henry, "to see you view the subject with so much philosophy."

"Why," said Charles, "you made a remark of your own, which enabled me, viewing the matter in its very worst and most hideous aspect, to gather hope."

"What was that?"

"You said, properly and naturally enough, that if ever we felt that there was such a weight of evidence in favour of a belief in the existence of vampyres that we are compelled to succumb to it, we might as well receive all the popular feelings and superstitions concerning them likewise."

"I did. Where is the mind to pause, when once we open it to the reception of such things?"

"Well, then, if that be the case, we will watch this vampire and catch it."

"Catch it?"

"Yes; surely it can be caught; as I understand, this species of being is not like an apparition, that may be composed of thin air, and utterly impalpable to the human touch, but it consists of a revivified corpse."

"Yes, yes."

"Then it is tangible and destructible. By Heaven! if ever I catch a glimpse of any such thing, it shall drag me to its home, be that where it may, or I will make it prisoner."

"Oh, Charles! you know not the feeling of horror that will come across you when you do. You have no idea of how the warm blood will seem to curdle in your veins, and how you will be paralysed in every limb."

"Did you feel so?"

"I did."

"I will endeavour to make head against such feelings. The love of Flora shall enable me to vanquish them. Think you it will come again to-morrow?"

"I can have no thought the one way or the other."

"It may. We must arrange among us all, Henry, some plan of watching which, without completely prostrating our health and strength, will always provide that one shall be up all night and on the alert."

"It must be done."

"Flora ought to sleep with the consciousness now that she has ever at hand some intrepid and well-armed protector, who is not only himself prepared to defend her, but who can in a moment give an alarm to us all, in case of necessity requiring it."

"It would be a dreadful capture to make to seize a vampyre," said Henry.

"Not at all; it would be a very desirable one. Being a corpse revivified, it is capable of complete destruction, so as to render it no longer a scourge to anyone."

"Charles, Charles, are you jesting with me, or do you really give any credence to the story?"

"My dear friend, I always make it a rule to take things at their worst, and then I cannot be disappointed. I am content to reason upon this matter as if the fact of the existence of a vampyre were thoroughly established, and then to think upon what is best to be done about it."

"You are right."

"If it should turn out then that there is an error in the fact, well and good—we are all the better off; but if otherwise, we are prepared, and armed at all points."

"Let it be so, then. It strikes me, Charles, that you will be the coolest and the calmest among us all on this emergency; but the hour now waxes late, I will get them to prepare a chamber for you, and at least to-night, after what has occurred already, I should think we can be under no apprehension."

"Probably not. But, Henry, if you would allow me to sleep in that room where the portrait hangs of him whom you suppose to be the vampyre, I should prefer it."

"Prefer it!"

"Yes; I am not one who courts danger for danger's sake, but I would rather occupy that room, to see if the vampyre, who perhaps has a partiality for it, will pay me a visit."

"As you please, Charles. You can have the apartment. It is in the same state as when occupied by Flora. Nothing has been, I believe, removed from it."

"You will let me, then, while I remain here, call it my room?"

"Assuredly."

This arrangement was accordingly made to the surprise of all the household, not one of whom would, indeed, have slept, or attempted to sleep there for any amount of reward. But Charles Holland had his own reasons for preferring that chamber, and he was conducted to it in the course of half an hour by Henry, who looked around it with a shudder, as he bade his young friend good night.

CHAPTER XII.

CHARLES HOLLAND'S SAD FEELINGS. —THE PORTRAIT. —THE OCCURRENCE OF THE NIGHT AT THE HALL.

Charles Holland wished to be alone, if ever any human being had wished fervently to be so. His thoughts were most fearfully oppressive.

The communication that had been made to him by Henry Bannerworth, had about it too many strange, confirmatory circumstances to enable him to treat it, in his own mind, with the disrespect that some mere freak of a distracted and weak imagination would, most probably, have received from him.

He had found Flora in a state of excitement which could arise only from some such terrible cause as had been mentioned by her brother, and then he was, from an occurrence which certainly never could have entered into his calculations, asked to forego the bright dream of happiness which he had held so long and so rapturously to his heart.

How truly he found that the course of true love ran not smooth; and yet how little would anyone have suspected that from such a cause as that which now oppressed his mind, any obstruction would arise.

Flora might have been fickle and false; he might have seen some other fairer face, which might have enchained his fancy, and woven for him a new heart's chain; death might have stepped between him and the realization of his fondest hopes; loss of fortune might have made the love cruel which would have yoked to its distresses a young and beautiful girl, reared in the lap of luxury, and who was not, even by those who loved her, suffered to feel, even in later years, any of the pinching necessities of the family.

All these things were possible—some of them were probable; and yet none of them had occurred. She loved him still; and he, although he had looked on many a fair face, and basked in the sunny smiles of beauty, had never for a moment forgotten her faith, or lost his devotion to his own dear English girl.

Fortune he had enough for both; death had not even threatened to rob him of the prize of such a noble and faithful heart which he had won. But a horrible superstition had arisen, which seemed to place at once an impassable abyss between them, and to say to him, in a voice of thundering denunciation,—

"Charles Holland, will you have a vampyre for your bride?"

The thought was terrific. He paced the gloomy chamber to and fro with rapid strides, until the idea came across his mind that by so doing he might not only be proclaiming to his kind entertainers how much he was mentally distracted, but he likewise might be seriously distracting them.

The moment this occurred to him he sat down, and was profoundly still for some time. He then glanced at the light which had been given to him, and he found himself almost unconsciously engaged in a mental calculation as to how long it would last him in the night.

Half ashamed, then, of such terrors, as such a consideration would seem to indicate, he was on the point of hastily extinguishing it, when he happened to cast his eyes on the now mysterious and highly interesting portrait in the panel.

The picture, as a picture, was well done, whether it was a correct likeness or not of the party whom it represented. It was one of those kind of portraits that seem so life-like, that, as you look at them, they seem to return your gaze fully, and even to follow you with their eyes from place to place.

By candle-light such an effect is more likely to become striking and remarkable than by daylight; and now, as Charles Holland shaded his own eyes from the light, so as to cast its full radiance upon the portrait, he felt wonderfully interested in its life-like appearance.

"Here is true skill," he said; "such as I have not before seen. How strangely this likeness of a man whom I never saw seems to gaze upon me."

Unconsciously, too, he aided the effect, which he justly enough called life-like, by a slight movement of the candle, such as anyone not blessed with nerves of iron would be sure to make, and such a movement made the face look as if it was inspired with vitality.

Charles remained looking at the portrait for a considerable period of time. He found a kind of fascination in it which prevented him from drawing his eyes away from it. It was not fear which induced him to continue gazing on it, but the circumstance that it was a likeness of the man who, after death, was supposed to have borrowed so new and so hideous an existence, combined with its artistic merits, chained him to the spot.

"I shall now," he said, "know that face again, let me see it where I may, or under what circumstances I may. Each feature is now indelibly fixed upon my memory—I never can mistake it."

He turned aside as he uttered these words, and as he did so his eyes fell upon a part of the ornamental frame which composed the edge of the panel, and which seemed to him to be of a different colour from the surrounding portion.

Curiosity and increased interest prompted him at once to make a closer inquiry into the matter; and, by a careful and diligent scrutiny, he was almost induced to come to the positive opinion, that it no very distant period in time past, the portrait had been removed from the place it occupied.

When once this idea, even vague and indistinct as it was, in consequence of the slight grounds he formed it on, had got possession of his mind, he felt most anxious to prove its verification or its fallacy.

He held the candle in a variety of situations, so that its light fell in different ways on the picture; and the more he examined it, the more he felt convinced that it must have been moved lately.

It would appear as if, in its removal, a piece of the old oaken carved framework of the panel had been accidentally broken off, which caused the new look of the fracture, and that this accident, from the nature of the broken bit of framing, could have occurred in any other way than from an actual or attempted removal of the picture, he felt was extremely unlikely.

He set down the candle on a chair near at hand, and tried if the panel was fast in its place. Upon the very first touch, he felt convinced it was not so, and that it easily moved. How to get it out, though, presented a difficulty, and to get it out was tempting.

"Who knows," he said to himself, "what may be behind it? This is an old baronial sort of hall, and the greater portion of it was, no doubt, built at a time when the construction of such places as hidden chambers and intricate staircases were, in all buildings of importance, considered a desiderata."

That he should make some discovery behind the portrait, now became an idea that possessed him strongly, although he certainly had no definite grounds for really supposing that he should do so. Perhaps the wish was more father to the thought than he, in the partial state of excitement he was in, really imagined; but so it was. He felt convinced that he should not be satisfied until he had removed that panel from the wall, and seen what was immediately behind it.

After the panel containing the picture had been placed where it was, it appeared that pieces of moulding had been inserted all around, which had had the effect of keeping it in its place, and it was a fracture of one of these pieces which had first called Charles Holland's attention to the probability of the picture having been removed. That he should have to get two, at least, of the pieces of moulding away, before he could hope to remove the picture, was to him quite apparent, and he was considering how he should accomplish such a result, when he was suddenly startled by a knock at his chamber door.

Until that sudden demand for admission at his door came, he scarcely knew to what a nervous state he had worked himself up. It was an odd sort of tap—one only—a single tap, as if someone demanded admittance, and wished to awaken his attention with the least possible chance of disturbing anyone else.

"Come in," said Charles, for he knew he had not fastened his door; "come in."

There was no reply, but after a moment's pause, the same sort of low tap came again.

Again he cried "come in," but, whoever it was, seemed determined that the door should be opened for him, and no movement was made from the outside. A third time the tap came, and Charles was very close to the door when he heard it, for with a noiseless step he had approached it intending to open it. The instant this third mysterious demand for admission came, he did open it wide. There was no one there! In an instant he crossed the threshold into the corridor, which ran right and left. A window at one end of it now sent in the moon's rays, so that it was tolerably light, but he could see no one. Indeed, to look for any one, he felt sure was needless, for he had opened his chamber-door almost simultaneously with the last knock for admission.

"It is strange," he said, as he lingered on the threshold of his room door for some moments; "my imagination could not so completely deceive me. There was most certainly a demand for admission."
Slowly, then, he returned to his room again, and closed the door behind him.

"One thing is evident," he said, "that if I am in this apartment to be subjected to these annoyances, I shall get no rest, which will soon exhaust me."

This thought was a very provoking one, and the more he thought that he should ultimately find a necessity for giving up that chamber he had himself asked as a special favour to be allowed to occupy, the more vexed he became to think what construction might be put upon his conduct for so doing.

"They will all fancy me a coward," he thought, "and that I dare not sleep here. They may not, of course, say so, but they will think that my appearing so bold was one of those acts of bravado which I have not courage to carry fairly out."

Taking this view of the matter was just the way to enlist a young man's pride in staying, under all circumstances, where he was, and, with a slight accession of colour, which, even although he was alone, would visit his cheeks, Charles Holland said aloud,—

"I will remain the occupant of this room come what may, happen what may . No terrors, real or unsubstantial, shall drive me from it: I will brave them all, and remain here to brave them."

Tap came the knock at the door again, and now, with more an air of vexation than fear, Charles turned again towards it, and listened. Tap in another minute again succeeded, and much annoyed, he walked close to the door, and laid his hand upon the lock, ready to open it at the precise moment of another demand for admission being made.

He had not to wait long. In about half a minute it came again, and, simultaneously with the sound, the door flew open. There was no one to be seen; but, as he opened the door, he heard a strange sound in the corridor—a sound which scarcely could be called a groan, and scarcely a sigh, but seemed a compound of both, having the agony of the one combined with the sadness of the other. From what direction it came he could not at the moment decide, but he called out,—

"Who's there? Who's there?"

The echo of his own voice alone answered him for a few moments, and then he heard a door open, and a voice, which he knew to be Henry's, cried,—

"What is it? who speaks?"

"Henry," said Charles.

"Yes—yes—yes."

"I fear I have disturbed you."

"You have been disturbed yourself, or you would not have done so. I shall be with you in a moment."

Henry closed his door before Charles Holland could tell him not to come to him, as he intended to do, for he felt ashamed to have, in a manner of speaking, summoned assistance for so trifling a cause of alarm as that to which he had been subjected. However, he could not go to Henry's chamber to forbid him from coming to his, and, more vexed than before, he retired to his room again to await his coming.

He left the door open now, so that Henry Bannerworth, when he had got on some articles of dress, walked in at once, saying,—

"What has happened, Charles?"

"A mere trifle, Henry, concerning which I am ashamed you should have been at all disturbed."

"Never mind that, I was wakeful."

"I heard a door open, which kept me listening, but I could not decide which door it was till I heard your voice in the corridor."

"Well, it was this door; and I opened it twice in consequence of the repeated taps for admission that came to it; someone has been knocking at it, and, when I go to it, lo! I can see nobody."

"Indeed!"

"Such is the case."

"You surprise me."

"I am very sorry to have disturbed you, because, upon such a ground, I do not feel that I ought to have done so; and, when I called out in the corridor, I assure you it was with no such intention."

"Do not regret it for a moment," said Henry; "you were quite justified in making an alarm on such an occasion."

"It's strange enough, but still it may arise from some accidental cause; admitting, if we did but know it, of some ready enough explanation."

"It may, certainly, but, after what has happened already, we may well suppose a mysterious connection between any unusual sight or sound, and the fearful ones we have already seen."

"Certainly we may."

"How earnestly that strange portrait seems to look upon us, Charles."

"It does, and I have been examining it carefully. It seems to have been removed lately."

"Removed!"

"Yes, I think, as far as I can judge, that it has been taken from its frame; I mean, that the panel on which it is painted has been taken out."

"Indeed!"

"If you touch it you will find it loose, and, upon a close examination, you will perceive that a piece of the moulding which holds it in its place has been chipped off, which is done in such a place that I think it could only have arisen during the removal of the picture."

"You must be mistaken."

"I cannot, of course, take upon myself, Henry, to say precisely such is the case," said Charles.

"But there is no one here to do so."

"That I cannot say. Will you permit me and assist me to remove it? I have a great curiosity to know what is behind it."

"If you have, I certainly will do so. We thought of taking it away altogether, but when Flora left this room the idea was given up as useless. Remain here a few moments, and I will endeavour to find something which shall assist us in its removal."

Henry left the mysterious chamber in order to search in his own for some means of removing the frame-work of the picture, so that the panel would slip easily out, and while he was gone, Charles Holland continued gazing upon it with greater interest, if possible, than before.

In a few minutes Henry returned, and although what he had succeeded in finding were very inefficient implements for the purpose, yet with this aid the two young men set about the task. It is said, and said truly enough, that "where there is a will there is a way," and although the young men had no tools at all adapted for the purpose, they did succeed in removing the moulding from the sides of the panel, and then by a little tapping at one end of it, and using a knife as a lever at the other end of the panel, they got it fairly out.

Disappointment was all they got for their pains. On the other side there was nothing but a rough wooden wall, against which the finer and more nicely finished oak panelling of the chamber rested.

"There is no mystery here," said Henry.

"None whatever," said Charles, as he tapped the wall with his knuckles, and found it all hard and sound. "We are foiled."

"We are indeed."

"I had a strange presentiment, now," added Charles, "that we should make some discovery that would repay us for our trouble. It appears, however, that such is not to be the case; for you see nothing presents itself to us but the most ordinary appearances."

"I perceive as much; and the panel itself, although of more than ordinary thickness, is, after all, but a bit of planed oak, and apparently fashioned for no other object than to paint the portrait on."

"True. Shall we replace it?"

Charles reluctantly assented, and the picture was replaced in its original position. We say Charles reluctantly assented, because, although he had now had ocular demonstration that there was really nothing behind the panel but the ordinary woodwork which might have been expected from the construction of the old house, yet he could not, even with such a fact staring him in the face, get rid entirely of the feeling that had come across him, to the effect that the picture had some mystery or another.

"You are not yet satisfied," said Henry, as he observed the doubtful look of Charles Holland's face.

"My dear friend," said Charles, "I will not deceive you. I am much disappointed that we have made no discovery behind that picture."

"Heaven knows we have mysteries enough in our family," said Henry.

Even as he spoke they were both startled by a strange clattering noise at the window, which was accompanied by a shrill, odd kind of shriek, which sounded fearful and preternatural on the night air.

"What is that?" said Charles.

"God only knows," said Henry.

The two young men naturally turned their earnest gaze in the direction of the window, which we have before remarked was one unprovided with shutters, and there, to their intense surprise, they saw, slowly rising up from the lower part of it, what appeared to be a human form. Henry would have dashed forward, but Charles restrained him, and drawing quickly from its case a large holster pistol, he levelled it carefully at the figure, saying in a whisper,—

"Henry, if I don't hit it, I will consent to forfeit my head."

He pulled the trigger—a loud report followed—the room was filled with smoke, and then all was still. A circumstance, however, had occurred, as a consequence of the concussion of air produced by the discharge of the pistol, which neither of the young men had for the moment calculated upon, and that was the putting out of the only light they there had.

In spite of this circumstance, Charles, the moment he had discharged the pistol, dropped it and sprang forward to the window. But here he was perplexed, for he could not find the old fashioned, intricate fastening which held it shut, and he had to call to Henry,—

"Henry! For God's sake open the window for me, Henry! The fastening of the window is known to you, but not to me. Open it for me."

Thus called upon, Henry sprung forward, and by this time the report of the pistol had effectually alarmed the whole household. The flashing of lights from the corridor came into the room, and in another minute, just as Henry succeeded in getting the window wide open, and Charles Holland had made his way on to the balcony, both George Bannerworth and Mr. Marchdale entered the chamber, eager to know what had occurred. To their eager questions Henry replied,—

"Ask me not now;" and then calling to Charles, he said,—"Remain where you are, Charles, while I run down to the garden immediately beneath the balcony."

"Yes—yes," said Charles.

Henry made prodigious haste, and was in the garden immediately below the bay window in a wonderfully short space of time. He spoke to Charles, saying,—

"Will you now descend? I can see nothing here; but we will both make a search."

George and Mr. Marchdale were both now in the balcony, and they would have descended likewise, but Henry said,—

"Do not all leave the house. God only knows, now, situated as we are, what might happen."

"I will remain, then," said George. "I have been sitting up to-night as the guard, and, therefore, may as well continue to do so."

Marchdale and Charles Holland clambered over the balcony, and easily, from its insignificant height, dropped into the garden. The night was beautiful, and profoundly still. There was not a breath of air sufficient to stir a leaf on a tree, and the very flame of the candle which Charles had left burning in the balcony burnt clearly and steadily, being perfectly unruffled by any wind.

It cast a sufficient light close to the window to make everything very plainly visible, and it was evident at a glance that no object was there, although had that figure, which Charles shot at, and no doubt hit, been flesh and blood, it must have dropped immediately below.

As they looked up for a moment after a cursory examination of the ground, Charles exclaimed,—

"Look at the window! As the light is now situated, you can see the hole made in one of the panes of glass by the passage of the bullet from my pistol."

They did look, and there the clear, round hole, without any starring, which a bullet discharged close to a pane of glass will make in it, was clearly and plainly discernible.

"You must have hit him," said Henry.

"One would think so," said Charles; "for that was the exact place where the figure was."

"And there is nothing here," added Marchdale. "What can we think of these events—what resource has the mind against the most dreadful suppositions concerning them?"

Charles and Henry were both silent; in truth, they knew not what to think, and the words uttered by Marchdale were too strikingly true to dispute for a moment. They were lost in wonder.

"Human means against such an appearance as we saw to-night," said Charles, "are evidently useless."

"My dear young friend," said Marchdale, with much emotion, as he grasped Henry Bannerworth's hand, and the tears stood in his eyes as he did so,—"my dear young friend, these constant alarms will kill you. They will drive you, and all whose happiness you hold dear, distracted. You must control these dreadful feelings, and there is but one chance that I can see of getting now the better of these."

"What is that?"

"By leaving this place forever."

"Alas! am I to be driven from the home of my ancestors from such a cause as this? And whither am I to fly? Where are we to find a refuge?

To leave here will be at once to break up the establishment which is now held together, certainly upon the sufferance of creditors, but still to their advantage, inasmuch as I am doing what no one else would do, namely, paying away to within the scantiest pittance the whole proceeds of the estate that spreads around me.”

“Heed nothing but an escape from such horrors as seem to be accumulating now around you.”

“If I were sure that such a removal would bring with it such a corresponding advantage, I might, indeed, be induced to risk all to accomplish it.”

“As regards poor dear Flora,” said Mr. Marchdale, “I know not what to say, or what to think; she has been attacked by a vampyre, and after this mortal life shall have ended, it is dreadful to think there may be a possibility that she, with all her beauty, all her excellence and purity of mind, and all those virtues and qualities which should make her the beloved of all, and which do, indeed, attach all hearts towards her, should become one of that dreadful tribe of beings who cling to existence by feeding, in the most dreadful manner, upon the life blood of others—oh, it is too dreadful to contemplate! Too horrible—too horrible!”

“Then wherefore speak of it?” said Charles, with some asperity. “Now, by the great God of Heaven, who sees all our hearts, I will not give in to such a horrible doctrine! I will not believe it; and were death itself my portion for my want of faith, I would this moment die in my disbelief of anything so truly fearful!”

“Oh, my young friend,” added Marchdale, “if anything could add to the pangs which all who love, and admire, and respect Flora Bannerworth must feel at the unhappy condition in which she is placed, it would be the noble nature of you, who, under happier auspices, would have been her guide through life, and the happy partner of her destiny.”

“As I will be still.”

“May Heaven forbid it! We are now among ourselves, and can talk freely upon such a subject. Mr. Charles Holland, if you wed, you would look forward to being blessed with children—those sweet ties which bind the sternest hearts to life with so exquisite a bondage. Oh, fancy, then, for a moment, the mother of your babes coming at the still hour of midnight to drain from their veins the very life blood she gave to them. To drive you and them mad with the expected horror of such visitations—to make your nights hideous—your days but so many hours of melancholy retrospection. Oh, you know not the world of terror, on the awful brink of which you stand, when you talk of making Flora Bannerworth a wife."

"Peace! oh, peace!" said Henry.

"Nay, I know my words are unwelcome," continued Mr. Marchdale. "It happens, unfortunately for human nature, that truth and some of our best and holiest feelings are too often at variance, and hold a sad contest—"

"I will hear no more of this," cried Charles Holland.—"I will hear no more."

"I have done," said Mr. Marchdale.

"And 'twere well you had not begun."

"Nay, say not so. I have but done what I considered was a solemn duty."

"Under that assumption of doing duty—a solemn duty—heedless of the feelings and the opinions of others," said Charles, sarcastically, "more mischief is produced—more heart-burnings and anxieties caused, than by any other two causes of such mischievous results combined. I wish to hear no more of this."

"Do not be angered with Mr. Marchdale, Charles," said Henry. "He can have no motive but our welfare in what he says. We should not condemn a speaker because his words may not sound pleasant to our ears."

"By Heaven!" said Charles, with animation, "I meant not to be illiberal; but I will not because I cannot see a man's motives for active interference in the affairs of others, always be ready, merely on account of such ignorance, to jump to a conclusion that they must be estimable."

"Tomorrow, I leave this house," said Marchdale.

"Leave us?" exclaimed Henry.

"Aye, forever."

"Nay, now, Mr. Marchdale, is this generous?"

"Am I treated generously by one who is your own guest, and towards whom I was willing to hold out the honest right hand of friendship?"

Henry turned to Charles Holland, saying,—

"Charles, I know your generous nature. Say you meant no offence to my mother's old friend."

"If to say I meant no offence," said Charles, "is to say I meant no insult, I say it freely."

"Enough," cried Marchdale; "I am satisfied."

"But do not," added Charles, "draw me any more such pictures as the one you have already presented to my imagination, I beg of you. From the storehouse of my own fancy I can find quite enough to make me wretched, if I choose to be so; but again and again do I say I will not allow this monstrous superstition to tread me down, like the tread of a giant on a broken reed. I will contend against it while I have life to do so."

"Bravely spoken."

"And when I desert Flora Bannerworth, may Heaven, from that moment, desert me!"

"Charles!" cried Henry, with emotion, "dear Charles, my more than friend—brother of my heart—noble Charles!"

"Nay, Henry, I am not entitled to your praises. I were base indeed to be other than that which I purpose to be. Come weal or woe—come what may, I am the affianced husband of your sister, and she, and she only, can break asunder the tie that binds me to her."

CHAPTER XIII.

THE OFFER FOR THE HALL.
—THE VISIT TO SIR FRANCIS VARNEY.
—THE STRANGE RESEMBLANCE.
—A DREADFUL SUGGESTION.

The party made a strict search through every nook and corner of the garden, but it proved to be a fruitless one: not the least trace of any one could be found. There was only one circumstance, which was pondered over deeply by them all, and that was that, beneath the window of the room in which Flora and her mother sat while the brothers were on their visit to the vault of their ancestors, were visible marks of blood to a considerable extent.

It will be remembered that Flora had fired a pistol at the spectral appearance, and that immediately upon that it had disappeared, after uttering a sound which might well be construed into a cry of pain from a wound.

That a wound then had been inflicted upon someone, the blood beneath the window now abundantly testified; and when it was discovered, Henry and Charles made a very close examination indeed of the garden, to discover what direction the wounded figure, be it man or vampyre, had taken.

But the closest scrutiny did not reveal to them a single spot of blood, beyond the space immediately beneath the window;—there the apparition seemed to have received its wound, and then, by some mysterious means, to have disappeared.

At length, wearied with the continued excitement, combined with want of sleep, to which they had been subjected, they returned to the hall.

Flora, with the exception of the alarm she experienced from the firing of the pistol, had met with no disturbance, and that, in order to spare her painful reflections, they told her was merely done as a precautionary measure, to proclaim to anyone who might be lurking in the garden that the inmates of the house were ready to defend themselves against any aggression.

Whether or not she believed this kind deceit they knew not. She only sighed deeply, and wept. The probability is, that she more than suspected the vampyre had made another visit, but they forbore to press the point; and, leaving her with her mother, Henry and George went from her chamber again—the former to endeavour to seek some repose, as it would be his turn to watch on the succeeding night, and the latter to resume his station in a small room close to Flora's chamber, where it had been agreed watch and ward should be kept by turns while the alarm lasted.

At length, the morning again dawned upon that unhappy family, and to none were its beams more welcome.

The birds sang their pleasant carols beneath the window. The sweet, deep-coloured autumnal sun shone upon all objects with a golden luster; and to look abroad, upon the beaming face of nature, no one could for a moment suppose, except from sad experience, that there were such things as gloom, misery, and crime, upon the earth.

"And must I," said Henry, as he gazed from a window of the hall upon the undulating park, the majestic trees, the flowers, the shrubs, and the many natural beauties with which the place was full,—"must I be chased from this spot, the home of myself and of my kindred, by a phantom—must I indeed seek refuge elsewhere, because my own home has become hideous?"

It was indeed a cruel and a painful thought! It was one he yet would not, could not be convinced was absolutely necessary. But now the sun was shining: it was morning; and the feelings, which found a home in his breast amid the darkness, the stillness, and the uncertainty of night, were chased away by those glorious beams of sunlight, that fell upon hill, valley, and stream, and the thousand sweet sounds of life and animation that filled that sunny air!

Such a revulsion of feeling was natural enough. Many of the distresses and mental anxieties of night vanish with the night, and those which oppressed the heart of Henry Bannerworth were considerably modified.

He was engaged in these reflections when he heard the sound of the lodge bell, and as a visitor was now somewhat rare at this establishment, he waited with some anxiety to see to whom he was indebted for so early a call.

In the course of a few minutes, one of the servants came to him with a letter in her hand.

It bore a large handsome seal, and, from its appearance, would seem to have come from some personage of consequence. A second glance at it showed him the name of "Varney" in the corner, and, with some degree of vexation, he muttered to himself, "Another condoling epistle from the troublesome neighbour whom I have not yet seen."

"If you please, sir," said the servant who had brought him the letter, "as I'm here, and you are here, perhaps you'll have no objection to give me what I'm to have for the day and two nights as I've been here, cos I can't stay in a family as is so familiar with all sorts o' ghostesses: I ain't used to such company."

"What do you mean?" said Henry.

The question was a superfluous one—: too well he knew what the woman meant, and the conviction came across his mind strongly that no domestic would consent to live long in a house which was subject to such dreadful visitations.

"What does I mean!" said the woman,—"Why, sir, if it's all the same to you, I don't myself come of a wampyre family, and I don't choose to remain in a house where there is sich things encouraged. That's what I means, sir."

"What wages are owing to you?" said Henry.

"Why, as to wages, I only comed here by the day."

"Go, then, and settle with my mother. The sooner you leave this house, the better."

"Oh, indeed. I'm sure I don't want to stay."

This woman was one of those who were always armed at all points for a row, and she had no notion of concluding any engagement, of any character whatever, without some disturbance; therefore, to see Henry take what she said with such provoking calmness was aggravating in the extreme; but there was no help for such a source of vexation. She could find no other ground of quarrel than what was connected with the vampyre, and, as Henry would not quarrel with her on such a score, she was compelled to give it up in despair.

When Henry found himself alone, and free from the annoyance of this woman, he turned his attention to the letter he held in his hand, and which, from the autograph in the corner, he knew came from his new neighbour, Sir Francis Varney, whom, by some chance or another, he had never yet seen.

To his great surprise, he found that the letter contained the following words:—

> *Dear Sir,—As a neighbour, by purchase of an estate contiguous to your own, I am quite sure you have excused, and taken in good part, the cordial offer I made to you of friendship and service some short time since; but now, in addressing to you a distinct proposition, I trust I shall meet with an indulgent consideration, whether such proposition be accordant with your views or not.*
>
> *What I have heard from common report induces me to believe that Bannerworth Hall cannot be a desirable residence for yourself, or your amiable sister. If I am right in that conjecture, and you have any serious thought of leaving the place, I would earnestly recommend you, as one having some experience in such descriptions of property, to sell it at once.*
>
> *Now, the proposition with which I conclude this letter is, I know, of a character to make you doubt the*

disinterestedness of such advice; but that it is disinterested, nevertheless, is a fact of which I can assure my own heart, and of which I beg to assure you. I propose, then, should you, upon consideration, decide upon such a course of proceeding, to purchase of you the Hall. I do not ask for a bargain on account of any extraneous circumstances which may at the present time depreciate the value of the property, but I am willing to give a fair price for it. Under these circumstances, I trust, sir, that you will give a kindly consideration to my offer, and even if you reject it, I hope that, as neighbours, we may live long in peace and amity, and in the interchange of those good offices which should subsist between us. Awaiting your reply,

Believe me to be, dear sir,

Your very obedient servant,

FRANCIS VARNEY.
To Henry Bannerworth, Esq.

Henry, after having read this most unobjectionable letter through, folded it up again, and placed it in his pocket. Clasping his hands, then, behind his back, a favourite attitude of his when he was in deep contemplation, he paced to and fro in the garden for some time in deep thought.

"How strange," he muttered. "It seems that every circumstance combines to induce me to leave my old ancestral home. It appears as if everything now that happened had that direct tendency. What can be the meaning of all this? 'Tis very strange—amazingly strange. Here arise circumstances which are enough to induce any man to leave a particular place. Then a friend, in whose single-mindedness and judgment I know I can rely, advises the step, and immediately upon the back of that comes a fair and candid offer."

There was an apparent connection between all these circumstances which much puzzled Henry. He walked to and fro for nearly an hour, until he heard a hasty footstep approaching him, and upon looking in the direction from whence it came, he saw Mr. Marchdale.

"I will seek Marchdale's advice," he said, "upon this matter. I will hear what he says concerning it."

"Henry," said Marchdale, when he came sufficiently near to him for conversation, "why do you remain here alone?"

"I have received a communication from our neighbour, Sir Francis Varney," said Henry.

"Indeed!"

"It is here. Peruse it for yourself, and then tell me, Marchdale, candidly what you think of it."

"I suppose," said Marchdale, as he opened the letter, "it is another friendly note of condolence on the state of your domestic affairs, which, I grieve to say, from the prattling of domestics, whose tongues it is quite impossible to silence, have become food for gossip all over the neighbouring villages and estates."

"If anything could add another pang to those I have already been made to suffer," said Henry, "it would certainly arise from being made the food of vulgar gossip. But read the letter, Marchdale. You will find its contents of a more important character than you anticipate."

"Indeed!" said Marchdale, as he ran his eyes eagerly over the note. When he had finished it he glanced at Henry, who then said,—

"Well, what is your opinion?"

"I know not what to say, Henry. You know that my own advice to you has been to get rid of this place."

"It has."

"With the hope that the disagreeable affair connected with it now may remain connected with it as a house, and not with you and yours as a family."

"It may be so."

"There appears to me every likelihood of it."

"I do not know," said Henry, with a shudder. "I must confess, Marchdale, that to my own perceptions it seems more probable that the infliction we have experienced from the strange visitor, who seems now resolved to pester us with visits, will rather attach to a family than to a house. The vampyre may follow us."

"If so, of course the parting with the Hall would be a great pity, and no gain."

"None in the least."

"Henry, a thought has struck me."

"Let's hear it, Marchdale."

"It is this:—Suppose you were to try the experiment of leaving the Hall without selling it. Suppose for one year you were to let it to someone, Henry."

"It might be done."

"Ay, and it might, with very great promise and candour, be proposed to this very gentleman, Sir Francis Varney, to take it for one year, to see how he liked it before becoming the possessor of it. Then if he found himself tormented by the vampyre, he need not complete the purchase, or if you found that the apparition followed you from hence, you might yourself return, feeling that perhaps here, in the spots familiar to your youth, you might be most happy, even under such circumstances as at present oppress you."

"Most happy!" ejaculated Henry.

"Perhaps I should not have used that word."

"I am sure you should not," said Henry, "when you speak of me."

"Well—well; let us hope that the time may not be very far distant when I may use the term happy, as applied to you, in the most conclusive and the strongest manner it can be used."

"Oh," said Henry, "I will hope; but do not mock me with it now, Marchdale, I pray you."

"Heaven forbid that I should mock you!"

"Well—well; I do not believe you are the man to do so to anyone. But about this affair of the house."

"Distinctly, then, if I were you, I would call upon Sir Francis Varney, and make him an offer to become a tenant of the Hall for twelve months, during which time you could go where you please, and test the fact of absence ridding you or not ridding you of the dreadful visitant who makes the night here truly hideous."

"I will speak to my mother, to George, and to my sister of the matter. They shall decide."

Mr. Marchdale now strove in every possible manner to raise the spirits of Henry Bannerworth, by painting to him the future in far more radiant colours than the present, and endeavouring to induce a belief in his mind that a short period of time might after all replace in his mind, and in the minds of those who were naturally so dear to him, all their wonted serenity.

Henry, although he felt not much comfort from these kindly efforts, yet could feel gratitude to him who made them; and after expressing such a feeling to Marchdale, in strong terms, he repaired to the house, in order to hold a solemn consultation with those whom he felt ought to be consulted as well as himself as to what steps should be taken with regard to the Hall.

The proposition, or rather the suggestion, which had been made by Marchdale upon the proposition of Sir Francis Varney, was in every respect so reasonable and just, that it met, as was to be expected, with the concurrence of every member of the family.

Flora's cheeks almost resumed some of their wonted colour at the mere thought now of leaving that home to which she had been at one time so much attached.

"Yes, dear Henry," she said, "let us leave here if you are agreeable so to do, and in leaving this house, we will believe that we leave behind us a world of terror."

"Flora," remarked Henry, in a tone of slight reproach, "if you were so anxious to leave Bannerworth Hall, why did you not say so before this proposition came from other mouths? You know your feelings upon such a subject would have been laws to me."

"I knew you were attached to the old house," said Flora; "and, besides, events have come upon us all with such fearful rapidity, there has scarcely been time to think."

"True—true."

"And you will leave, Henry?"

"I will call upon Sir Francis Varney myself, and speak to him upon the subject."

A new impetus to existence appeared now to come over the whole family, at the idea of leaving a place which always would be now associated in their minds with so much terror. Each member of the family felt happier, and breathed more freely than before, so that the change which had come over them seemed almost magical. And Charles Holland, too, was much better pleased, and he whispered to Flora,—

"Dear Flora, you will now surely no longer talk of driving from you the honest heart that loves you?"

"Hush, Charles, hush!" she said; "meet me an hour hence in the garden, and we will talk of this."

"That hour will seem an age," he said.

Henry, now, having made a determination to see Sir Francis Varney, lost no time in putting it into execution. At Mr. Marchdale's own request, he took him with him, as it was desirable to have a third person present in the sort of business negotiation which was going on. The estate which had been so recently entered upon by the person calling himself Sir Francis Varney, and which common report said he had purchased, was a small, but complete property, and situated so close to the grounds connected with Bannerworth Hall, that a short walk soon placed Henry and Mr. Marchdale before the residence of this gentleman, who had shown so kindly a feeling towards the Bannerworth family.

"Have you seen Sir Francis Varney?" asked Henry of Mr. Marchdale, as he rung the gate-bell.

"I have not. Have you?"

"No; I never saw him. It is rather awkward our both being absolute strangers to his person."

"We can but send in our names, however; and, from the great vein of courtesy that runs through his letter, I have no doubt but we shall receive the most gentlemanly reception from him."

A servant in handsome livery appeared at the iron-gates, which opened upon a lawn in the front of Sir Francis Varney's house, and to this domestic Henry Bannerworth handed his card, on which he had written, in pencil, likewise the name of Mr. Marchdale.

"If your master," he said, "is within, we shall be glad to see him."

"Sir Francis is at home, sir," was the reply, "although not very well. If you will be pleased to walk in, I will announce you to him."

Henry and Marchdale followed the man into a handsome enough reception-room, where they were desired to wait while their names were announced.

"Do you know if this gentleman be a baronet," said Henry, "or a knight merely?"

"I really do not; I never saw him in my life, or heard of him before he came into this neighbourhood."

"And I have been too much occupied with the painful occurrences of this hall to know anything of our neighbours. I dare say Mr. Chillingworth, if we had thought to ask him, would have known something concerning him."

"No doubt."

This brief colloquy was put an end to by the servant, who said,—

"My master, gentlemen, is not very well; but he begs me to present his best compliments, and to say he is much gratified with your visit, and will be happy to see you in his study."

Henry and Marchdale followed the man up a flight of stone stairs, and then they were conducted through a large apartment into a smaller one. There was very little light in this small room; but at the moment of their entrance a tall man, who was seated, rose, and, touching the spring of a blind that was to the window, it was up in a moment, admitting a broad glare of light. A cry of surprise, mingled with terror, came from Henry Bannerworth's lip. *The original of the portrait on the panel stood before him!* There was the lofty stature, the long, sallow face, the slightly projecting teeth, the dark, lustrous, although somewhat sombre eyes; the expression of the features—all were alike.

"Are you unwell, sir?" said Sir Francis Varney, in soft, mellow accents, as he handed a chair to the bewildered Henry.

"God of Heaven!" said Henry; "how like!"

"You seem surprised, sir. Have you ever seen me before?"

Sir Francis drew himself up to his full height, and cast a strange glance upon Henry, whose eyes were riveted upon his face, as if with a species of fascination which he could not resist.

"Marchdale," Henry gasped; "Marchdale, my friend, Marchdale. I—I am surely mad."

"Hush! be calm," whispered Marchdale.

"Calm—calm—can you not see? Marchdale, is this a dream? Look—look—oh! look."

"For God's sake, Henry, compose yourself."

"Is your friend often thus?" said Sir Francis Varney, with the same mellifluous tone which seemed habitual to him.

"No, sir, he is not; but recent circumstances have shattered his nerves; and, to tell the truth, you bear so strong a resemblance to an old portrait in his house, that I do not wonder so much as I otherwise should at his agitation."

"Indeed."

"A resemblance!" said Henry; "a resemblance! God of Heaven! it is the face itself."

"You much surprise me," said Sir Francis.

Henry sunk into the chair which was near him, and he trembled violently. The rush of painful thoughts and conjectures that came through his mind was enough to make any one tremble. "Is this the vampyre?" was the horrible question that seemed impressed upon his very brain, in letters of flame. "Is this the vampyre?"

"Are you better, sir?" said Sir Francis Varney, in his bland, musical voice. "Shall I order any refreshment for you?"

"No—no," gasped Henry; "for the love of truth tell me! Is—is your name really Varney!"

"Sir?"

"Have you no other name to which, perhaps, a better title you could urge?"

"Mr. Bannerworth, I can assure you that I am too proud of the name of the family to which I belong to exchange it for any other, be it what it may."

"How wonderfully like!"

"I grieve to see you so much distressed. Mr. Bannerworth. I presume ill health has thus shattered your nerves?"

"No; ill health has not done the work. I know not what to say, Sir Francis Varney, to you; but recent events in my family have made the sight of you full of horrible conjectures."

"What mean you, sir?"

"You know, from common report, that we have had a fearful visitor at our house."

"A vampyre, I have heard," said Sir Francis Varney, with a bland, and almost beautiful smile, which displayed his white glistening teeth to perfection.

"Yes; a vampyre, and—and—"

"I pray you go on, sir; you surely are far above the vulgar superstition of believing in such matters?"

"My judgment is assailed in too many ways and shapes for it to hold out probably as it ought to do against so hideous a belief, but never was it so much bewildered as now."

"Why so?"

"Because—"

"Nay, Henry," whispered Mr. Marchdale, "it is scarcely civil to tell Sir Francis to his face, that he resembles a vampyre."

"I must, I must."

"Pray, sir," interrupted Varney to Marchdale, "permit Mr. Bannerworth to speak here freely. There is nothing in the whole world I so much admire as candour."

"Then you so much resemble the vampyre," added Henry, "that—that I know not what to think."

"Is it possible?" said Varney.

"It is a damning fact."

"Well, it's unfortunate for me, I presume? Ah!" Varney gave a twinge of pain, as if some sudden bodily ailment had attacked him severely.

"You are unwell, sir?" said Marchdale.

"No, no—no," he said; "I—hurt my arm, and happened accidentally to touch the arm of this chair with it."

"A hurt?" said Henry.

"Yes, Mr. Bannerworth."

"A—a wound?"

"Yes, a wound, but not much more than skin deep. In fact, little beyond an abrasion of the skin."

"May I inquire how you came by it?"

"Oh, yes. A slight fall."

"Indeed."

"Remarkable, is it not? Very remarkable. We never know a moment when, from same most trifling cause, we may receive really some serious bodily harm. How true it is, Mr. Bannerworth, that in the midst of life we are in death."

"And equally true, perhaps," said Henry, "that in the midst of death there may be found a horrible life."

"Well, I should not wonder. There are really so many strange things in this world, that I have left off wondering at anything now."

"There are strange things," said Henry. "You wish to purchase of me the Hall, sir?"

"If you wish to sell."

"You—you are perhaps attached to the place? Perhaps you recollected it, sir, long ago?"

"Not very long," smiled Sir Francis Varney. "It seems a nice comfortable old house; and the grounds, too, appear to be amazingly well wooded, which, to one of rather a romantic temperament like myself, is always an additional charm to a place. I was extremely pleased with it the first time I beheld it, and a desire to call myself the owner of it took possession of my mind. The scenery is remarkable for its beauty, and, from what I have seen of it, it is rarely to be excelled. No doubt you are greatly attached to it."

"It has been my home from infancy," returned Henry, "and being also the residence of my ancestors for centuries, it is natural that I should be so."

"True—true."

"The house, no doubt, has suffered much," said Henry, "within the last hundred years."

"No doubt it has. A hundred years is a tolerable long space of time, you know."

"It is, indeed. Oh, how any human life which is spun out to such an extent, must lose its charms, by losing all its fondest and dearest associations."

"Ah, how true," said Sir Francis Varney. He had some minutes previously touched a bell, and at this moment a servant brought in on a tray some wine and refreshments.

CHAPTER XIV.

HENRY'S AGREEMENT WITH SIR FRANCIS VARNEY. —THE SUDDEN ARRIVAL AT THE HALL. —FLORA'S ALARM.

On the tray which the servant brought into the room, were refreshments of different kinds, including wine, and after waving his hand for the domestic to retire, Sir Francis Varney said,—

"You will be better, Mr. Bannerworth, for a glass of wine after your walk, and you too, sir. I am ashamed to say, I have quite forgotten your name."

"Marchdale."

"Mr. Marchdale. Aye, Marchdale. Pray, sir, help yourself."

"You take nothing yourself?" said Henry.

"I am under a strict regimen," replied Varney. "The simplest diet alone does for me, and I have accustomed myself to long abstinence."

"He will not eat or drink," muttered Henry, abstractedly.

"Will you sell me the Hall?" said Sir Francis Varney.

Henry looked in his face again, from which he had only momentarily withdrawn his eyes, and he was then more struck than ever with the resemblance between him and the portrait on the panel of what had been Flora's chamber. What made that resemblance, too, one about which there could scarcely be two opinions, was the mark or cicatrix of a wound in the forehead, which the painter had slightly indented in the portrait, but which was much more plainly visible on the forehead of Sir Francis Varney. Now that Henry observed this distinctive mark, which he had not done before, he could feel no doubt, and a sickening sensation came over him at the thought that he was actually now in the presence of one of those terrible creatures, vampyres.

"You do not drink," said Varney. "Most young men are not so modest with a decanter of unimpeachable wine before them. I pray you help yourself."

"I cannot."

Henry rose as he spoke, and turning to Marchdale, he said, in addition,—

"Will you come away?"

"If you please," said Marchdale, rising.

"But you have not, my dear sir," said Varney, "given me yet any answer about the Hall?"

"I cannot yet," answered Henry, "I will think. My present impression is, to let you have it on whatever terms you may yourself propose, always provided you consent to one of mine."

"Name it."

"That you never show yourself in my family."

"How very unkind. I understand you have a charming sister, young, beautiful, and accomplished. Shall I confess, now, that I had hopes of making myself agreeable to her?"

"You make yourself agreeable to her? The sight of you would blast her forever, and drive her to madness."

"Am I so hideous?"

"No, but—you are—"

"What am I?"

"Hush, Henry, hush," cried Marchdale. "Remember you are in this gentleman's house."

"True, true. Why does he tempt me to say these dreadful things? I do not want to say them."

"Come away, then—come away at once. Sir Francis Varney, my friend, Mr. Bannerworth, will think over your offer, and let you know. I think you may consider that your wish to become the purchaser of the Hall will be complied with."

"I wish to have it," said Varney, "and I can only say, that if I am master of it, I shall be very happy to see any of the family on a visit at any time."

"A visit!" said Henry, with a shudder. "A visit to the tomb were far more desirable. Farewell, sir."

"Adieu," said Sir Francis Varney, and he made one of the most elegant bows in the world, while there came over his face a peculiarity of expression that was strange, if not painful, to contemplate. In another minute Henry and Marchdale were clear of the house, and with feelings of bewilderment and horror, which beggar all description, poor Henry allowed himself to be led by the arm by Marchdale to some distance, without uttering a word. When he did speak, he said,—

"Marchdale, it would be charity of someone to kill me."

"To kill you!"

"Yes, for I am certain otherwise that I must go mad."

"Nay, nay; rouse yourself."

"This man, Varney, is a vampyre."

"Hush! hush!"

"I tell you, Marchdale," cried Henry, in a wild, excited manner, "he is a vampyre. He is the dreadful being who visited Flora at the still hour of midnight, and drained the life-blood from her veins. He is a vampyre. There are such things. I cannot doubt now. Oh, God, I wish now that your lightnings would blast me, as here I stand, for over into annihilation, for I am going mad to be compelled to feel that such horrors can really have existence."

"Henry—Henry."

"Nay, talk not to me. What can I do? Shall I kill him? Is it not a sacred duty to destroy such a thing? Oh, horror—horror. He must be killed—destroyed—burnt, and the very dust to which he is consumed must be scattered to the winds of Heaven. It would be a deed well done, Marchdale."

"Hush! hush! These words are dangerous."

"I care not."

"What if they were overheard now by unfriendly ears? What might not be the uncomfortable results? I pray you be more cautious what you say of this strange man."

"I must destroy him."

"And wherefore?"

"Can you ask? Is he not a vampyre?"

"Yes; but reflect, Henry, for a moment upon the length to which you might carry out so dangerous an argument. It is said that vampyres are made by vampyres sucking the blood of those who, but for that circumstance, would have died and gone to decay in the tomb along with ordinary mortals; but that being so attacked during life by a vampyre, they themselves, after death, become such."

"Well—well, what is that to me?"

"Have you forgotten Flora?"

A cry of despair came from poor Henry's lips, and in a moment he seemed completely, mentally and physically, prostrated.

"God of Heaven!" he moaned, "I had forgotten her!"

"I thought you had."

"Oh, if the sacrifice of my own life would suffice to put an end to all this accumulating horror, how gladly would I lay it down. Aye, in any way—in any way. No mode of death should appall me. No amount of pain make me shrink. I could smile then upon the destroyer, and say, 'welcome—welcome—most welcome.' "

"Rather, Henry, seek to live for those whom you love than die for them. Your death would leave them desolate. In life you may ward off many a blow of fate from them."

"I may endeavour so to do."

"Consider that Flora may be wholly dependent upon such kindness as you may be able to bestow upon her."

"Charles clings to her."

"Humph!"

"You do not doubt him?"

"My dear friend, Henry Bannerworth, although I am not an old man, yet I am so much older than you that I have seen a great deal of the world, and am, perhaps, far better able to come to accurate judgments with regard to individuals."

"No doubt—no doubt; but yet—"

"Nay, hear me out. Such judgments, founded upon experience, when uttered have all the character of prophecy about them. I, therefore, now prophecy to you that Charles Holland will yet be so stung with horror at the circumstance of a vampire visiting Flora, that he will never make her his wife."

"Marchdale, I differ from you most completely," said Henry. "I know that Charles Holland is the very soul of honour."

"I cannot argue the matter with you. It has not become a thing of fact. I have only sincerely to hope that I am wrong."

"You are, you may depend, entirely wrong. I cannot be deceived in Charles. From you such words produce no effect but one of regret that you should so much err in your estimate of anyone. From anyone but yourself they would have produced in me a feeling of anger I might have found it difficult to smother."

"It has often been my misfortune through life," said Mr. Marchdale, sadly, "to give the greatest offence where I feel the truest friendship, because it is in such quarters that I am always tempted to speak too freely."

"Nay, no offence," said Henry. "I am distracted, and scarcely know what I say. Marchdale, I know you are my sincere friend—but, as I tell you, I am nearly mad.”

“My dear Henry, be calmer. Consider upon what is to be said concerning this interview at home.”

“Aye; that is a consideration.”

“I should not think it advisable to mention the disagreeable fact, that in your neighbor you think you have found out the nocturnal disturber of your family.”

“No—no.”

“I would say nothing of it. It is not at all probable that, after what you have said to him this Sir Francis Varney, or whatever his real name may be will obtrude himself upon you.”

“If he should he die.”

“He will, perhaps, consider that such a step would be dangerous to him.”

“It would be fatal, so help me. However, and then would I take especial care that no power of resuscitation should ever enable that man again to walk the earth.”

“They say that only way of destroying a vampyre is to fix him to the earth with a stake, so that he cannot move, and then, of course, decomposition will take its course, as in ordinary cases.”

“Fire would consume him, and be a quicker process,” said Henry. “But these are fearful reflections, and, for the present, we will not pursue them. Now to play the hypocrite, and endeavour to look composed and serene to my mother, and to Flora while my heart is breaking.”

The two friends had by this time reached the hall, and leaving his friend Marchdale, Henry Bannerworth, with feelings of the most unenviable description, slowly made his way to the apartment occupied by his mother and sister.

CHAPTER XV.

THE OLD ADMIRAL AND HIS SERVANT.
—THE COMMUNICATION FROM THE LANDLORD
OF THE NELSON'S ARMS.

While those matters of most grave and serious import were going on at the Hall, while each day, and almost each hour in each day, was producing more and more conclusive evidence upon a matter which at first had seemed too monstrous to be at all credited, it may well be supposed what a wonderful sensation was produced among the gossip-mongers of the neighbourhood by the exaggerated reports that had reached them.

The servants, who had left the Hall on no other account, as they declared, but sheer fright at the awful visits of the vampyre, spread the news far and wide, so that in the adjoining villages and market-towns the vampyre of Bannerworth Hall became quite a staple article of conversation.

Such a positive godsend for the lovers of the marvelous had not appeared in the countryside within the memory of that sapient individual—the oldest inhabitant.

And, moreover, there was one thing which staggered some people of better education and maturer judgments, and that was, that the more they took pains to inquire into the matter, in order, if possible, to put an end to what they considered a gross lie from the commencement, the more evidence they found to stagger their own senses upon the subject.

Everywhere then, in every house, public as well as private, something was being continually said of the vampyre. Nursery maids began to think a vampyre vastly superior to "old scratch and old bogie" as a means of terrifying their infant charges into quietness, if not to sleep, until they themselves became too much afraid upon the subject to mention it.

But nowhere was gossiping carried on upon the subject with more systematic fervour than at an inn called the Nelson's Arms, which was in the high street of the nearest market town to the Hall.

There, it seemed as if the lovers of the horrible made a point of holding their headquarters, and so thirsty did the numerous discussions make the guests, that the landlord was heard to declare that he, from his heart, really considered a vampyre as very nearly equal to a contested election.

It was towards evening of the same day that Marchdale and Henry made their visit to Sir Francis Varney, that a postchaise drew up to the inn we have mentioned. In the vehicle were two persons of exceedingly dissimilar appearance and general aspect.

One of these people was a man who seemed fast verging upon seventy years of age, although, from his still ruddy and embrowned complexion and stentorian voice, it was quite evident he intended yet to keep time at arm's-length for many years to come.

He was attired in ample and expensive clothing, but every article had a naval animus about it, if we may be allowed such an expression with regard to clothing. On his buttons was an anchor, and the general assortment and colour of the clothing as nearly assimilated as possible to the undress naval uniform of an officer of high rank some fifty or sixty years ago.

His companion was a younger man, and about his appearance there was no secret at all. He was a genuine sailor, and he wore the shore costume of one. He was hearty-looking, and well dressed, and evidently well fed.

As the chaise drove up to the door of the inn, this man made an observation to the other to the following effect,—

"A-hoy!"

"Well, you lubber, what now?" cried the other.

"They call this the Nelson's Arms; and you know, shiver me, that for the best half of his life he had but one."

"D—n you!" was the only rejoinder he got for this observation; but, with that, he seemed very well satisfied.

"Heave to!" he then shouted to the postilion, who was about to drive the chaise into the yard. "Heave to, you lubberly son of a gun! we don't want to go into dock."

"Ah!" said the old man, "Let's get out, Jack. This is the port; and, do you hear, and be cursed to you, let's have no swearing, d—n you, nor bad language, you lazy swab."

"Aye, aye," cried Jack; "I've not been ashore now a matter o' ten years, and not larnt a little shore-going politeness, admiral, I ain't been your *walley de sham* without larning a little about land reckonings. Nobody would take me for a sailor now, I'm thinking, admiral."

"Hold your noise!"

"Aye, aye, sir."

Jack, as he was called, bundled out of the chaise when the door was opened, with a movement so closely resembling what would have ensued had he been dragged out by the collar, that one was tempted almost to believe that such a feat must have been accomplished all at once by some invisible agency.

He then assisted the old gentleman to alight, and the landlord of the inn commenced the usual profusion of bows with which a passenger by a postchaise is usually welcomed in preference to one by a stage coach.

"Be quiet, will you!" shouted the admiral, for such indeed he was. "Be quiet."

"Best accommodation, sir—good wine—well-aired beds—good attendance—fine air—"

"Belay there," said Jack; and he gave the landlord what no doubt he considered a gentle admonition, but which consisted of such a dig in the ribs, that he made as many evolutions as the clown in a pantomime when he vociferates hot codlings.

"Now, Jack, where's the sailing instructions?" said his master.

"Here, sir, in the locker," said Jack, as he took from his pocket a letter, which he handed to the admiral.

"Won't you step in, sir?" said the landlord, who had begun now to recover a little from the dig in the ribs.

"What's the use of coming into port and paying harbour dues, and all that sort of thing, till we know if it's the right, you lubber, eh?"

"No; oh, dear me, sir, of course—God bless me, what can the old gentleman mean?"

The admiral opened the letter, and read:—

If you stop at the Nelson's Aims at Uxotter, you will hear of me, and I can be sent for, when I will tell you more.

Yours, very obediently and humbly,
JOSIAH CRINKLES.

"Who the deuce is he?"

"This is Uxotter, sir," said the landlord; "and here you are, sir, at the Nelson's Arms. Good beds—good wine—good—"

"Silence!"

"Yes, sir—oh, of course."

"Who the devil is Josiah Crinkles?"

"Ha! ha! ha! ha! Makes me laugh, sir. Who the devil indeed! They do say the devil and lawyers, sir, know something of each other—makes me smile."

"I'll make you smile on the other side of that d———d great hatchway of a mouth of yours in a minute. Who is Crinkles?"

"Oh, Mr. Crinkles, sir, everybody knows, most respectable attorney, sir, indeed, highly respectable man, sir."

"A lawyer?"

"Yes, sir, a lawyer."

"Well, I'm d———d!"

Jack gave a long whistle, and both master and man looked at each other aghast.

"Now, hang me!" cried the admiral, "if ever I was so taken in in all my life."

"Aye, aye, sir," said Jack.

"To come a hundred and seventy miles to see a d———d swab of a rascally lawyer."

"Aye, aye, sir."

"I'll smash him—Jack!"

"Yer honour?"

"Get into the chaise again."

"Well, but where's Master Charles? Lawyers, in course, sir, is all blessed rogues; but, howsomdever, he may have for once in his life this here one of 'em have told us of the right channel, and if so be as he has, don't be the Yankee to leave him among the pirates. I'm ashamed on you."

"You infernal scoundrel; how dare you preach to me in such a way, you lubberly rascal?"

"Cos you desarves it."

"Mutiny—mutiny—by Jove! Jack, I'll have you put in irons—you're a scoundrel, and no seaman."

"No seaman!—no seaman!"

"Not a bit of one."

"Very good. It's time, then, as I was off the purser's books. Good bye to you; I only hopes as you may get a better seaman to stick to you and be your *walley de sham* nor Jack Pringle, that's all the harm I wish you. You didn't call me no seaman in the Bay of Corfu, when the bullets were scuttling our nobs."

"Jack, you rascal, give us your fin. Come here, you d——d villain. You'll leave me, will you?"

"Not if I know it."

"Come in, then."

"Don't tell me I'm no seaman. Call me a wagabone if you like, but don't hurt my feelings. There I'm as tender as a baby, I am.—Don't do it."

"Confound you, who is doing it?"

"The devil."

"Who is?"

"Don't, then."

Thus wrangling, they entered the inn, to the great amusement of several bystanders, who had collected to hear the altercation between them.

"Would you like a private room, sir?" said the landlord.

"What's that to you?" said Jack.

"Hold your noise, will you?" cried his master. "Yes, I should like a private room, and some grog."

"Strong as the devil!" put in Jack.

"Yes, sir-yes, sir. Good wines—good beds—good—"

"You said all that before, you know," remarked Jack, as he bestowed upon the landlord another terrific dig in the ribs.

"Hilloa!" cried the admiral, "you can send for that infernal lawyer, Mister Landlord."

"Mr. Crinkles, sir?"

"Yes, yes."

"Who may I have the honour to say, sir, wants to see him?"

"Admiral Bell."

"Certainly, admiral, certainly. You'll find him a very conversible, nice, gentlemanly little man, sir."

"And tell him as Jack Pringle is here, too," cried the seaman.

"Oh, yes, yes—of course," said the landlord, who was in such a state of confusion from the digs in the ribs he had received and the noise his guests had already made in his house, that, had he been suddenly put upon his oath, he would scarcely have liked to say which was the master and which was the man.

"The idea now, Jack," said the admiral, "of coming all this way to see a lawyer."

"Aye, aye, sir."

"If he'd said he was a lawyer, we would have known what to do. But it's a take in, Jack."

"So I think. Howsomdever, we'll serve him out when we catch him, you know."

"Good—so we will."

"And, then, again, he may know something about Master Charles, sir, you know. Lord love him, don't you remember when he came aboard to see you once at Portsmouth?"

"Ah! I do, indeed."

"And how he said he hated the French, and quite a baby, too. What perseverance and sense. 'Uncle,' says he to you, 'when I'm a big man, I'll go in a ship, and fight all the French in a heap,' says he. 'And beat 'em, my boy, too,' says you; cos you thought he'd forgot that; and then he says, 'what's the use of saying that, stupid?—don't we always beat 'em?' "

The admiral laughed and rubbed his hands, as he cried aloud,—

"I remember, Jack—I remember him. I was stupid to make such a remark."

"I know you was—a d——d old fool I thought you."

"Come, come. Hilloa, there!"

"Well, then, what do you call me no seaman for?"

"Why, Jack, you bear malice like a marine."

"There you go again. Goodbye. Do you remember when we were yard arm to yard arm with those two Yankee frigates, and took 'em both! You didn't call me a marine then, when the scuppers were running with blood. Was I a seaman then?"

"You were, Jack—you were; and you saved my life."

"I didn't."

"You did."

"I say I didn't—it was a marlin-spike."

"But I say you did, you rascally scoundrel.—I say you did, and I won't be contradicted in my own ship."

"Call this your ship?"

"No, d—n it—I—"

"Mr. Crinkles," said the landlord, flinging the door wide open, and so at once putting an end to the discussion which always apparently had a tendency to wax exceedingly warm.

"The shark, by G—d!" said Jack.

A little, neatly dressed man made his appearance, and advanced rather timidly into the room. Perhaps he had heard from the landlord that the parties who had sent for him were of rather a violent sort.

"So you are Crinkles, are you?" cried the admiral. "Sit down, though you are a lawyer."

"Thank you, sir. I am an attorney, certainly, and my name as certainly is Crinkles."

"Look at that."

The admiral placed the letter in the little lawyer's hands, who said,—

"Am I to read it?"

"Yes, to be sure."

"Aloud?"

"Read it to the devil, if you like, in a pig's whisper, or a West India hurricane."

"Oh, very good, sir. I—I am willing to be agreeable, so I'll read it aloud, if it's all the same to you."

He then opened the letter, and read as follows:—

"To Admiral Bell.

Admiral,—Being, from various circumstances, aware that you take a warm and a praiseworthy interest in your nephew, Charles Holland, I venture to write to you concerning a matter in which your immediate and active co-operation with others may rescue him from a condition which will prove, if allowed to continue, very much to his detriment, and ultimate unhappiness.

You are, then, hereby informed, that he, Charles Holland, has, much earlier than he ought to have done, returned to England, and that the object of his return is to contract a marriage into a family in every way objectionable, and with a girl who is highly objectionable.

You, admiral, are his nearest and almost his only relative in the world; you are the guardian of his

The lawyer ceased to read, and the amazed look with which he glanced at the face of Admiral Bell would, under any other circumstances, have much amused him. His mind, however, was by far too much engrossed with a consideration of the danger of Charles Holland, his nephew, to be amused at anything; so, when he found that the little lawyer said nothing, he bellowed out,—

"Well, sir?"

"We—we—well," said the attorney.

"I've sent for you, and here you are, and here I am, and here's Jack Pringle. What have you got to say?"

"Just this much," said Mr. Crinkles, recovering himself a little, "just this much, sir, that I never saw that letter before in all my life."

"You—never—saw—it?"

"Never."

"Didn't you write it?"

"On my solemn word of honour, sir, I did not."

Jack Pringle whistled, and the admiral looked puzzled. Like the admiral in the song, too, he "grew paler," and then Mr. Crinkles added,—

"Who has forged my name to a letter such as this, I cannot imagine. As for writing to you, sir, I never heard of your existence, except publicly, as one of those gallant officers who have spent a long life in nobly fighting their country's battles, and who are entitled to the admiration and the applause of every Englishman."

Jack and the admiral looked at each other in amazement, and then the latter exclaimed,—

"What! This from a lawyer?"

"A lawyer, sir," said Crinkles, "may know how to appreciate the deeds of gallant men, although he may not be able to imitate them. That letter, sir, is a forgery, and I now leave you, only much gratified at the incident which has procured me the honour of an interview with a gentleman, whose name will live in the history of his country. Good day, sir! Good day!"

"No! I'm d——d if you go like that," said Jack, as he sprang to the door, and put his back against it. "You shall take a glass with me in honour of the wooden walls of Old England, d—— ye, if you was twenty lawyers."

"That's right, Jack," said the admiral. "Come, Mr. Crinkles, I'll think, for your sake, there may be two decent lawyers in the world, and you one of them. We must have a bottle of the best wine the ship—I mean the house—can afford together."

"If it is your command, admiral, I obey with pleasure," said the attorney; "and although I assure you, on my honour, I did not write that letter, yet some of the matters mentioned in it are so generally notorious here, that I can afford you information concerning them."

"Can you?"

"I regret to say I can, for I respect the parties."

"Sit down, then—sit down. Jack, run to the steward's room and get the wine. We will go into it now starboard and larboard. Who the deuce could have written that letter?"

"I have not the least idea, sir."

"Well—well, never mind; it has brought me here, that's something, so I won't grumble much at it. I didn't know my nephew was in England, and I dare say he didn't know I was; but here we both are, and I won't rest till I've seen him, and ascertained how the what's-its-name—"

"The vampyre."

"Ah! the vampyre."

"Shiver my timbers!" said Jack Pringle, who now brought in some wine much against the remonstrances of the waiters of the establishment, who considered that he was treading upon their vested interests by so doing.—"Shiver my timbers, if I knows what a *wamphigher* is, unless he's some distant relation to Davy Jones!"

"Hold your ignorant tongue," said the admiral; "nobody wants you to make a remark, you great lubber!"

"Very good," said Jack, and he sat down the wine on the table, and then retired to the other end of the room, remarking to himself that he was not called a great lubber on a certain occasion, when bullets were scuttling their nobs, and they were yard arm and yard arm with God knows who.

"Now, mister lawyer," said Admiral Bell, who had about him a large share of the habits of a rough sailor. "Now, mister lawyer, here is a glass first to our better acquaintance, for d——e, if I don't like you!"

"You are very good, sir."

"Not at all. There was a time, when I'd just as soon have thought of asking a young shark to supper with me in my own cabin as a lawyer, but I begin to see that there may be such a thing as a decent, good sort of a fellow seen in the law; so here's good luck to you, and you shall never want a friend or a bottle while Admiral Bell has a shot in the locker."

"Gammon," said Jack.

"D—n you, what do you mean by that?" roared the admiral, in a furious tone.

"I wasn't speaking to you," shouted Jack, about two octaves higher. "It's two boys in the street as is pretending they're a going to fight, and I know d——d well they won't."

"Hold your noise."

"I'm going. I wasn't told to hold my noise, when our nobs were being scuttled off Beirut."

"Never mind him, mister lawyer," added the admiral. "He don't know what he's talking about. Never mind him. You go on and tell me all you know about the—the—"

"The vampyre!"

"Ah! I always forget the names of strange fish. I suppose, after all, it's something of the mermaid order?"

"That I cannot say, sir; but certainly the story, in all its painful particulars, has made a great sensation all over the country."

"Indeed!"

"Yes, sir. You shall hear how it occurred. It appears that one night Miss Flora Bannerworth, a young lady of great beauty, and respected and admired by all who knew her was visited by a strange being who came in at the window."

"My eye," said Jack, "it waren't me, I wish it had a been."

"So petrified by fear was she, that she had only time to creep half out of the bed, and to utter one cry of alarm, when the strange visitor seized her in his grasp."

"D—n my pig tail," said Jack, "what a squall there must have been, to be sure."

"Do you see this bottle?" roared the admiral.

"To be sure, I does; I think as it's time I seed another."

"You scoundrel, I'll make you feel it against that d——d stupid head of yours, if you interrupt this gentleman again."

"Don't be violent."

"Well, as I was saying," continued the attorney, "she did, by great good fortune, manage to scream, which had the effect of alarming the whole house. The door of her chamber, which was fast, was broken open."

"Yes, yes—"

"Ah," cried Jack.

"You may imagine the horror and the consternation of those who entered the room to find her in the grasp of a fiend-like figure, whose teeth were fastened on her neck, and who was actually draining her veins of blood."

"The devil!"

"Before anyone could lay hands sufficiently upon the figure to detain it, it had fled precipitately from its dreadful repast. Shots were fired after it in vain."

"And they let it go?"

"They followed it, I understand, as well as they were able, and saw it scale the garden wall of the premises; there it escaped, leaving, as you may well imagine, on all their minds, a sensation of horror difficult to describe."

"Well, I never did hear anything the equal of that. Jack, what do you think of it?"

"I haven't begun to think, yet," said Jack.

"But what about my nephew, Charles?" added the admiral.

"Of him I know nothing."

"Nothing?"

"Not a word, admiral. I was not aware you had a nephew, or that any gentleman bearing that, or any other relationship to you, had any sort of connection with these mysterious and most unaccountable circumstances. I tell you all I have gathered from common report about this vampyre business. Further I know not, I assure you."

"Well, a man can't tell what he don't know. It puzzles me to think who could possibly have written me this letter."

"That I am completely at a loss to imagine," said Crinkles. "I assure you, my gallant sir, that I am much hurt at the circumstance of anyone using my name in such a way. But, nevertheless, as you are here, permit me to say, that it will be my pride, my pleasure, and the boast of the remainder of my existence, to be of some service to so gallant a defender of my country, and one whose name, along with the memory of his deeds, is engraved upon the heart of every Briton."

"Quite ekal to a book, he talks," said Jack. "I never could read one myself, on account o' not knowing how, but I've heard 'em read, and that's just the sort o' incomprehensible gammon."

"We don't want any of your ignorant remarks," said the admiral, "so you be quiet."

"Aye, aye, sir."

"Now, Mister Lawyer, you are an honest fellow, and an honest fellow is generally a sensible fellow."

"Sir, I thank you."

"If so be as what this letter says is true, my nephew Charles has got a liking for this girl, who has had her neck bitten by a vampyre, you see."

"I perceive, sir."

"Now what would you do?"

"One of the most difficult, as well, perhaps, as one of the most ungracious of tasks," said the attorney, "is to interfere with family affairs. The cold and steady eye of reason generally sees things in such very different lights to what they appear to those whose feelings and whose affections are much compromised in their results."

"Very true. Go on."

"Taking, my dear sir, what in my humble judgment appears to be a reasonable view of this subject, I should say it would be a dreadful thing for your nephew to marry into a family any member of which was liable to the visitations of a vampyre."

"It wouldn't be pleasant."

"The young lady might have children."

"Oh, lots," cried Jack.

"Hold your noise, Jack."

"Aye, aye, sir."

"And she might herself actually, when after death she became a vampyre, come and feed on her own children."

"Become a vampyre! What, is she going to be a vampyre too?"

"My dear sir, don't you know that it is a remarkable fact, as regards the physiology of vampyres, that whoever is bitten by one of those dreadful beings, becomes a vampyre?"

"The devil!"

"It is a fact, sir."

"Whew!" whistled Jack; "she might bite us all, and we should be a whole ship's crew o' *wamphighers*. There would be a confounded go!"

"It's not pleasant," said the admiral, as he rose from his chair, and paced to and fro in the room, "it's not pleasant. Hang me up at my own yard-arm if it is."

"Who said it was?" cried Jack.

"Who asked you, you brute?"

"Well, sir," added Mr. Crinkles, "I have given you all the information I can; and I can only repeat what I before had the honour of saying more at large, namely, that I am your humble servant to command, and that I shall be happy to attend upon you at any time."

"Thank ye—thank ye, Mr.—a—a—"

"Crinkles."

"Ah, Crinkles. You shall hear from me again, sir, shortly. Now that I am down here, I will see to the very bottom of this affair, were it deeper than fathom ever sounded. Charles Holland was my poor sister's son; he's the only relative I have in the wide world, and his happiness is dearer to my heart than my own."

Crinkles turned aside, and, by the twinkle of his eyes, one might premise that the honest little lawyer was much affected.

"God bless you, sir," he said; "farewell."

"Good day to you."

"Good-bye, lawyer," cried Jack. "Mind how you go. D—n me, if you don't seem a decent sort of fellow, and, after all, you may give the devil a clear berth, and get into heaven's straits with a flowing sheet, provided as you don't, towards the end of the voyage, make any lubberly blunders."

The old admiral threw himself into a chair with a deep sigh.

"Jack," said he.

"Aye, aye, sir."

"What's to be done now?"

Jack opened the window to discharge the superfluous moisture from an enormous quid he had indulged himself with while the lawyer was telling about the vampyre, and then again turning his face towards his master, he said,—

"Do! What shall we do? Why, go at once and find out Charles, our *nevy*, and ask him all about it, and see the young lady, too, and lay hold o' the *wamphigher* if we can, as well, and go at the whole affair broadside to broadside, till we make a prize of all the particulars, after which we can turn it over in our minds agin, and see what's to be done."

"Jack, you are right. Come along."

"I knows I am. Do you know now which way to steer?"

"Of course not. I never was in this latitude before, and the channel looks intricate. We will hail a pilot, Jack, and then we shall be all right, and if we strike it will be his fault."

"Which is a mighty great consolation," said Jack. "Come along."

CHAPTER XVI.

THE MEETING OF THE LOVERS IN THE GARDEN. —AN AFFECTING SCENE. —THE SUDDEN APPEARANCE OF SIR FRANCIS VARNEY.

Our readers will recollect that Flora Bannerworth had made an appointment with Charles Holland in the garden of the hall. This meeting was looked forward to by the young man with a variety of conflicting feelings, and he passed the intermediate time in a most painful state of doubt as to what would be its result.

The thought that he should be much urged by Flora to give up all thoughts of making her his, was a most bitter one to him, who loved her with so much truth and constancy, and that she would say all she could to induce such a resolution in his mind he felt certain. But to him the idea of now abandoning her presented itself in the worst of aspects.

"Shall I," he said, "sink so low in my own estimation, as well as in hers, and in that of all honourable-minded persons, as to desert her now in the hour of affliction? Dare I be so base as actually or virtually to say to her, 'Flora, when your beauty was undimmed by sorrow—when all around you seemed life and joy, I loved you selfishly for the increased happiness which you might bestow upon me; but now the hand of misfortune presses heavily upon you—you are not what you were, and I desert you?' Never—never—never!"

Charles Holland, it will be seen by some of our more philosophic neighbours, felt more acutely than he reasoned; but let his errors of argumentation be what they may, can we do other than admire the nobility of soul which dictated such a self-denying generous course as that he was pursuing?

As for Flora, Heaven only knows if at that precise time her intellect had completely stood the test of the trying events which had nearly overwhelmed it.

The two grand feelings that seemed to possess her mind were fear of the renewed visit of the vampyre, and an earnest desire to release Charles Holland from his repeated vows of constancy towards her.

Feeling, generosity, and judgment, all revolted holding a young man to such a destiny as hers. To link him to her fate, would be to make him to a real extent a sharer in it, and the more she heard fall from his lips in the way of generous feelings of continued attachment to her, the more severely did she feel that he would suffer most acutely if united to her.

And she was right. The very generosity of feeling which would have now prompted Charles Holland to lead Flora Bannerworth to the altar, even with the marks of the vampyre's teeth upon her throat, gave an assurance of a depth of feeling which would have made him an ample haven in all her miseries, in all her distresses and afflictions.

What was familiarly in the family at the Hall called the garden was a semicircular piece of ground shaded in several directions by trees, and which was exclusively devoted to the growth of flowers. The piece of ground was nearly hidden from the view of the house, and in its center was a summer-house, which at the usual season of the year was covered with all kinds of creeping plants of exquisite perfumes, and rare beauty. All around, too, bloomed the fairest and sweetest of flowers, which a rich soil and a sheltered situation could produce.

Alas! though, of late many weeds had straggled up among their more estimable floral culture, for the decayed fortunes of the family had prevented them from keeping the necessary servants, to place the Hall and its grounds in a state of neatness, such as it had once been the pride of the inhabitants of the place to see them. It was then in this flower-garden that Charles and Flora used to meet.

As may be supposed, he was on the spot before the appointed hour, anxiously expecting the appearance of her who was so really and truly dear to him. What to him were the sweet flowers that there grew in such happy luxuriance and heedless beauty? Alas, the flower that to his mind was fairer than them all, was blighted, and in the wan cheek of her whom he loved, he sighed to see the lily usurping the place of the radiant rose.

"Dear, dear Flora," he ejaculated, "you must indeed be taken from this place, which is so full of the most painful remembrance; now, I cannot think that Mr. Marchdale somehow is a friend to me, but that conviction, or rather impression, does not paralyze my judgment sufficiently to induce me not to acknowledge that his advice is good. He might have couched it in pleasanter words—words that would not, like daggers, each have brought a deadly pang home to my heart, but still I do think that in his conclusion he was right."

A light sound, as of some fairy footstep among the flowers, came upon his ears, and turning instantly to the direction from whence the sound proceeded, he saw what his heart had previously assured him of, namely, that it was his Flora who was coming.

Yes, it was she; but, ah, how pale, how wan—how languid and full of the evidences of much mental suffering was she. Where now was the elasticity of that youthful step? Where now was that lustrous beaming beauty of mirthfulness, which was wont to dawn in those eyes?

Alas, all was changed. The exquisite beauty of form was there, but the light of joy which had lent its most transcendent charms to that heavenly face, was gone. Charles was by her side in a moment. He had her hand clasped in his, while his disengaged one was wound tenderly around her taper waist.

"Flora, dear, dear Flora," he said, "you are better. Tell me that you feel the gentle air revives you?"

She could not speak. Her heart was too full of woe.

"Oh; Flora, my own, my beautiful," he added, in those tones which come so direct from the heart, and which are so different from any assumption of tenderness. "speak to me, dear, dear Flora—speak to me if it be but a word."

"Charles," was all she could say, and then she burst into a flood of tears, and leant so heavily upon his arm, that it was evident but for that support she must have fallen.

Charles Holland welcomed those, although the grieved him so much that he could have accompanied them with his own, but then he knew that she would be soon now more composed, and that they would relieve the heart whose sorrows called them into existence.

He forbore to speak to her until he found this sudden gush of feeling was subsiding into sobs, and then in low, soft accents, he again endeavoured to breathe comfort to her afflicted and terrified spirit.

"My Flora," he said, "remember that there are warm hearts that love you. Remember that neither time nor circumstance can change such endearing affection as mine. Ah, Flora, what evil is there in the whole world that love may not conquer, and in the height of its noble feelings laugh to scorn."

"Oh, hush, hush, Charles, hush."

"Wherefore, Flora, would you still the voice of pure affection? I love you surely, as few have ever loved. Ah, why would you forbid me to give such utterance as I may to those feelings which fill up my whole heart?"

"No—no—no."

"Flora, Flora, wherefore do you say no?"

"Do not, Charles, now speak to me of affection or love. Do not tell me you love me now."

"Not tell you I love you! Ah, Flora, if my tongue, with its poor eloquence to give utterance to such a sentiment, were to do its office, each feature of my face would tell the tale. Each action would show to all the world how much I loved you."

"I must not now hear this. Great God of Heaven give me strength to carry out the purpose of my soul."

"What purpose is it, Flora, that you have to pray thus fervently for strength to execute? Oh, if it savour aught of treason against love's majesty, forget it. Love is a gift from Heaven. The greatest and the most glorious gift it ever bestowed upon its creatures. Heaven will not aid you in repudiating that which is the one grand redeeming feature that rescues human nature from a world of reproach."

Flora wrung her hands despairingly as she said,—

"Charles, I know I cannot reason with you. I know I have not power of language, aptitude of illustration. nor depth of thought to hold a mental contention with you."

"Flora, for what do I contend?"

"You, you speak of love."

"And I have, ere this, spoken to you of love unchecked."

"Yes, yes. Before this."

"And now, wherefore not now? Do not tell me you are changed."

"I am changed, Charles. Fearfully changed. The curse of God has fallen upon me, I know not why. I know not that in word or in thought I have done evil, except perchance unwittingly, and yet—the vampyre."

"Let not that affright you."

"Affright me! It has killed me."

"Nay, Flora,—you think too much of what I still hope to be susceptible of far more rational explanation."

"By your own words, then, Charles, I must convict you. I cannot, I dare not be yours, while such a dreadful circumstance is hanging over me, Charles; if a more rational explanation than the hideous one which my own fancy gives to the form that visits me can be found, find it, and rescue me from despair and from madness."

They had now reached the summer-house, and as Flora uttered these words she threw herself on to a seat, and covering her beautiful face with her hands, she sobbed convulsively.

"You have spoken," said Charles, dejectedly. "I have heard that which you wished to say to me."

"No, no. Not all, Charles."

"I will be patient, then, although what more you may have to add should tear my very heart-strings."

"I—I have to add, Charles," she said, in a tremulous voice, "that justice, religion, mercy—every human attribute which bears the name of virtue, calls loudly upon me no longer to hold you to vows made under different auspices."

"Go on, Flora."

"I then implore you, Charles, finding me what I am, to leave me to the fate which it has pleased Heaven to cast upon me. I do not ask you, Charles, not to love me."

"'Tis well. Go on, Flora."

"Because I should like to think that, although I might never see you more, you loved me still. But you must think seldom of me, and you must endeavour to be happy with some other—"

"You cannot, Flora, pursue the picture you yourself would draw. These words come not from your heart."

"Yes—yes—yes."

"Did you ever love me?"

"Charles, Charles, why will you add another pang to those you know must already rend my heart?"

"No, Flora, I would tear my own heart from my bosom ere I would add one pang to yours. Well I know that gentle maiden modesty would seal your lips to the soft confession that you loved me. I could not hope the joy of hearing you utter these words. The tender devoted lover is content to see the truthful passion in the speaking eyes of beauty. Content is he to translate it from a thousand acts, which, to eyes that look not so acutely as a lover's, bear no signification; but when you tell me to seek happiness with another, well may the anxious question burst from my throbbing heart of, 'Did you ever love me, Flora?' "

Her senses hung entranced upon his words. Oh, what a witchery is in the tongue of love. Some even of the former colour of her cheek returned as forgetting all for the moment but that she was listening to the voice of him, the thoughts of whom had made up the day dream of her happiness, she gazed upon his face.

His voice ceased. To her it seemed as if some music had suddenly left off in its most exquisite passage. She clung to his arm—she looked imploringly up to him. Her head sunk upon his breast as she cried, "Charles, Charles, I did love you. I do love you now."

"Then let sorrow and misfortune shake their grisly locks in vain," he cried. "Heart to heart—hand to hand with me, defy them."

He lifted up his arms towards Heaven as he spoke, and at the moment came such a rattling peal of thunder that the very earth seemed to shake upon its axis.

A half scream of terror burst from the lips of Flora, as she cried,—

"What was that?"

"Only thunder," said Charles, calmly.

"'Twas an awful sound."

"A natural one."

"But at such a moment, when you were defying Fate to injure us. Oh! Charles, is it ominous?"

"Flora, can you really give way to such idle fancies?"

"The sun is obscured."

"Ay, but it will shine all the brighter for its temporary eclipse. The thunder-storm will clear the air of many noxious vapours; the forked lightning has its uses as well as its powers of mischief. Hark! there again!"

Another peal, of almost equal intensity to the other, shook the firmament. Flora trembled.

"Charles," she said, "this is the voice of Heaven. We must part—we must part for ever. I cannot be yours."

"Flora, this is madness. Think again, dear Flora. Misfortunes for a time will hover over the best and most fortunate of us; but, like the clouds that now obscure the sweet sunshine, will pass away, and leave no trace behind them. The sunshine of joy will shine on you again."

There was a small break in the clouds, like a window looking into Heaven. From it streamed one beam of sunlight, so bright, so dazzling, and so beautiful, that it was a sight of wonder to look upon. It fell upon the face of Flora; it warmed her cheek; it lent lustre to her pale lips and tearful eyes; it illumined that little summer-house as if it had been the shrine of some saint.

"Behold!" cried Charles, "Where is your omen now?"

"God of Heaven!" cried Flora; and she stretched out her arms.

"The clouds that hover over your spirit now," said Charles, "shall pass away. Accept this beam of sunlight as a promise from God."

"I will—I will. It is going."

"It has done its office."

The clouds closed over the small orifice, and all was gloom again as before.

"Flora," said Charles, "you will not ask me now to leave you?"

She allowed him to clasp her to his heart. It was beating for her, and for her only.

"You will let me, Flora, love you still?"

Her voice, as she answered him, was like the murmur of some distant melody the ears can scarcely translate to the heart.

"Charles we will live, love, and die together."

And now there was a rapt stillness in that summer-house for many minutes—a trance of joy. They did not speak, but now and then she would look into his face with an old familiar smile, and the joy of heart was near to bursting in tears from his eyes.

A shriek burst from Flora's lips—a shriek so wild and shrill that it awakened echoes far and near. Charles staggered back a step, as if shot, and then in such agonised accents as he was long indeed in banishing the remembrance of, she cried,—

"The vampyre! the vampyre!"

CHAPTER XVII.

THE EXPLANATION. —THE ARRIVAL OF THE ADMIRAL AT THE HOUSE. —A SCENE OF CONFUSION, AND SOME OF ITS RESULTS.

So sudden and so utterly unexpected a cry of alarm from Flora, at such a time might well have the effect of astounding the nerves of any one, and no wonder that Charles was for a few seconds absolutely petrified and almost unable to think.

Mechanically, then, he turned his eyes towards the door of the summer-house, and there he saw a tall, thin man, rather elegantly dressed, whose countenance certainly, in its wonderful resemblance to the portrait on the panel, might well appall anyone.

The stranger stood in the irresolute attitude on the threshold of the summer-house of one who did not wish to intrude, but who found it as awkward, if not more so now, to retreat than to advance.

Before Charles Holland could summon any words to his aid, or think of freeing himself from the clinging grasp of Flora, which was wound around him, the stranger made a very low and courtly bow, after which he said, in winning accents,—

"I very much fear that I am an intruder here. Allow me to offer my warmest apologies, and to assure you, sir, and you, madam, that I had no idea any one was in the arbour. You perceive the rain is falling smartly, and I made towards here, seeing it was likely to shelter me from the shower."

These words were spoken in such a plausible and courtly tone of voice, that they might well have become any drawing-room in the kingdom.

Flora kept her eyes fixed upon him during the utterance of these words; and as she convulsively clutched the arm of Charles, she kept on whispering,—

"The vampyre! the vampyre!"

"I much fear," added the stranger, in the same bland tones, "that I have been the cause of some alarm to the young lady!"

"Release me," whispered Charles to Flora. "Release me; I will follow him at once."

"No, no—do not leave me—do not leave me. The vampyre—the dreadful vampyre!"

"But, Flora—"

"Hush—hush—hush! It speaks again."

"Perhaps I ought to account for my appearance in the garden at all," added the insinuating stranger. "The fact is, I came on a visit—" Flora shuddered. "—to Mr. Henry Bannerworth," continued the stranger; "and finding the garden-gate open, I came in without troubling the servants, which I much regret, as I can perceive I have alarmed and annoyed the lady. Madam, pray accept of my apologies."

"In the name of God, who are you?" said Charles.

"My name is Varney."

"Oh, yes. You are the Sir Francis Varney, residing close by, who bears so fearful a resemblance to—"

"Pray go on, sir. I am all attention."

"To a portrait here."

"Indeed! Now I reflect a moment, Mr. Henry Bannerworth did incidentally mention something of the sort. It's a most singular coincidence."

The sound of approaching footsteps was now plainly heard, and in a few moments Henry and George, along with Mr. Marchdale, reached the spot. Their appearance showed that they had made haste, and Henry at once exclaimed,—

"We heard, or fancied we heard, a cry of alarm."

"You did hear it," said Charles Holland. "Do you know this gentleman?"

"It is Sir Francis Varney."

"Indeed!"

Varney bowed to the new comers, and was altogether as much at his ease as everybody else seemed quite the contrary. Even Charles Holland found the difficulty of going up to such a well-bred, gentlemanly man, and saying, "Sir, we believe you to be a vampyre"— to be almost, if not wholly, insurmountable.

"I cannot do it," he thought, "but I will watch him."

"Take me away," whispered Flora. "'Tis he—'tis he. Oh, take me away, Charles."

"Hush, Flora, hush. You are in some error; the accidental resemblance should not make us be rude to this gentleman."

"The vampyre!—it is the vampyre!"

"Are you sure, Flora?"

"Do I know your features—my own—my brother's? Do not ask me to doubt—I cannot. I am quite sure. Take me from his hideous presence, Charles."

"The young lady, I fear, is very much indisposed," remarked Sir Francis Varney, in a sympathetic tone of voice. "If she will accept of my arm, I shall esteem it a great honour."

"No—no—no!—God! no," cried Flora.

"Madam, I will not press you."

He bowed, and Charles led Flora from the summer-house towards the hall.

"Flora," he said, "I am bewildered—I know not what to think. That man most certainly has been fashioned after the portrait which is on the panel in the room you formerly occupied; or it has been painted from him."

"He is my midnight visitor!" exclaimed Flora. "He is the vampyre;—this Sir Francis Varney is the vampyre."

"Good God! What can be done?"

"I know not. I am nearly distracted."

"Be calm, Flora. If this man be really what you name him, we now know from what quarter the mischief comes, which is, at all events, a point gained. Be assured we shall place a watch upon him."

"Oh, it is terrible to meet him here."

"And he is so wonderfully anxious, too, to possess the Hall."

"He is—he is."

"It looks strange, the whole affair. But, Flora, be assured of one thing, and that is, of your own safety."

"Can I be assured of that?"

"Most certainly. Go to your mother now. Here we are, you see, fairly within doors. Go to your mother, dear Flora, and keep yourself quiet. I will return to this mysterious man now with a cooler judgment than I left him."

"You will watch him, Charles?"

"I will, indeed."

"And you will not let him approach the house here alone?"

"I will not."

"Oh, that the Almighty should allow such beings to haunt the earth!"

"Hush, Flora, hush! we cannot judge of his all-wise purpose."

"'Tis hard that the innocent should be inflicted with its presence."

Charles bowed his head in mournful assent.

"Is it not very, very dreadful?"

"Hush——hush! Calm yourself, dearest, calm yourself. Recollect that all we have to go upon in this matter is a resemblance, which, after all, may be accidental. But leave it all to me, and be assured that now I have some clue to this affair, I will not lose sight of it, or of Sir Francis Varney."

So saying, Charles surrendered Flora to the care of her mother, and then was hastening back to the summer-house, when he met the whole party coming towards the Hall, for the rain was each moment increasing in intensity.

"We are returning," remarked Sir Francis Varney, with a half bow and a smile, to Charles.

"Allow me," said Henry, "to introduce you, Mr. Holland, to our neighbour, Sir Francis Varney."

Charles felt himself compelled to behave with courtesy, although his mind was so full of conflicting feelings as regarded Varney; but there was no avoiding, without such brutal rudeness as was inconsistent with all his pursuits and habits, replying in something like the same strain to the extreme courtly politeness of the supposed vampyre.

"I will watch him closely," thought Charles. "I can do no more than watch him closely."

Sir Francis Varney seemed to be a man of the most general and discursive information. He talked fluently and pleasantly upon all sorts of topics, and notwithstanding he could not but have heard what Flora had said of him, he asked no questions whatever upon that subject.

This silence as regarded a matter which would at once have induced some sort of inquiry from any other man, Charles felt told much against him, and he trembled to believe for a moment that, after all, it really might be true.

"Is he a vampyre?" he asked himself. "Are there vampyres, and is this man of fashion—this courtly, talented, educated gentleman one?" It was a perfectly hideous question.

"You are charmingly situated here," remarked Varney, as, after ascending the few steps that led to the hall door, he turned and looked at the view from that slight altitude.

"The place has been much esteemed," said Henry, "for its picturesque beauties of scenery."

"And well it may be. I trust, Mr. Holland, the young lady is much better?"

"She is, sir," said Charles.

"I was not honoured by an introduction."

"It was my fault," said Henry, who spoke to his extraordinary guest with an air of forced hilarity.

"It was my fault for not introducing you to my sister."

"And that was your sister?"

"It was, sir."

"Report has not belied her—she is beautiful. But she looks rather pale, I thought. Has she bad health?"

"The best of health."

"Indeed! Perhaps the little disagreeable circumstance, which is made so much food for gossip in the neighbourhood, has affected her spirits?"

"It has."

"You allude to the supposed visit here of a vampyre?" said Charles, as he fixed his eyes upon Varney's face.

"Yes, I allude to the supposed appearance of a supposed vampyre in this family," said Sir Francis Varney, as he returned the earnest gaze of Charles, with such unshrinking assurance, that the young man was compelled, after about a minute, nearly to withdraw his own eyes.

"He will not be cowed," thought Charles. "Use has made him familiar to such cross-questioning."

It appeared now suddenly to occur to Henry that he had said something at Varney's own house which should have prevented him from coming to the Hall, and he now remarked, "We scarcely expected the pleasure of your company here, Sir Francis Varney."

"Oh, my dear sir, I am aware of that; but you roused my curiosity. You mentioned to me that there was a portrait here amazingly like me."

"Did I?"

"Indeed you did, or how could I know it? I wanted to see if the resemblance was so perfect."

"Did you hear, sir," added Henry, "that my sister was alarmed at your likeness to that portrait?"

"No, really."

"I pray you walk in, and we will talk more at large upon that matter."

"With great pleasure. One leads a monotonous life in the country, when compared with the brilliancy of a court existence. Just now I have no particular engagement. As we are near neighbours I see no reason why we should not be good friends, and often interchange such civilities as make up the amenities of existence, and which, in the country, more particularly, are valuable."

Henry could not be hypocrite enough to assent to this; but still, under the present aspect of affairs, it was impossible to return any but a civil reply; so he said,—

"Oh, yes, of course—certainly. My time is very much occupied, and my sister and mother see no company."

"Oh, now, how wrong."

"Wrong, sir?"

"Yes, surely. If anything more than another tends to harmonize individuals, it is the society of that fairer half of the creation which we love for their very foibles. I am much attached to the softer sex—to young persons full of health. I like to see the rosy checks, where the warm blood mantles in the superficial veins, and all is loveliness and life."

Charles shrank back, and the word "Demon" unconsciously escaped his lips.

Sir Francis took no manner of notice of the expression, but went on talking, as if he had been on the very happiest terms with every one present.

"Will you follow me, at once, to the chamber where the portrait hangs," said Henry, "or will you partake of some refreshment first?"

"No refreshment for me," said Varney. "My dear friend, if you will permit me to call you such, this is a time of the day at which I never do take any refreshment."

"Nor at any other," thought Henry.

They all went to the chamber where Charles had passed one very disagreeable night, and when they arrived, Henry pointed to the portrait on the panel, saying—

"There, Sir Francis Varney, is your likeness."

He looked, and, having walked up to it, in an undertone, rather as if he were conversing with himself than making a remark for anyone else to hear, he said—

"It is wonderfully like."

"It is, indeed," said Charles.

"If I stand beside it, thus," said Varney, placing himself in a favourable attitude for comparing the two faces, "I dare say you will be more struck with the likeness than before."

So accurate was it now, that the same light fell upon his face as that under which the painter had executed the portrait, that all started back a step or two.

"Some artists," remarked Varney, "have the sense to ask where a portrait is to be hung before they paint it, and then they adapt their lights and shadows to those which would fall upon the original, were it similarly situated."

"I cannot stand this," said Charles to Henry; "I must question him farther."

"As you please, but do not insult him."

"I will not."

"He is beneath my roof now, and, after all, it is but a hideous suspicion we have of him."

"Rely upon me."

Charles stepped forward, and once again confronting Varney, with an earnest gaze, he said—

"Do you know, sir, that Miss Bannerworth declares the vampyre she fancies to have visited this chamber to be, in features, the exact counterpart of this portrait?"

"Does she indeed?"

"She does, indeed."

"And perhaps, then, that accounts for her thinking that I am the vampyre, because I bear a strong resemblance to the portrait."

"I should not be surprised," said Charles.

"How very odd."

"Very."

"And yet entertaining. I am rather amused than otherwise. The idea of being a vampyre. Ha! ha! If ever I go to a masquerade again, I shall certainly assume the character of a vampyre."

"You would do it well."

"I dare say, now, I should make quite a sensation."

"I am certain you would. Do you not think, gentlemen, that Sir Francis Varney would enact the character to the very life? By Heavens, he would do it so well that one might, without much difficulty, really imagine him a vampyre."

"Bravo—bravo," said Varney, as he gently folded his hands together, with that genteel applause that may even be indulged in in a box at the opera itself. "Bravo. I like to see young persons enthusiastic; it looks as if they had some of the real fire of genius in their composition. Bravo—bravo."

This was, Charles thought, the very height and acme of impudence, and yet what could he do? What could he say? He was foiled by the downright coolness of Varney.

As for Henry, George, and Mr. Marchdale, they had listened to what was passing between Sir Francis and Charles in silence. They feared to diminish the effect of anything Charles might say, by adding a word of their own; and, likewise, they did not wish to lose one observation that might come from the lips of Varney.

But now Charles appeared to have said all he had to say, he turned to the window and looked out. He seemed like a man who had made up his mind, for a time, to give up some contest in which he had been engaged.

And, perhaps, not so much did he give it up from any feeling or consciousness of being beaten, as from a conviction that it could be the more effectually, at some other and far more eligible opportunity, renewed.

Varney now addressed Henry, saying,—

"I presume the subject of our conference, when you did me the honour of a call, is no secret to anyone here?"

"None whatever," said Henry.

"Then, perhaps, I am too early in asking you if you have made up your mind?"

"I have scarcely, certainly, had time to think."

"My dear sir, do not let me hurry you; I much regret, indeed, the intrusion."

"You seem anxious to possess the Hall," remarked Mr. Marchdale to Varney.

"I am."

"Is it new to you?"

"Not quite. I have some boyish recollections connected with this neighbourhood, among which Bannerworth Hall stands sufficiently prominent."

"May I ask how long ago that was?" said Charles Howard, rather abruptly.

"I do not recollect, my enthusiastic young friend," said Varney. "How old are you?"

"Just about twenty-one."

"You are, then, for your age, quite a model of discretion."

It would have been difficult for the most accurate observer of human nature to have decided whether this was said truthfully or ironically, so Charles made no reply to it whatever.

"I trust," said Henry, "we shall induce you, as this is your first visit, Sir Francis Varney, to the Hall, to partake of something."

"Well, well, a cup of wine—"

"Is at your service."

Henry now led the way to a small parlour, which, although by no means one of the showiest rooms of the house, was, from the care and exquisite carving with which it abounded, much more to the taste of any who possessed an accurate judgment in such works of art.

Then wine was ordered, and Charles took an opportunity of

whispering to Henry,—

"Notice well if he drinks."

"I will."

"Do you see that beneath his coat there is a raised place, as if his arm was bound up?"

"I do."

"There, then, was where the bullet from the pistol fired by Flora, when we were at the church, hit him."

"Hush! for God's sake, hush! you are getting into a dreadful state of excitement, Charles; hush! hush!"

"And can you blame—"

"No, no; but what can we do?"

"You are right. Nothing can we do at present. We have a clue now, and be it our mutual inclination, as well as duty, to follow it. Oh, you shall see how calm I will be!"

"For Heaven's sake, be so. I have noted that his eyes flash upon yours with no friendly feeling."

"His friendship were a curse."

"Hush! he drinks!"

"Watch him."

"I will."

"Gentlemen all," said Sir Francis Varney, in such soft, dulcet tones, that it was quite a fascination to hear him speak; "gentlemen all, being as I am, much delighted with your company, do not accuse me of presumption, if I drink now, poor drinker as I am, to our future merry meetings."

He raised the wine to his lips, and seemed to drink, after which he replaced the glass upon the table.

Charles glanced at it; it was still full.

"You have not drank, Sir Francis Varney," he said.

"Pardon me, enthusiastic young sir," said Varney, "perhaps you will have the liberality to allow me to take my wine how I please and when I please."

"Your glass is full."

"Well, sir?"

"Will you drink it?"

"Not at any man's bidding, most certainly. If the fair Flora Bannerworth would grace the board with her sweet presence, methinks I could then drink on, on, on."

"Hark you, sir," cried Charles, "I can bear no more of this. We have had in this house most horrible and damning evidence that there are such things as vampyres."

"Have you really? I suppose you eat raw pork at supper, and so had the nightmare?"

"A jest is welcome in its place, but pray hear me out, sir, if it suit your lofty courtesy to do so."

"Oh, certainly."

"Then I say we believe, as far as human judgment has a right to go, that a vampyre has been here."

"Go on, it's interesting. I always was a lover of the wild and the wonderful."

"We have, too," continued Charles, "some reason to believe that you are the man."

Varney tapped his forehead as he glanced at Henry, and said,—"Oh, dear, I did not know. You should have told me he was a little wrong about the brain; I might have quarreled with the lad. Dear me, how lamentable for his poor mother."

"This will not do, Sir Francis Varney *alias* Bannerworth."

"Oh—oh! Be calm—be calm."

"I defy you to your teeth, sir! No, God, no! Your teeth!"

"Poor lad! Poor lad!"

"You are a cowardly demon, and here I swear to devote myself to your destruction."

Sir Francis Varney drew himself up to his full height, and that was immense, as he said to Henry,—

"I pray you, Mr. Bannerworth, since I am thus grievously insulted beneath your roof, to tell me if your friend here be mad or sane?"

"He's not mad."

"Then—"

"Hold, sir! The quarrel shall be mine. In the name of my persecuted sister—in the name of Heaven. Sir Francis Varney, I defy you."

Sir Francis, in spite of his impenetrable calmness, appeared somewhat moved, as he said,—

"I have already endured insult sufficient—I will endure no more. If there are weapons at hand—"

"My young friend," interrupted Mr. Marchdale, stepping between the excited men, "is carried away by his feelings, and knows not what he says. You will look upon it in that light, Sir Francis."

"We need no interference," exclaimed Varney, his hitherto bland voice changing to one of fury.

"The hot blooded fool wishes to fight, and he shall—to the death—to the death."

"And I say he shall not," exclaimed Mr. Marchdale, taking Henry by the arm. "George," he added, turning to the young man, "assist me in persuading your brother to leave the room. Conceive the agony of your sister and mother if anything should happen to him."

Varney smiled with a devilish sneer, as he listened to these words, and then he said,—

"As you will—as you will. There will be plenty of time, and perhaps better opportunity, gentlemen. I bid you good day."

And with provoking coolness, he then moved towards the door, and quitted the room.

"Remain here," said Marchdale; "I will follow him, and see that he quits the premises."

He did so, and the young men, from the window, beheld Sir Francis walking slowly across the garden, and then saw Mr. Marchdale follow on his track.

While they were thus occupied, a tremendous ringing came at the gate, but their attention was so riveted to what was passing in the garden, that they paid not the least attention to it.

CHAPTER XVIII.

THE ADMIRAL'S ADVICE.—
THE CHALLENGE TO THE VAMPYRE.—
THE NEW SERVANT AT THE HALL.

The violent ringing of the bell continued uninterruptedly until at length George volunteered to answer it. The fact was, that now there was no servant at all in the place for, after the one who had recently demanded of Henry her dismissal had left, the other was terrified to remain alone, and had precipitately gone from the house, without even going through the ceremony of announcing her intention to. To be sure, she sent a boy for her money afterwards, which may be considered a great act of condescension.

Suspecting, then, this state of things, George himself hastened to the gate, and, being not over well pleased at the continuous and unnecessary ringing which was kept up at it, he opened it quickly, and cried, with more impatience, by a vast amount, than was usual with him.

"Who is so impatient that he cannot wait a seasonable time for the door to be opened?"

"And who the d——l are you?" cried one who was immediately outside.

"Who do you want?" cried George.

"Shiver my timbers!" cried Admiral Bell, for it was no other than that personage. "What's that to you?"

"Aye, aye," added Jack, "answer that if you can, you shore-going-looking swab."

"Two madmen, I suppose," ejaculated George, and he would have closed the gate upon them; but Jack introduced between it and the post the end of a thick stick, saying,—

"Avast there! None of that; we have had trouble enough to get in. If you are the family lawyer, or the chaplain, perhaps you'll tell us where

Mister Charley is."

"Once more I demand of you who you want?" said George, who was now perhaps a little amused at the conduct of the impatient visitors.

"We want the admiral's *nevey*," said Jack.

"But how do I know who is the admiral's *nevey* as you call him."

"Why, Charles Holland, to be sure. Have you got him aboard or not?"

"Mr. Charles Holland is certainly here; and, if you had said at once, and explicitly, that you wished to see him, I could have given you a direct answer."

"He is here?" cried the admiral.

"Most certainly."

"Come along, then; yet, stop a bit. I say, young fellow, just before we go any further, tell us if he has maimed the vampyre?"

"The what?"

"The *wamphigher*," said Jack, by way of being, as he considered, a little

more explanatory than the admiral.

"I do not know what you mean," said George; "if you wish to see Mr. Charles Holland walk in and see him. He is in this house; but, for myself, as you are strangers to me, I decline answering any questions, let their import be what they may."

"Hilloa! who are they?" suddenly cried Jack, as he pointed to two figures some distance off in the meadows, who appeared to be angrily conversing.

George glanced in the direction towards which Jack pointed, and there he saw Sir Francis Varney and Mr. Marchdale standing within a few paces of each other, and apparently engaged in some angry discussion.

His first impulse was to go immediately towards them; but, before he could execute even that suggestion of his mind, he saw Varney strike Marchdale, and the latter fell to the ground.

"Allow me to pass," cried George, as he endeavoured to get by the rather unwieldy form of the admiral. But, before he could accomplish this, for the gate was narrow, he saw Varney, with great swiftness, make off, and Marchdale, rising to his feet, came towards the Hall.

When Marchdale got near enough to the garden-gate to see George, he motioned to him to remain where he was, and then, quickening his pace, he soon came up to the spot.

"Marchdale," cried George, "you have had an encounter with Sir Francis Varney."

"I have," said Marchdale, in an excited manner. "I threatened to follow him, but he struck me to the earth as easily as I could a child. His strength is superhuman."

"I saw you fall."

"I believe, but that he was observed, he would have murdered me."

"Indeed!"

"What, do you mean to say that lanky, horse-marine looking fellow is as bad as that!" said the admiral.

Marchdale now turned his attention to the two new comers, upon whom he looked with some surprise, and then, turning to George, he said,—"Is this gentleman a visitor?"

"To Mr. Holland, I believe he is," said George; "but I have not the pleasure of knowing his name."

"Oh, you may know my name as soon as you like," cried the admiral. "The enemies of old England know it, and I don't care if all the world knows it. I'm old Admiral Bell, something of a hulk now, but still able to head a quarter-deck if there was any need to do so."

"Aye, aye," cried Jack, and taking from his pocket a boatswain's whistle, he blew a blast so long, and loud, and shrill, that George was fain to cover his ears with his hands to shut out the brain-piercing, and, to him, unusual sound.

"And are you, then, a relative," said Marchdale, "of Mr. Holland's, sir, may I ask?"

"I'm his uncle, and be d——d to him, if you must know, and someone has told me that the young scamp thinks of marrying a mermaid, or a ghost, or a vampyre, or some such thing, so, for the sake of the memory of his poor mother, I've come to say no to the bargain, and d—n me, who cares.”

“Come in, sir,” said George, “I will conduct you to Mr. Holland. I presume this is your servant?”

“Why, not exactly. That’s Jack Pringle, he was my boatswain, you see, and now he’s a kind o’ something betwixt and between. Not exactly a servant.”

“Aye, aye, sir,” said Jack. “Have it all your own way, though we is paid off.”

“Hold your tongue, you audacious scoundrel, will you.”

“Oh, I forgot, you don’t like anything said about paying off, cos it puts you in mind of—”

“Now, d—n you, I’ll have you strung up to the yard-arm, you dog, if you don’t belay there.”

“I’m done. All’s right.”

By this time the party, including the admiral, Jack, George Bannerworth, and Marchdale, had got more than half-way across the garden, and were observed by Charles Holland and Henry, who had come to the steps of the hall to see what was going on. The moment Charles saw the admiral a change of colour came over his face, and he exclaimed,—

“By all that’s surprising, there is my uncle!”

“Your uncle!” said Henry.

“Yes, as good a hearted a man as ever drew breath, and yet, withal, as full of prejudices, and as ignorant of life, as a child.”

Without waiting for any reply from Henry, Charles Holland rushed forward, and seizing his uncle by the hand, he cried, in tones of genuine affection,—

“Uncle, dear uncle, how came you to find me out?”

“Charley, my boy,” cried the old man, “bless you; I mean, confound your d——d impudence; you rascal, I'm glad to see you; no, I ain’t, you young mutineer. What do you mean by it, you ugly, ill-looking, d——d fine fellow—my dear boy. Oh, you infernal scoundrel.”

All this was accompanied by a shaking of the hand, which was enough to dislocate anybody’s shoulder, and which Charles was compelled to bear as well as he could. It quite prevented him from speaking, however, for a few moments, for it nearly shook the breath out of him. When, then, he could get in a word, he said,—

"Uncle, I dare say you are surprised."

"Surprised! D—n me, I am surprised."

"Well, I shall be able to explain all to your satisfaction, I am sure. Allow me now to introduce you to my friends."

Turning then to Henry, Charles said,—

"This is Mr. Henry Bannerworth, uncle; and this Mr. George Bannerworth, both good friends of mine; and this is Mr. Marchdale, a friend of theirs, uncle."

"Oh, indeed!"

"And here you see Admiral Bell, my most worthy, but rather eccentric uncle."

"Confound your impudence."

"What brought him here I cannot tell; but he is a brave officer, and a gentleman."

"None of your nonsense," said the admiral.

"And here you sees Jack Pringle," said that individual, introducing himself, since no one appeared inclined to do that office for him, "a tar for all weathers. One as hates the French, and is never so happy as when he's alongside o' some o' those lubberly craft blazing away."

"That's uncommonly true," remarked the admiral.

"Will you walk in, sir?" said Henry, courteously. "Any friend of Charles Holland's is most welcome here. You will have much to excuse us for, because we are deficient in servants at present, in consequence of some occurrences in our family, which your nephew has our full permission to explain to you in full."

"Oh, very good, I tell you what it is, all of you, what I've seen of you, d——e, I like, so here goes. Come along, Jack."

The admiral walked into the house, and as he went, Charles Holland said to him,—

"How came you to know I was here, uncle?"

"Some fellow wrote me a despatch."

"Indeed!"

"Yes, saying at you was a going to marry some odd sort of fish as it wasn't at all the thing to introduce into the family."

"Was—was a vampyre mentioned?"

"That's the very thing."

"Hush, uncle—hush."

"What for?"

"Do not, I implore, hint at such a thing before these kind friends of mine. I will take an opportunity within the next hour of explaining all to you, and you shall form your own kind and generous judgement upon circumstances in which my honour and my happiness are so nearly concerned."

"Gammon," said the admiral.

"What, uncle?"

"Oh, I know you want to palaver me into saying it's all right. I suppose if my judgment and generosity don't like it, I shall be an old fool, and a cursed goose?"

"Now, uncle."

"Now, *nevey.*"

"Well, well—no more at present. We will talk over this at leisure. You promise me to say nothing about it until you have heard my explanation, uncle?"

"Very good. Make it as soon as you can, and as short as you can, that's all I ask of you."

"I will, I will."

Charles was to the full as anxious as his uncle could be to enter upon the subject, some remote information of which, he felt convinced, had brought the old man down to the Hall. Who it could have been that so far intermeddled with his affairs as to write to him, he could not possibly conceive.

A very few words will suffice to explain the precise position in which Charles Holland was. A considerable sum of money had been left to him, but it was saddled with the condition that he should not come into possession of it until he was one year beyond the age which is usually denominated that of discretion, namely, twenty-one. His uncle, the admiral, was the trustee of his fortune, and he, with rare discretion, had got the active and zealous assistance of a professional gentleman of great honour and eminence to conduct the business for him.

This gentleman had advised that for the two years between the ages of twenty and twenty-two, Charles Holland should travel, inasmuch as in English society he would find himself in an awkward position, being for one whole year of age, and yet waiting for his property.

Under such circumstances, reasoned the lawyer, a young man, unless he is possessed of very rare discretion indeed, is almost sure to get fearfully involved with money-lenders. Being of age, his notes, and bills, and bonds would all be good, and he would be in a ten times worse situation than a wealthy minor.

All this was duly explained to Charles, who, rather eagerly than otherwise, caught at the idea of a two years wander on the continent, where he could visit so many places, which to a well-read young man like himself, and one of a lively imagination, were full of the most delightful associations.

But the acquaintance with Flora Bannerworth effected a great revolution in his feelings. The dearest, sweetest spot on earth became that which she inhabited. When the Bannerworths left him abroad, he knew not what to do with himself. Everything, and every pursuit in which he had before taken a delight, became most distasteful to him. He was, in fact, in a short time, completely "used up," and then he determined upon returning to England, and finding out the dear object of his attachment at once. This resolution was no sooner taken, than his health and spirits returned to him, and with what rapidity he could, he now made his way to his native shores.

The two years were so nearly expired, that he made up his mind he would not communicate either with his uncle, the admiral, or the professional gentleman upon whose judgment he set so high and so just a value. And at the Hall he considered he was in perfect security from any interruption, and so he would have been, but for that letter which was written to Admiral Bell, and signed Josiah Crinkles, but which Josiah Crinkles so emphatically denied all knowledge of. Who wrote it, remains at present one of those mysteries which time, in the progress of our narrative, will clear up.

The opportune, or rather the painful juncture at which Charles Holland had arrived at Bannerworth Hall, we are well cognisant of. Where he expected to find smiles he found tears, and the family with whom he had fondly hoped he should pass a time of uninterrupted happiness, he found plunged in the gloom incidental to an occurrence of the most painful character.

Our readers will perceive, too, that coming as he did with an utter disbelief in the vampyre, Charles had been compelled, in some measure, to yield to the overwhelming weight of evidence which had been brought to bear upon the subject, and although he could not exactly be said to believe in the existence and the appearance of the vampyre at Bannerworth Hall, he was upon the subject in a most painful state of doubt and indecision.

Charles now took an opportunity to speak to Henry privately, and inform him exactly how he stood with his uncle, adding—

"Now, my dear friend, if you forbid me, I will not tell my uncle of this sad affair, but I must own I would rather do so fully and freely, and trust to his own judgment upon it."

"I implore you to do so," said Henry. "Conceal nothing. Let him know the precise situation and circumstances of the family by all means. There is nothing so mischievous as secrecy: I have the greatest dislike to it. I beg you tell him all."

"I will; and with it, Henry, I will tell him that my heart is irrevocably Flora's."

"Your generous clinging to one whom your heart saw and loved, under very different auspices," said Henry, "believe me, Charles, sinks deep into my heart. She has related to me something of a meeting she had with you."

"Oh, Henry, she may tell you what I said; but there are no words which can express the depth of my tenderness. 'Tis only time which can prove how much I love her."

"Go to your uncle," said Henry, in a voice of emotion. "God bless you, Charles. It is true you would have been fully justified in leaving my sister; but the nobler and the more generous path you have chosen has endeared you to us all."

"Where is Flora now?" said Charles.

"She is in her own room. I have persuaded her, by some occupation, to withdraw her mind from a too close and consequently painful contemplation of the distressing circumstances in which she feels herself placed."

"You are right. What occupation best pleases her?"

"The pages of romance once had a charm for her gentle spirit."

"Then come with me, and, from among the few articles I brought with me here, I can find some papers which may help her to pass some merry hours."

Charles took Henry to his room, and, unstrapping a small valise, he took from it some manuscript papers, one of which he handed to Henry, saying—

"Give that to her: it contains an account of a wild adventure, and shows that human nature may suffer much more—and that wrongfully too—than came ever under our present mysterious affliction."

"I will," said Henry; "and, coming from you, I am sure it will have a more than ordinary value in her eyes."

"I will now," said Charles, "seek my uncle. I will tell him how I love her; and at the end of my narration, if he should not object, I would fain introduce her to him, that he might himself see that, let what beauty may have met his gaze, her peer he never yet met with, and may in vain hope to do so."

"You are partial, Charles."

"Not so. 'Tis true I look upon her with a lover's eyes, but I look still with those of truthful observation.

"Well, I will speak to her about seeing your uncle, and let you know. No doubt, he will not be at all averse to an interview with anyone who stands high in your esteem."

The young men now separated—Henry, to seek his beautiful sister;

and Charles, to communicate   to his uncle the strange particulars connected with Varney, the Vampyre.

CHAPTER XIX.

FLORA IN HER CHAMBER. —HER FEARS. —THE MANUSCRIPT. —AN ADVENTURE.

Henry found Flora in her chamber. She was in deep thought when he tapped at the door of the room, and such was the state of nervous excitement in which she was that even the demand for admission made by him to the room was sufficient to produce from her a sudden cry of alarm.

"Who—who is there?" she then said, in accents full of terror.

"'Tis I, dear Flora," said Henry.

She opened the door in an instant, and, with a feeling of grateful relief, exclaimed—

"Oh, Henry, is it only you?"

"Who did you suppose it was, Flora?"

She shuddered.

"I—I—do not know; but I am so foolish now, and so weak-spirited, that the slightest noise is enough to alarm me."

"You must, dear Flora, fight up, as I had hoped you were doing, against this nervousness."

"I will endeavour. Did not some strangers come a short time since, brother?"

"Strangers to us, Flora, but not to Charles Holland. A relative of his—an uncle whom he much respects, has found him out here, and has now come to see him."

"And to advise him," said Flora, as she sunk into a chair, and wept bitterly; "to advise him, of course, to desert, as he would a pestilence, a vampyre bride."

"Hush, hush! for the sake of Heaven, never make use of such a phrase, Flora. You know not what a pang it brings to my heart to hear you."

"Oh, forgive me, brother."

"Say no more of it, Flora. Heed it not. It may be possible—in fact, it may well be supposed as more than probable—that the relative of Charles Holland may shrink from sanctioning the alliance, but do you rest securely in the possession of the heart which I feel convinced is wholly yours, and which, I am sure, would break ere it surrendered you."

A smile of joy came across Flora's pale but beautiful face, as she cried,—

"And you, dear brother—you think so much of Charles's faith?"

"As Heaven is my judge, I do."

"Then I will bear up with what strength God may give me against all things that seek to depress me; I will not be conquered."

"You are right, Flora; I rejoice to find in you such a disposition. Here is some manuscript which Charles thinks will amuse you, and he bade me ask you if you would be introduced to his uncle."

"Yes, yes—willingly."

"I will tell him so; I know he wishes it, and I will tell him so. Be patient, dear Flora, and all may yet be well."

"But, brother, on your sacred word, tell me do you not think this Sir Francis Varney is the vampyre?"

"I know not what to think, and do not press me for a judgment now. He shall be watched."

Henry left his sister, and she sat for some moments in silence with the papers before her that Charles had sent her.

"Yes," she then said, gently, "he loves me—Charles loves me; I ought to be very, very happy. He loves me. In those words are concentrated a whole world of joy—Charles loves me—he will not forsake me. Oh, was there ever such dear love—such fond devotion?—never, never. Dear Charles. He loves me—he loves me!"

The very repetition of these words had a charm for Flora—a charm which was sufficient to banish much sorrow; even the much-dreaded vampyre was forgotten while the light of love was beaming upon her, and she told herself,—

"He is mine!—he is mine! He loves me truly."

After a time, she turned to the manuscript which her brother had brought her, and, with a far greater concentration of mind than she had thought it possible she could bring to it, considering the many painful subjects of contemplation that she might have occupied herself with, she read the pages with very great pleasure and interest.

*　　*　　*　　*

...and even as she did so, she heard a footstep approaching her chamber door.

CHAPTER XX.

THE DREADFUL MISTAKE.
—THE TERRIFIC INTERVIEW IN THE CHAMBER.
—THE ATTACK OF THE VAMPYRE.

The footstep which Flora, upon the close of the tale she had been reading, heard approaching her apartment, came rapidly along the corridor.

"It is Henry, returned to conduct me to an interview with Charles's uncle," she said. "I wonder, now, what manner of man he is. He should in some respects resemble Charles; and if he do so, I shall bestow upon him some affection for that alone."

Tap—tap came upon the chamber door. Flora was not at all alarmed now, as she had been when Henry brought her the manuscript. From some strange action of the nervous system, she felt quite confident, and resolved to brave everything. But then she felt quite sure that it was Henry, and before the knocking had taken her by surprise.

"Come in," she said, in a cheerful voice. "Come in."

The door opened with wonderful swiftness—a figure stepped into the room, and then closed it as rapidly, and stood against it. Flora tried to scream, but her tongue refused its office; a confused whirl of sensations passed through her brain—she trembled, and an icy coldness came over her. It was Sir Francis Varney, the vampyre!

He had drawn up his tall, gaunt frame to its full height, and crossed his arms upon his breast; there was a hideous smile upon his sallow countenance, and his voice was deep and sepulchral, as he said,—

"Flora Bannerworth, hear that which I have to say, and hear it calmly. You need have nothing to fear. Make an alarm—scream, or shout for help, and, by the hell beneath us, you are lost!"

There was a death-like, cold, passionless manner about the utterance of these words, as if they were spoken mechanically, and came from no human lips.

Flora heard them, and yet scarcely comprehended them; she stepped slowly back till she reached a chair, and there she held for support. The only part of the address of Varney that thoroughly reached her ears, was that if she gave any alarm some dreadful consequences were to ensue. But it was not on account of these words that she really gave no alarm; it was because she was utterly unable to do so.

"Answer me," said Varney. "Promise that you will hear that which I have to say. In so promising you commit yourself to no evil, and you shall hear that which shall give you much peace."

It was in vain she tried to speak; her lips moved, but she uttered no sound.

"You are terrified," said Varney, "and yet I know not why. I do not come to do you harm, although harm have you done me. Girl, I come to rescue you from a thralldom of the soul under which you now labour."

There was a pause of some moments' duration, and then, faintly, Flora managed to say,—

"Help! help! Oh, help me, Heaven!"

Varney made a gesture of impatience, as he said,—

"Heaven works no special matters now. Flora Bannerworth, if you have as much intellect as your nobility and beauty would warrant the world in supposing, you will listen to me."

"I—I hear," said Flora, as she still, dragging the chair with her, increased the distance between them.

"'Tis well. You are now more composed."

She fixed her eyes upon the face of Varney with a shudder. There could be no mistake. It was the same which, with the strange, glassy looking eyes, had glared upon her on that awful night of the storm when she was visited by the vampyre. And Varney returned that gaze unflinchingly There was a hideous and strange contortion of his face now as he said,—

"You are beautiful. The most cunning statuary might well model some rare work of art from those rounded limbs, that were surely made to bewitch the gazer. Your skin rivals the driven snow—what a face of loveliness, and what a form of enchantment."

She did not speak, but a thought came across her mind, which at once crimsoned her cheek—she knew she had fainted on the first visit of the vampyre, and now he, with a hideous reverence, praised beauties which he might have cast his demoniac eyes over at such a time.

"You understand me," he said. "Well, let that pass. I am something allied to humanity yet."

"Speak your errand," gasped Flora, "or come what may, I scream for help to those who will not be slow to render it."

"I know it."

"You know I will scream?"

"No; you will hear me. I know they would not be slow to tender help to you, but you will not call for it; I will present to you no necessity."

"Say on—say on."

"You perceive I do not attempt to approach you; my errand is one of peace."

"Peace from you! Horrible being, if you be really what even now my appalled imagination shrinks from naming you, would not even to you absolute annihilation be a blessing?"

"Peace, peace. I came not here to talk on such a subject. I must be brief, Flora Bannerworth, for time presses. I do not hate you. Wherefore should I? You are young, and you are beautiful, and you bear a name which should command, and does command, some portion of my best regard."

"There is a portrait," said Flora, "in this house."

"No more—no more. I know what you would say."

"It is yours."

"The house, and all within, I covet," he said, uneasily. "Let that suffice. I have quarreled with your brother—I have quarrelled with one who just now fancies he loves you."

"Charles Holland loves me truly."

"It does not suit me now to dispute that point with you. I have the means of knowing more of the secrets of the human heart than common men. I tell you, Flora Bannerworth, that he who talks to you of love, loves you not but with the fleeting fancy of a boy; and there is one who hides deep in his heart a world of passion, one who has never spoken to you of love, and yet who loves you with a love as far surpassing the evanescent fancy of this boy Holland, as does the mighty ocean the most placid lake that ever basked in idleness beneath a summer's sun."

There was a wonderful fascination in the manner now of Varney. His voice sounded like music itself. His words flowed from his tongue, each gently and properly accented, with all the charm of eloquence. Despite her trembling horror of that man—despite her fearful opinion, which might be said to amount to a conviction of what he really was, Flora felt an irresistible wish to hear him speak on. Aye, despite too, the ungrateful theme to her heart which he had now chosen as the subject of his discourse, she felt her fear of him gradually dissipating, and now when he made a pause, she said,—

"You are much mistaken. On the constancy and truth of Charles Holland, I would stake my life."

"No doubt, no doubt."

"Have you spoken now that which you had to say?"

"No, no. I tell you I covet this place, I would purchase it, but having with your bad-tempered brothers quarrelled, they will hold no further converse with me."

"And well they may refuse."

"Be, that as it may, sweet lady, I come to you to be my mediator. In the shadow of the future I can see many events which are to come."

"Indeed."

"It is so. Borrowing some wisdom from the past, and some from resources I would not detail to you, I know that if I have inflicted much misery upon you, I can spare you much more. Your brother or your lover will challenge me."

"Oh, no, no."

"I say such will happen, and I can kill either. My skill as well as my strength is superhuman."

"Mercy! mercy!" gasped Flora.

"I will spare either or both on a condition."

"What fearful condition?"

"It is not a fearful one. Your terrors go far before the fact. All I wish, maiden, of you is to induce these imperious brothers of yours to sell or let the Hall to me."

"Is that all?"

"It is. I ask no more, and, in return, I promise you not only that I will not fight with them, but that you shall never see me again. Rest securely, maiden, you will be undisturbed by me."

"Oh, God! That were indeed an assurance worth the striving for," said Flora.

"It is one you may have. But—"

"Oh, I knew—my heart told me there was yet some fearful condition to come."

"You are wrong again. I only ask of you that you keep this meeting a secret."

"No, no, no—I cannot."

"Nay, what so easy?"

"I will not; I have no secrets from those I love."

"Indeed, you will find soon the expediency of a few at least; but if you will not, I cannot urge it longer. Do as your wayward woman's nature prompts you."

There was a slight, but a very slight, tone of aggravation in these words, and the manner in which they were uttered.

As he spoke, he moved from the door towards the window, which opened into a kitchen garden. Flora shrunk as far from him as possible, and for a few moments they regarded each other in silence.

"Young blood," said Varney, "mantles in your veins."

She shuddered with terror.

"Be mindful of the condition I have proposed to you. I covet Bannerworth Hall."

"I—I hear."

"And I must have it. I will have it, although my path to it be through a sea of blood. You understand me, maiden? Repeat what has passed between us or not, as you please. I say, beware of me, if you keep not the condition I have proposed."

"Heaven knows that this place is becoming daily more hateful to us all," said Flora.

"Indeed!"

"You well might know so much. It is no sacrifice to urge it now. I will urge my brother."

"Thanks—a thousand thanks. You may not live to regret even having made a friend of Varney—"

"The vampyre!" said Flora.

He towards her a step, and she involuntarily uttered a scream of terror.

In an instant his hand clasped her waist with the power of an iron vice; she felt his hot breath flushing on her cheek. Her senses reeled, and she found herself sinking. She gathered all her breath and all her energies into one piercing shriek, and then she fell to the floor. There was a sudden crash of broken glass, and then all was still.

CHAPTER XXXIV.
THE THREAT.—ITS CONSEQUENCES.—THE RESCUE, AND SIR FRANCIS VARNEY'S DANGER.

Sir Francis Varney now paused again, and he seemed for a few moments to gloat over the helpless condition of her whom he had so determined to make his victim; there was no look of pity in his face, no one touch of human kindness could be found in the whole expression of those diabolical features; and if he delayed making the attempt to strike terror into the heart of that unhappy, but beautiful being, it could not be from any relenting feeling, but simply, that he wished for a few moments to indulge his imagination with the idea of perfecting his villainy more effectually.

Alas! and they who would have flown to her rescue,—they, who for her would have chanced all accidents, ay, even life itself, were sleeping, and knew not of the loved one's danger. She was alone, and far enough from the house, to be driven to that tottering verge where sanity ends, and the dream of madness, with all its terrors, commences.

But still she slept—if that half-waking sleep could indeed be considered as anything akin to ordinary slumber—still she slept, and called mournfully upon her lover's name; and in tender, beseeching accents, that should have melted even the stubbornest hearts, did she express her soul's conviction that he loved her still.

The very repetition of the name of Charles Holland seemed to be galling to Sir Francis Varney. He made a gesture of impatience, as she again uttered it, and then, stepping forward, he stood within a pace of where she sat, and in a fearfully distinct voice he said,—

"Flora Bannerworth, awake! awake! and look upon me, although the sight blast and drive you to despair. Awake! awake!"

It was not the sound of the voice which aroused her from that strange slumber. It is said that those who sleep in that eccentric manner, are insensible to sounds, but that the lightest touch will arouse them in an instant; and so it was in this case, for Sir Francis Varney, as he spoke, laid upon the hand of Flora two of his cold, corpse-like looking fingers. A shriek burst from her lips, and although the confusion of her memory and conceptions was immense, yet she was awake, and the somnambulistic trance had left her.

"Help, help!" she cried. "Gracious Heavens! Where am I?"

Varney spoke not, but he spread out his long, thin arms in such a manner that he seemed almost to encircle her, while he touched her not, so that escape became a matter of impossibility, and to attempt to do so, must have been to have thrown herself into his hideous embrace.

She could obtain but a single view of the face and figure of him who opposed her progress, but, slight as that view was, it more than sufficed. The very extremity of fear came across her, and she sat like one paralysed; the only evidence of existence she gave consisting in the words,—

"The vampyre—the vampyre!"

"Yes," said Varney, "the vampyre. You know me, Flora Bannerworth—Varney, the vampyre; your midnight guest at that feast of blood. I am the vampyre. Look upon me well; shrink not from my gaze. You will do well not to shun me, but to speak to me in such a shape that I may learn to love you."

Flora shook as in a convulsion, and she looked as white as any marble statue.

"This is horrible!" she said. "Why does not Heaven grant me the death I pray for?"

"Hold!" said Varney. "Dress not up in the false colours of the imagination that which in itself is sufficiently terrific to need none of the allurements of romance. Flora Bannerworth, you are persecuted—persecuted by me, the vampyre. It is my fate to persecute you; for there are laws to the invisible as well as the visible creation that force even such a being as I am to play my part in the great drama of existence. I am a vampyre; the sustenance that supports this frame must be drawn from the life-blood of others."

"Oh, horror—horror!"

"But most I do affect the young and beautiful. It is from the veins of such as thou art, Flora Bannerworth, that I would seek the sustenance I'm compelled to obtain for my own exhausted energies. But never yet, in all my long career—a career extending over centuries of time—never yet have I felt the soft sensation of human pity till I looked on thee, exquisite piece of excellence. Even at the moment when the reviving fluid from the gushing fountain of your veins was warming at my heart, I pitied and I loved you. Oh, Flora! even I can now feel the pang of being what I am!"

There was a something in the tone, a touch of sadness in the manner, and a deep sincerity in these words, that in some measure disabused Flora of her fears. She sobbed hysterically, and a gush of tears came to her relief, as, in almost inarticulate accents, she said,—

"May the great God forgive even you!"

"I have need of such a prayer," exclaimed Varney—"Heaven knows I have need of such a prayer. May it ascend on the wings of the night air to the throne of Heaven. May it be softly whispered by ministering angels to the ear of Divinity. God knows I have need of such a prayer!"

"To hear you speak in such a strain," said Flora, "calms the excited fancy, and strips even your horrible presence of some of its maddening influence."

"Hush," said the vampyre, "you must hear more—you must know more ere you speak of the matters that have of late exercised an influence of terror over you."

"But how came I here?" said Flora, "tell me that. By what more than earthly power have you brought me to this spot? If I am to listen to you, why should it not be at some more likely time and place?"

"I have powers," said Varney, assuming from Flora's words that she would believe such arrogance—"I have powers which suffice to bend many purposes to my will—powers incidental to my position, and therefore is it I have brought you here to listen to that which should make you happier than you are."

"I will attend," said Flora. "I do not shudder now; there's an icy coldness through my veins, but it is the night air—speak, I will attend you."

"I will. Flora Bannerworth, I am one who has witnessed time's mutations on man and on his works, and I have pitied neither; I have seen the fall of empires, and sighed not that high reaching ambition was toppled to the dust. I have seen the grave close over the young and the beautiful—those whom I have doomed by my insatiable thirst for human blood to death, long ere the usual span of life was past, but I never loved till now."

"Can such a being as you," said Flora "be susceptible of such an earthly passion?"

"And wherefore not?"

"Love is either too much of heaven, or too much of earth to find a home with thee."

"No, Flora, no! it may be that the feeling is born of pity. I will save you—I will save you from a continuance of the horrors that are assailing you."

"Oh! then may Heaven have mercy in your hour of need!"

"Amen!"

"May you even yet know peace and joy above."

"It is a faint and straggling hope—but if achieved, it will be through the interposition of such a spirit as thine, Flora, which has already exercised so benign an influence upon my tortured soul, as to produce the wish within my heart, to do a least one unselfish action."

"That wish," said Flora, "shall be father to the deed. Heaven has boundless mercy yet."

"For thy sweet sake, I will believe so much, Flora Bannerworth; it is a condition with my hateful race, that if we can find one human heart to love us, we are free. If, in the face of Heaven, you will consent to be mine, you will snatch me from a continuance of my frightful doom, and for your pure sake, and on your merits, shall I yet know heavenly happiness. Will you be mine?"

A cloud swept from off the face of the moon, and a slant ray fell upon the hideous features of the vampire. He looked as if just rescued from some charnel-house, and endowed for a space with vitality to destroy all beauty and harmony in nature, and drive some benighted soul to madness.

"No, no, no!" shrieked Flora, "never!"

"Enough," said Varney, "I am answered. It was a bad proposal. I am a vampyre still."

"Spare me! spare me!"

"Blood!"

Flora sank upon her knees, and uplifted her hands to heaven. "Mercy, mercy!" she said.

"Blood!" said Varney, and she saw his hideous, fang-like teeth. "Blood! Flora Bannerworth, the vampyre's motto. I have asked you to love me, and you will not—the penalty be yours."

"No, no!" said Flora. "Can it be possible that even you, who have already spoken with judgment and precision, can be so unjust? You must feel that, in all respects, I have been a victim, most gratuitously— a sufferer, while there existed no just cause that I should suffer; one who has been tortured, not from personal fault, selfishness, lapse of integrity, or honourable feelings, but because you have found it necessary, for the prolongation of your terrific existence, to attack me as you have done. By what plea of honour, honesty, or justice, can I be blamed for not embracing an alternative which is beyond all human control?—I cannot love you."

"Then be content to suffer. Flora Bannerworth, will you not, even for a time, to save yourself and to save me, become mine?"

"Horrible proposition!"

"Then am I doomed yet, perhaps, for many a cycle of years, to spread misery and desolation around me; and yet I love you with a feeling which has in it more of gratefulness and unselfishness than ever yet found a home within my breast. I would fain have you, although you cannot save me; there may yet be a chance, which shall enable you to escape from the persecution of my presence."

"Oh! glorious chance!" said Flora. "Which way can it come? tell me how I may embrace it, and such grateful feelings as a heart-stricken mourner can offer to him who has rescued her from her deep affliction, shall yet be yours."

"Hear me, then, Flora Bannerworth, while I state to you some particulars of mysterious existence, of such beings as myself, which never yet have been breathed to mortal ears."

Flora looked intently at him, and listened, while, with a serious earnestness of manner, he detailed to her something of the physiology of the singular class of beings which the concurrence of all circumstances tended to make him appear.

"Flora," he said, "it is not that I am so enamoured of an existence to be prolonged only by such frightful means, which induces me to become a terror to you or to others. Believe me, that if my victims, those whom my insatiable thirst for blood make wretched, suffer much, I, the vampyre, am not without my moments of unutterable agony. But it is a mysterious law of our nature, that as the period approaches when the exhausted energies of life require a new support from the warm, gushing fountain of another's veins, the strong desire to live grows upon us, until, in a paroxysm of wild insanity, which will recognise no obstacles, human or divine, we seek a victim."

"A fearful state!" said Flora.

"It is so; and, when the dreadful repast is over, then again the pulse beats healthfully, and the wasted energies of a strange kind of vitality are restored to us, we become calm again, but with that calmness comes all the horror, all the agony of reflection, and we suffer far more than tongue can tell."

"You have my pity," said Flora; "even you have my pity."

"I might well demand it, if such a feeling held a place within your breast. I might well demand your pity, Flor a Bannerworth, for never crawled an abject wretch upon the earth's rotundity, so pitiable as I."

"Go on, go on."

"I will, and with such brief conclusions as I may. Having once attacked any human being, we feel a strange, but terribly impulsive desire again to seek that person for more blood. But I love you, Flora; the small amount of sensibility that still lingers about my preternatural existence, acknowledges in you a pure and better spirit. I would fain save you."

"Oh! tell me how I may escape the terrible infliction."

"That can only be done by flight. Leave this place, I implore you! leave it as quickly as the movement may be made. Linger not—cast not one regretful look behind you on your ancient home. I shall remain in this locality for years. Let me lose sight of you, I will not pursue you; but, by force of circumstances, I am myself compelled to linger here. Flight is the only means by which you may avoid a doom as terrific as that which I endure."

"But tell me," said Flora, after a moment's pause, during which she appeared to be endeavouring to gather courage to ask some fearful question; "tell me if it be true that those who have once endured the terrific attack of a vampyre, become themselves, after death, one of that dread race?"

"It is by such means," said Varney, "that the frightful brood increases; but time and circumstances must aid the development of the new and horrible existence. You, however, are safe."

"Safe! Oh! say that word again."

"Yes, safe; not once or twice will the vampyre's attack have sufficient influence on your mortal frame, as to induce a susceptibility on your part to become coexistent with such as he. The attacks must be often repeated, and the termination of mortal existence must be a consequence essential, and direct from those attacks, before such a result may be anticipated."

"Yes, yes; I understand."

"If you were to continue my victim from year to year, the energies of life would slowly waste away, and, till like some faint taper's gleam, consuming more sustenance than it received, the veriest accident would extinguish your existence, and then, Flora Bannerworth, you might become a vampyre."

"Oh! horrible! most horrible!"

"If by chance, or by design, the least glimpse of the cold moonbeams rested on your apparently lifeless remains, you would rise again and be one of us—a terror to yourself and a desolation to all around."

"Oh! I will fly from here," said Flora. "The hope of escape from so terrific and dreadful a doom shall urge me onward; if flight can save me—flight from Bannerworth Hall, I will pause not until continents and oceans divide us."

"It is well. I'm able now thus calmly to reason with you. A few short months more and I shall feel the languor of death creeping over me, and then will come that mad excitement of the brain, which, were you hidden behind triple doors of steel, would tempt me again to seek your chamber—again to seize you in my full embrace—again to draw from your veins the means of prolonged life—again to convulse your very soul with terror."

"I need no incentives," said Flora, with a shudder, "in the shape of descriptions of the past, to urge me on."

"You will fly from Bannerworth Hall?"

"Yes, yes!" said Flora, "it shall be so; its very chambers now are hideous with the recollection of scenes enacted in them. I will urge my brothers, my mother, all to leave, and in some distant clime we will find security and shelter. There even we will learn to think of you with more of sorrow than of anger—more pity than reproach—more curiosity than loathing."

"Be it so," said the vampyre; and he clasped his hands, as if with a thankfulness that he had done so much towards restoring peace at least to one, who, in consequence of his acts, had felt such exquisite despair. "Be it so; and even I will hope that the feelings which have induced so desolated and so isolated a being as myself to endeavour to bring peace to one human heart, will plead for me, trumpet-tongued, to Heaven!"

"It will—it will," said Flora.

"Do you think so?"

"I do; and I will pray that the thought may turn to certainty in such a cause."

The vampyre appeared to be much affected; and then he added,—

"Flora, you know that this spot has been the scene of a catastrophe fearful to look back upon, in the annals of your family?"

"It has," said Flora. "I know to what you allude; 'tis a matter of common knowledge to all—a sad theme to me, and one I would not court."

"Nor would I oppress you with it. Your father, here, on this very spot, committed that desperate act which brought him uncalled for to the judgment seat of God. I have a strange, wild curiosity upon such subjects. Will you, in return for the good that I have tried to do you, gratify it?"

"I know not what you mean," said Flora.

"To be more explicit, then, do you remember the day on which your father breathed his last?"

"Too well—too well."

"Did you see him or converse with him shortly before that desperate act was committed?"

"No; he shut himself up for some time in a solitary chamber."

"Ha! what chamber?"

"The one in which I slept myself on the night—"

"Yes, yes; the one with the portrait—that speaking portrait—the eyes of which seem to challenge an intruder as he enters the apartment."

"The same."

"For hours shut up there!" added Varney, musingly; "and from thence he wandered to the garden, where, in this summer-house, he breathed his last?"

"It was so."

"Then, Flora, ere I bid you adieu—"

These words were scarcely uttered, when there was a quick, hasty footstep, and Henry Bannerworth appeared behind Varney, in the very entrance of the summer-house.

"Now," he cried, "for revenge! Now, foul being, blot upon the earth's surface, horrible imitation of humanity, if mortal arm can do aught against you, you shall die!"

A shriek came from the lips of Flora, and flinging herself past Varney, who stepped aside, she clung to her brother, who made an unavailing pass with his sword at the vampyre. It was a critical moment; and had the presence of mind of Varney deserted him in the least, unarmed as he was, he must have fallen beneath the weapon of Henry. To spring, however, up the seat which Flora had vacated, and to dash out some of the flimsy and rotten wood-work at the back of the summer-house by the propulsive power of his whole frame, was the work of a moment; and before Henry could free himself from the clinging embrace of Flora, Varney, the vampyre was gone, and there was no greater chance of his capture than on a former occasion, when he was pursued in vain from the Hall to the wood, in the intricacies of which he was so entirely lost.

GLOSSARY

Admiral..."*grew paler*": Reference to the 19th century song "The Return of the Admiral" by Barry Cornwall.
"*Decay's offensive fingers*": quoted from Byron's poem *The Giaour*.
Desiderata: Latin for "a thing to be desired."
"*Do as you think. You are fertile in expedients. Do as you think...*" The text for this line in Chapter IV was "Do you think." I have added the "as" in both cases for what I think it clarity.
Dr. Johnson: Samuel Johnson published his *Dictionary* in 1755; another reason to suspect the story of *Varney* to be set in the early 19th

century. However, Dr. Johnson did *not* include a definition for "vampyre" or "vampire"—the "quotation" is fictitious.

Gammon: A smoked ham-haunch; but in the way Admiral Bell uses it, an 18th century slang term meaning "nonsense" or "rubbish."

Levant: A wide-ranging term; the general area of the Eastern Mediterranean, from Greece to Syria.

"He holds her with his glittering eye.": Rymer steals one of the most famous lines from Coleridge's 1798 poem. *The Rime of the Ancient Mariner:*

> *He holds him with his glittering eye—*
> *The Wedding-Guest stood still,*
> *And listens like a three years' child:*
> *The Mariner hath his will.*

The Romantics—and the penny dreadful writers—loved the idea of an overpowering will. Vampires in the mid-1840s do not yet have the power of instant hypnosis or telepathy, but Varney's force of will is practically supernatural.

Mahometans: Muslims.

Mantle: Used here in the sense of spreading over something.

Meed of praise: "Meed" is an appropriate or deserved share or reward.

Nelson's Arms: Admiral Horatio Nelson, Britain's greatest naval hero, lived 1758-1805. Bell and Pringle's talk of long-ago battles near Corfu (probably a reference to naval engagements of 1798) and Yankee ships, indicates an early 19th century setting.

Old Scratch and Old Bogie: "Scratch" is a nickname for the devil; a "bogie" hides in corners and makes strange sounds.

Postchaise: A four-wheeled carriage.

Postillion: Carriage driver.

Travels in Norway and Sweden: A made-up book, though possibly based on Samuel Laing's *Journal of a Residence in Norway in the Years 1834, 1835, and 1836.* Norway and Sweden were actually hotbeds of vampire lore, although the Viking Sagas are full of the *draugr,* or *aptrgangr* ("after-walkers"), the recently dead returning to bother and even infect the living,—without, however, actually sucking their blood. Rymer is conflating two different superstitions. However, it's intriguing that Rymer is hinting that his English vampire is not originally from Poland or Serbia or somewhere else in the East, but, rather, might have a Nordic background.ir Walter Scott published a summary in English of some of the sagas in 1814, and this may be were Rymer got his information, although the saga called *Heimskringla* was translated into English in 1844 by Laing, a year before *Varney.*

Undress Naval Uniform: a uniform worn on non-formal occasions; possibly a frock coat.

Wagabone: Jack's cockney version of "vagabond."

AFTERWORD

A note for concerned readers: Varney never does vampirize Flora; she comes out of the whole nightmarish ordeal alive and well.

The events concerning Flora and her family eventually conclude, but Varney's adventures continue. Some of his further exploits are found in Volume II: The Vampire Ladies, where another aristocratic young lady is vampirized with tragic results. Rymer tries, with Victorian rigor, to build on the treatises of the 1700s, to go deeper into the mythology of vampirism, to explain exactly how a vampire's victim becomes a vampire—something Polidori neglected, and, frankly, something that has never been standardized in the genre. How many bites does it take to turn a victim? How much blood needs to be taken? How long a process is it? Well, it all depends on who's writing the story, and, even then, there can be inconsistencies.

As far as undead attributes are concerned, Sir Francis Varney is clearly a literary descendant of Lord Ruthven; not just because of his title, but because of his dependence on moonlight for revival. But while Lord Ruthven is the first vampire in fiction to leave tell-tale bite marks, Sir Francis Varney is the first to have true fangs.

Varney also precedes Dracula in not drinking a glass of wine; and, as pointed out earlier, he's the first vampire whose survival through the centuries is a major point of the plot and his character. Speaking of character: Varney is the first male vampire whose villainy is shaded with feelings of deep regret, which makes him even more Byronic than Ruthven. At other times in Varney, vampirism is spoken of as an addiction.

Although Sir Francis Varney was popular enough to run through two solid years of penny dreadfuls in the 1840's, and to have his saga reprinted in 1853, he then fell into near-oblivion; it was probably a mention by Montague Summers in his 1928 historical study, The Vampire: His Kith and Kin, *that started the search to recover the complete story among fans of Gothic fiction.*

Full reprints of the Varney penny dreadfuls were made available in the early 1970's; and now, Sir Francis Varney is online. He deserves to be better known than he is.

The next, and final, story in this volume takes us, for the first time in the genre, to the Carpathian mountains; it features a resourceful heroine and a vampire Count...but the tale was written almost fifty years before Dracula.

And, although written by two men, the story is told from a woman's point of view: another first in vampire fiction...

COUNT KOSTAKI

My door opened slowly, noiselessly, as if pushed inward by a supernatural force…

The Pale Lady *continues a peculiar sub-theme of early vampire literature: that of the secret author. While Ossenfelder and John Stagg proudly signed their short vampire poems, no one knows* who wrote the first English newspaper accounts of Arnold Paul *(although the local investigators signed the official report); Byron was thought to be the author of* The Vampyre; *Tolstoy published his novel of aristocratic vampires under another name;* Varney *was published without a byline and the identity of the author or authors was debated for more than a hundred years...and* The Pale Lady *first appeared in 1849 as the sole work of Alexandre Dumas, already renowned for* The Three Musketeers *and* The Count of Monte Cristo, *although, like those works, it was written with a collaborator.*

Instead of Auguste Maquet, the co-author of Monte Cristo *and the adventures of D'Artagnan and his friends, Dumas wrote his vampire story with Paul Bocage. We don't know the details of the collaboration, but it's likely that Bocage worked on the plot and set out the characters, then handed it over to Dumas for dialogue, colorful descriptions and actions, etc.*

La Dame Pâle *is the concluding story, told over several chapters, in* Les Mille et uns fantômes. *That's* The Thousand and One Ghosts, *although there are actually only a handful of stories. The conceit is that various people are gathered in a room in Paris to talk about supernatural events that they know about or experienced first-hand.*

Hedwig, the narrator and heroine, recounts her story in the "present," that is, the late 1840's, but the events themselves take place in 1825 and 1826, and a few historical notes may be useful to 21st century readers:

Hedwig is Polish, although there was no independent Poland in the 19th century. Various parts of the Polish state (and Lithuania) were absorbed into Prussia, Russia, or Austria-Hungary during three "partitions" in 1772, 1793, and 1795. In December 1825, Nicholas I became tsar of Russia—and its Polish territories. His coronation was the signal for a rebellion in Poland. The "Decembrists" fought for Polish independence, legal reforms, and either a republic or a limited monarchy. But they were ill-organized, and Russian forces crushed the rebellion. There would be no independent Polish state again until 1918.

By making their heroine a Pole, Dumas and Bocage give Hedwig a foothold in both the civilized, skeptical West and the more primitive, superstitious, tribal East. As a Pole, she thirsts for independence and personal liberty, and is more than capable of leading men in an impromptu cavalry charge. She does faint more than might be expected; but her essential strength and intelligence make her victimization by supernatural forces all the more powerful.

THE PALE LADY

Alexandre Dumas & Paul Bocage

"Listen," said the pale lady, with a strange solemnity, "since everyone here has told a story, I want to tell one too. Doctor, you will not say that the story is not true, for it is mine. You shall know why I am so pale."

At that moment, a ray of moonlight slid out of the window through the curtains, and, coming to play on the couch where she lay, enveloped her in a bluish light that seemed to make her a black marble statue lying on a tomb. Not a voice was raised; but the deep silence which reigned in the drawing-room announced that everyone anxiously awaited her tale....

THE CARPATHIAN MOUNTAINS

I am Polish, born in Sandomir; that is to say, in a country where legends become articles of faith, where we believe in our family traditions as much, perhaps more, than in the Gospel. There is not one of our castles that does not have its spectre, not one of our cottages without its familiar spirit.

Both rich and poor, in the castle as in the cottage, recognize the principles of good and evil. Sometimes these two principles come into conflict. Then there are such mysterious noises in the corridors, such terrible roars in the old towers, such frightful tremors in the walls, that one flees from the cottage as one does the castle, and peasants and gentlemen run to the church to seek the blessed cross or the holy relics, the only protections against the demons that torment us.

But, in this land, two other principles, more terrible, more fierce, more implacable, are also in opposition: tyranny and liberty.

The year 1825 saw one of those struggles between Russia and

Poland in which one would think that all the blood of a people would be drained, as the blood of a family is often drained.

My father and my two brothers joined the revolt against the new tsar, and rode under the flag of Polish independence, always struck down, always raised up again.

One day I learned that my youngest brother had been killed; another day, I was told that my older brother was mortally wounded; finally, after a day during which I had listened with terror to the sound of ever-nearing cannon, I saw my father arrive with a hundred horsemen, the debris of the three thousand men he once commanded.

He came to shut himself up in our castle, with the intention of being buried under its ruins when the enemy destroyed it. My father, who feared nothing for himself, was trembling for me. He looked forward to nothing but death, because he was determined not to fall alive into the hands of his enemies; but my fate would be slavery, dishonor, shame.

My father, among the hundred men who remained, chose ten, called the steward, gave him all the gold and jewels we possessed, and, remembering how, during the second division of Poland, my mother, then but a child, had found an impregnable refuge in the monastery of Sahastru, situated in the middle of the Carpathian mountains, he ordered him to take me to this monastery, which, hospitable to the mother, would not be less hospitable, no doubt, to the girl.

Despite the great love my father had for me, the goodbyes were not long. In all likelihood, the Russians would be in sight of the castle by the next day. There was no time to lose.

I hastily put on a riding habit, with which I used to accompany my brothers on the hunt. The men saddled me the safest horse in the stable; my father slipped his own pistols, a masterpiece of the Tula factory, into my holsters, kissed me, and gave the order to leave. That night and the following day, we traveled twenty leagues, following the banks of one of those nameless rivers which flung themselves into the Vistula. This hard riding put us out of reach of the Russians.

At the last rays of the sun, we saw the snowy peaks of the Carpathian mountains sparkle. Towards the end of the next day we reached their base; finally, on the morning of the third day, we entered one of their winding gorges.

Our Carpathian mountains do not resemble the civilized mountains of your West. All that nature has of the strange and grandiose presents itself to the eyes in the most complete majesty. Their stormy peaks are lost in the clouds, covered with eternal snows; their immense forests of fir trees lean over the polished mirrors of lakes like seas; never has a keel furrowed these lakes, never has the net of a fisherman disturbed their crystal waters, as deep as the azure of the sky. The human voice is rarely heard, although from time to time Moldavian peasants sing a song to which the cries of wild animals respond. Singing and shouting will awaken some solitary echo, astonished that any rumor has taught him his own existence.

For many miles we traveled under the dark vaults of wood cut by the unexpected marvels that solitude revealed to us at every step, and which made our minds pass from astonishment to admiration. There, danger is everywhere, and consists of a thousand different perils; but one feels no fear, for the dangers are so grand and sublime. Sometimes there are cascades flowing from the melting ice, which, leaping from rock to rock, suddenly invade the narrow path that you follow, a path drawn by the passage of the wild beast and the hunter pursuing it; sometimes there are weather-tortured trees that stand out from the ground and fall with a terrible crash that seems to be that of an earthquake; and, sometimes, the hurricanes envelop you in clouds, in the midst of which the lightning flashes, stretches, and twists, like a serpent of fire.

Then, after these alpine peaks, after these primitive forests, where you once had giant mountains and boundless woods, you now have endless steppes, like a sea with its waves and storms, arid and rolling savannahs where the view is lost in a boundless horizon; then it is no longer the terror that seizes you, it is the sadness that inundates you; it is a vast and profound melancholy from which nothing can distract; for the aspect of the country, as far as your gaze may extend, is always the same. You go up and down similar slopes twenty times, vainly searching for a marked path: seeing yourself thus lost in your isolation, in the midst of deserts, you believe yourself alone in nature, and your melancholy becomes desolation; indeed, the march seems to have become an iniquitous thing which will lead you to nothing. You meet neither village, nor castle, nor cottage, no trace of human habitation; sometimes only, like another sorrow in this bleak landscape, a small lake without reeds, without bushes, asleep at the bottom of a ravine, like another Dead Sea, blocks the road with its green waters, above which, at your approach, some water birds raise long and discordant cries. Then, you make a detour; you climb the hill in front of you, you go down into another valley, you climb another hill, and it lasts until you have exhausted the chain of ever-receding foothills. But, once this chain is exhausted, if you make a turn towards the south, then the landscape recovers its grandeur. Then you see another, higher, mountain range, of more picturesque form, of richer aspect; this one is all covered with forests, cut through with streams: with the shadow and the water, life is reborn in the landscape; we hear the bell of a hermitage; we see a caravan meandering on the mountainside. Finally, at the last rays of the sun, one can distinguish, like a band of white birds leaning against each other, the houses of a village which seem to have grouped together to protect themselves from some nocturnal attack. With the sight of human life, our danger returned, for it was no longer, as in the first mountains that we crossed, bands of bears and wolves to be feared, but hordes of Moldavian brigands to fight.

Despite the danger, we went on. Ten days of travel had passed without incident. We could already see the summit of Mount Pion, which surpasses the whole family of giants, on the southern slope of which is located the convent of Sahastru, my destination.

Another three days, and we had arrived. We were at the end of July; the day had been very hot, and it was with unparalleled pleasure that at about four o'clock we began to inhale the first chill of the evening. We passed the ruined towers of Niantzo, and rode down to a plain that we began to see through the opening of the mountains. We could already, from where we were, follow the course of the Bistriza, with its enameled red banks and large bellflowers with their white petals. We made our way alongside a precipice, at the bottom of which rolled the river in torrent. Our horses had barely enough space to walk two abreast. Our guide preceded us, lying sideways on his horse, singing a song with monotonous modulations. I followed the words with singular interest. The singer was also the composer. As for the air, it would be necessary to be one of these men of the mountains to make you understand all its wild sadness, all its dark simplicity. Here are the words:

"In the swamp of Stavila,
Where so much warrior blood flowed,
Do you see that corpse!
He is not a son of Illyria;
He's a raging brigand
Who, deceiving sweet Marie,
Exterminated, deceived, burned.

A bullet in the heart of the brigand
Has passed like a hurricane,
In his throat is a yatagan.

But for three days, oh mystery,
Under the sad and lonely pine,
His warm blood is watering the earth
And darkening the pale Ovigan.

His blue eyes forever stare;
Let's all flee, woe to he
Who goes to the swamp near him.

It's a vampire! The tawny wolf
Far from the unclean corpse fleeing,

And on the bald-faced mountain,
The frightened vulture fled.

Suddenly the explosion of a gun was heard, and a bullet whistled. The song was interrupted, and the guide, struck to death, rolled from the saddle and tumbled to the bottom of the precipice. His horse extended his head over the abyss where his master had disappeared.

At the same time a loud cry arose, and we saw some thirty bandits standing on the sides of the mountain; we were completely surrounded.

Everyone seized his weapon, and although taken unexpectedly, those who accompanied me were old soldiers accustomed to battle, and did not allow themselves to be intimidated. They returned fire. I myself, setting an example, seized a pistol, and, feeling the disadvantage of our position, cried, "Forward!" and spurred my horse down towards the flat plain.

But we were dealing with mountaineers who leapt among the rocks like true demons of the abyss, firing while leaping, always keeping their position on our flank.

Worse, our attempted escape had been expected. At a place where the road widened into a plateau, a young man was waiting for us at the head of a dozen people on horseback. As soon as they saw us, they set their horses on a gallop, and struck us head-on, while those who pursued us were rolling down the sides of the mountain, and, having cut off our retreat, enveloped us on all sides. The situation was serious, and yet, accustomed from my childhood to scenes of war, I could observe it without missing a single detail. All these men were dressed in sheepskins, and wore huge round hats crowned with wildflowers, like those of the Hungarians. They each had in their hands a long Turkish rifle, which they waved after firing, uttering wild cries, and each man at his waist wore a curved sword and a pair of pistols.

As for their leader, he was a young man of only twenty-two years of age, with a pale complexion, large black eyes, and curling hair on his shoulders. His costume consisted of the Moldavian dress trimmed with furs and tied at the waist with a red and gold silk scarf. A curved saber shone in his hand, and four pistols glittered at his belt. During the fight, he uttered hoarse and inarticulate cries that seemed not to belong to the human tongue and yet expressed his wishes, because at these cries his men obeyed, throwing themselves on the ground to avoid our soldiers' fire, rising to fire in their turn, shooting down those who were still standing, finishing the wounded and finally changing the fight into a butcher's shop.

I had seen two-thirds of my defenders fall one by one. Four were still standing, ranging themselves around me, not asking for a grace that they were certain not to get, and only thinking of one thing, to sell their lives as dearly as possible. Then the young chief uttered a louder cry and aimed the point of his saber towards us. No doubt this order was to wrap this last group with a circle of fire, and shoot us all together, for the long Moldavian muskets were lowered in the same movement. I realized that our last hour had come. I raised my eyes and hands to heaven with one last prayer, and waited for death.

At that moment I saw, leaping down from higher in the mountain, a young man, who stopped and stood on an outcropping that dominated the scene. He was like a statue on a pedestal as he put out his hand over the field of battle, and uttered only this one word: "Enough."

At this voice, all eyes rose, each one seeming to obey this new master. Only one bandit put his rifle back to his shoulder and fired. One of our men screamed; the bullet had broken his left arm. He turned at once to charge at the man who had wounded him; but before his horse had taken four steps, a flash of lightning shone over our heads, and the rebellious bandit fell, his head shattered by a bullet.

So many different emotions had led me to the end of my strength, I fainted.

When I came back to myself, I was lying on the grass, my head resting on a man's knees. He held his very white hand, covered with rings, around my waist; while, in front of us, standing with his saber under one of his crossed arms, was the young Moldavian leader who had directed the attack against us.

"Kostaki, withdraw your men," the man holding me said in French, with a tone of authority, "and leave me the care of this young woman."

"Brother, my brother," replied the one to whom these words were addressed, and who seemed to restrain himself with difficulty, "my brother, beware of wearying my patience: I leave you the castle, leave me the forest. At the castle, you are the master, but here I am almighty. Here, I would just need a word to force you to obey me."

"Kostaki, I am the eldest, so I am the master everywhere, in the forest as in the castle, there as here. Oh! I am of the blood of the Brankovans, like you, the royal blood that is in the habit of commanding, and I command."

"You order, you, Gregoriska, to your valets, yes; to my soldiers, no."

"Your soldiers are brigands, Kostaki. Robbers whom I will have hanged in the battlements of our towers, if they do not obey me this instant."

"Well! try to order them."

Then I felt the one who supported me pull his knee away and gently place my head on a stone. I watched him anxiously, and I recognized the same young man who had fallen, so to speak, from the sky in the middle of the fray, and whom I had only been able to glimpse, having fainted at the very moment he had spoken.

He was a young man of twenty-four, of tall stature, with large blue eyes in which one read a singular resolution and firmness. His long blond hair, a clue to his Slav ancestry, fell on his shoulders like those of the archangel Michael, framing young and fresh cheeks; his lips were raised by a disdainful smile, and showed a double row of pearls; his gaze was that of the eagle, crossed with lightning. He was dressed in a sort of tunic of black velvet; a little cap like that of Raphael, adorned with an eagle feather, covered his head; he had close-fitting pants and embroidered boots. His waist was tightened by a belt supporting a hunting knife; he wore a small double-barreled rifle over his shoulder, which one of the bandits had just had the opportunity to appreciate.

He extended his hand, and this hand seemed to command even

his brother. He spoke a few words in the Moldavian language. These words seemed to make a deep impression on the bandits. Then, in the same language, the young chief spoke in his turn, and I guessed that his words were mixed with threats and imprecations. But at this long and burning speech, the eldest of the two brothers answered only one word.

The bandits bowed. He made a gesture, and the bandits assembled behind us.

"Well! So it is, Gregoriska," said Kostaki, returning to the French language. "This woman will not go to the cave, but she will be none the less mine. I find her beautiful, I conquered her and I want her." And saying these words, he threw himself on me and lifted me into his arms.

"This woman will be taken to the castle and handed over to my mother, and I will not leave her until then," replied my protector.

Kostaki cried out in Moldavian. Ten bandits hastened to obey, and brought to their master the horse he was asking for. Gregoriska looked around him, grasped the bridle of a horse without a master, and jumped on it without touching the stirrups.

Kostaki seated himself almost as lightly as his brother, though he still held me in his arms, and set off at a gallop.

Gregoriska's horse seemed to have received the same impulse, and stuck his head and flank to Kostaki's head and flank.

It was a curious thing to see these two riders flying side by side, determined, silent, not losing sight of the other for a moment, though without seeming to look at each other. They gave free rein to their horses, as their desperate race carried them through the woods and along the rocks and the precipices. My head, thrown back, allowed me to see Gregoriska's beautiful eyes fixed on mine. Kostaki noticed it, and raised my head, so that I saw only his dark gaze devouring me. I lowered my eyelids, but it was useless; through their veil, I continued to see that throbbing glance that penetrated to the bottom of my chest and pierced my heart. Then a strange hallucination took possession of me; I seemed to be the Lenore of Burger's ballad, carried away by the ghost horse and rider, and when I felt that we were stopping, it was only with terror that I opened my eyes, so much I was convinced that I was going to see around me only broken crosses and open tombs.

What I saw was hardly more cheerful, it was the inner courtyard of a Moldavian castle, built in the fourteenth century.

CASTLE BRANKOVAN

Kostaki let me slide from his arms to the ground, and almost instantly jumped down beside me; but, quick as his movement had been, he had only followed that of Gregoriska. As Gregoriska had said, at the castle he was the master. On seeing the two young men arrive, and that stranger whom they brought, the servants ran up; but, although the care was shared between Kostaki and Gregoriska, it was felt that the greatest consideration, that the most profound respects, were for the latter. Two women approached; Gregoriska gave them an order in the Moldavian language and waved me to follow them. There was so much respect in the look that accompanied this sign that I did not hesitate.

Five minutes later I was in a room, which, though it might have seemed bare and uninhabitable to the most exacting of men, was evidently the most beautiful of the castle.

It was a large square room, with a sort of green serge couch: a sofa during the day, and a bed at night. Five or six large oak armchairs, a large sideboard, and, in one corner of this room, a canopied chair looking like a large and magnificent church stall. There were no curtains on the bed or over the windows.

The way to the room was up a staircase, along which, in niches, stood three larger-than-life statues of the Brankovans.

In this room, after a very little time, my luggage was brought, including my trunks. The women offered me their services. I repaired the disorder which this event had wrought on my outfit, but I kept on my riding-habit, a costume more in harmony with that of my guests than any of those which I could have taken from my trunks.

Hardly were these small changes made, when I heard a gentle knock on my door.

"Come in," I said in French; French, as you know, being to us Poles an almost maternal language.

Gregoriska entered. "Ah! madame, I am happy that you speak French."

"And I, too, sir," replied I, "I am happy to speak this language, since I have been able, by chance, to appreciate your generous conduct towards me. It is in this language that you have defended me against the designs of your brother; it is in this language that I offer you the expression of my sincere gratitude."

"Thank you, Madam. It was only natural that I was interested in a woman in the position you were in. I was hunting in the mountains when I heard irregular and continuous gunfire; I understood that it was some armed attack, and I walked on fire, as they say in the military. I arrived in time, thanks to heaven. But will you allow me to ask you, madam, by what chance did a woman of distinction such as yourself venture into our mountains?"

"I am Polish, sir," replied I, "my two brothers have just been killed in the war against Russia; my father, whom I left ready to defend our castle against the enemy, has no doubt rejoined them by now. I, on his orders, fled the massacres. I came to seek refuge at the Sahastru monastery, where my mother, in her youth and under similar circumstances, had found a safe haven."

"You are the enemy of the Russians; so much the better," said the young man. "This fact will be a strong point in your favor at the castle, and we need all our strength to support the struggle that is coming. First of all, since I know who you are, know, madam, who we are: Brankovan's name is not foreign to you, is it, madam?" I bowed. "My mother is the last princess of that name, the last descendant of that illustrious chief whom the Cantimir, those miserable courtiers of Peter I, had killed. My mother first married my father, Serban Waivady, a prince like her, but of less illustrious race. My father had been raised in Vienna; he had been able to appreciate the advantages of civilization.

"He resolved to make me a European. We left for France, Italy,

Spain and Germany. My mother (it is not for a son, I know it well, to tell you what I am about to say to you, but as it is necessary that you know us well, you will appreciate the causes of this revelation); my mother, who, during my father's first travels, when I was in my youngest childhood, had guilty relations with a leader of…partisans. That is how," added Gregoriska with a smile, "this country calls the men who attacked you; so, I say, my mother had guilty relations with Count Giordaki Koproli, half Greek, half Moldavian. She wrote to my father to tell him everything and ask him to divorce her; saying, in this demand, that she, a Brankovan, did not wish to remain the wife of a man who day by day became more foreign to his country. Alas! my father did not need to give his consent to this request—a request which may seem strange to you, but which, in our country, is the most common and the most natural thing in the world—for my father had just died of an aneurysm from which he had long suffered. I had nothing to do except convey my sincere wishes for her happiness to my mother. These vows were in the letter from me to her, announcing that she was a widow. This same letter asked her for permission to continue my travels, which permission was granted to me. My very firm intention was to settle in France or Germany, so as not to find myself in the presence of a man who hated me and whom I could not love, that is, my mother's second husband; when, suddenly, I learned that Count Giordaki Koproli had just been murdered, as it was said, by the old Cossacks of my father. I hastened to return; I loved my mother; I understood her isolation, her need to have with her, at such a time, the people who could be dear to her. Although she had never had any tender affection for me, I was her son. I returned one morning, without being expected, to the castle of our fathers. I found a young man whom I first took for a stranger, and whom I afterwards knew to be my brother.

"It was Kostaki, the son of adultery, that a second marriage legitimized, Kostaki, that is to say the indomitable creature you saw, whose passions are his only law, who holds nothing sacred in this world but his mother, who obeys me like the tiger obeys the arm that has tamed him—with an eternal roar, sustained by the vague hope of one day devouring me. In the interior of the castle, in the house of Brankovan and Waivady, I am still the master; but once outside this enclosure, once in the open country, he becomes again the savage child of the woods and the mountains, who wants to bend everything under his iron will. How did he give in today, how did his men give in? I do not know; an old habit, a remnant of respect. But I would not venture another test. Stay here, do not leave this room, this courtyard, the inside of the walls. Here, I am the final answer for everything; take a step out of the castle, I cannot answer for anything…except that I would die to defend you."

"Cannot I, according to the wishes of my father, continue my journey to the convent of Sahastru?"

"Order me, and I will accompany you; but I will remain on the road, and you, you ... you will not arrive."

"What to do, then?"

"Rest here, wait on events and take advantage of circumstances. Suppose you have fallen into a bandit den, and only your courage can help you, only your coolness can save you. My mother, despite her preference for Kostaki, the son of her love, is good and generous. Besides, she's a Brankovan, which means she is a true princess. You will see it; she will defend you from Kostaki's brutal passions. Put yourself under her protection; you are beautiful, she will love you. Besides," he looked at me with an indefinable expression, "who could see you and not love you? Come to the dining room now, where she is waiting for us. Do not show embarrassment or distrust; speak in Polish: nobody knows this language here; I will translate your words to my mother, and rest assured, I will say only what must be said. Above all, not a word about what I have just revealed to you, or of what we understand of each other. You are still ignorant of the cunning and dissimulation of the most sincere among us. Come."

I followed him down that staircase, lit by torches of resin burning in iron hands mounted on the walls. It was obvious that it was for me that he had made this unusual illumination.

We arrived at the dining room.

As soon as Gregoriska had opened the door, and had, in Moldavian, uttered a word, which I have since known to mean "the stranger," a great woman advanced towards us. It was Princess Brankovan. Her white hair was wound around her head; she wore a little sable cap, surmounted by an egret, a testimony of her princely origin. She wore a sort of tunic of gold cloth, and her bodice, beaded with precious stones, covered a long robe of Turkish stuff, trimmed with fur like that of her cap.

She held in her hand a rosary with amber beads, which she rolled very fast between her fingers.

Beside her was Kostaki, wearing the splendid and majestic Magyar costume, which made him seem even more exotic than before. It was a green velvet dress, with wide sleeves, falling below the knee. He wore pantaloons of red cashmere, slippers of Moroccan leather embroidered with gold; his head was uncovered, and his long hair, so black it was almost blue, fell on his bare neck, which was covered by only the light white thread of a silk shirt. (Gregoriska wore the Magyar tunic like his brother; only this tunic was of garnet velvet with blue cashmere trousers. A magnificent decoration hung around his neck: it was Sultan Mahmoud's Nishan.)

Kostaki greeted me awkwardly, and pronounced, in Moldavian, some words which remained unintelligible to me.

"You can speak French, my brother," said Gregoriska. "Madame is Polish, and understands that language."

Then Kostaki pronounced, in French, some words which were almost as unintelligible to me as those he had said in Moldavian; but the mother, gravely extending her arm, interrupted him. It was obvious to me that she was telling both her sons that it was her place to receive me. Then, in Moldavian, she began a welcome speech, to which her smiling face gave a meaning that needed no translation.

She showed me the table, offered me a seat near her, and gestured to the whole house, as if to say that it was mine; and, sitting first with a benevolent dignity, she made a sign of the cross, and began a prayer.

Then each took his place, as fixed by etiquette. Gregoriska sat just below me. I was the foreigner, and consequently I was given a place of honor next to Kostaki, who sat by his mother Smerande. This was the name of the Countess.

The rest of the servants of the house supped at the same table, each sitting according to their rank.

The supper was grave; not once did Kostaki speak to me, although his brother was always ready to translate anything for me in French. As for the mother, she offered me everything herself with that solemn air which never left her. As Gregoriska had said, she was a true princess.

After supper, Gregoriska approached his mother. He explained to her, in Moldavian, the need I had to be alone, and how much rest was necessary after the emotions of such a day. Smerande nodded her approval, held out her hand, kissed me on the forehead, as she would have done with her daughter, and wished me a good night in her castle.

Gregoriska was not mistaken: I longed for some time by myself. So I thanked the princess, who brought me back to the door, where the two women who had already taken me to my room waited for me.

I thanked her and her two sons, and returned to the same chamber from which I had gone an hour before.

The sofa had been made into a bed. That was the only change.

I thanked the serving-women. With gestures, I told them that I would undress by myself; they went out at once with gestures of respect which indicated that they had orders to obey me in all things. I remained in that immense room, of which my light, while I walked, illuminated only the parts that I traversed, without ever being able to enlighten all. A strange play of the light made a struggle between the glow of my candle and the rays of the moon, which passed through my curtainless window. In addition to the door by which I had entered, which looked out on the staircase, two other doors opened into my room; but enormous bolts secured them from the inside, and assured me of my safety. I went to the front door, and tried it. Like the other doors, it was a firm defense. I opened my window; it overlooked a precipice. I realized that Gregoriska had been very thoughtful in choosing to give me this room. At last, returning to my sofa, I found on a table placed at my bedside a little folded note. I opened it, and I read, in Polish: *"Sleep easy; you will have nothing to fear as long as you live in the interior of the castle. - Gregoriska."* I followed the advice given to me, and, as tiredness overcame my preoccupations, I went to bed, and fell asleep.

THE TWO BROTHERS

From that moment on, I was established at the castle, and from that moment began the tragedy I am about to tell you.

The two brothers fell in love with me, each according to his character.

Kostaki, the next day, told me that he loved me, declared that I should be his and not another's, and that he would kill me rather than let me belong to anyone else.

Gregoriska said nothing; but he enveloped me with care and attention. All the resources of a brilliant education, all the memories of a youth spent in the most noble courts of Europe, were employed to please me. Alas! it was not difficult: at the first sound of his voice, I felt that voice caressing my soul; at the first glance of his eyes, I felt that his look penetrated to my heart.

After three months, Kostaki had told me a hundred times that he loved me, and I hated him; at the end of three months Gregoriska had not yet said a single word of love, and I felt that, when he would demand it, I would be all his own.

Kostaki had given up his outside duties. He no longer left the castle. He had temporarily abdicated his rule over the bandits in favor of a sort of lieutenant, who from time to time came to ask his orders, and then disappeared.

Smerande also loved me with a passionate friendship, the expression of which frightened me. She was obviously protecting Kostaki, and seemed to be more jealous of me than he was. Only, since she understood neither Polish nor French, and I did not understand

Moldavian, she could not make very pressing arguments for her son; but she had learned to say three words in French, which she repeated to me each time her lips rested on my forehead: "Kostaki loves Hedwig."

One day, I learned terrible news that came to overpower my misfortunes: liberty had been restored to these four men who had survived the fight; they had gone back to Poland, pledging their word that one of them would return, before three months, to give me news of my father. One of them reappeared one morning. Our castle had been taken and burned. My father had been killed by defending it.

I was left completely alone in the world.

Kostaki redoubled his authority, and Smerande her tenderness; but this time I offered my need to mourn for my father, alone. Kostaki insisted that the more isolated I was, the more support I needed; his mother insisted on his behalf perhaps even more strongly than he did himself. As for Gregoriska, he had told me about the power that Moldavians have over themselves when they do not want their feelings read plainly. He was a living example. It was impossible to be more certain of the love of a man than I was of his, and yet, if I had been asked on what proof this certainty rested, it would have been impossible for me to say; no one in the castle had seen his hand touch mine, or his eyes seeking mine. Jealousy alone could enlighten Kostaki on this rivalry, just as my love alone could enlighten me on Gregoriska's love. However, I confess, this mastery of Gregoriska over himself worried me. I certainly believed; but it was not enough. I needed to be convinced.

Then, one evening, as I had just returned to my room, I heard a soft knock on one of those two doors that are bolted from the inside. From the manner of the knocking, I guessed that this call was that of a friend. I went over, and asked who was there.

"Gregoriska," answered a voice that I could not mistake.

"What do you want from me?" I asked, trembling.

"If you trust me," said Gregoriska, "if you think me a man of honor, grant me my request."

"What is it?"

"Turn off your light, as if you were lying down, and in half an hour, open your door."

"Come back in half an hour," was my only answer.

I turned off my light, and waited.

My heart beat violently, because I understood that it was some important event.

Half an hour passed; I heard knocking more gently than the first time. During the interval I had pulled the bolts; I had only to open the door.

Gregoriska entered. Saying nothing, I closed the door behind him, and fastened the bolts.

He remained silent and motionless for a moment, entreating my silence with a gesture. Then, when he had ascertained that no urgent danger threatened us, he took me to the middle of the vast room, and, feeling at my trembling that I could not remain standing, he went to fetch me a chair. I sat down, or rather I dropped into the chair.

"Oh! my God!" I said to him, "What is this, and why so many precautions?"

"Because my life—which is nothing—because yours maybe too, depends on the conversation we are going to have."

I grabbed his hand, frightened. He raised my hand to his lips, while looking at me, to ask for forgiveness for such audacity. I lowered my eyes in consent.

"I love you," he said in his melodious voice. "Do you love me?"

"Yes," I told him.

"Would you like to be my wife?"

"Yes."

He ran his hand over his forehead with a deep sigh of happiness.

"Then you will not refuse to follow me?"

"I will follow you everywhere!"

"You understand," he went on, "that we can only be happy by running away."

"Oh yes!" I exclaimed, "Let us flee!"

"Silence!" he said, shuddering. "Silence!"

"You are right." And I moved tremblingly close to him.

"This is what I did," he said to me; "here is what made me take so long without confessing to you that I loved you. Because I wanted, once sure of your love, that nothing could oppose our union. I am rich, Hedwig, immensely rich, but like the Moldavian lords: rich in lands, cattle, serfs. Well! I sold, at the Hango monastery, for a million francs, some of my cattle and villages. They gave me three hundred thousand francs in jewels, a hundred thousand francs in gold, and the rest in bills of exchange in Vienna. Will one million be enough?"

I pressed his hand.

"Your love would have sufficed for me, Gregoriska, judge if it would not."

"Well! Listen: tomorrow I'm going to the Hango monastery to make my last arrangements with the Superior. He keeps horses ready for me; these horses will be waiting for us at nine o'clock, hidden a hundred yards from the castle. After dinner, come back here to your room as you did tonight; as tonight, extinguish your light; like tonight, I will come in. But tomorrow, instead of my leaving you alone, you follow me. We reach the gate which overlooks the country, we find our horses, we throw ourselves on them, and the day after tomorrow, by dawn, we have traveled thirty leagues."

"Why is it not already tomorrow?"

"Dear Hedwig!"

Gregoriska hugged me against his heart, and our lips met.

Oh! he had said it well: he was a man of honor to whom I had opened the door of my room; but he understood it well: if I did not belong to him in a body, I belonged to him with a soul.

The night passed without me being able to sleep for a moment. I saw myself running away with Gregoriska; I felt carried away by him as I had been by Kostaki, only this time, that terrible, frightening, funereal race changed into a sweet and lovely embrace to which speed added voluptuousness.

The day came.

I went down.

It seemed to me that there was something darker than usual in the way Kostaki greeted me. His smile was not even an irony, it was a threat.

Smerande, though, seemed to me the same as usual.

During lunch, Gregoriska ordered his horses. Kostaki did not seem to pay any attention to this order.

About eleven o'clock he bade us farewell, saying he would return in the evening and begging his mother not to hold dinner for him; then, turning towards me, he begged me, in turn, to accept his excuses.

He left. His brother's eye followed him until he was gone from the room, and at that moment there blazed from that eye a flash of hatred, which made me shudder.

The day passed in the midst of such terrible fears as may be conceived. I had not confided our plans to anyone; scarcely even in my prayers had I dared to speak to God about it, yet it seemed to me that these projects were known to everybody; that every gaze that was fixed on me could penetrate and read the depths of my heart.

Dinner was a torture: dark and taciturn, Kostaki rarely spoke; this time, he contented himself with addressing his mother in Moldavian two or three times, and each time the accent of his voice made me tremble. When I got up to go up to my room, Smerande, as usual, kissed me, and, kissing me, she told me this sentence, that for eight days I had not heard out of her mouth: "Kostaki loves Hedwig!" This phrase pursued me as a threat; once in my room, it seemed to me that a fatal voice whispered in my ear: Kostaki loves Hedwig! But Kostaki's love, Gregoriska told me, was death.

About seven o'clock in the evening, as the day was beginning to wane, I saw Kostaki cross the courtyard He turned to look at me, but I threw myself back, so that he could not see me. He went to the stables. He then took his favorite horse out of it, and saddled it with his own hands, with the care of a man who attaches the greatest importance to every detail. He had the same costume under which he had appeared to me for the first time, except that his only weapon was his sword.

As he saddled his horse, he cast his eyes once more on the window of my room. Then, not seeing me, he jumped into the saddle, opened the same door through which his brother had gone, and galloped off towards the monastery of Hango.

Then my heart sank in a terrible way, a fatal presentiment told me that Kostaki was going to meet his brother.

I remained at this window as long as I could make out the road, which, a quarter of a league from the castle, turned into the edge of the forest. But the night grew darker moment by moment, and the road finally disappeared altogether.

I still stayed where I was.

At last my anxiety, by its very excesses, restored my strength, and as it was evidently in the hall below that I was to have the first news of the two brothers, I went downstairs.

I first looked for Smerande. I saw, in the calmness of her face, that she felt no apprehension; she gave her orders for the usual supper, and the cutlery for the two brothers were in their places.

I did not dare to question anyone. Besides, who would I have questioned? No one in the castle, except Kostaki and Gregoriska, spoke any of the only two languages I spoke.

At the slightest sound, I flinched.

It was usually at nine o'clock that they sat down for supper.

I went down at half-past eight; I watched with my eyes the minute hand, whose progress was almost visible on the vast dial of the clock.

The second hand crossed the distance that separated it from the quarter.

The quarter struck. The vibration sounded dark and sad, then the hand resumed its silent march, and I saw it again traveling the distance with the regularity and slowness of a compass point. A few minutes before nine o'clock, I seemed to hear the galloping of a horse in the yard. Smerande heard it too, for she turned her head towards the window; but the night was too thick for her to see. Oh! if she had looked at me now, she could have guessed what was happening in my heart. We had only heard the trot of a single horse, and I knew that only one rider would come back.

But which one?

Footsteps echoed in the antechamber. These steps were slow and seemed to weigh on my heart.

The door opened, I saw in the dark draw a shadow.

This shadow stopped for a moment on the door. My heart was hanging.

The shadow advanced, and as it entered the circle of light, I breathed.

I recognized Gregoriska.

One more moment of pain, and my heart was breaking. I recognized Gregoriska, but pale as a dead man. Just seeing him, we guessed that something terrible had happened.

"Is it you, Kostaki?" asked Smerande.

"No, mother," said Gregoriska in a muffled voice.

"Ah! here you are," said she. "And since when does your mother have to wait for you?"

"Mother," said Gregoriska, glancing at the clock, "it is only nine o'clock." And at the same time, indeed, nine o'clock struck.

"That's true," said Smerande. "Where is your brother?"

In spite of myself, I thought it was the same question that God had made to Cain. Gregoriska did not answer.

"Has no one seen Kostaki?" asked Smerande.

The vatar, or butler, inquired about him. "Seven o'clock," he said, "the Count has been to the stables, saddled his horse himself, and has gone on the road to Hango."

At that moment, my eyes met Gregoriska's eyes. I do not know if it was a reality or a hallucination, but it seemed to me that he had a drop of blood in the middle of his forehead. I slowly carried my finger to my own forehead, indicating where I thought I saw that spot. Gregoriska understood me; he took his handkerchief and wiped himself.

"Yes, yes," murmured Smerande, "he has met some bear, some wolf, whom he has amused himself with pursuing. That's why a child makes his mother wait. Where did you leave him, Gregoriska? Say."

"My mother," Gregoriska said in a voice that was emotional but steady, "my brother and I did not go out together."

"Very good!" said Smerande. "Let us have supper, sit down and close the doors; those who will be outside will sleep outside."

The first two parts of this order were executed to the letter. Smerande took Kostaki's place, Gregoriska sat on her right, and I on his left.

Then the servants went out to fulfill the third command, that is, to close the gates of the castle.

At that moment, a loud noise was heard in the courtyard, and a very frightened valet entered the room, saying: "Princess, Count Kostaki's horse has just returned to the yard, alone, and covered with blood."

"Oh!" murmured Smerande, rising pale and threatening, "Just as his father's horse returned one evening."

I cast my eyes on Gregoriska: he was no longer pale, he was livid. In fact, Count Koproli's horse had returned one evening to the castle courtyard, all covered with blood, and an hour later the servants had found and brought back the body covered with wounds.

Smerande took a torch from the hands of one of the valets, went to the door, opened it, and descended into the courtyard. The terrified horse was being calmed by the combined efforts of three or four servants. Smerande advanced towards the animal, looked at the blood staining his saddle, and saw an injury at the top of the horse's head.

"Kostaki was killed from the front," she said, "in a duel and by one enemy. Look for his body, children, later we will look for his murderer."

As the horse had come in through the gate that opened on the road to Hango, all the servants, bearing torches, rushed out. They spread through the countryside and into the forest, as on a fine summer evening one sees glimmering fireflies in the plains of Nice and Pisa.

Smerande, as if she had been convinced that the search would not belong, waited at the door. Not a tear flowed from the eyes of that desolate mother, and yet one felt despair rumble deep in her heart.

Gregoriska was standing behind her, and I was near Gregoriska. There was a moment, as he was about to leave the room, when he was about to offer me his arm, but he had not dared.

At the end of a quarter of an hour, at the turn of the road, a torch reappeared, then two, then all the torches. Only this time, instead of scattering in the countryside, they were massed around a common center. This common center, we could soon see, consisted of a litter with a man lying on it.

The deathly procession advanced slowly, but it advanced. After ten minutes Kostaki's body was at the door. On seeing the living mother who was waiting for the dead son, those who bore the litter instinctively uncovered their heads, and then they returned silently into the courtyard.

Smerande followed them, and we followed Smerande. Thus we reached the great hall, into which the body was laid.

Then, making a gesture of supreme majesty, Smerande dismissed everyone, and, approaching the corpse, she went down on one knee in front of him, moving aside the hair that fell like a veil over his face, and contemplated him for a long time with dry eyes. Then, opening the Moldavian dress, she spread apart the blood-stained shirt.

The injury was on the right side of the chest. It had to have been made by a straight and sharp two-edged blade.

I remembered seeing, that very day, Gregoriska's long hunting knife that served as a bayonet for his rifle.

I looked for this weapon; but it was gone.

Smerande asked for water, soaked her handkerchief, and washed the wound. Fresh, pure blood blushed the lips of the wound.

The sight I had before me presented something at once atrocious and sublime. This vast room, smoked by resin torches, those barbarous faces, those fierce brilliant eyes, those strange costumes, that mother who calculated, at the sight of the still hot blood, how long had death taken her son from her, this great silence, interrupted only by the sobs of these brigands, of which Kostaki was the chief, all this, I repeat, was both atrocious and sublime to see. Finally Smerande drew her lips to her son's forehead; then, getting up, and throwing back the long strands of her white hair that had come undone: "Gregoriska!" she said.

Gregoriska shuddered, shook his head, and emerging from his stony silence: "Mother," he replied.

"Come here, my son, and listen to me."

Gregoriska obeyed with a shudder, but he obeyed. As he approached the body, the blood, more abundant and more ruddy, came out of the wound. Fortunately, Smerande did not see this, for at the sight of this accusing blood, she would no longer have needed to ask who the murderer was.

"Gregoriska," she said, "I know that you and Kostaki do not love each other. I know you're Waivady by your father, and he, Koproli by his; but, by your mother, you were both Brankovan. I know that you are a man of the cities of the West, and he is a child of the Eastern mountains; but finally, by the womb that carried you both, you are brothers. Well! Gregoriska, I want to know if we will take my son to lie by his father without the oath of vengeance being pronounced, or if I can cry quietly, as a woman, depending on you, as a man, to punish."

"Tell me the name of the murderer of my brother, madame, and order me; I swear to you, that before one o'clock, if you demand it, he will have ceased to live."

"Swear, Gregoriska, swear, on pain of my curse, do you hear, my son? Swear that the murderer will die, that you will not leave a stone of his house; that his mother, his children, his brothers, his wife, or his beloved will perish from your hand. Swear, and, swearing, call upon you the wrath of heaven if you break this sacred oath. If you break this sacred oath, you will submit to misery, to the execration of your friends, to the curse of your mother."

Gregoriska stretched out his hand on the corpse.

"I swear the murderer will die," he said.

At this strange oath, of which I and the dead alone, perhaps, could understand the true meaning, I saw, or thought I saw, a terrible prodigy. The eyes of the corpse opened again and attached themselves to me more alive than I had ever seen them, and, as if this double ray had been palpable, I felt burning iron pierce my heart.

It was more than I could bear, and I fainted dead away.

THE HANGO MONASTERY

When I woke up, I was in my room, lying on my bed; one of the two servant women was watching near me. I asked where Smerande was; I was told that she was standing vigil near the body of her son. I asked where Gregoriska was; I was told that he was at the Hango monastery. It was no longer a question of flight. Was not Kostaki dead? It was no longer a question of marriage. Could I marry the fratricide? Three days and three nights passed thus in the midst of strange dreams. In my waking moments or in my sleep, I always saw these two eyes alive in the middle of this dead face: it was a horrible vision.

It was on the third day that Kostaki's burial was to take place. On the morning of that day, Smerande brought me a complete widow's costume. I got dressed and went downstairs. The house seemed empty; everyone was in the chapel. I went to join them. At the moment when I crossed the threshold, Smerande crossed the threshold and came to me. She seemed like a statue of pain. With a slow and stiff motion, she placed her icy lips on my forehead, and in a voice that seemed already to come out of the grave, she uttered these usual words: "Kostaki loves Hedwig."

You can have no idea of the effect these words produced on me. This protest of love made in the present tense, instead of the past; this *loves you* instead of *loved you*, this love from beyond the grave, which came to seek me in life, produced on me a terrible impression.

At the same time, a strange feeling took possession of me, as if I had indeed been the wife of the one who had died, and not the fiancée of him who was alive. This coffin drew me to him, despite myself, painfully, as it is said that the snake attracts the bird it fascinates. I looked for Gregoriska's eyes. I saw him, pale and standing, against a column; his eyes were raised to heaven. I cannot say if he saw me. The monks of the convent of Hango surrounded the body singing psalms of the Greek Orthodox rite, sometimes harmonious, more often in monotone. I wanted to pray too; but the prayer died on my lips, my mind was so upset that it seemed rather to be attending a gathering of demons than a meeting of priests. At the moment when the body was removed, I wanted to follow it, but my strength refused. I felt my legs crack under me, and I leaned on the door. Then Smerande came to me, and made a sign to Gregoriska. Gregoriska obeyed, and approached. Then Smerande spoke to me in the Moldavian language.

"My mother orders me to repeat word for word what she will say," said Gregoriska. Then Smerande spoke again; when she had finished: "Here are the words of my mother," said he, "you mourn my son, Hedwig, you loved him, did not you? I thank you for your tears and your love; now you are as much my daughter as if Kostaki had been your husband; you now have a fatherland, a mother, a family. Let's shed the tears we owe to the dead, and then again become worthy of the one who is no longer…me his mother, you his wife! Farewell! go home; I will follow my son to his last home; on my return, I will shut myself up with my grief, and you will see me only when I have conquered it; fear not, I will kill it, for I do not want it to kill me." I could not answer these words of Smerande, translated by Gregoriska, with anything but a groan. I went back to my room, the funeral procession passed on. I saw them disappear around the corner of the road. The convent of Hango was only half a league from the castle; but the obstacles on the ground forced the road to deviate, and, following the road, it was nearly two hours away. We were in November. The days had become cold and short again. At five o'clock it was dark night.

About seven o'clock I saw torches reappear. It was the funeral cortege returning. The corpse lay in the tomb of his fathers. All the rites had been performed. I have told you what strange feelings had been preying on me ever since the fatal event that had dressed us all in mourning, and especially since I had seen those eyes that death had closed open once more and fix themselves on me. That night, overwhelmed by the emotions of the day, I was sadder still. I listened to the different hours at the castle clock, and I felt sorry for myself as the flying time brought me closer to the moment when Kostaki must have died.

I heard a quarter to nine. Then a strange sensation took hold of me. It was a shuddering terror that ran through my body, and froze me; then, along with this terror, came something like an invincible sleep that weighed upon my senses; my chest went down, my eyes closed. I stretched out my arms, and lay backwards on my bed. However, my senses were not so overcome that I could not hear a footstep approaching my door; then it seemed to me that my door was opening; after that I saw and heard nothing. But I felt a sharp pain in my neck. After which I fell into the deepest sleep.

At midnight I woke up. My lamp was still burning. I wanted to get up, but I was so weak that I had to go back to bed twice. However, I finally overcame this weakness, and realized that, awake, I felt the same pain in my neck that I felt in my sleep.

I dragged myself, leaning against the wall, to the mirror and I looked.

Something like a pin-prick marked the artery of my neck.

I thought that some insect had bitten me during my sleep, and, as I was crushed with fatigue, I went to bed and fell back asleep.

The next day I woke up as usual. As usual, I wanted to get up as soon as my eyes were opened; but I felt a weakness that I had experienced only once in my life, after one of my monthly bleedings.

I went up to my mirror and was struck by my pallor.

The day passed sad and dark. I was too fatigued to leave my room.

Night came, and the serving-women brought me my lamp; they offered, by their gestures, to stay near me. I thanked them: they went out.

At the same time as the night before, I experience the same symptoms. I wanted to get up then and call for help; but I could not go to the door. I vaguely heard the clock ticking at a quarter to nine; the footsteps sounded, the door opened; but I saw and heard nothing; as the night before, I remained motionless on my bed.

Just like the night before, I felt a sharp pain in the same place.

Just like the night before, I woke up at midnight; only, I woke up even weaker and paler.

The next day I felt once more the horrible sense of oppressive evil.

I was determined to go down to Smerande, as weak as I was, when one of my serving-women entered my room, and pronounced the name of Gregoriska. Gregoriska came behind her. I wanted to get up to receive him, but I fell back in my chair. He uttered a cry when he saw me, and I knew that he wanted to rush towards me; but I found the strength to extend a warning arm.

"What are you doing here?" I asked him.

"Alas!" he said, "I came to say goodbye! I came to tell you that I am leaving this world that is unbearable to me without your love and without your presence; I came to tell you that I am retiring to the monastery of Hango."

"You may take away my presence, Gregoriska," I exclaimed, "but not my love. Alas! I still love you, and my great sorrow is that henceforth this love will almost be a crime."

"Then I can hope that you will pray for me, Hedwig."

"Yes; only I will not pray long," I added with a smile.

"What do you mean? And why are you so pale?"

"I...God takes pity on me, no doubt, and he calls me to him!"

Gregoriska approached me, took my hand, which I had not the strength to withdraw, and, staring at me, said: "This pallor is not natural, Hedwig; what caused it?"

"If I told you, Gregoriska, you would think I'm mad."

"No, no, say, Hedwig, I beg you. We are in a country that is unlike any other country, in a family that is not like any other family. Say, say everything, I beg you!"

I told him everything: the strange hallucination which possessed me at the hour when Kostaki must have died; that terror, that numbness, that chill of ice, that paralysis that laid me on my bed, that footstep that I thought I heard, that door that I thought I saw opening, and finally that acute pain followed by a pallor and an ever increasing weakness.

I had thought that my story would appear to Gregoriska like the onset of madness, and I finished it with a certain shyness. But, on the contrary, I saw that he was giving my story the most profound attention. After I stopped talking, he thought for a moment. "So," he asked, "do you fall asleep every evening at a quarter to nine?"

"Yes, no matter what effort I make to stay awake."

"So you think you see your door open?"

"Yes, although I lock it shut."

"So you feel a sharp pain in your neck?"

"Yes, though my neck scarcely shows any injury."

"Will you allow me to see?" he said.

I threw my head on my shoulder. He examined this scar. "Hedwig," he said after a moment, "do you trust me? Do you believe in my word?"

I replied, "As I believe in the holy Gospels."

"Well! Hedwig, on my word, I swear to you that you have not eight days to live, if you do not consent to do, today, what I am going to say to you!"

"And if I consent to it?"

"If you consent, you may be saved."

"*May* be?"

He was silent.

"Whatever may come, Gregoriska," I said, "I will do what you order me to do."

"Listen," he said, "and above all, do not be frightened. In your country, as in Hungary, as in our Romania, there is a tradition."

I shuddered because I remembered what that tradition was.

"Ah!" he said, "you know what I mean?"

"Yes," I replied, "I've seen people in Poland who are subject to this horrible fatality."

"You mean vampires, do you not?"

"Yes. When I was a child, I saw forty people dead in the cemetery of a village belonging to my father, who all died in a fortnight, without anyone being able to guess the cause of their deaths. Seventeen gave all the signs of vampirism, that is to say that they were found fresh, rosy, and looking as though they were alive; the others were their victims."

"And what was done to save the village?"

"They were staked through the heart and burned."

"Yes, that is what is done ordinarily; but for you and I, that is not enough. To deliver you from this phantom, I must know who he is. By heaven I will know him! Yes, and, if necessary, I will fight hand-to-hand with him, whoever he may be."

"Gregoriska," I exclaimed, frightened.

"I said, whoever he may be, and I repeat it. But in order to carry out this terrible adventure, you must consent to all that I am going to require of you."

"Say."

"Be ready at seven o'clock. Go down to the chapel; go down alone; you must overcome your weakness, Hedwig, you must. There, we will receive the nuptial blessing. Consent to it, my beloved; in order for me to defend you, I must, before God and men, have the right to watch over you. We'll come back here after the ritual, and then…we'll see…"

"Oh! Gregoriska," I said, "if it is he, he will kill you."

"Do not be afraid, my dear Hedwig. Only, consent."

"You know very well that I will do all that you wish, Gregoriska."

"Until tonight, then."

"Yes, do what you must, and I will help. Go, now."

He went. A quarter of an hour later I saw a horseman charging up the road to the monastery; it was him! I had scarcely lost sight of him when I fell on my knees, and prayed as one no longer prays in your country without belief, and waited seven hours, offering to God and the saints the holocaust of my thoughts. I did not get up until seven o'clock struck. I was as weak as a dying woman, pale as a dead woman. I threw a large black veil over my head, went down the stairs, supporting myself against the walls, and went to the chapel without having met anyone.

Gregoriska was waiting for me with Father Bazile, Superior of the convent of Hango. My bridegroom wore at his side a holy sword, the relic of an old Crusader who had taken Constantinople with Ville-Hardouin and Beaudoin of Flanders. "Hedwig," he said, clapping his hand to the sword, "with the help of God, this will break the spell that threatens your life. Approach, therefore, resolutely; here is a holy man who, after having received my confession, will receive our oaths."

The ceremony began; never, perhaps, was there anything simpler and more solemn at the same time. No one assisted the priest; he himself placed the wedding crowns on our heads. Both of us, still dressed in mourning, circled the altar with a candle in our hands; then the priest, having pronounced the words of the holy rite, added: "Go now, my children, and may God give you strength and courage to fight against the enemy of the human race. You are armed with your innocence and justice; you will defeat the devil. Go, and be blessed."

We kissed the holy books and went out of the chapel. For the first time, I leaned on Gregoriska's arm, and it seemed to me that by the touch of that valiant arm, that at the touch of his noble heart, life was returning to my veins. I thought myself certain to triumph, since Gregoriska was with me.

We went back to my room.

Eight-thirty sounded.

"Hedwig," Gregoriska told me, "we have no time to lose. Do you want to fall asleep as before and have everything happen while you sleep? Or do you want to stay awake and witness everything?"

"Near you, I'm not afraid. I want to stay awake. I want to see everything."

Gregoriska drew from his bosom a blessed sprig of boxwood, still moist with holy water, and gave it to me. "Take this, then, lie down on your bed, recite your prayers to the Virgin, and wait without fear. God is with us. Above all, do not put down the boxwood; with it, you will be able to command hell itself. Do not call me, do not shout; pray, hope and wait."

I lay down on the bed, and folded my hands on my chest, on which I pressed the blessed branch. As for Gregoriska, he hid behind the canopied chair of which I spoke, which cut off the corner of my room. I counted the minutes, and Gregoriska probably counted them too.

The sound of the clock vibrated again, and then I felt the same numbness, the same terror, the same icy coldness; but I brought the blessed branch to my lips, and the feeling passed. Then I distinctly heard the sound of that slow, measured step that echoed on the staircase as it approached my door. My door opened slowly, noiselessly, as if pushed inward by a supernatural force, and then…

…And then I saw Kostaki, pale as I had seen him on the litter; his long black hair, scattered over his shoulders, was dripping with blood; he wore his usual costume; only his shirt was open at the breast, exposing his bleeding wound. He looked like a corpse. Everything about him was dead, his flesh, his clothes, the way he walked… only his eyes, those terrible eyes, were alive.

At this sight, strange thing! instead of feeling my fear renewed, I felt my courage grow. God doubtless sent it to me so that I could see my position clearly and defend myself against hell. At the first step the phantom made towards my bed, my eyes boldly met his leaden gaze, and I held out the blessed branch. The spectre tried to advance; but a stronger power than his held him in his place.

He stopped himself: "Oh!" he murmured; "she does not sleep, she knows everything."

He spoke in Moldavian, and yet I heard him as if these words had been spoken in a language I knew. We were face to face, the vampire and I. I could not detach my eyes from his. Then, without my needing to turn my head in his direction, Gregoriska appeared from behind the canopied chair, like an exterminating angel, brandishing his sword in his hand. He made the sign of the cross with his left hand and slowly advanced with his blade aimed at the vampire; the latter, at the sight of his brother, had drawn his own sword with a terrible laugh; but scarcely had his sword touched Gregoriska's consecrated iron, than the arm of the phantom fell helplessly by his side.

Kostaki uttered a sigh full of struggle and despair. "What do you want?" he said to his brother.

"In the name of the living God," said Gregoriska, "I adjure you to answer."

"Speak," said the phantom, grinding his teeth.

"Did I wait for you? Did I attack you?"

"…No."

"Did I strike you?"

"…No."

"You threw yourself on my knife, and that's all that happened. Therefore, in the eyes of God and of men, I am not guilty of the crime of fratricide; therefore you have not received a divine but an infernal mission; so you came out of the grave, not as a holy shadow, but as a cursed spectre, and you shall go back into your grave!"

"With her, yes!" cried Kostaki, making a supreme effort to seize me.

"Alone!" cried Gregoriska in his turn; "This woman belongs to me!"

And in pronouncing these words, with the tip of the blessed iron, he touched the living wound.

Kostaki uttered a cry as if a sword of flame had struck him, and, carrying his left hand to his breast, he took a step back.

At the same time, and with a motion that mirrored Kostaki's, Gregoriska took a step forward; then, meeting with his gaze the eyes of the dead, pressing his sword against the breast of his brother, he began a slow, terrible, solemn march; something like the passage of Don Juan and the Commander. The vampire recoiling before the sacred sword, wielded by the irresistible will of the champion of God, who followed him step by step without a word. Both were breathless and livid, as the living man prodded the dead man before him, forcing him to abandon the castle which was his abode in the past, for the tomb which was his abode in the future.

Oh! it was horrible to see; and yet, moved myself by a superior force, invisible, unknown, without realizing what I was doing, I got up and followed them.

We descended the stairs, lighted only by the fiery eyes of Kostaki. We thus crossed the gallery, then the court. We crossed though the door with this same measured step: the vampire backwards, Gregoriska following with arm extended, I following them.

This fantastic race lasted a full hour: it was necessary to return the dead to his grave; only, instead of following the usual path, Kostaki and

Gregoriska had cut the ground in a straight line, caring little for the obstacles along the way, which ceased to exist: under their feet, the ground itself flattened, the torrents dried up, the trees fell back, the rocks parted; the same miracle took place for me as for them; only the whole sky seemed to me covered with a black crepe, the moon and the stars had disappeared, and the only light I could see shining in the night were the fiery eyes of the vampire.

So we arrived at Hango, so we passed through the arbutus hedge which served as a fence at the cemetery. As soon as I entered, I saw, in the darkness, Kostaki's tomb, placed next to his father's; I had never seen it before, and yet I recognized it. That night I understood everything.

At the edge of the open tomb, Gregoriska stopped. "Kostaki," he said, "all is not over yet for you, and a voice from heaven tells me that you will be forgiven if you repent: do you promise to return to your grave? Do you promise not to go out? Do you promise to finally devote to God the worship which you have devoted to hell?"

"No!" Kostaki replied.

"Do you repent?" demanded Gregoriska.

"No!"

"For the last time, Kostaki?"

"No!"

"Well! Call Satan to your aid, as I call God to mine, and see who will win!"

Two cries echoed at the same time; the blades crossed each other, striking sparks, and the fight lasted a minute which seemed to me a century.

Kostaki fell; I saw the terrible sword rise, I saw it sinking into his body and nailing it to the freshly stirred earth. A final cry, which was not human, rent the air.

I ran to Gregoriska. He had remained standing, but he faltered. I supported him in my arms.

"Are you hurt?" I asked him anxiously.

"No," he said to me; "but in such a duel, dear Hedwig, it is not the wound that kills, it is the struggle. I struggled with death, I belong to death."

"Friend, friend," I exclaimed, "let us go away, get away from here, and life may come back."

"No," said he, "here is my grave, Hedwig; but do not waste time; take a little of this earth stained with his blood, and apply it to the bite he gave you; it is the only way to preserve you in the future from his horrible love."

I obeyed, shuddering. I stooped to pick up the bloody earth, and, bending down, saw the corpse nailed to the ground; the blessed sword pierced his heart, and black and abundant blood came out of his wound, as if he had just died a moment before.

I kneaded a little earth with the blood, and I applied the horrible talisman to my wound.

"Now, my beloved Hedwig," said Gregoriska, in a weak voice, "listen carefully to my last instructions: leave the country as soon as you can. Distance alone is your safety. Father Bazile has today received my last instructions, and he will perform them. Hedwig! a kiss! the last, the only one, Hedwig! I die."

And, saying these words, Gregoriska fell near his brother.

In all other circumstances, in the middle of this cemetery, near this open tomb, with these two corpses lying next to each other, I had gone mad; but, as I have already said, God had placed in me a force equal to the events of which he made me not only the witness, but the actor.

As I looked around for help, I saw the cloister door open, and the monks, led by Father Bazile, came forward two by two, carrying lighted torches and singing the prayers for the dead.

Father Bazile had just arrived; he had foreseen what had happened, and at the head of the whole community he went to the cemetery.

He found me alive near the two dead men.

Kostaki's face was twisted in a last convulsion. Gregoriska, on the contrary, was calm and almost smiling.

As Gregoriska had recommended, he was buried near his brother, the Christian guarding the damned.

Smerande, on learning of this new misfortune, and the part I had taken, wished to see me; she came to visit me at the cloister of Hango, and learned from my mouth all that had happened that terrible night. I told her in all its details the fantastic story; but she listened to me as Gregoriska had listened to me, without astonishment or fear.

"Hedwig," she replied after a moment's silence, "strange as you may have said, you have only said pure truth. The Brankovan race is cursed until the third and fourth generations because a Brankovan killed a priest. But the end of the curse has arrived; for though you were married, you are a virgin, and in me the race is extinguished. If my son has left you a million, take it. As for me, apart from some pious legacies I intend to make, you will have the rest of my fortune. Now, follow your husband's advice as soon as possible. Return as quickly as you can to the countries where God does not allow these terrible wonders to be accomplished. I do not need anyone to mourn my sons with me. Farewell, do not inquire of me anymore. My future destiny belongs only to me and to God." And kissing my forehead as usual, she left me and shut herself up at Castle Brankovan.

Eight days later, I left for France. As Gregoriska had hoped, there were no more night-time visits from the terrible phantom. Even my health has been restored, and I have kept from these events only the pallor of mortality that accompanies to the grave every creature who has been kissed by a vampire.

"…and prayed as one no longer prays in your country without belief…" : A reminder that Hedwig is narrating her tale to a group of skeptical Frenchmen, 20 years after the fact.

Arbutus: A flowering plant or tree.

"As he approached the body, the blood, more abundant and more ruddy, came out of the wound": It was an old belief that a murdered corpse would bleed in the presence of the murderer. There are notable examples in *The Nibelungenlied* and Shakespeare's *Richard III*. (However, since we learn, later, that Kostaki's death was an accident, so the accusation seems unfair…)

"A word, which I have since known to mean 'the stranger': The word is "strain."

Bistriza: A river in the Romanian region of Moldavia.

Boxwood: In some translations of the Bible, boxwood is included in the Book of Isaiah (Chapter 30, verse 8) as one of three trees that will be part of the Temple of the New Jerusalem: *"The glory of Lebanon shall come to thee, the fir tree, and the box tree, and the pine tree together, to beautify the place of my sanctuary: and I will glorify the place of my feet."* Therefore, some considered boxwood to be a tree with sacred connections. In the 1497 book *Margarita Medicine*, Johann Tollat of Vochenberg wrote, "Boxwood drives out the devil…so that he can have no place in the house."

Brankovans: Constantin Brâncoveanu was Prince of Wallachia (see below) from 1688 until he was deposed and executed, along with his sons, by the Turks in 1714. They were all declared saints by the Russian Orthodox Church in 2018.

Burger's Ballad: In 1774, the German poet Gottfried August Burger published a short poem, *Lenore*, that became one of the triggers of the Romantic movement. The ballad tells of a young woman, Lenore, whose beloved William seems to return from a war, riding up to her at night and invites her to elope. She gets on his horse and they gallop through an increasingly nightmarish landscape—until they reach a cemetery, where William's face turns into a skull and the living dead man drags Lenore to the grave with him. *Lenore* dazzled everyone from Goethe to

Scott to Byron and Shelley. Poe fixated on the name, and Bram Stoker memorably translated one of Burger's lines—*"die Todten reisen schnell,"* as "the dead travel fast"—in the first chapter of *Dracula.*

Cantimiri: Allies of the Moldavian Prince Dimitrie Cantemir, a political rival of Prince Constantin Brâncoveanu ("Brankovan").

Carpathian Mountains: A 932-mile mountain range stretching from Romania to what is now the Czech Republic.

Cossacks: Members of a semi-independent, militaristic community in southern Russia and Ukraine.

Don Juan and the Commander: In Mozart's opera *Don Giovanni,* the protagonist (Giovanni being Italian for Juan) kills the Commander, the old father of a woman the Don wants to seduce. Later, a statue of the Commander comes to life, threatens Don Giovanni, and has him dragged to hell by demons.

Hango: Apparently a fictitious name.

Illyria: Originally, an ancient region in the Balkans; in the early 19th century, "a son of Illyria" meant a Slav.

Iron: Early 19th century French stories often use "iron" as a synonym for "sword," even though it's more likely that a Crusader's sword would be of finely-tempered steel.

"Kostaki's tomb, placed next to his father's…": As in *Varney,* the aristocratic vampire has an above-ground tomb, making it easier to come and go from his resting-place.

Lenore: See *Burger's Ballad,* above.

Magyar: A tribe of people in Hungary.

Mount Pion: That mountain is actually in Ephesus (currently part of Turkey), almost 900 miles south of the monastery Hedwig heads for.

Niantzo: Niantzo is Neamt; the monastery and surrounding area was burned by the Turks in 1821; it was rebuilt from 1824 to 1826.

Nishan: An Islamic decoration for bravery in battle. The Sultan would be Mahmud II (ruled 1808-1839). He was a reformer, who in 1826

replaced the traditional Janissary troops with a more modern military force; the Janissaries revolted and were violently defeated. It seems that Gregoriska fought on the side of the Sultan—that is, on the side of westernizing modernity against the forces of eastern tradition.

Peter I: Tsar of Russia, 1682-1725.

"…Relic of an old Crusader who had taken Constantinople with Ville-Hardouin and Beaudoin of Flanders.": Frankly, this is an odd event to celebrate. The Fourth Crusade was launched in 1202 as the latest Catholic attempt to take back Jerusalem from the Muslims. But after a series of arguments, mistakes, and misunderstandings, the Catholic Crusaders instead sacked the Eastern Orthodox city of Constantinople in April 1204. One of the leaders of the campaign was Count Baldwin (Beaudoin) of Flanders and Hainault; Geoffroi de Villehardouin, "Marshal of Champagne and of Romania," was a knight and historian, who participated in the sack and wrote an eyewitness account. Constantinople is now the Turkish city of Istanbul.

Sahastru: Sihastri Putnei monastery, in the Romanian district of Neamt (part of Bukovina).

Sandomir: Sandomierz, a town in South-Eastern Poland.

"…the struggle that is coming." Russia had effective control over Moldavia, and Nicholas I was preparing to institute harsh measures against local autonomy, including attempting to suppress languages other than Russian.

Tula factory: Russian arms plant founded in 1712 by Peter the Great.

Vistula: The longest river in Poland (651 miles).

Wallachia: A Romanian principality that includes Transylvania; ruled by Dracula (Vlad Tepes) three times in the mid-1400's.

Yatagan: Or yataghan, ataghan; a curved, single-bladed Turkish sword.

AFTERWORD

As a vampire, Count Kostaki is much more monstrous than Ruthven or Varney; there's no sense that he would ever be able to pretend to live as a normal man among mortals. Of course, he wasn't the most civilized of men even as a human: he can barely speak French!

The way Kostaki actually becomes vampirized is we've seen repeatedly in this book, rather vague. His death as a human might resemble a suicide, which according to tradition could turn one into a vampire, but falling on Gregoriski's blade seems to have really been an accident. The vampirism is perhaps the result of some last-second hellish curse or pact…or maybe just the result of his relentless, resentful personality.

Once undead, Kostaki exhibits many traits that were by then part of vampire lore: he's deathly pale, but rather sexy; his eyes exert a special fascination; and he seems to have the telepathic power to send Hedwig into a trance-like state. He apparently also has the unique power to unlock a door from the outside.

Dumas and Bocage make up some vampire rules, especially in the way Kostaki becomes a vampire and in the way Gregoriska kills him; but there is a Christianized echo of Stagg's Herman and Sigismund at the conclusion, and it's obvious that Dumas and Bocage have read Calmet and his report on Arnold Paul, when Hedwig prevents herself from turning undead (or of somehow summoning Kostaki back from the tomb?) by rubbing her neck wound with bloody dirt from the vampire's grave. Fortunately for her and the reader, she doesn't have to eat Kostaki's dirt, as Arnold Paul ate the dirt of the Turkish vampire's grave.

It's notable that Kostaki is specifically weakened by Gregoriska making the sign of the cross, and by Christian prayers and talismans. French writers of vampire fiction, being for the most part Catholic, were familiar with holy objects that were not part of the culture of English writers, who were, in the 19th century, essentially Protestant. Whereas Aubrey or the Bannerworths, being English, have to be forcibly dragged into believing in vampires, the Polish Hedwig is already aware that such things exist in her part of the world. She has a relatively happy ending because she re-locates to Western Europe, where it seems there are no vampires.

When Stoker's Dracula comes to London, his English opponents are not only unfamiliar with the idea of the vampire, but they have to learn how Catholic objects like the cross can be used to fight these foreign bloodsuckers. (Gilbert and Sullivan's 1887 operetta Ruddigore *satirize the entire idea of sacred objects by having the hero hold the demonic, though not vampiric, Sir Ruthven Murgatroyd at bay with the mightiest talisman of all: a Union Jack.)*

As noted earlier, Dumas returned to vampires in 1851, when he and his main collaborator Auguste Maquet wrote Le Vampire, *a sequel to Polidori's* The Vampyre *featuring the evil Lord Ruthwen (note the spelling). The climactic swordfight is similar to the confrontation between Gregoriska and Kostaki; with the addition that, when Ruthwen is sealed in his tomb, the hero traces a cross on the stone— which then glows with holy light.*

Vampires hung on as a sub-category of French literature into the 1870's, but their popularity definitely cooled in the English-speaking world. The renaming of Dion Boucicault's play The Vampire *as* The Phantom *was done to mute any suggestion of vampirism; and it kept that title during a successful revival in Chicago in the 1870's.*

Bram Stoker's Dracula *revitalized vampire fiction, and Gothic fiction in general, in 1897. Stoker, with the brilliance of a natural storyteller who had a really good story to tell, combined old and new elements into a modern classic.*

But, as these stories make clear, Bram Stoker was planting fresh seeds in a garden that had already been tended.

James Grant Goldin has written numerous non-fiction television programs about fantasy and popular culture, including *Comic Book Super-Heroes Unmasked*; *The Return of the King—A Filmmaker's Journey*; *Zombie Apocalypse*; and *Hollywood's Ultimate Super Vixens*.